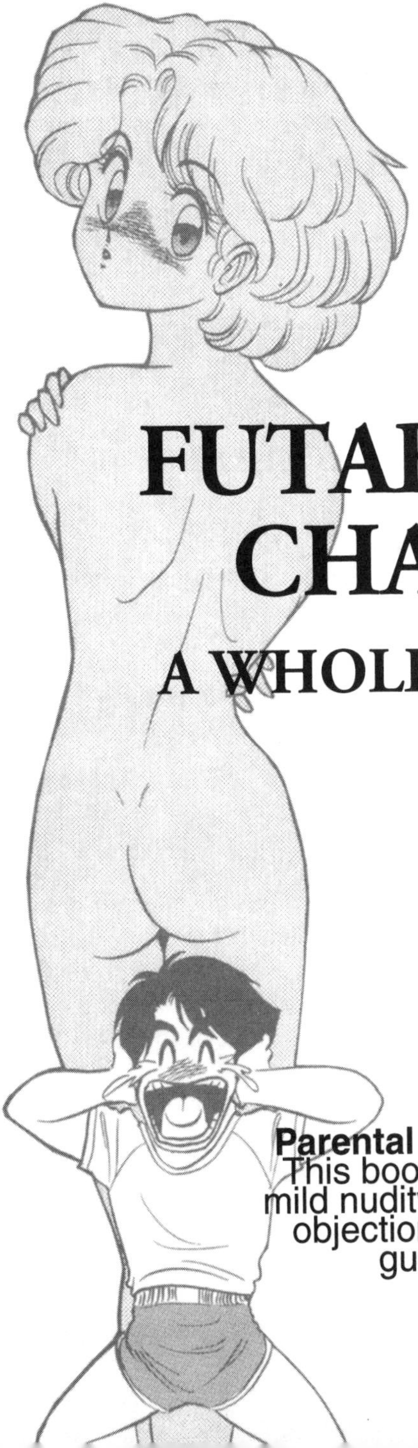

Studio Ironcat
Presents:

FUTABA-KUN CHANGE:

A WHOLE NEW YOU!

Story and Art by
HIROSHI ARO

Parental Advisory:
This book contains mild nudity and some objectionable language.

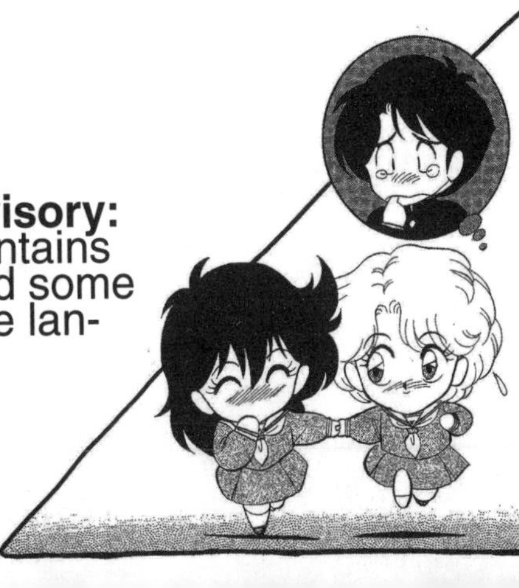

TABLE OF CONTENTS

STORY AND ART BY HIROSHI ARO

TOUCH-UP ART BY STEPHEN R. BENNETT IV
RETRANSLATION BY SACHIKO UCHIDA
EDITED BY KEVIN BENNETT
COVER BY DOUGLAS SMITH
SECOND EDITION ASSISTS BY STEPHANIE BROWN
AND KRISSY WHITE

This volume contains Futaba-kun Change Volume 1 in its entirety.

Futaba-kun Change™: "A Whole New You!" Graphic Novel Vol 1.
March1999. ©1990 Hiroshi Aro. Original Japanese Edition published by
Shueisha Pub. Co, Inc.; Tokyo, Japan. All rights reserved. Nothing from
this book may be reproduced without written consent from the copyright
holder(s). Violators will be prosecuted to the full extent of the laws of the
United States of America. All persons and events depicted are fictitious.
Any similarity to actual persons and/or events is unintentional.
Printed in CANADA.

PUBLISHED BY
STUDIO IRONCAT
607 WILLIAM STREET, SUITE 213
FREDERICKSBURG, VA 22401

THIRD PRINTING

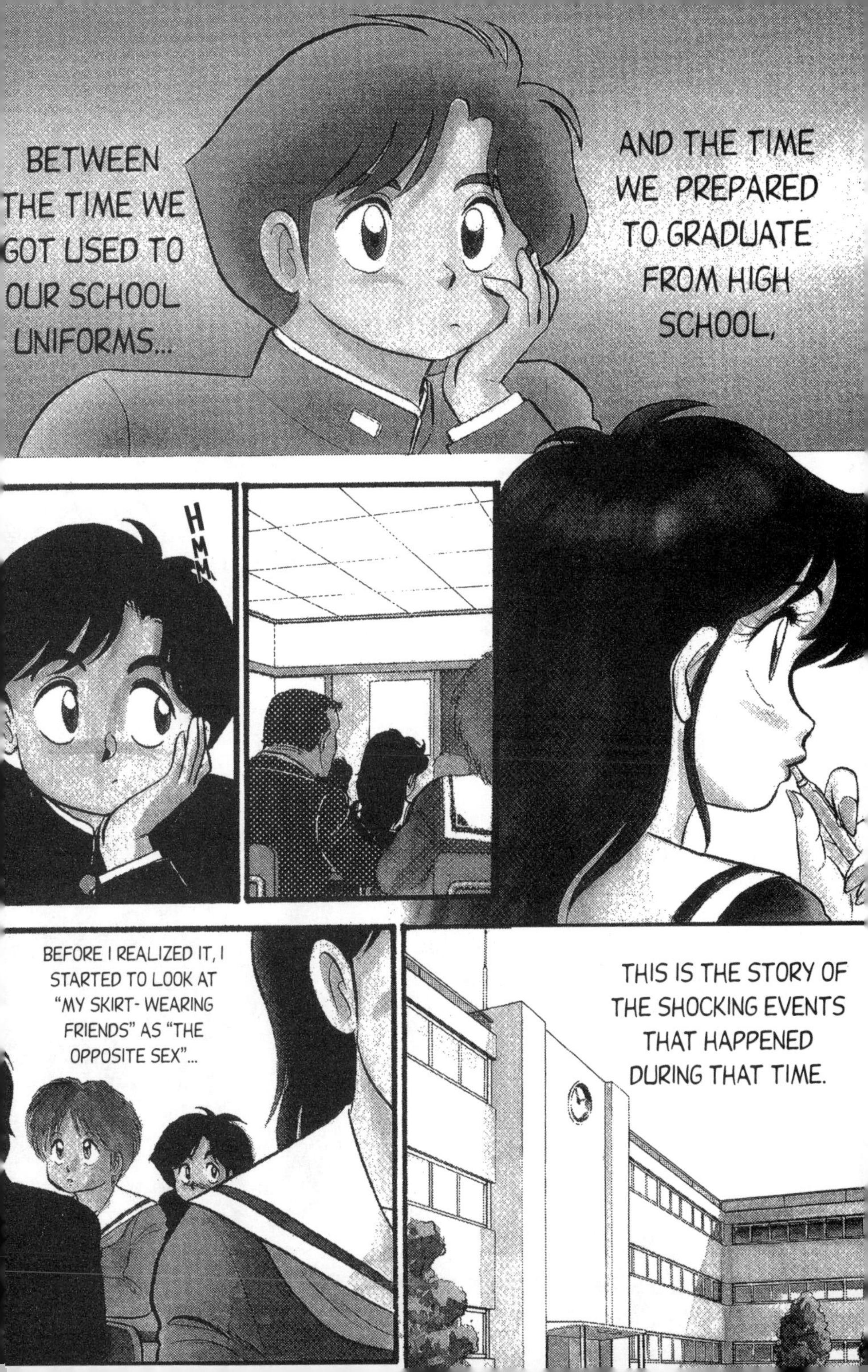

BETWEEN THE TIME WE GOT USED TO OUR SCHOOL UNIFORMS...
AND THE TIME WE PREPARED TO GRADUATE FROM HIGH SCHOOL,
HMMM
BEFORE I REALIZED IT, I STARTED TO LOOK AT "MY SKIRT- WEARING FRIENDS" AS "THE OPPOSITE SEX"...
THIS IS THE STORY OF THE SHOCKING EVENTS THAT HAPPENED DURING THAT TIME.

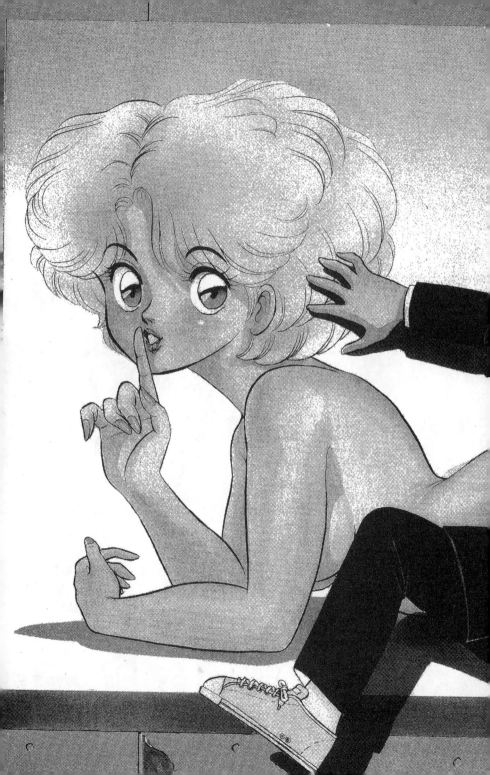

Futaba-kun Changes!!

Note: The name is pronounced "Foo-tah-bah" and "kun" is a suffix used after boys names, while "chan" is used after girls names.

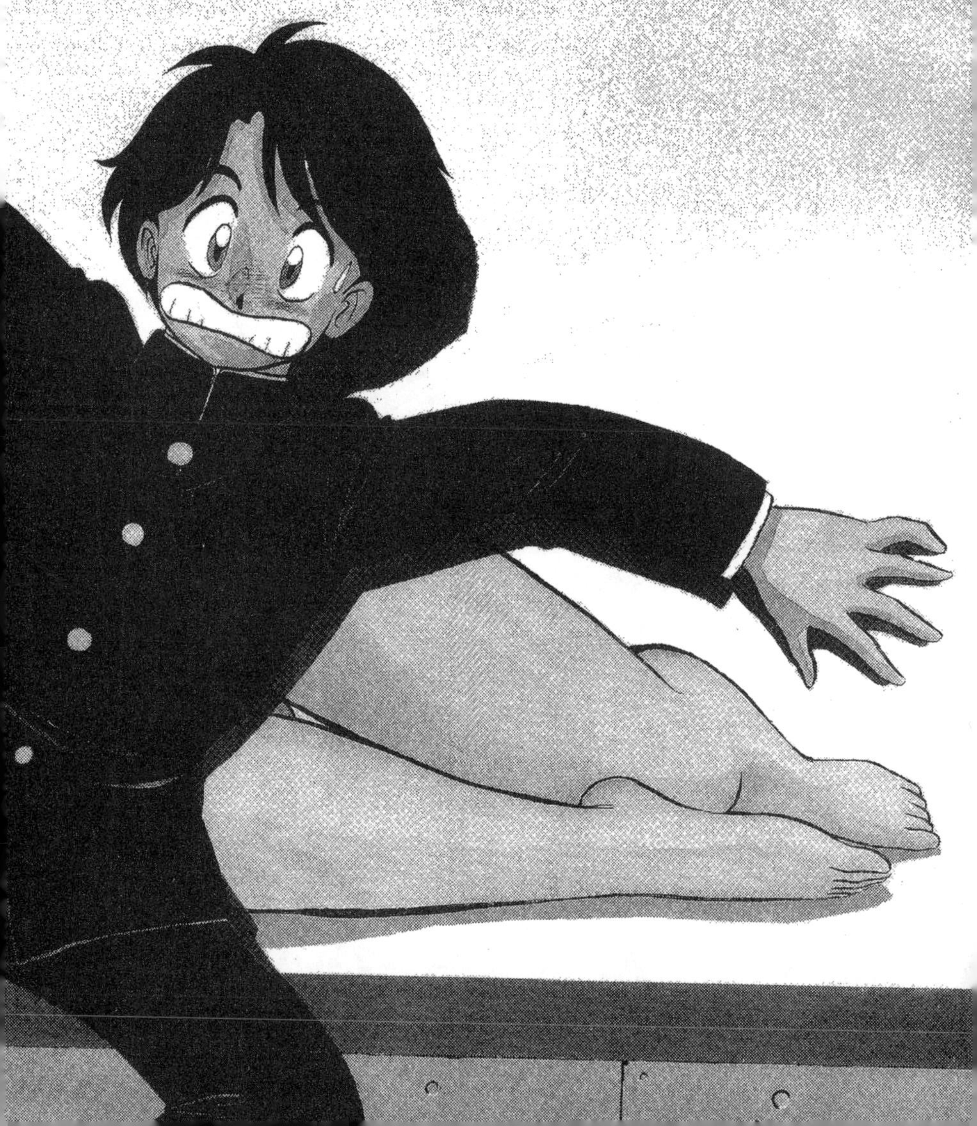

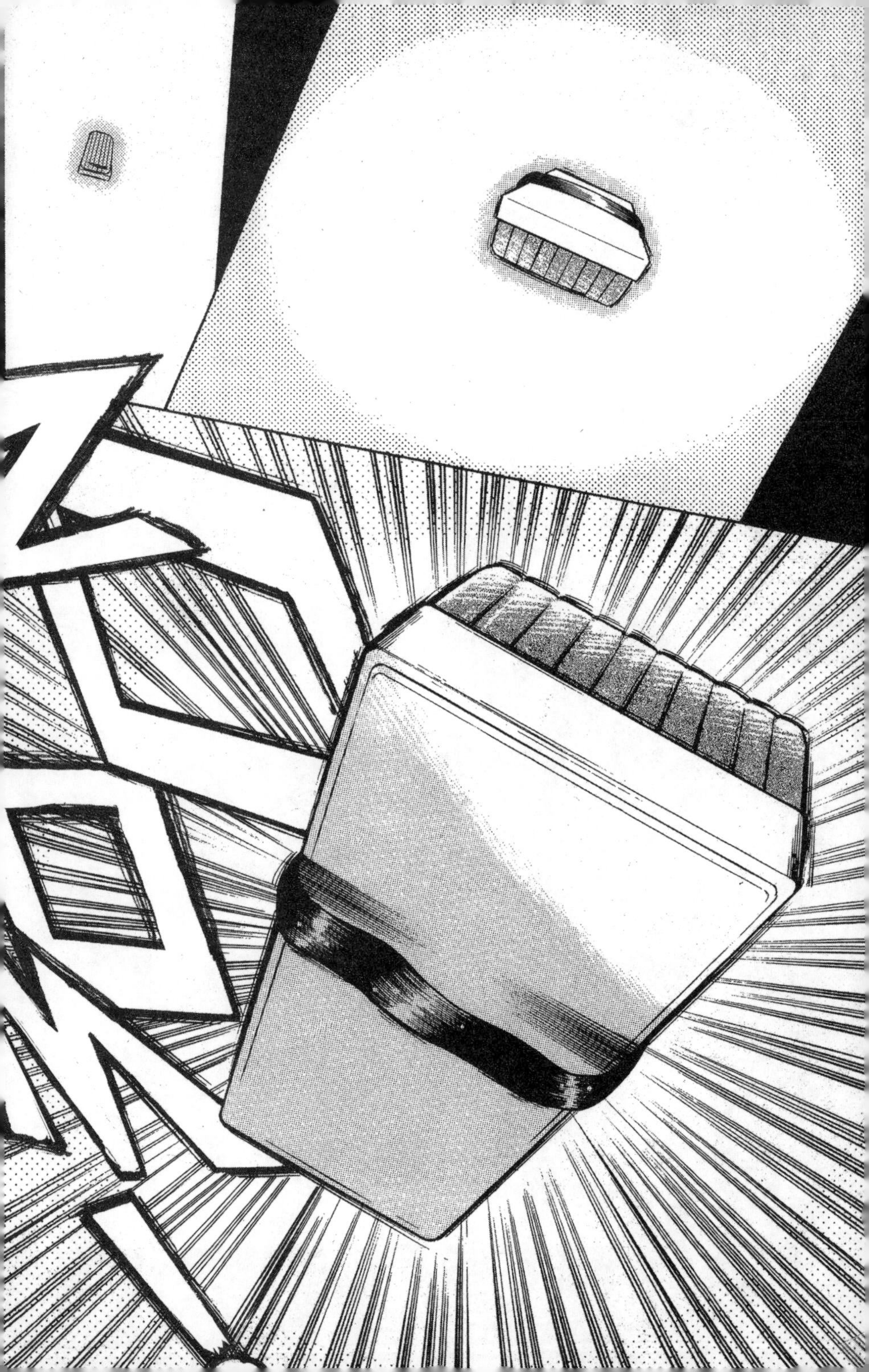

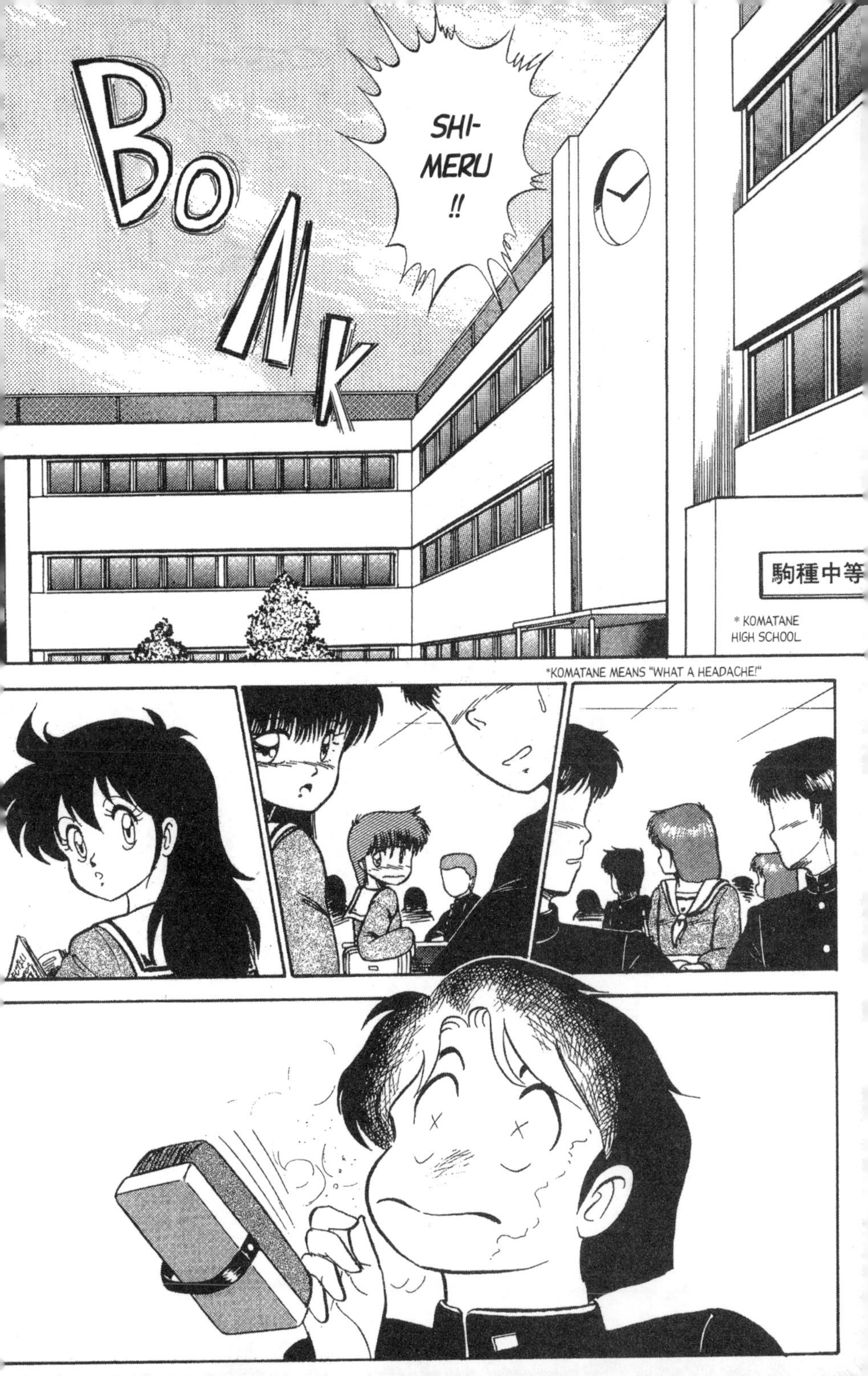
BONK
SHI-MERU !!
駒種中等
* KOMATANE HIGH SCHOOL
*KOMATANE MEANS "WHAT A HEADACHE!"

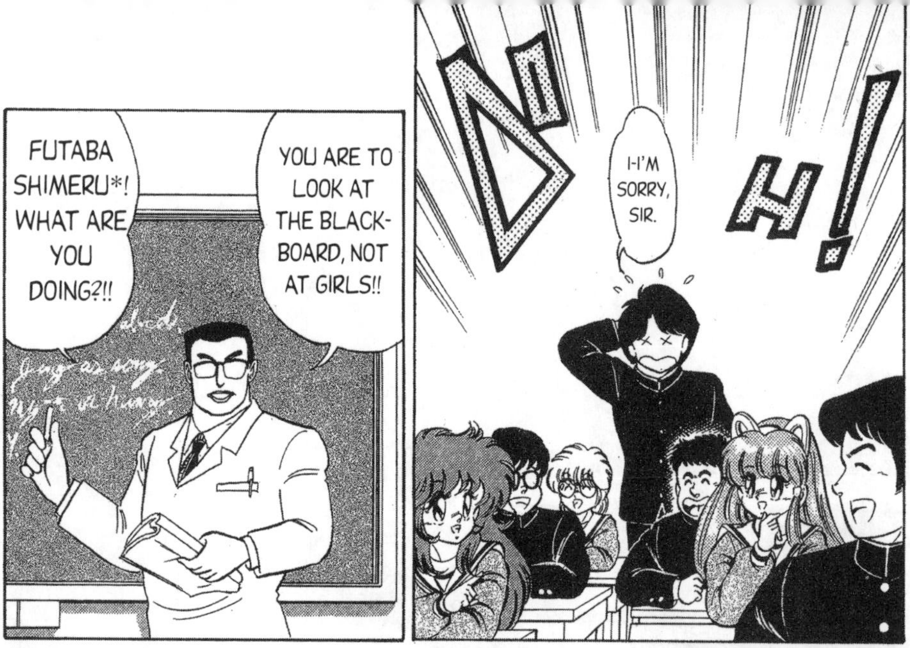
FUTABA SHIMERU*! WHAT ARE YOU DOING?!!
YOU ARE TO LOOK AT THE BLACK-BOARD, NOT AT GIRLS!!
DOH!
I-I'M SORRY, SIR.

*Literally means "two tied up leaves"

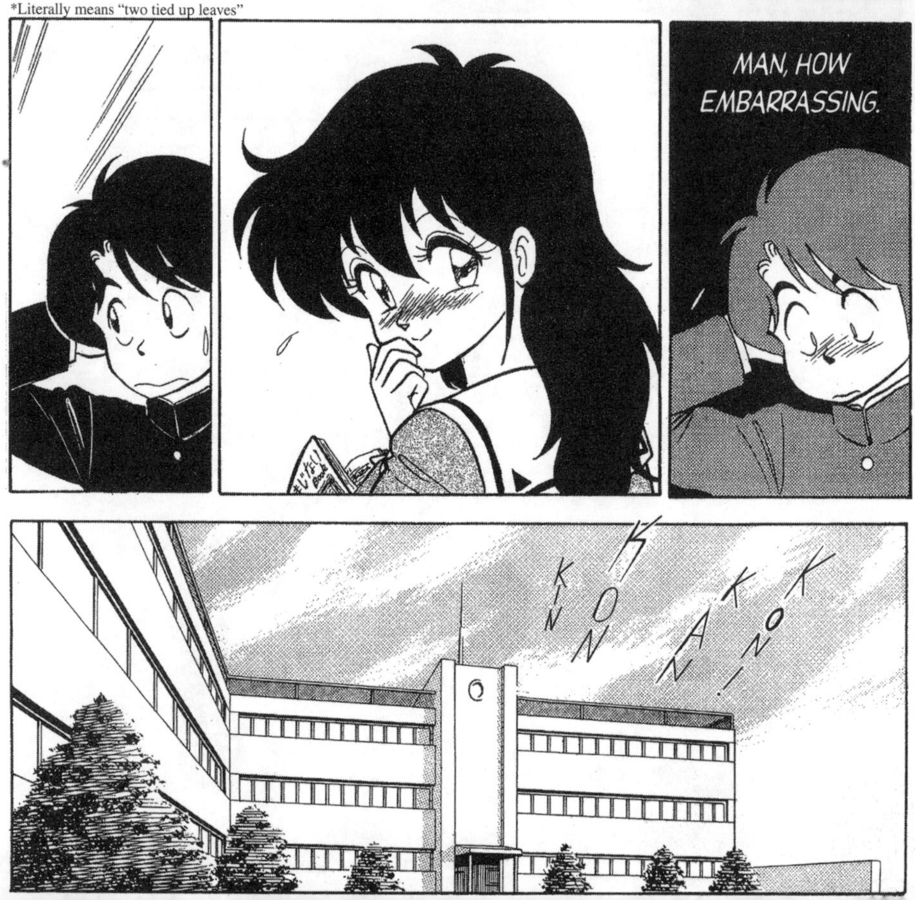
MAN, HOW EMBARRASSING.
KIN KON KAN KON!

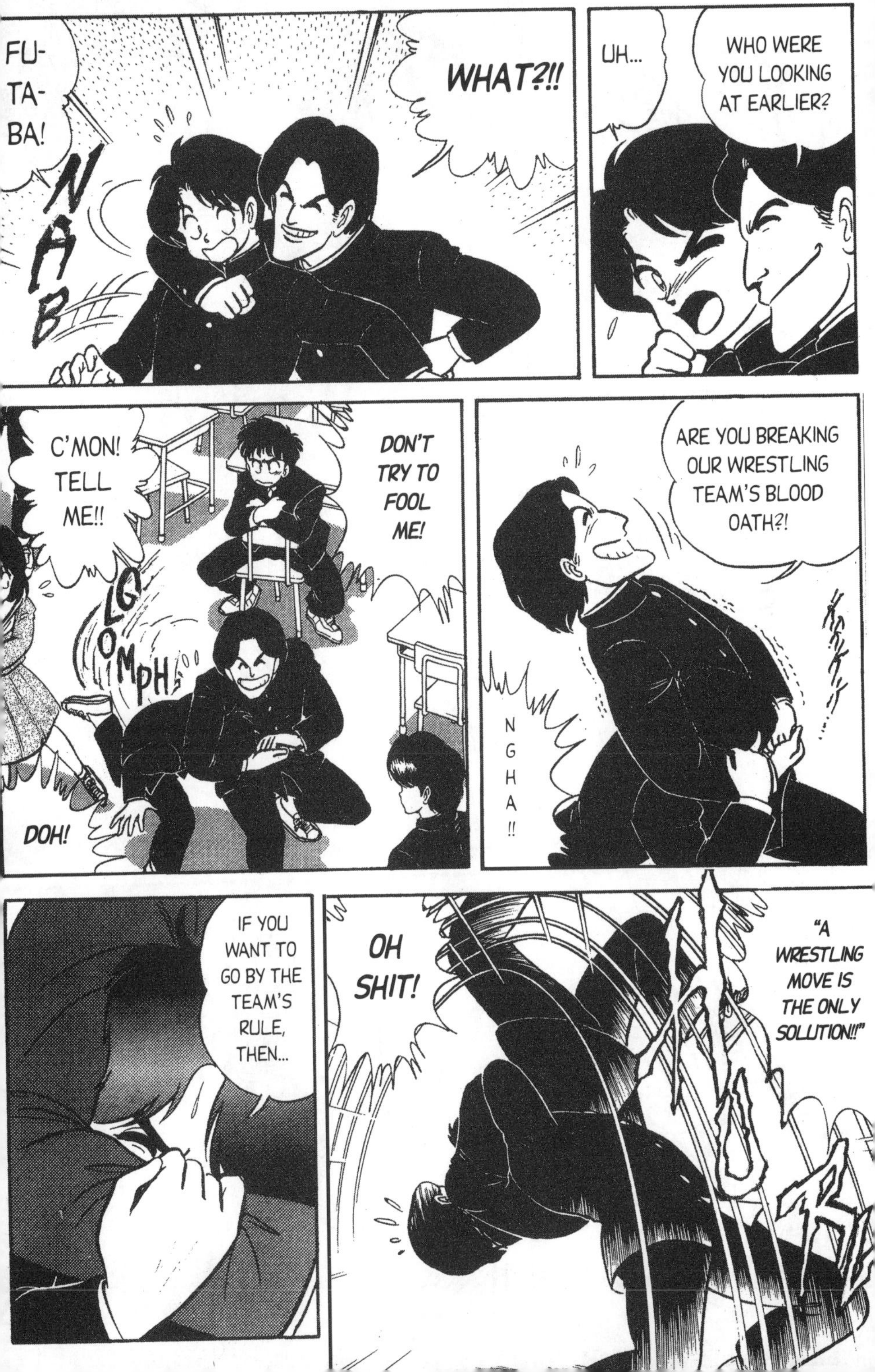
FU-TA-BA!
NAB
WHAT?!!
UH...
WHO WERE YOU LOOKING AT EARLIER?
C'MON! TELL ME!!
DON'T TRY TO FOOL ME!
DOH!
ARE YOU BREAKING OUR WRESTLING TEAM'S BLOOD OATH?!
NGHA!!
IF YOU WANT TO GO BY THE TEAM'S RULE, THEN...
OH SHIT!
"A WRESTLING MOVE IS THE ONLY SOLUTION!!"

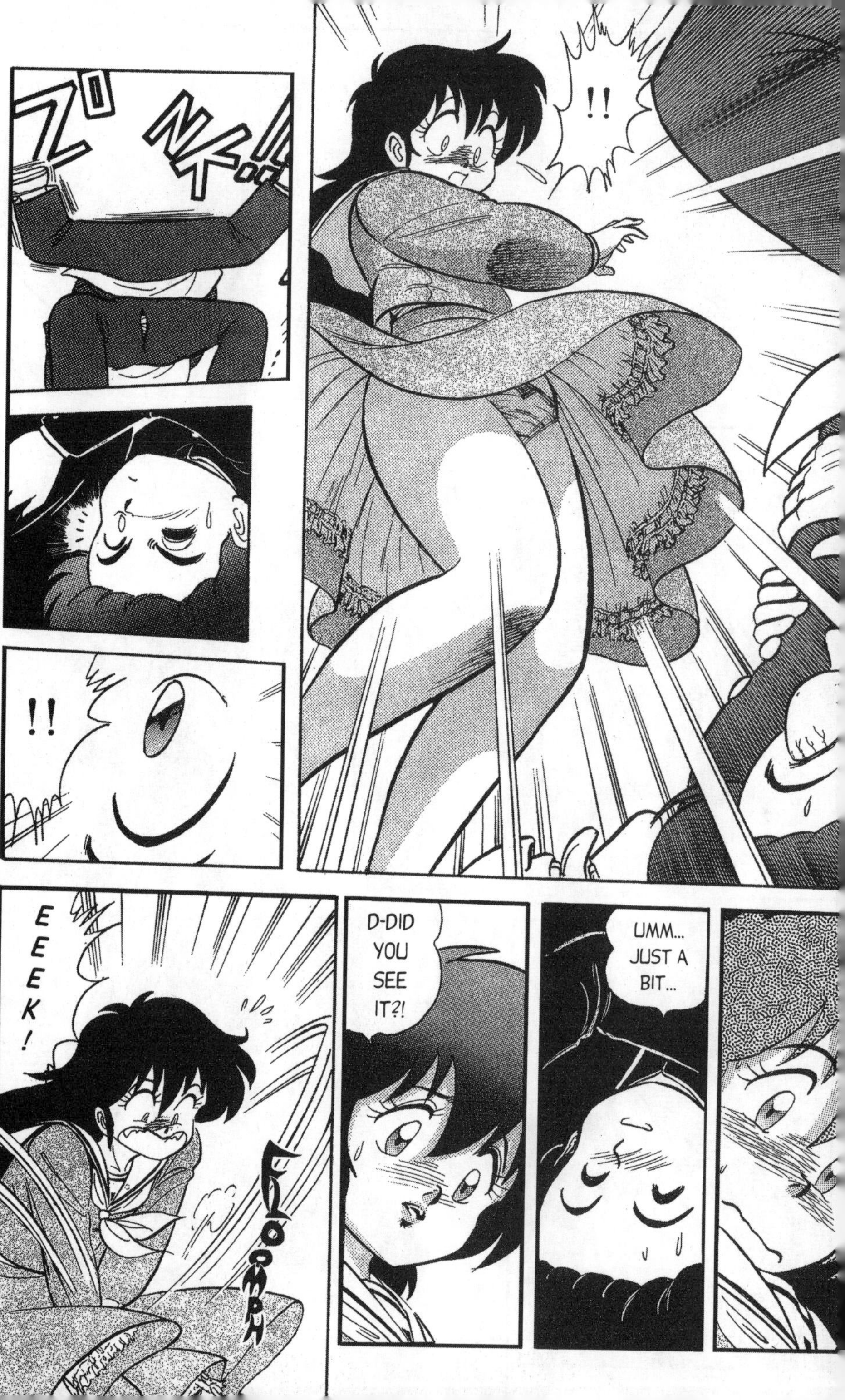
!!
ZONK!!
!!
EEEEK!
FLOOOMPH
D-DID YOU SEE IT?!
UMM... JUST A BIT...

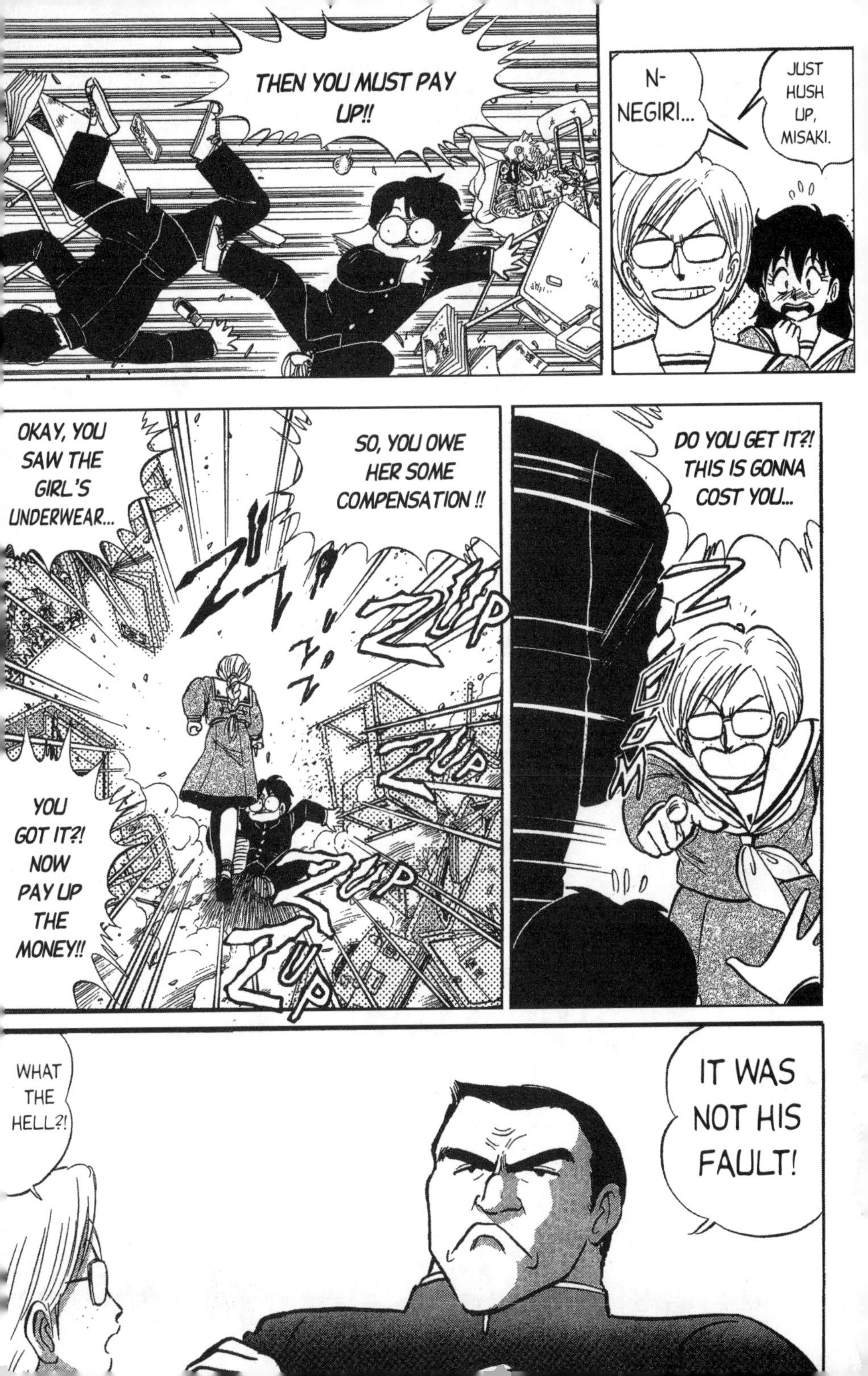
THEN YOU MUST PAY UP!!
N-NEGIRI...
JUST HUSH UP, MISAKI.
OKAY, YOU SAW THE GIRL'S UNDERWEAR...
SO, YOU OWE HER SOME COMPENSATION !!
ZUP
ZUP
YOU GOT IT?! NOW PAY UP THE MONEY!!
ZUP
ZUP
DO YOU GET IT?! THIS IS GONNA COST YOU...
ZOOOOM
WHAT THE HELL?!
IT WAS NOT HIS FAULT!

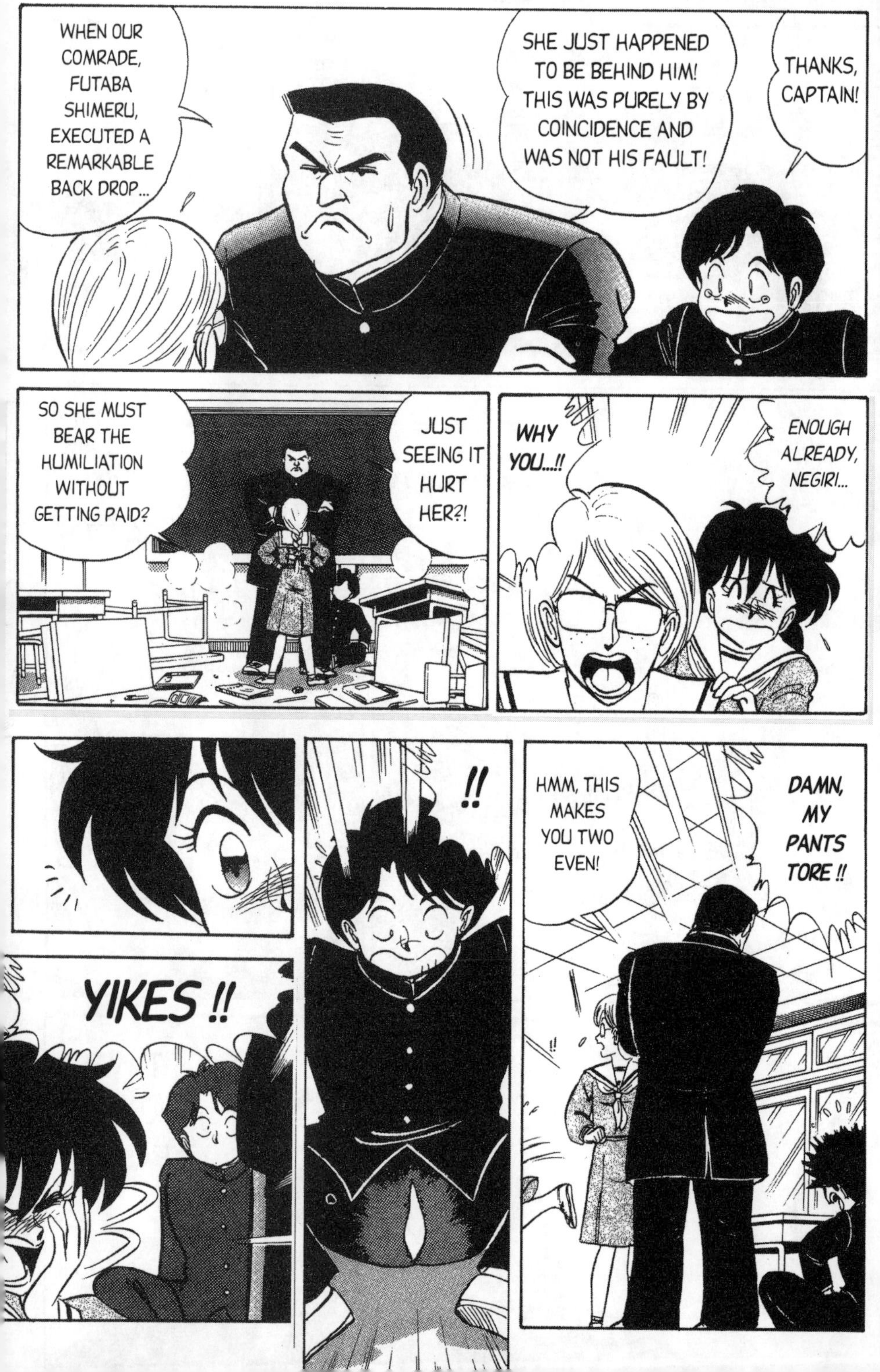
THANKS, CAPTAIN!
SHE JUST HAPPENED TO BE BEHIND HIM! THIS WAS PURELY BY COINCIDENCE AND WAS NOT HIS FAULT!
WHEN OUR COMRADE, FUTABA SHIMERU, EXECUTED A REMARKABLE BACK DROP...
ENOUGH ALREADY, NEGIRI...
WHY YOU...!!
JUST SEEING IT HURT HER?!
SO SHE MUST BEAR THE HUMILIATION WITHOUT GETTING PAID?
DAMN, MY PANTS TORE !!
HMM, THIS MAKES YOU TWO EVEN!
!!
YIKES !!

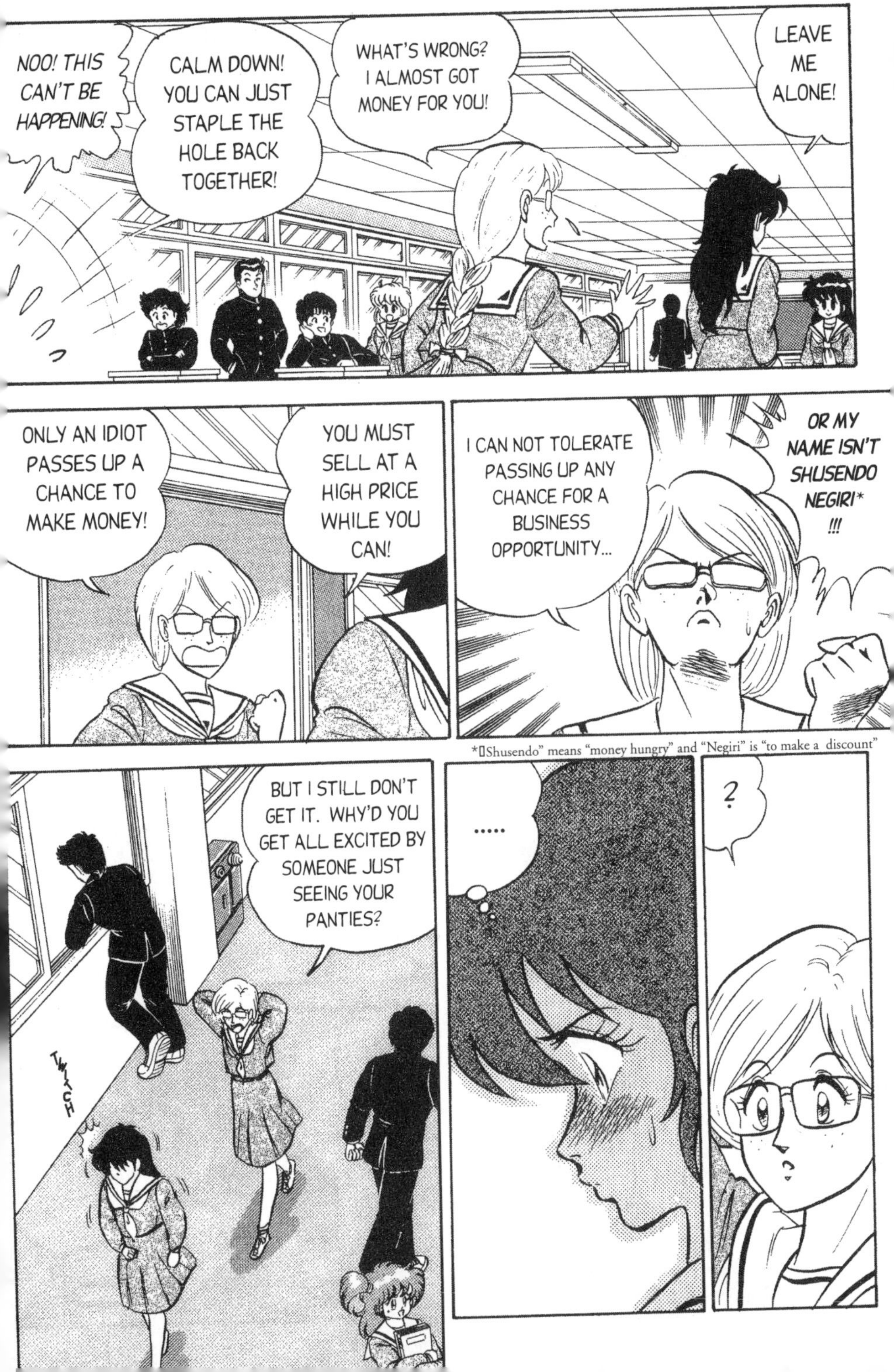
NOO! THIS CAN'T BE HAPPENING!
CALM DOWN! YOU CAN JUST STAPLE THE HOLE BACK TOGETHER!
WHAT'S WRONG? I ALMOST GOT MONEY FOR YOU!
LEAVE ME ALONE!
ONLY AN IDIOT PASSES UP A CHANCE TO MAKE MONEY!
YOU MUST SELL AT A HIGH PRICE WHILE YOU CAN!
I CAN NOT TOLERATE PASSING UP ANY CHANCE FOR A BUSINESS OPPORTUNITY...
OR MY NAME ISN'T SHUSENDO NEGIRI* !!!
BUT I STILL DON'T GET IT. WHY'D YOU GET ALL EXCITED BY SOMEONE JUST SEEING YOUR PANTIES?
TWITCH
.....
?

*"Shusendo" means "money hungry" and "Negiri" is "to make a discount"

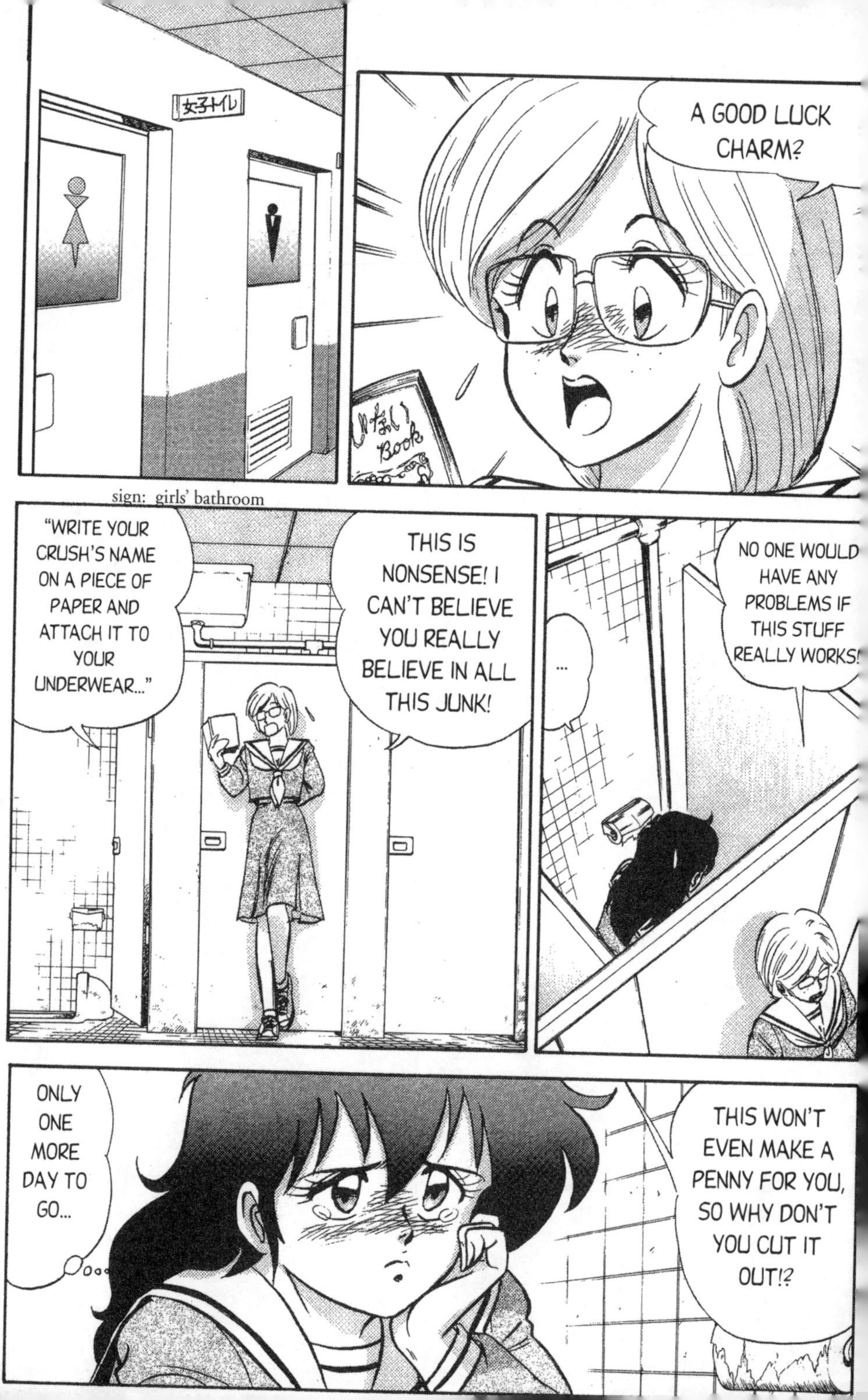
女子トイレ
A GOOD LUCK CHARM?
"WRITE YOUR CRUSH'S NAME ON A PIECE OF PAPER AND ATTACH IT TO YOUR UNDERWEAR..."
THIS IS NONSENSE! I CAN'T BELIEVE YOU REALLY BELIEVE IN ALL THIS JUNK!
...
NO ONE WOULD HAVE ANY PROBLEMS IF THIS STUFF REALLY WORKS!
ONLY ONE MORE DAY TO GO...
THIS WON'T EVEN MAKE A PENNY FOR YOU, SO WHY DON'T YOU CUT IT OUT!?

sign: girls' bathroom

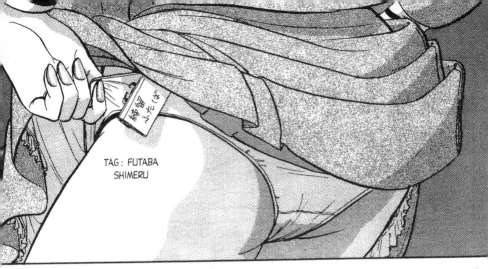

TAG : FUTABA
SHIMERU

COULD HE HAVE SEEN THE TAG?

I DOUBT IF HE COULD READ IT THOUGH...

BUT WHY DID IT HAVE TO BE HIM ?!

WHAT'RE YOU DOING? LUNCH BREAK IS ALMOST OVER!

I'M COMING!

HUFF!

I MADE A FOOL OF MYSELF IN FRONT OF HER AGAIN...

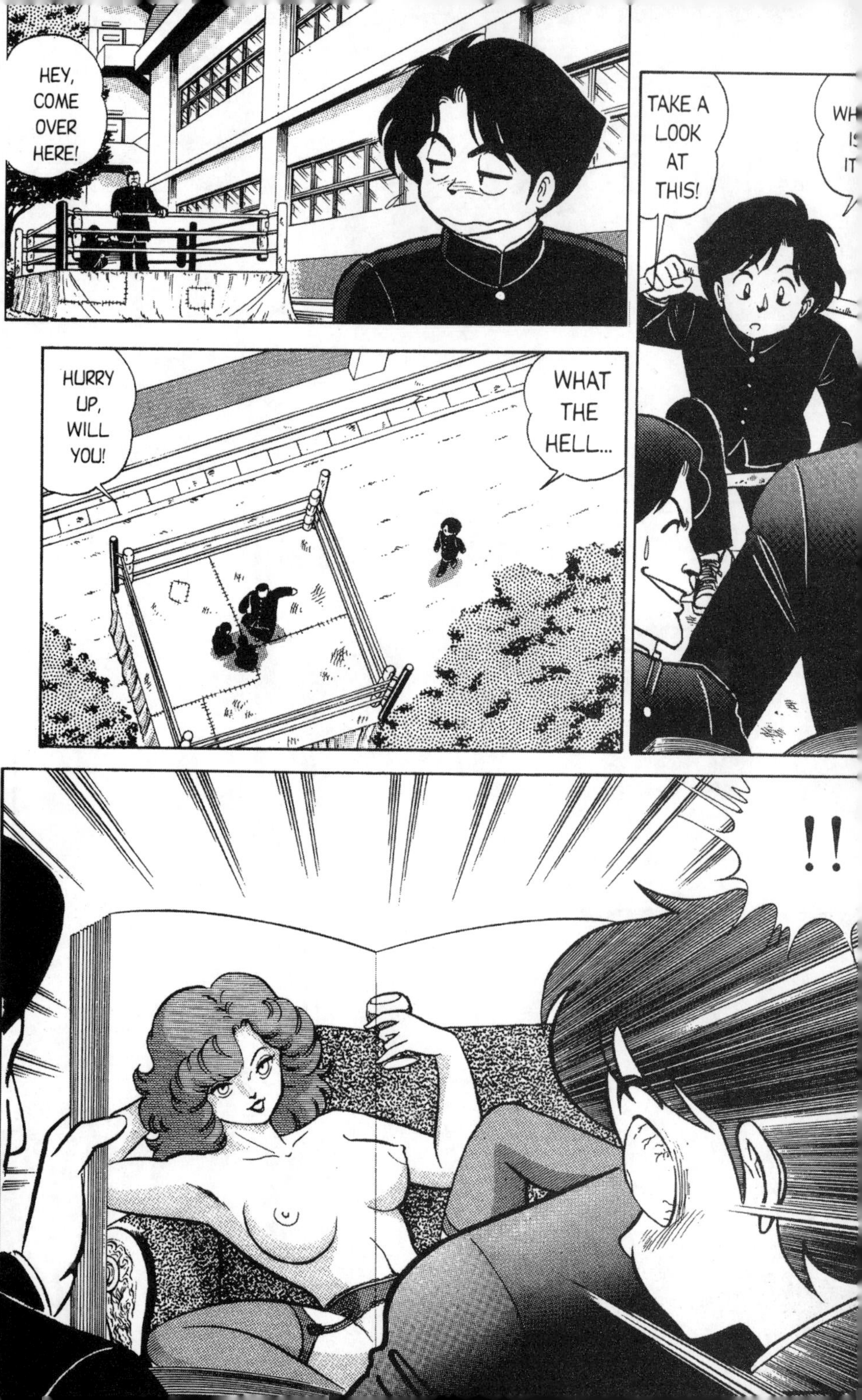
HEY, COME OVER HERE!
TAKE A LOOK AT THIS!
HURRY UP, WILL YOU!
WHAT THE HELL...
!!

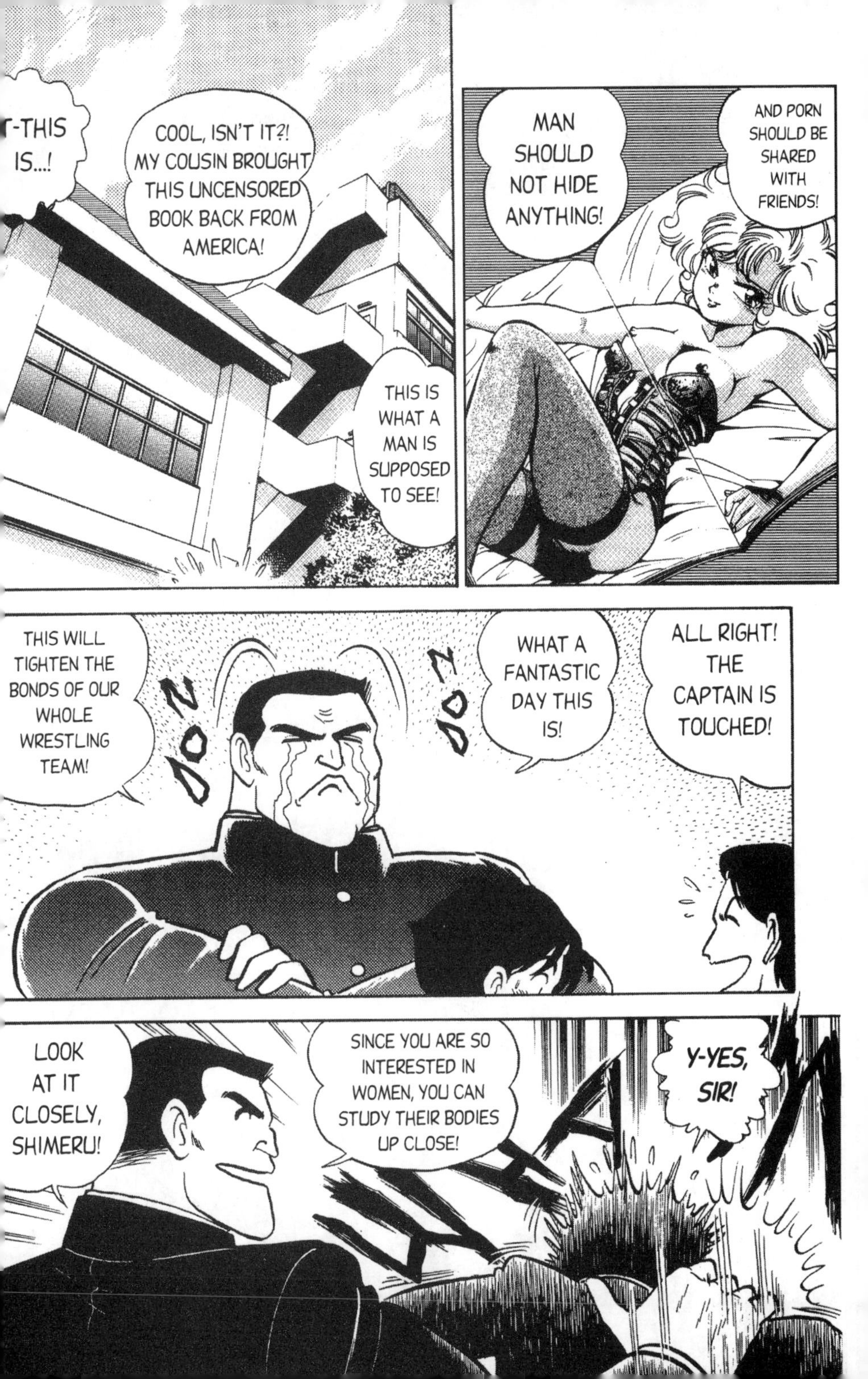
T-THIS IS...!
COOL, ISN'T IT?! MY COUSIN BROUGHT THIS UNCENSORED BOOK BACK FROM AMERICA!
THIS IS WHAT A MAN IS SUPPOSED TO SEE!
MAN SHOULD NOT HIDE ANYTHING!
AND PORN SHOULD BE SHARED WITH FRIENDS!
THIS WILL TIGHTEN THE BONDS OF OUR WHOLE WRESTLING TEAM!
NOD
NOD
WHAT A FANTASTIC DAY THIS IS!
ALL RIGHT! THE CAPTAIN IS TOUCHED!
LOOK AT IT CLOSELY, SHIMERU!
SINCE YOU ARE SO INTERESTED IN WOMEN, YOU CAN STUDY THEIR BODIES UP CLOSE!
Y-YES, SIR!

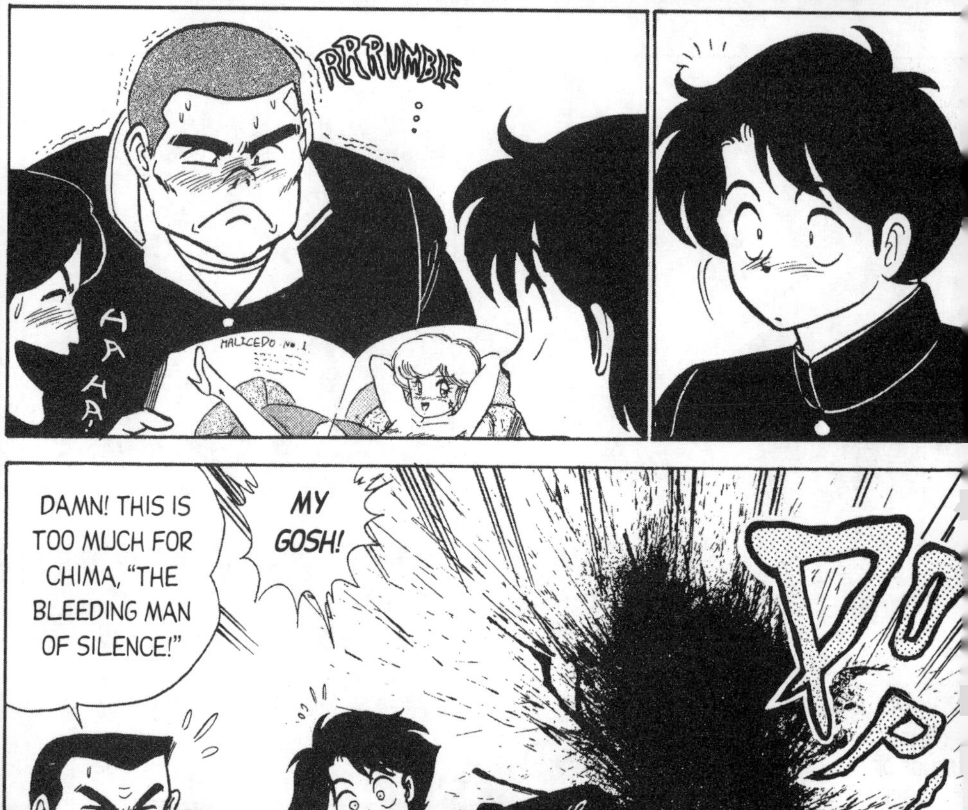
RRRUMBLE
HA HA HA!
MALICEDO No. 1
DAMN! THIS IS TOO MUCH FOR CHIMA, "THE BLEEDING MAN OF SILENCE!"
MY GOSH!
POP!

Note: A bloody nose signifies extreme excitement, as in "the blood is flowing."

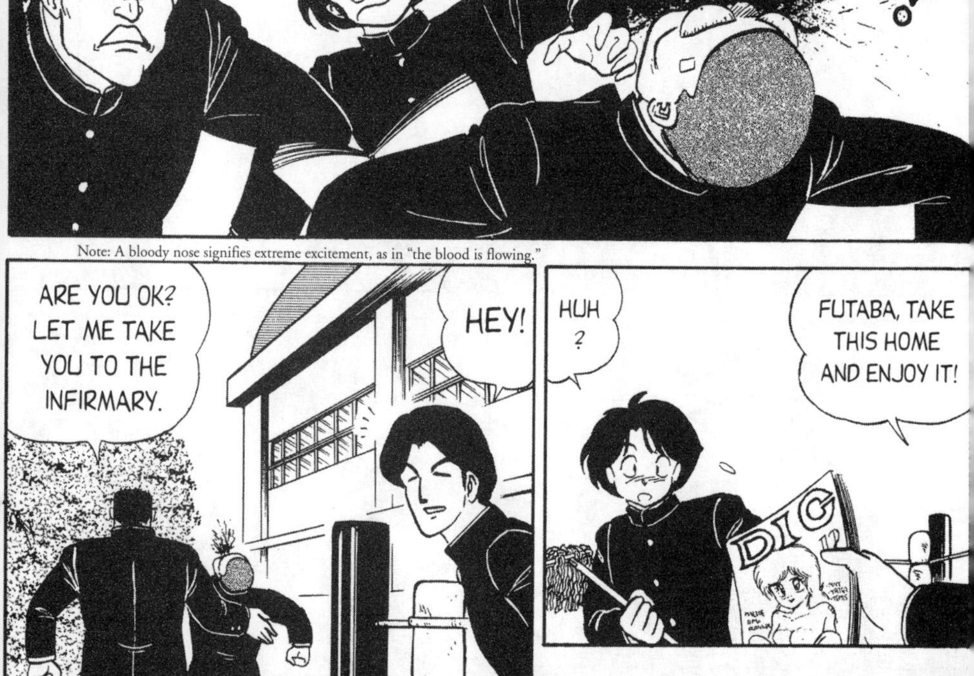
ARE YOU OK? LET ME TAKE YOU TO THE INFIRMARY.
HEY!
HUH?
FUTABA, TAKE THIS HOME AND ENJOY IT!
DIG

BUT DON'T STAIN IT UP!

....

MALE BONDING IS REALLY COOL!

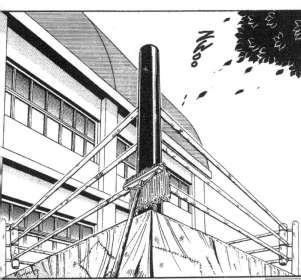

男子トイレ

女子トイレ

I CAN'T WAIT TO CHECK THIS OUT...

I'LL JUST TAKE A PEEK BEFORE I GO TO CLASS...

THIS IS KICK ASS STUFF!

MAN!

COOL!

WOW!

MMM

I WON- DER...

BTHUMP THUMP KTHUMP THUMP THUMP THUMP BTHUMP THUMP

IF AL WOM ARE L THIS

IF SO, IS MISAKI LIKE THIS, TOO!?!

THUMP

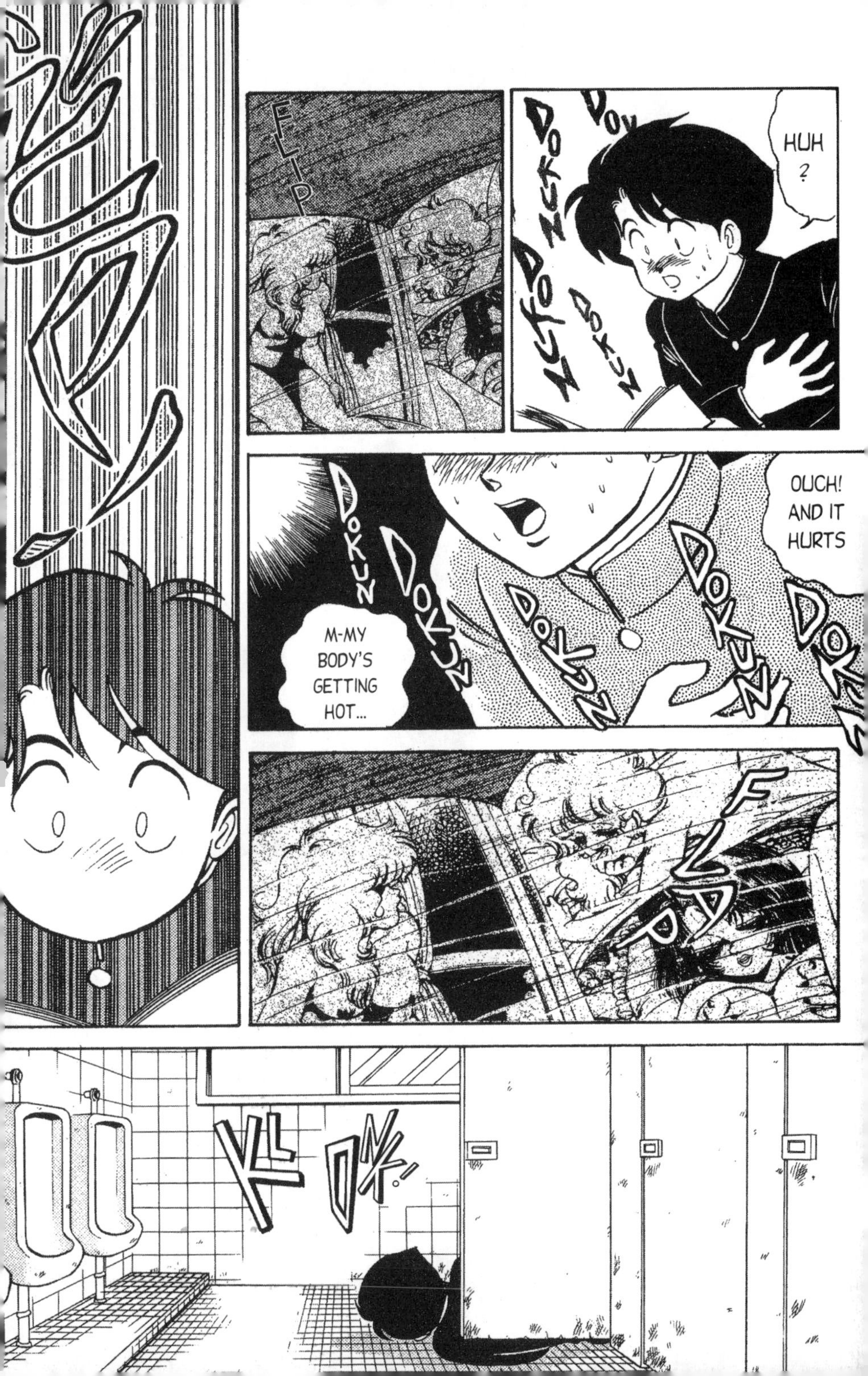

DOKUN DOKUN
DOKUN
DOKUN
HUH ?
FLIP
OUCH! AND IT HURTS
DOKUN DOKUN
DOKUN DOKUN
M-MY BODY'S GETTING HOT...
DOKUN DOKUN
FLAP
KLONK!

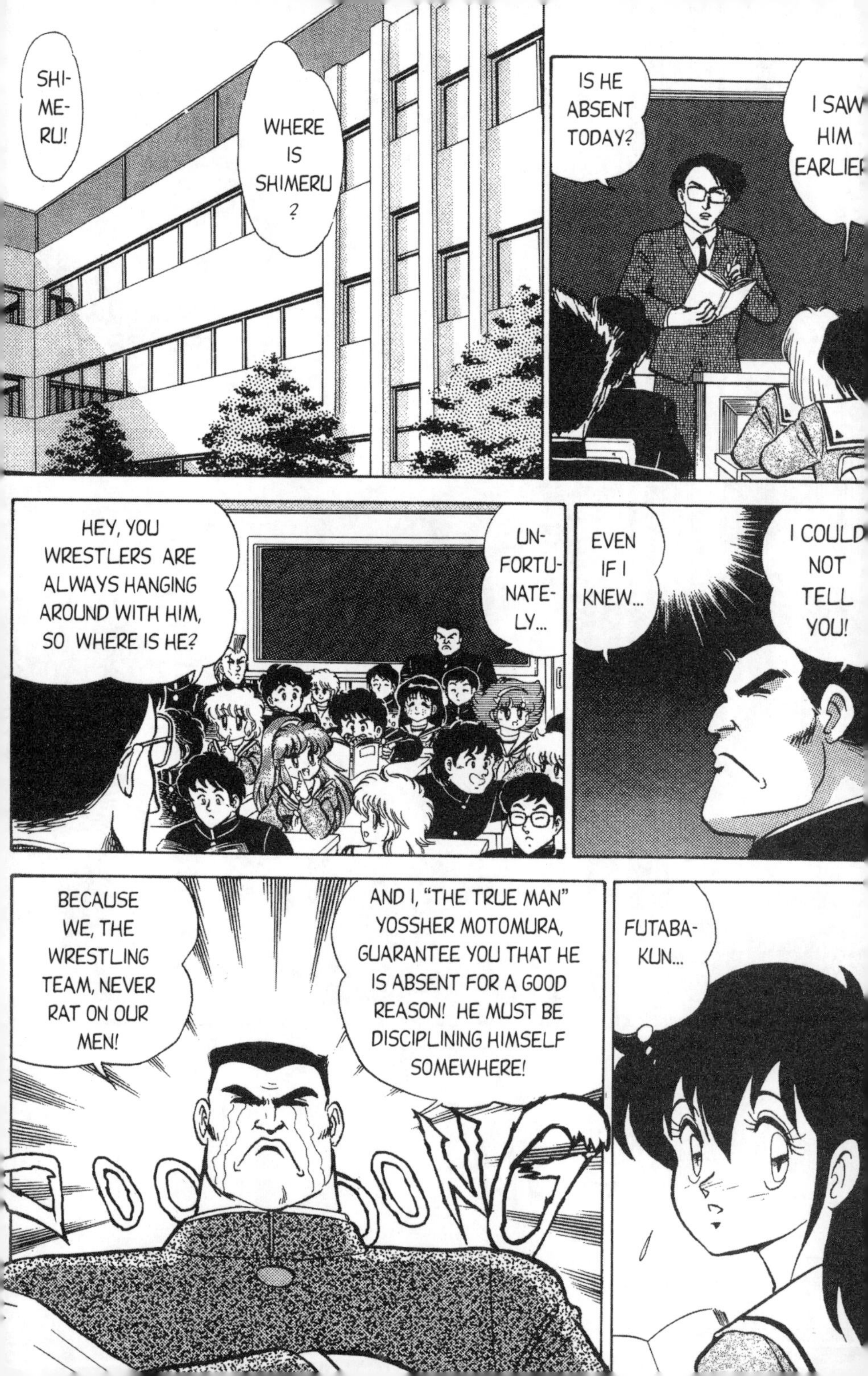
SHI-ME-RU!
WHERE IS SHIMERU?
IS HE ABSENT TODAY?
I SAW HIM EARLIEF
HEY, YOU WRESTLERS ARE ALWAYS HANGING AROUND WITH HIM, SO WHERE IS HE?
UN-FORTU-NATE-LY...
EVEN IF I KNEW...
I COULD NOT TELL YOU!
BECAUSE WE, THE WRESTLING TEAM, NEVER RAT ON OUR MEN!
AND I, "THE TRUE MAN" YOSSHER MOTOMURA, GUARANTEE YOU THAT HE IS ABSENT FOR A GOOD REASON! HE MUST BE DISCIPLINING HIMSELF SOMEWHERE!
DOOOOONG
FUTABA-KUN...

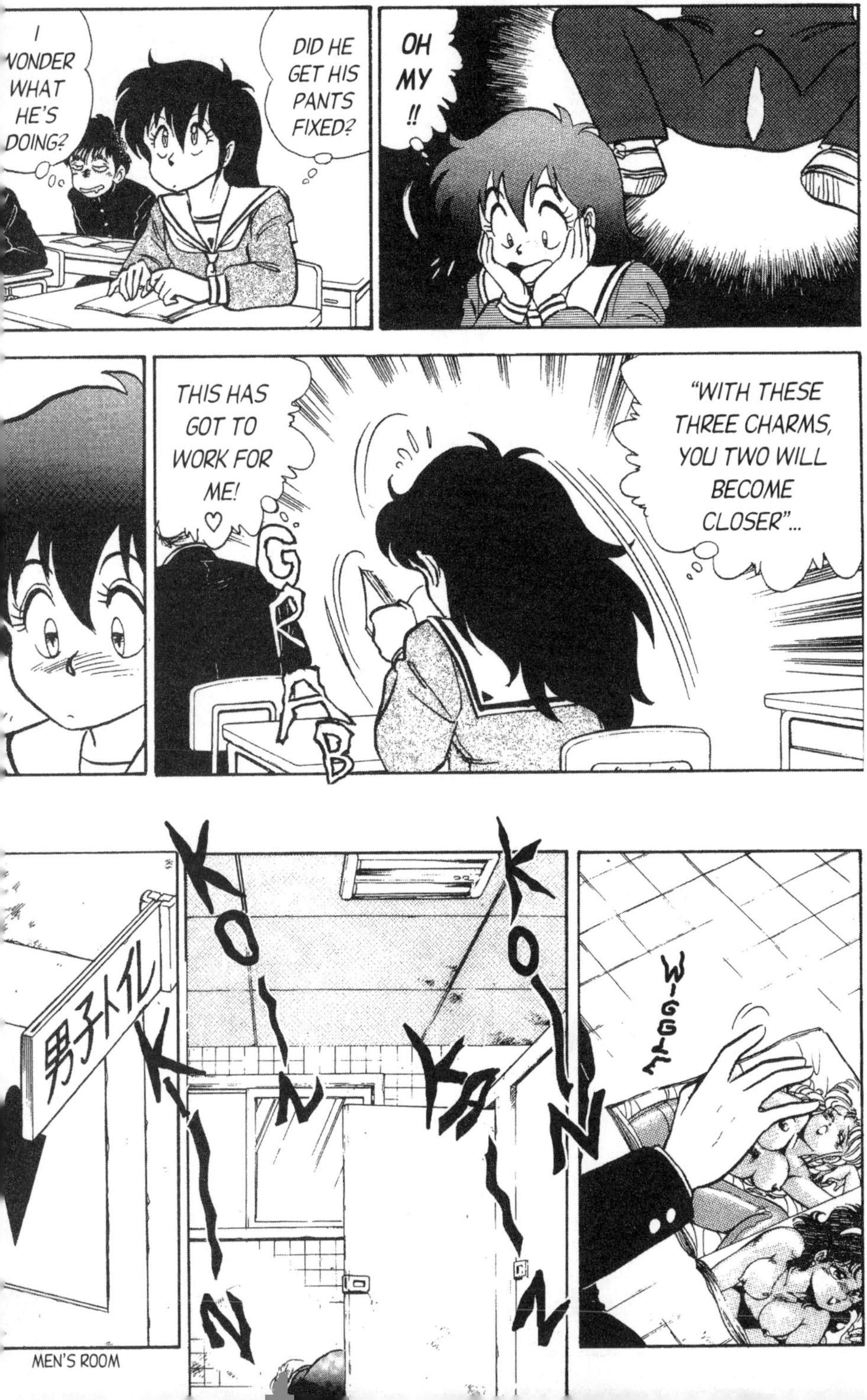

DID HE GET HIS PANTS FIXED?
I WONDER WHAT HE'S DOING?
OH MY !!
"WITH THESE THREE CHARMS, YOU TWO WILL BECOME CLOSER"...
THIS HAS GOT TO WORK FOR ME! ♡
GRABB
WIGGLE
KOI-N KA-N
KOI-N KI-N
男子トイレ
MEN'S ROOM

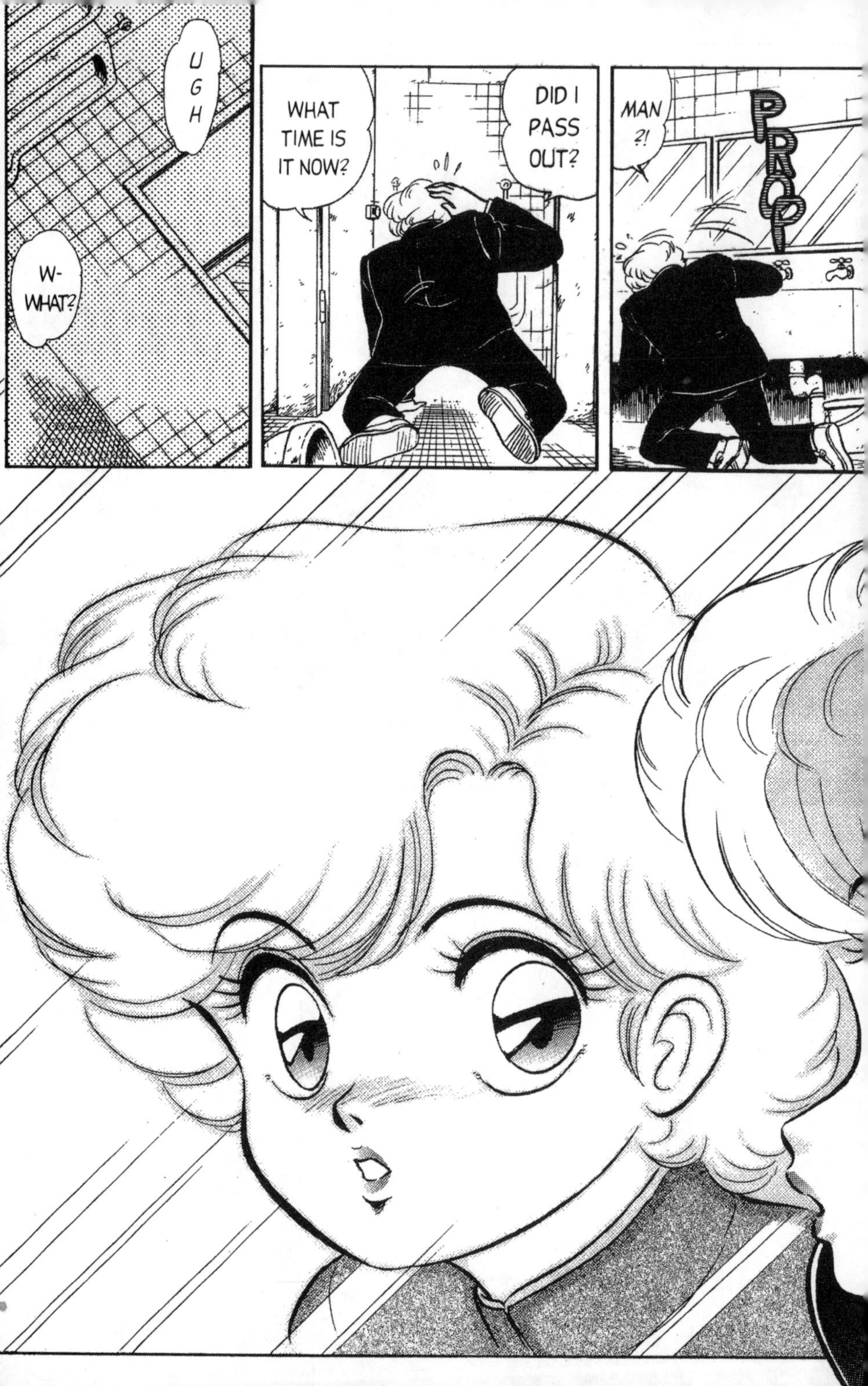
PROP
MAN ?!
DID I PASS OUT?
WHAT TIME IS IT NOW?
UGH
W-WHAT?

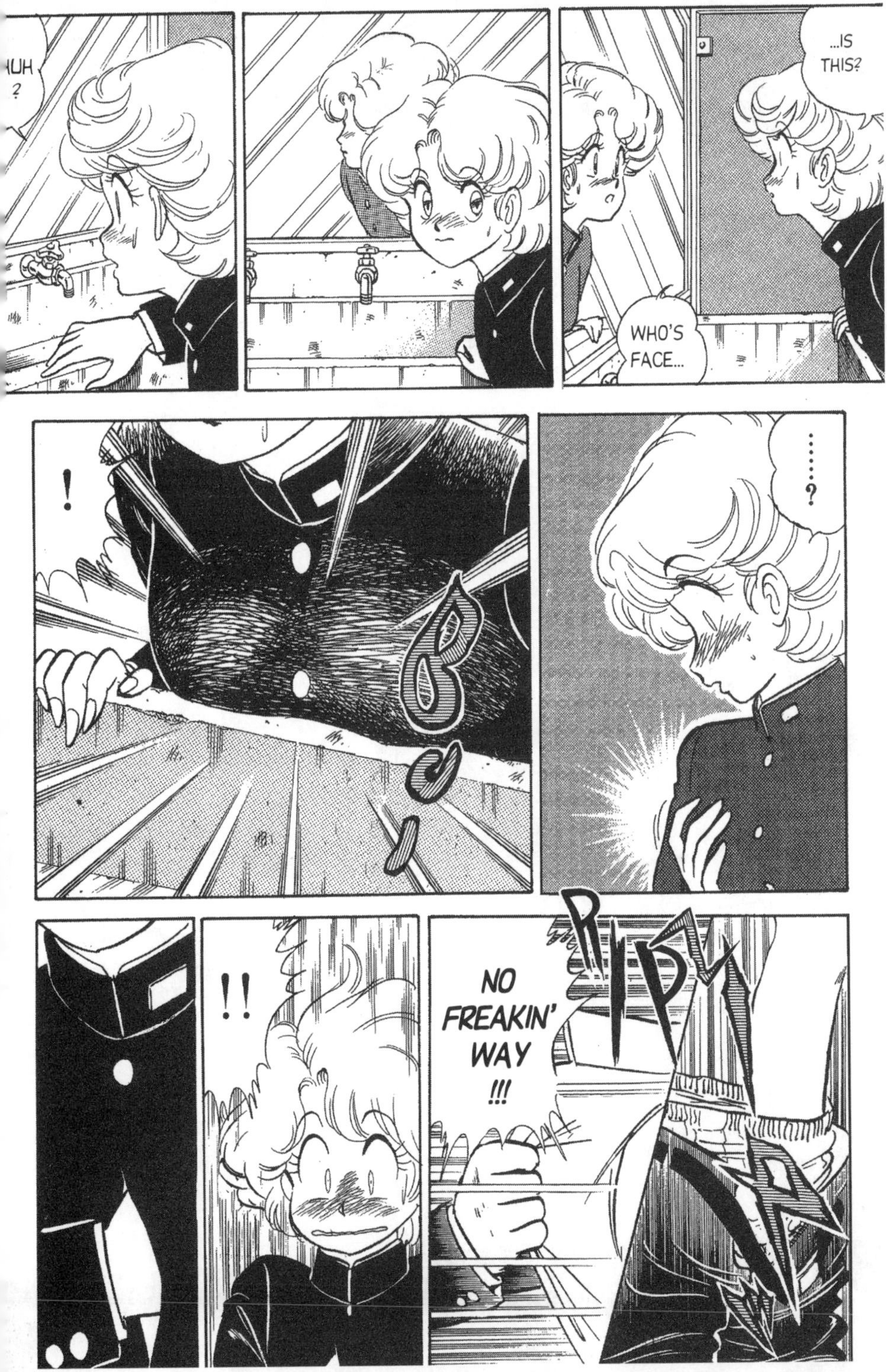

...IS THIS?
WHO'S FACE...
HUH ?
!
......?
NO FREAKIN' WAY !!!
!!
RIP

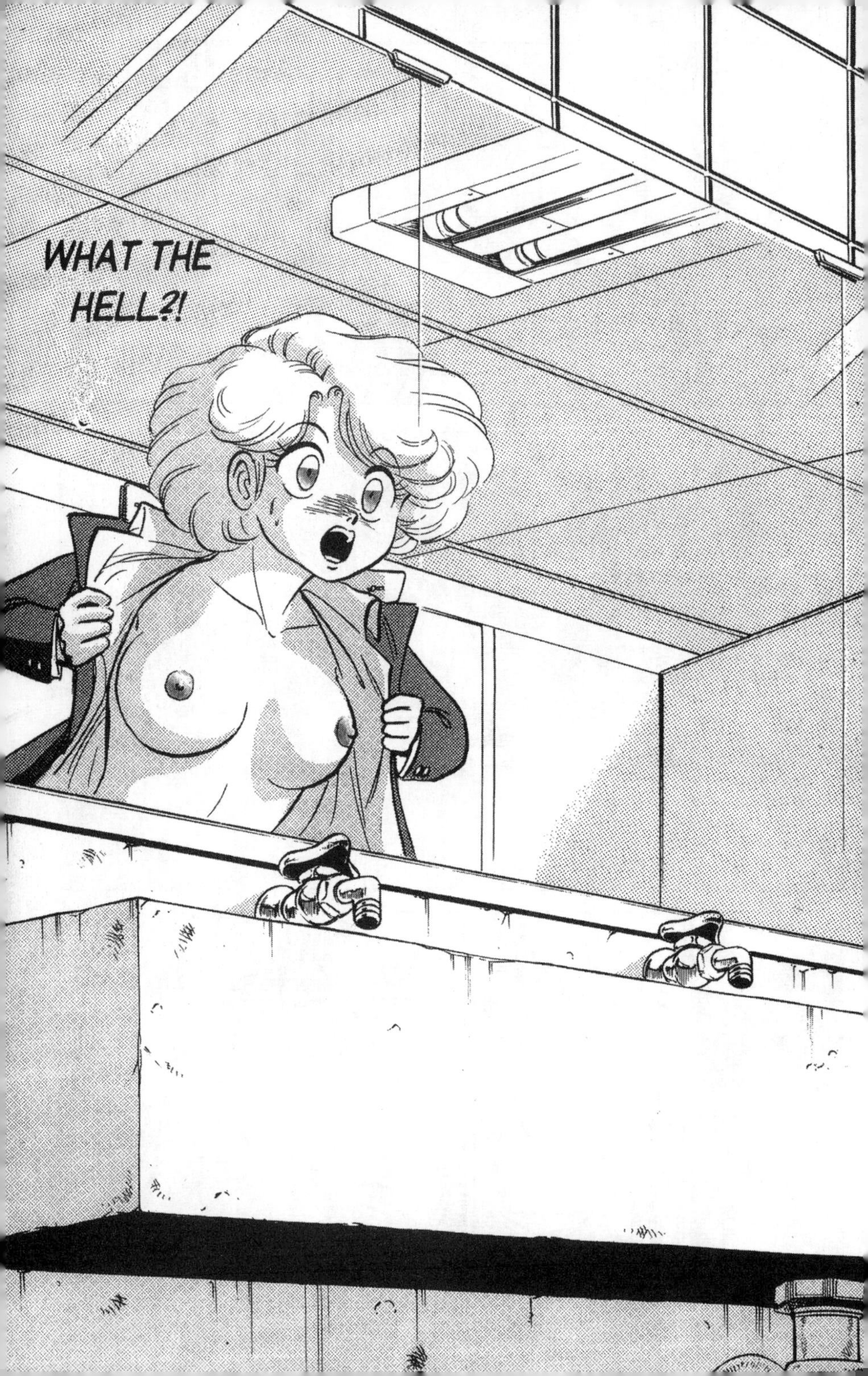
WHAT THE HELL?!

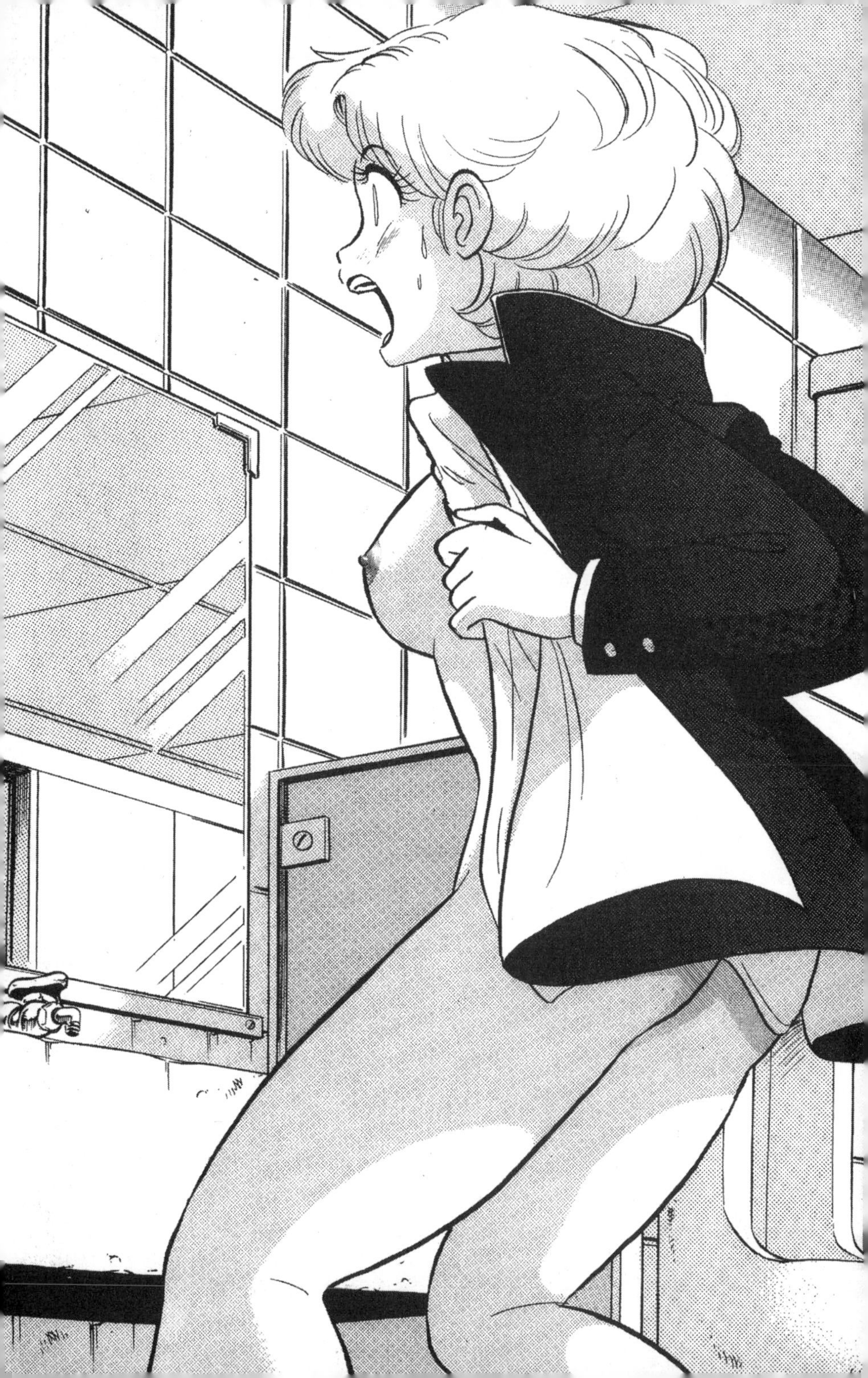

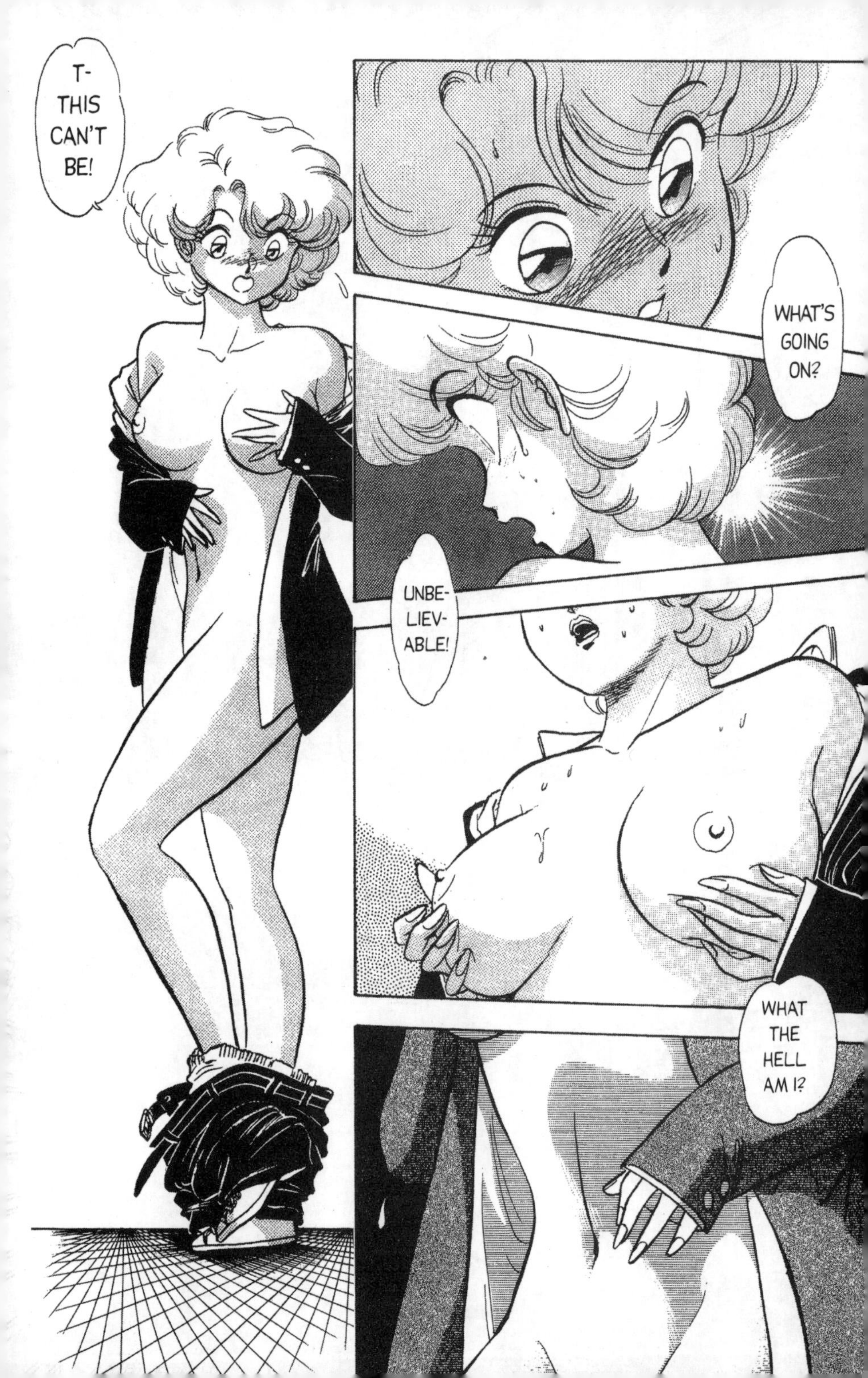
T- THIS CAN'T BE!
WHAT'S GOING ON?
UNBE- LIEV- ABLE!
WHAT THE HELL AM I?

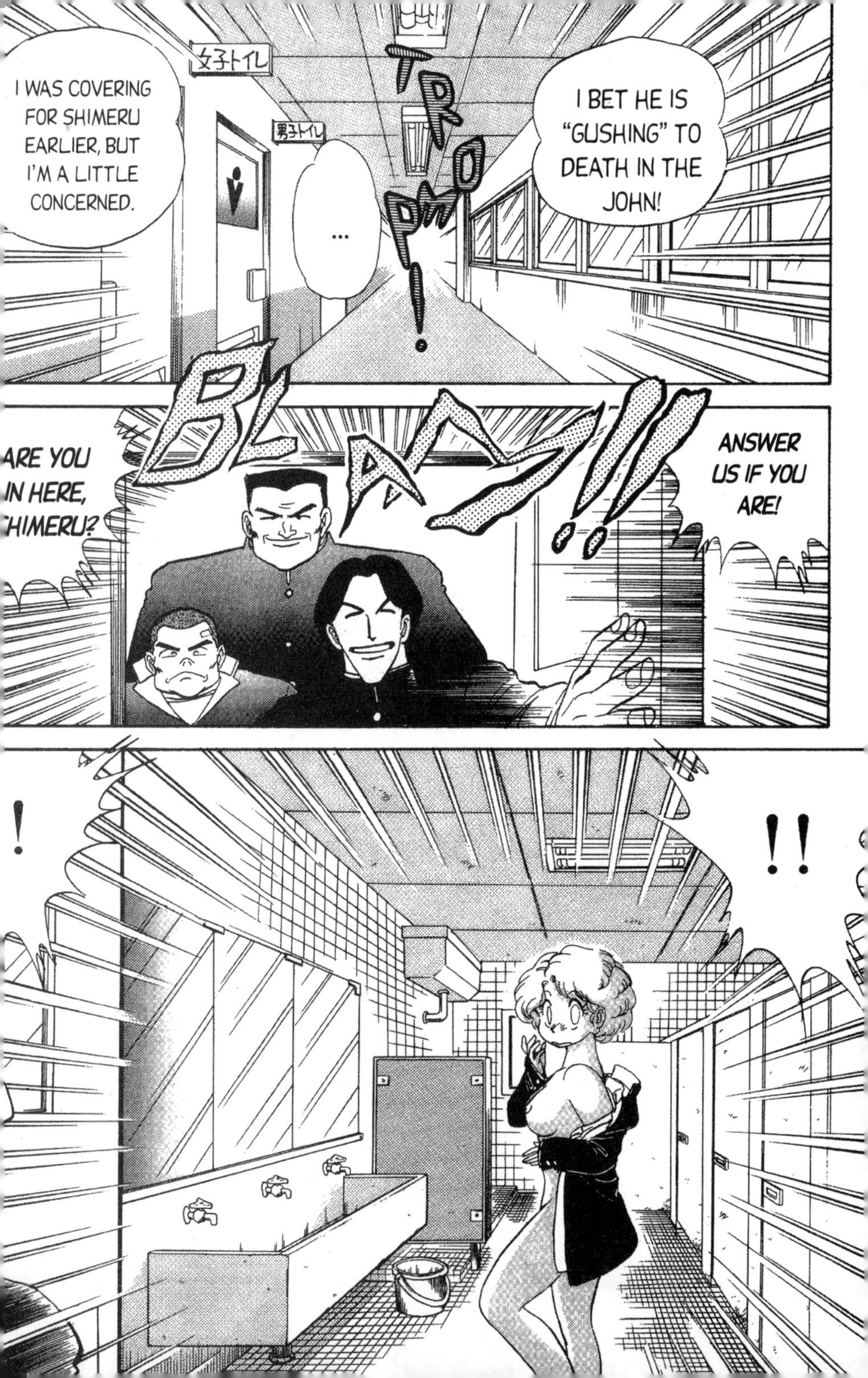

女子トイレ
男子トイレ
I BET HE IS "GUSHING" TO DEATH IN THE JOHN!
...
I WAS COVERING FOR SHIMERU EARLIER, BUT I'M A LITTLE CONCERNED.
BLAM!!
ANSWER US IF YOU ARE!
ARE YOU IN HERE, HIMERU?
!!
!

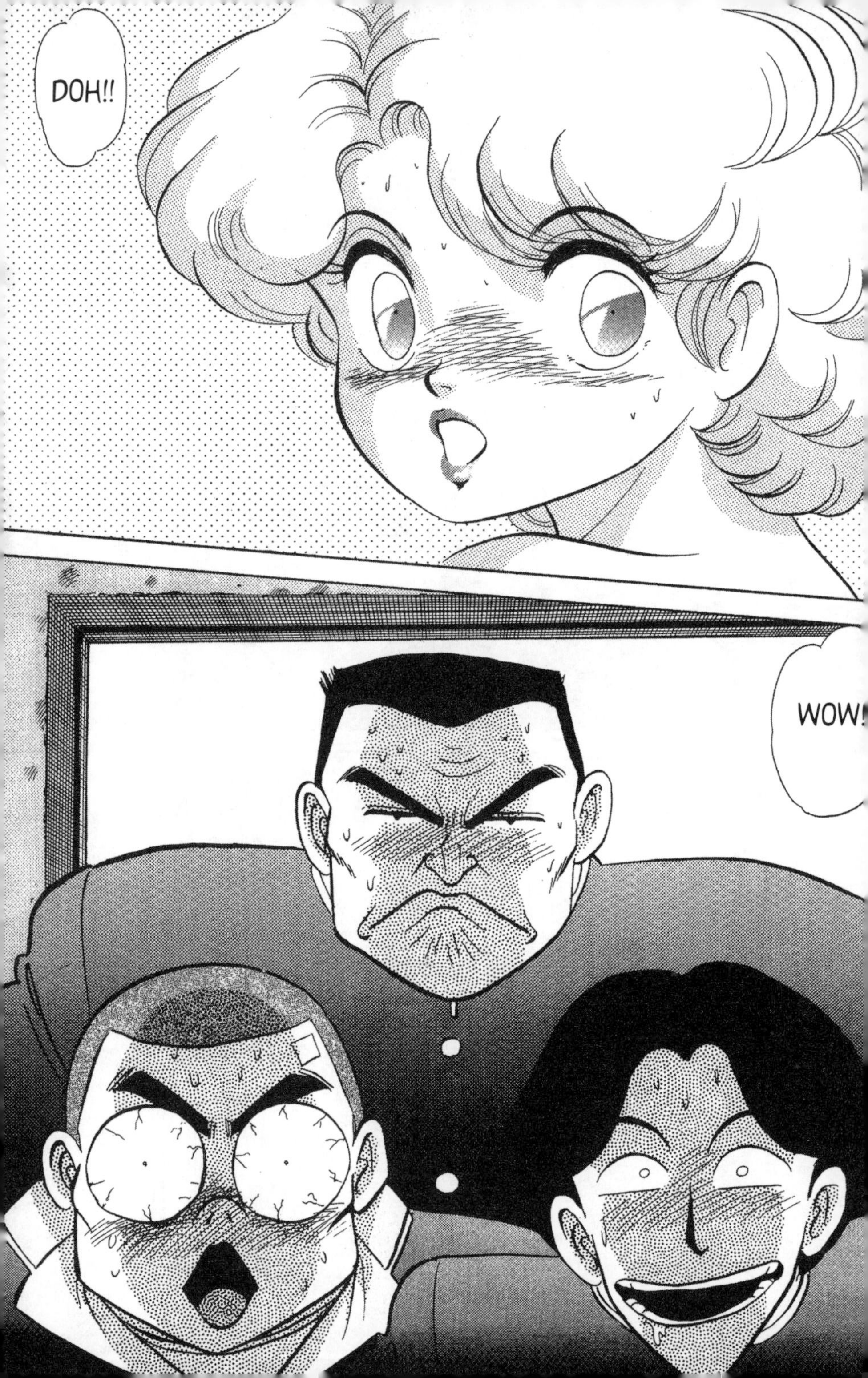
DOH!!
WOW!

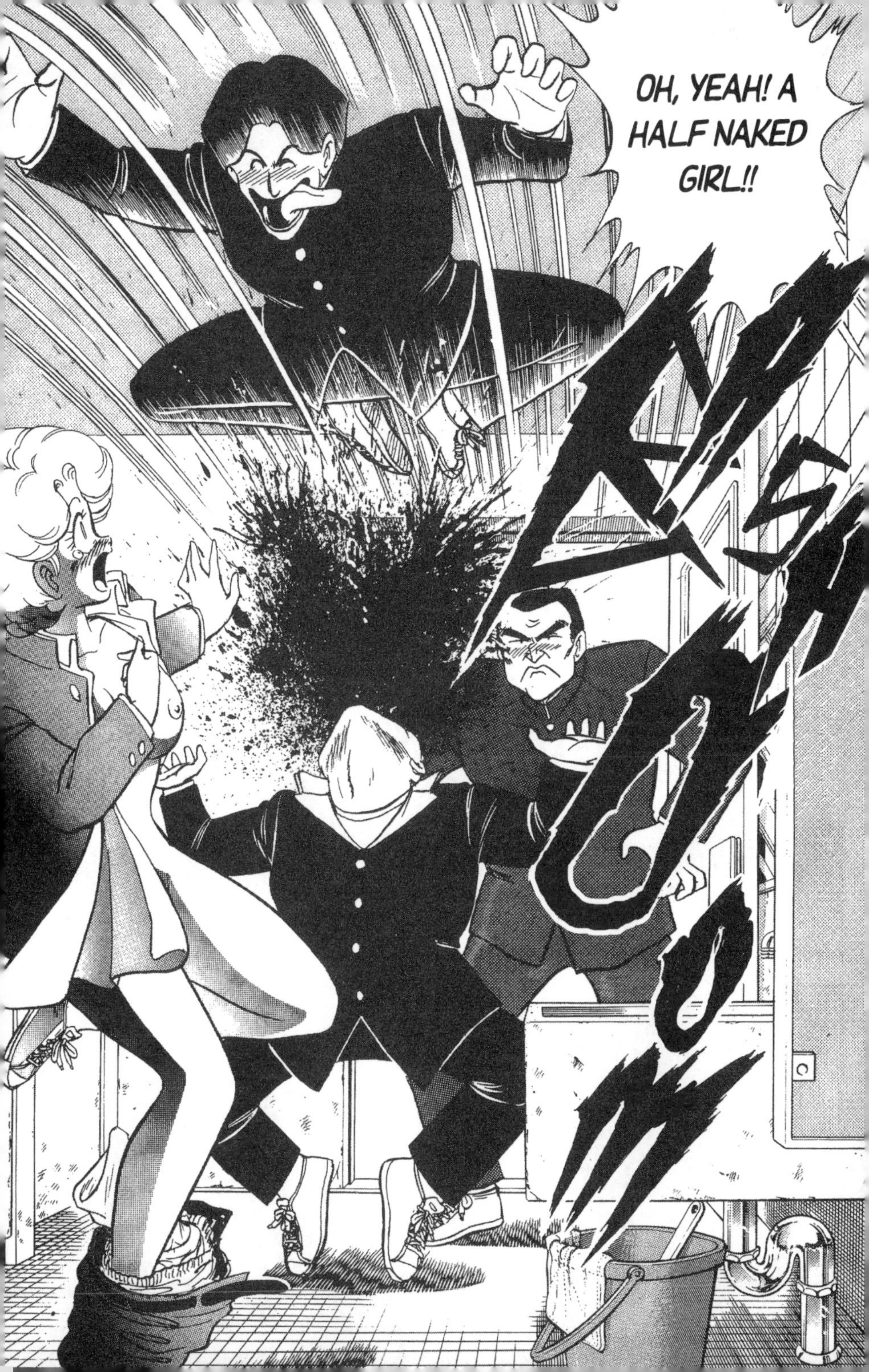
OH, YEAH! A HALF NAKED GIRL!!

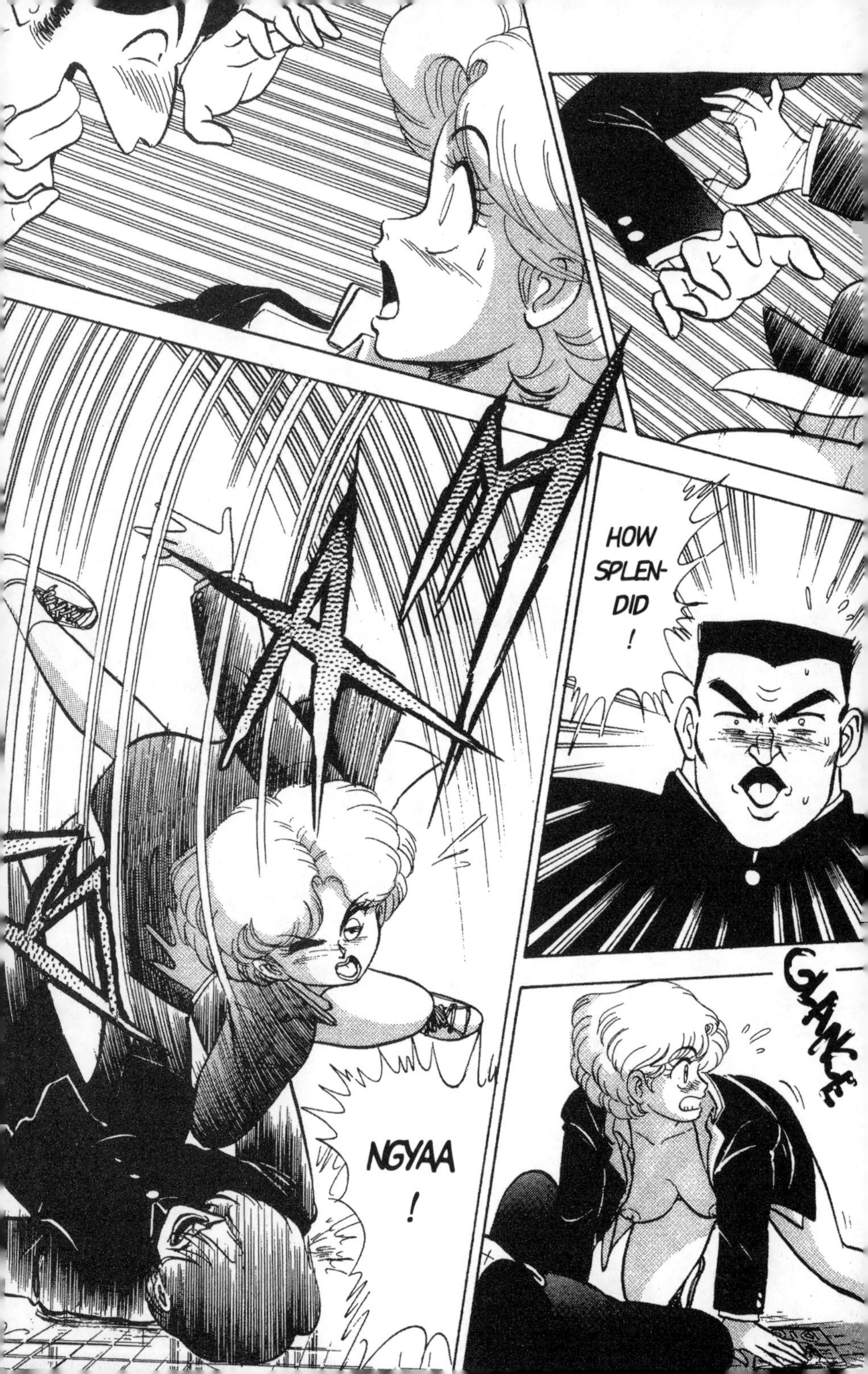

HOW SPLEN-DID !
GLANCE
NGYAA !

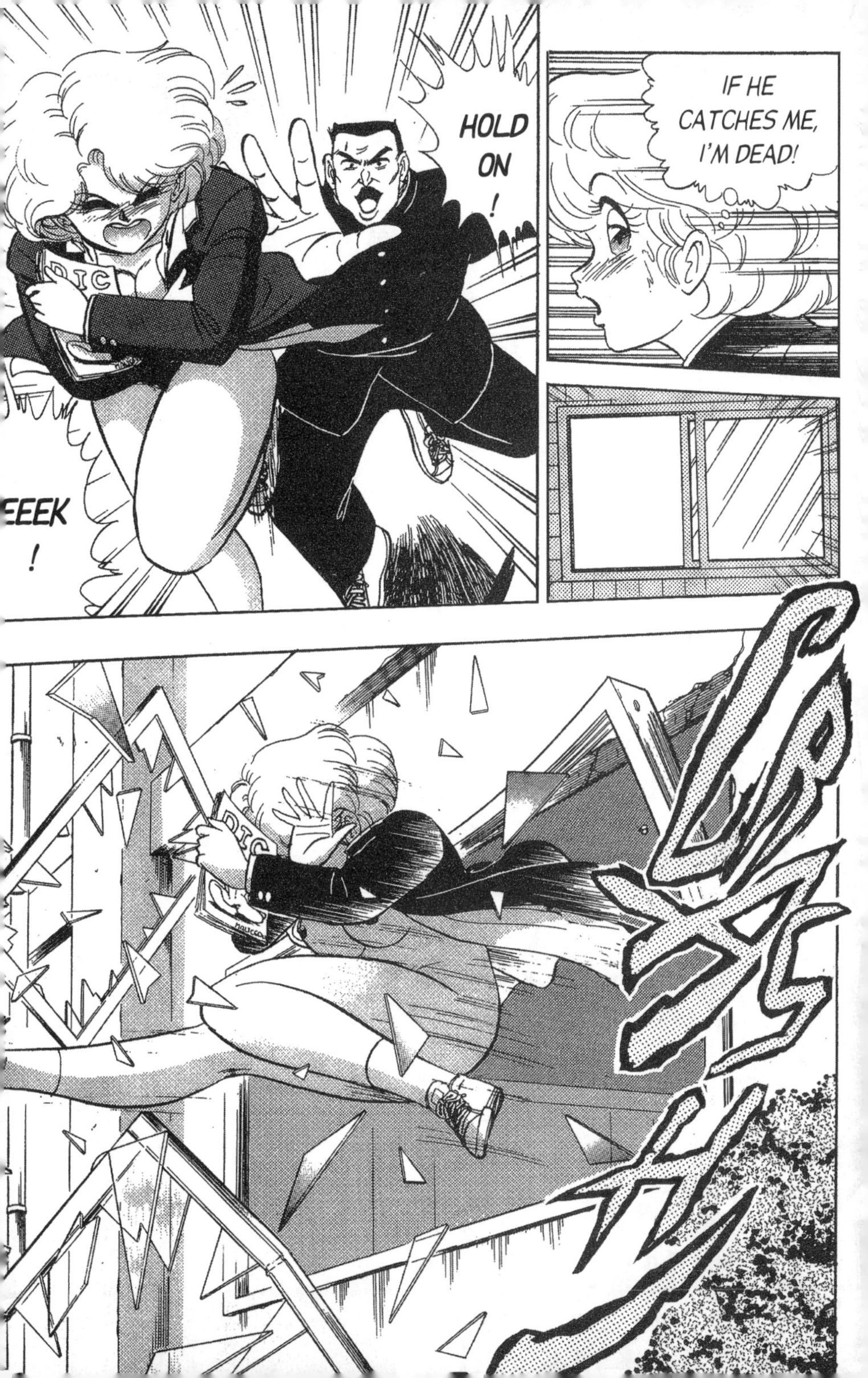
HOLD ON !
EEEK !
IF HE CATCHES ME, I'M DEAD!

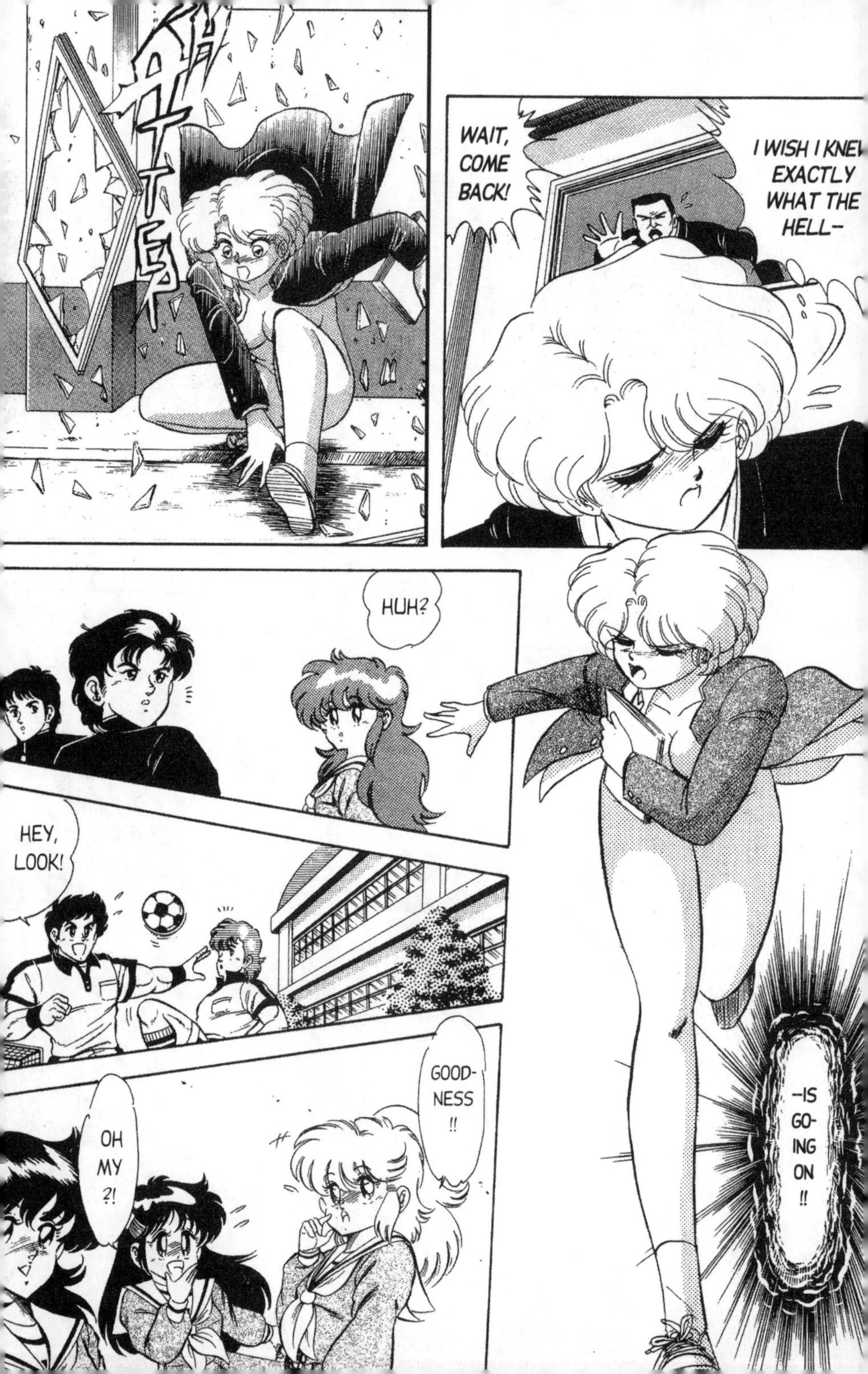

WAIT, COME BACK!
I WISH I KNEW EXACTLY WHAT THE HELL–
HUH?
HEY, LOOK!
GOODNESS !!
OH MY ?!
--IS GOING ON !!

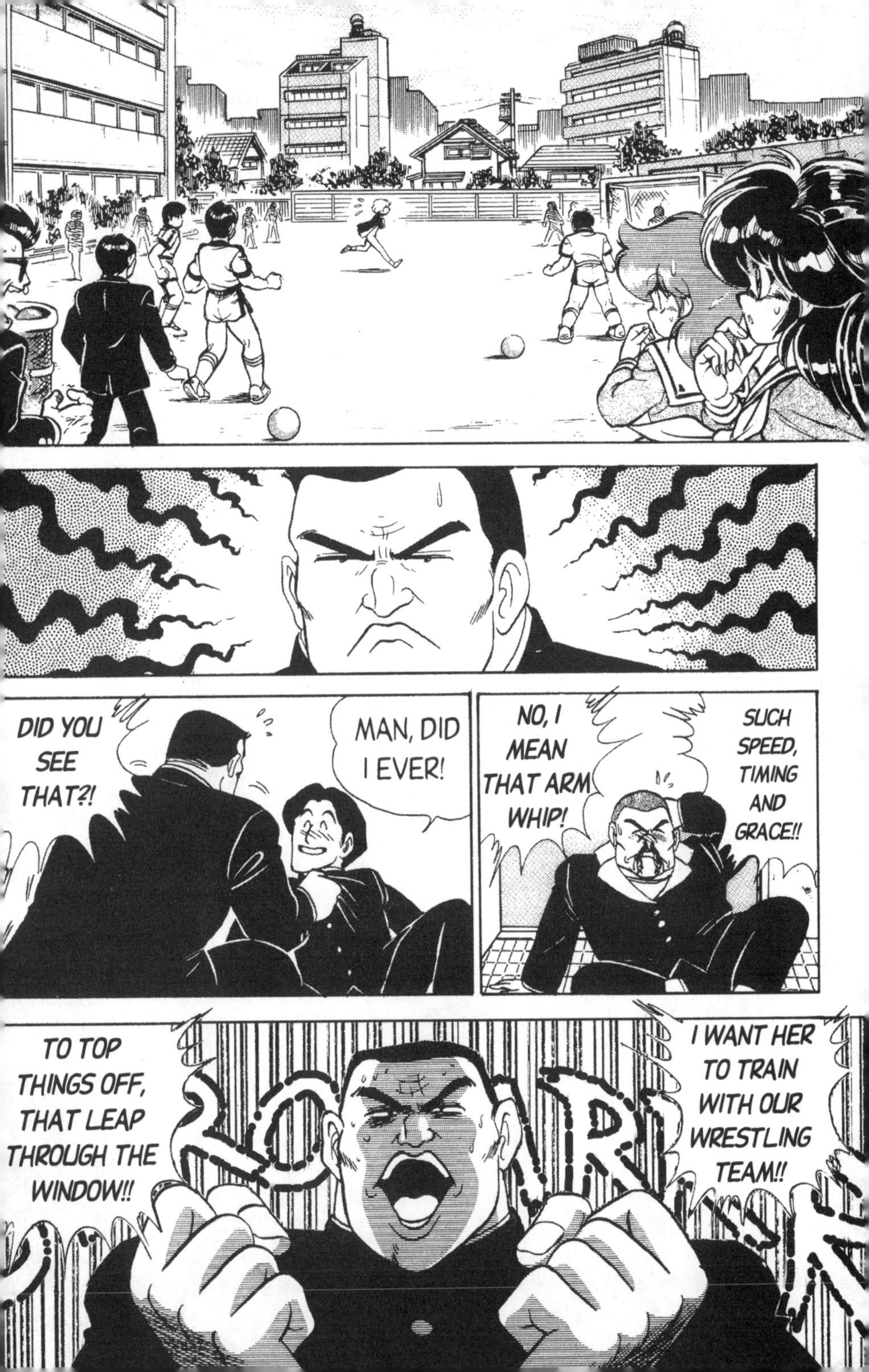
DID YOU SEE THAT?!
MAN, DID I EVER!
NO, I MEAN THAT ARM WHIP!
SUCH SPEED, TIMING AND GRACE!!
TO TOP THINGS OFF, THAT LEAP THROUGH THE WINDOW!!
I WANT HER TO TRAIN WITH OUR WRESTLING TEAM!!

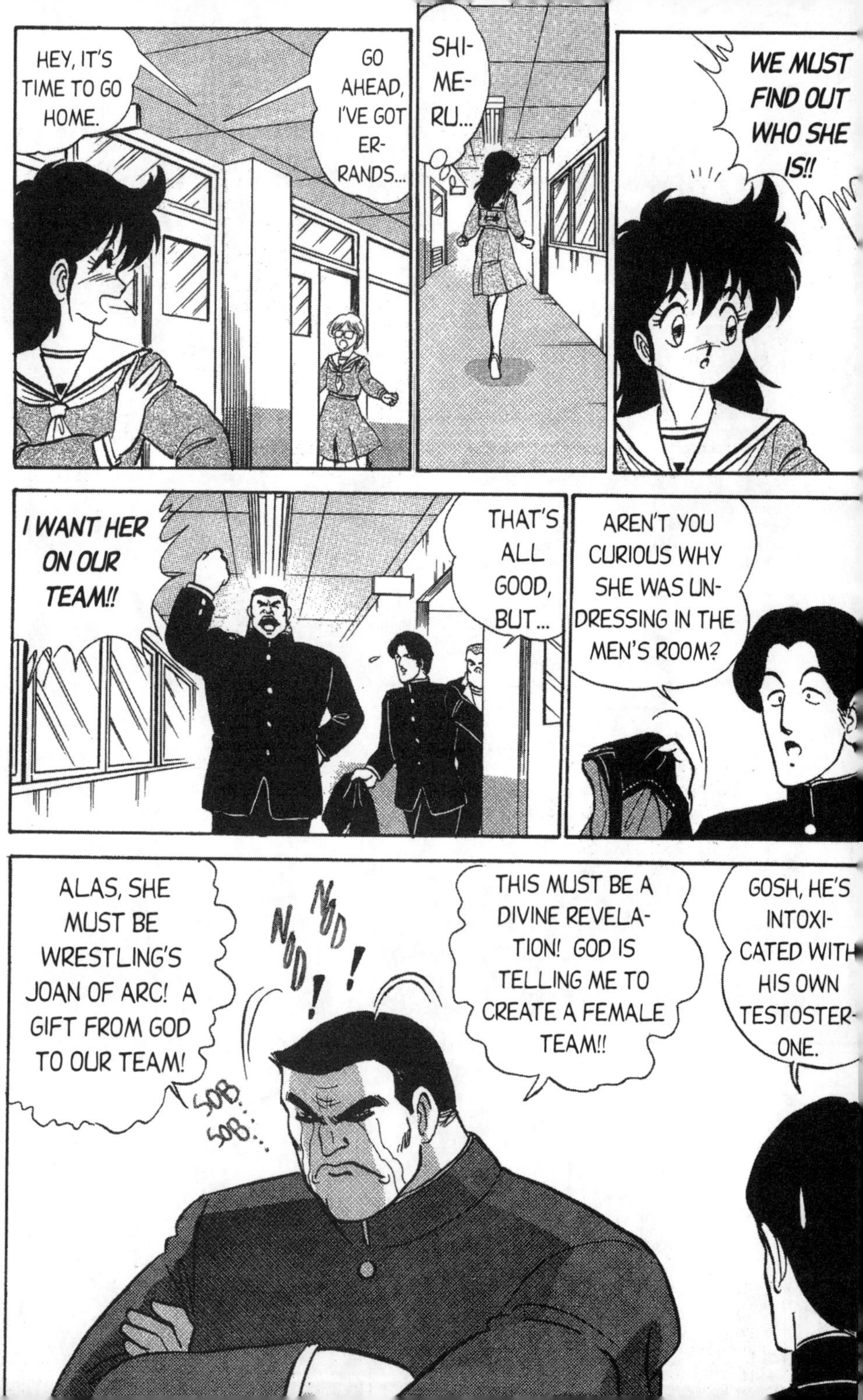
HEY, IT'S TIME TO GO HOME.
GO AHEAD, I'VE GOT ER-RANDS...
SHI-ME-RU...
WE MUST FIND OUT WHO SHE IS!!
I WANT HER ON OUR TEAM!!
THAT'S ALL GOOD, BUT...
AREN'T YOU CURIOUS WHY SHE WAS UN-DRESSING IN THE MEN'S ROOM?
ALAS, SHE MUST BE WRESTLING'S JOAN OF ARC! A GIFT FROM GOD TO OUR TEAM!
NOD NOD!!
SOB SOB...
THIS MUST BE A DIVINE REVELA-TION! GOD IS TELLING ME TO CREATE A FEMALE TEAM!!
GOSH, HE'S INTOXI-CATED WITH HIS OWN TESTOSTER-ONE.

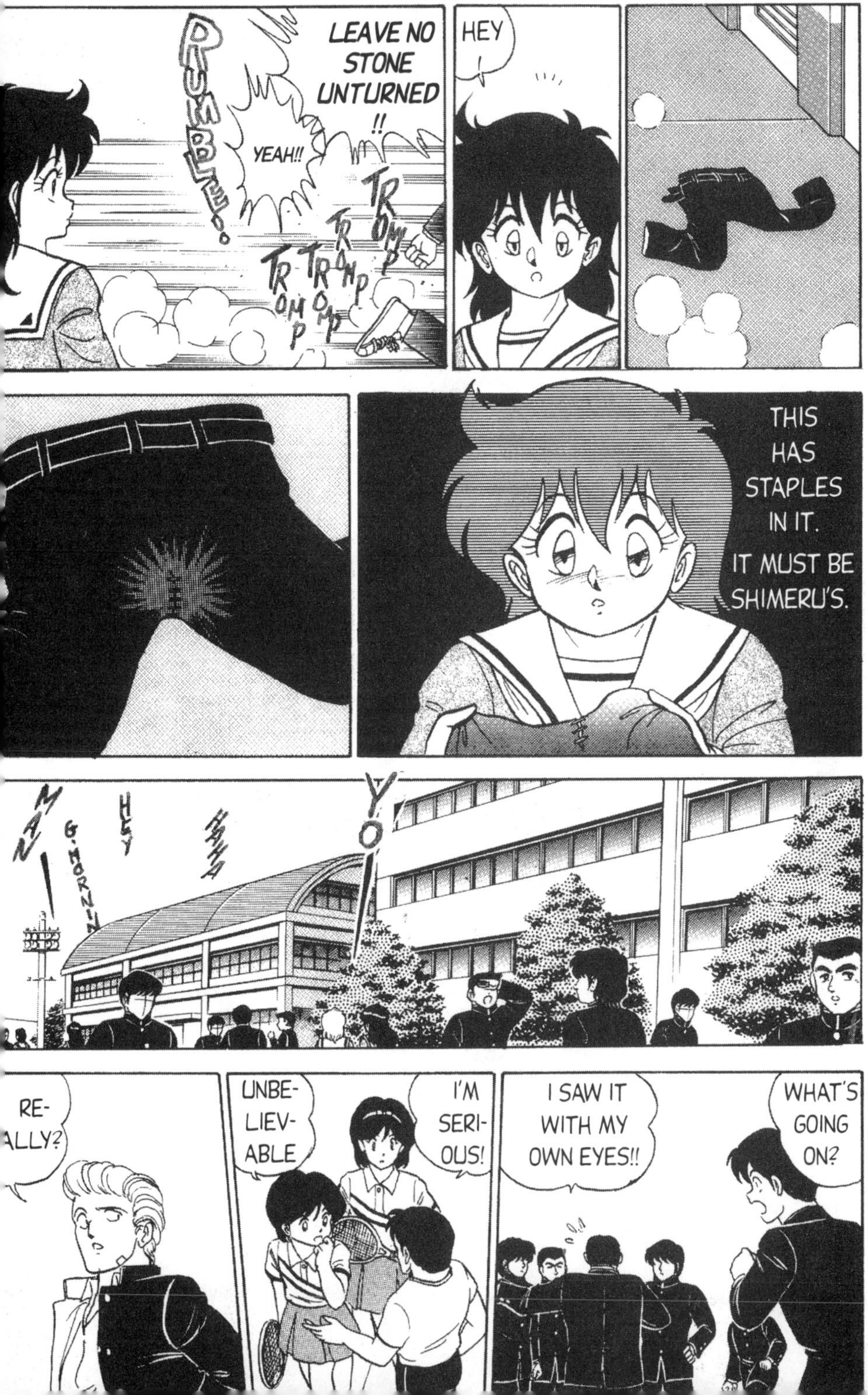

RUMBLE...
LEAVE NO STONE UNTURNED !!
YEAH!!
TROMP TROMP TROMP TROMP
HEY !
THIS HAS STAPLES IN IT.
IT MUST BE SHIMERU'S.
MAN !
G-MORNIN
HEY
HAHA
YO !
RE-ALLY?
UNBE-LIEV-ABLE
I'M SERI-OUS!
I SAW IT WITH MY OWN EYES!!
WHAT'S GOING ON?

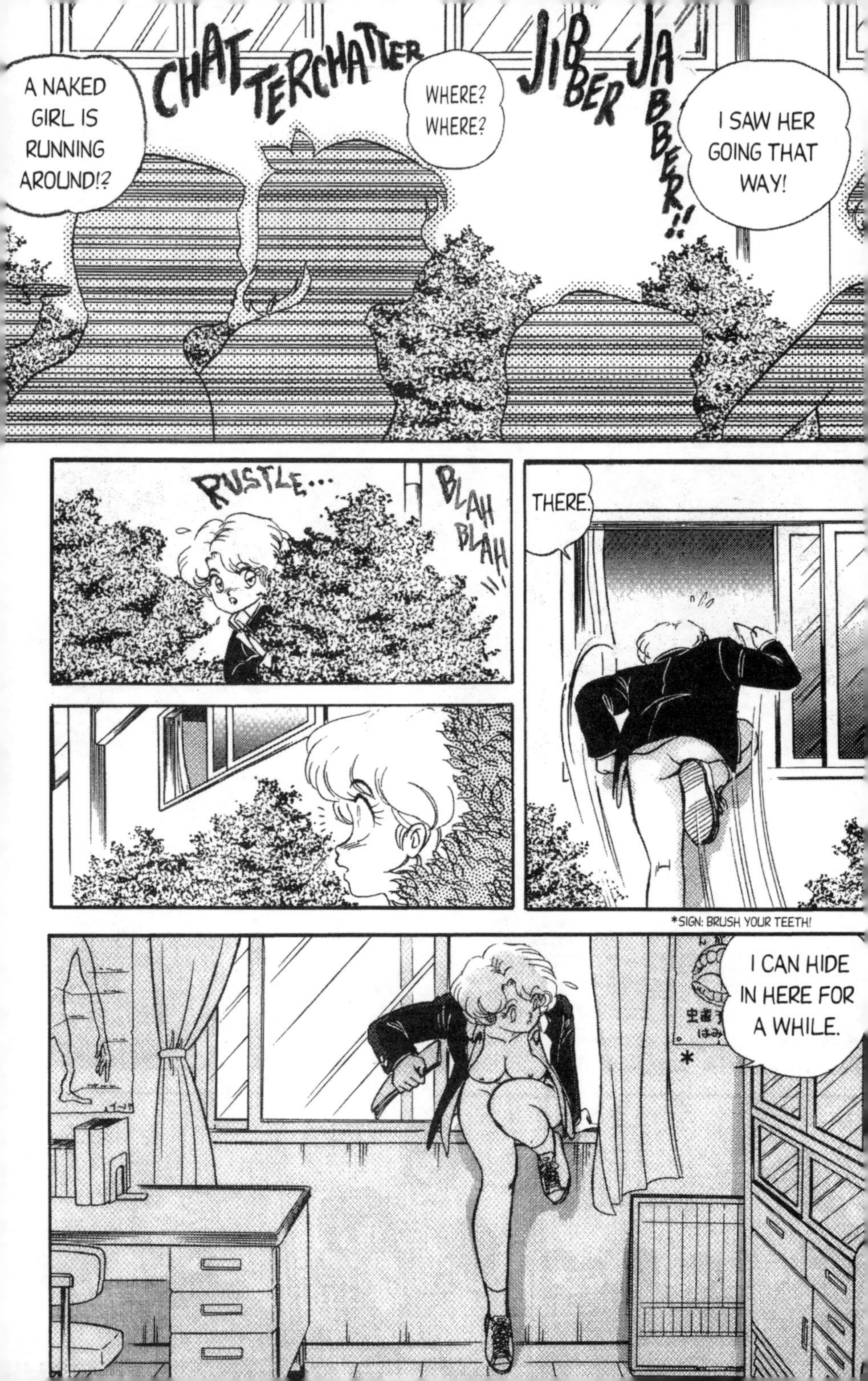

A NAKED GIRL IS RUNNING AROUND!?
CHATTERCHATTER
WHERE? WHERE?
JIBBER JABBER!!
I SAW HER GOING THAT WAY!
RUSTLE...
BLAH BLAH
THERE.
*SIGN: BRUSH YOUR TEETH!
I CAN HIDE IN HERE FOR A WHILE.

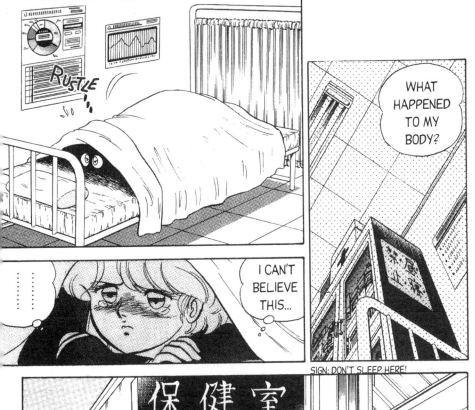

RUSTLE

WHAT HAPPENED TO MY BODY?

I CAN'T BELIEVE THIS...

SIGN: DON'T SLEEP HERE!

保健室

SIGN: INFIRMARY

THIS IS THE ONLY PLACE WE HAVEN'T CHECKED.

SLAM

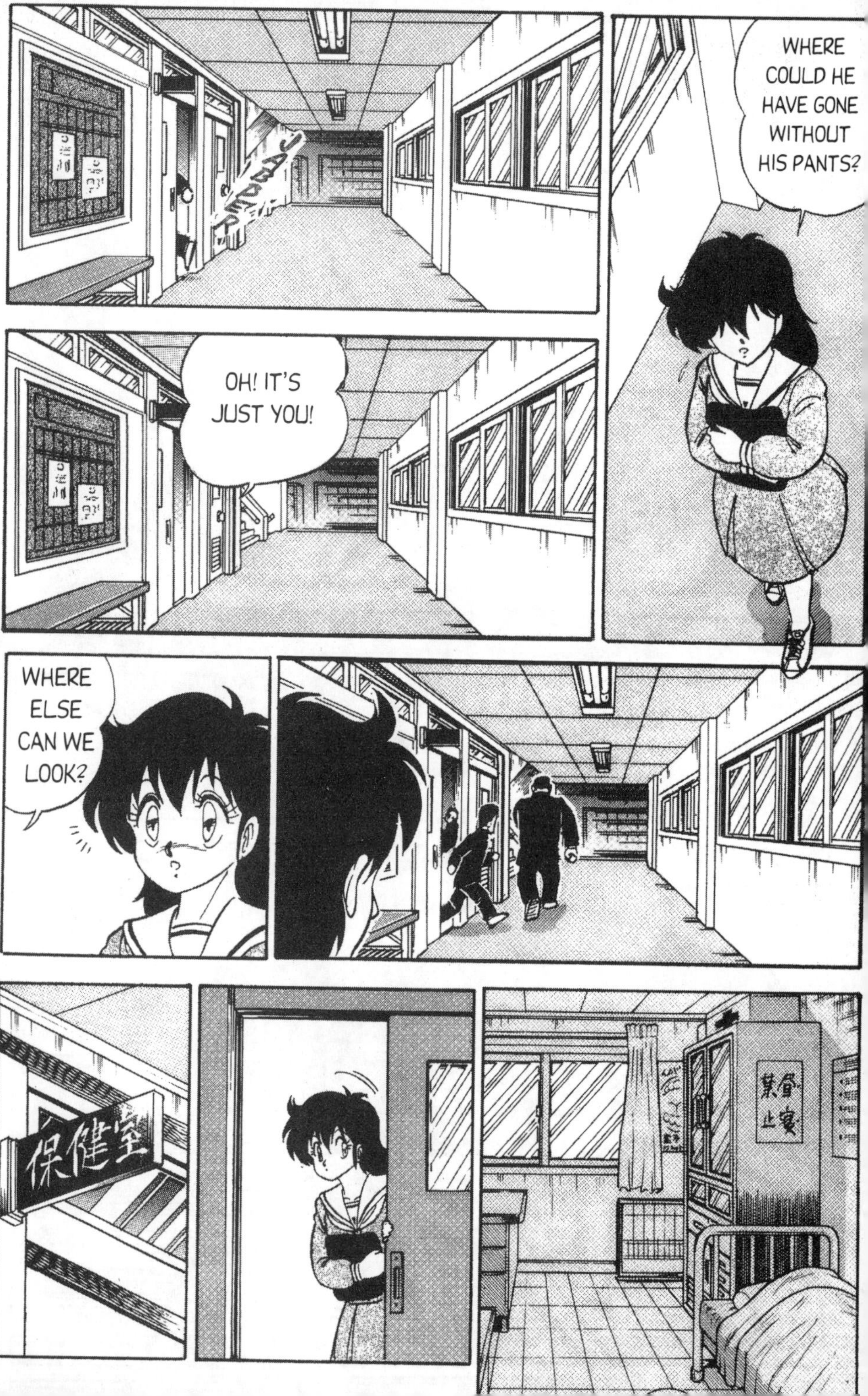

WHERE COULD HE HAVE GONE WITHOUT HIS PANTS?
JABBER
OH! IT'S JUST YOU!
WHERE ELSE CAN WE LOOK?
保健室

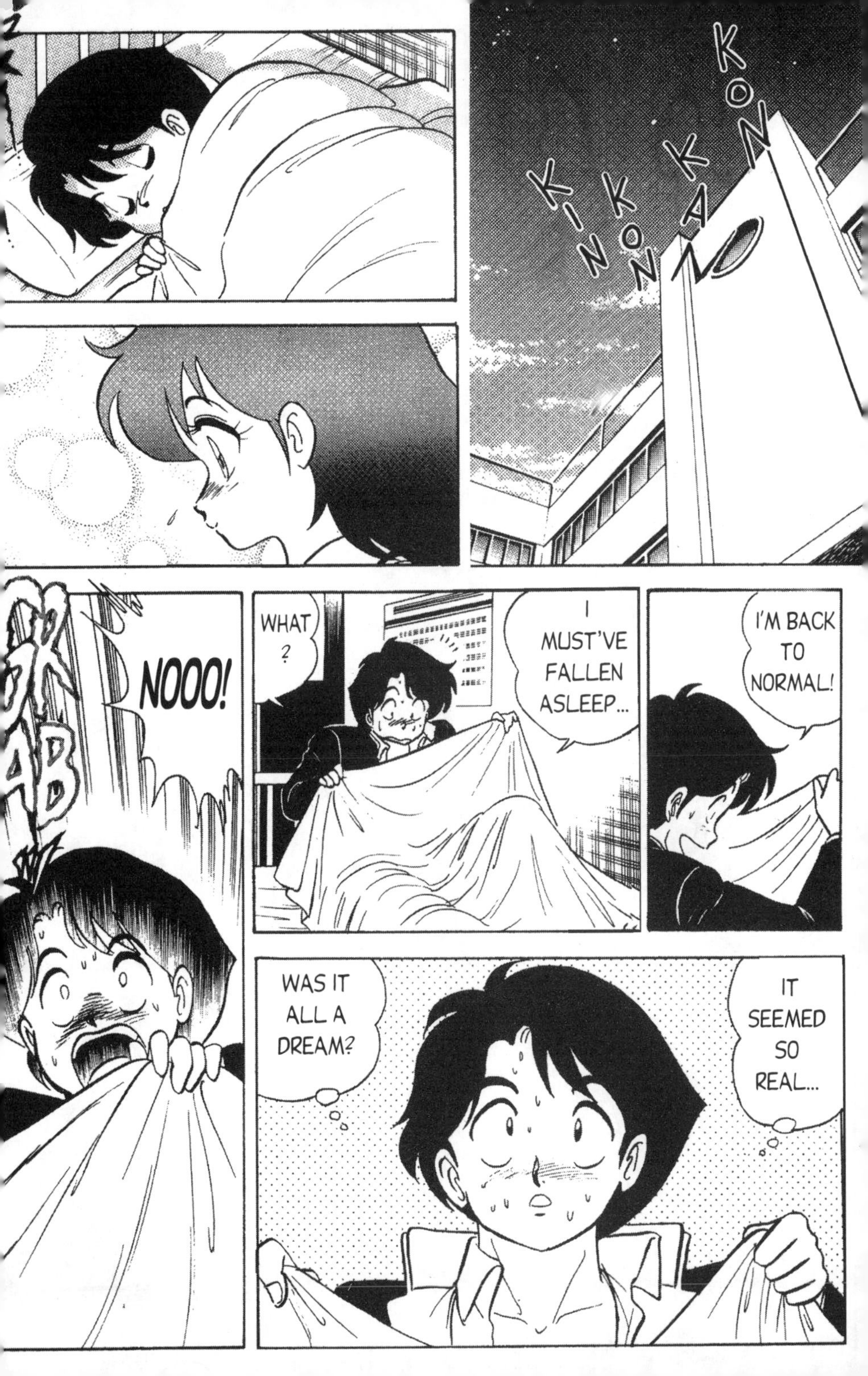
KIN KON KAN KON
NOOO!
WHAT?
I MUST'VE FALLEN ASLEEP...
I'M BACK TO NORMAL!
WAS IT ALL A DREAM?
IT SEEMED SO REAL...

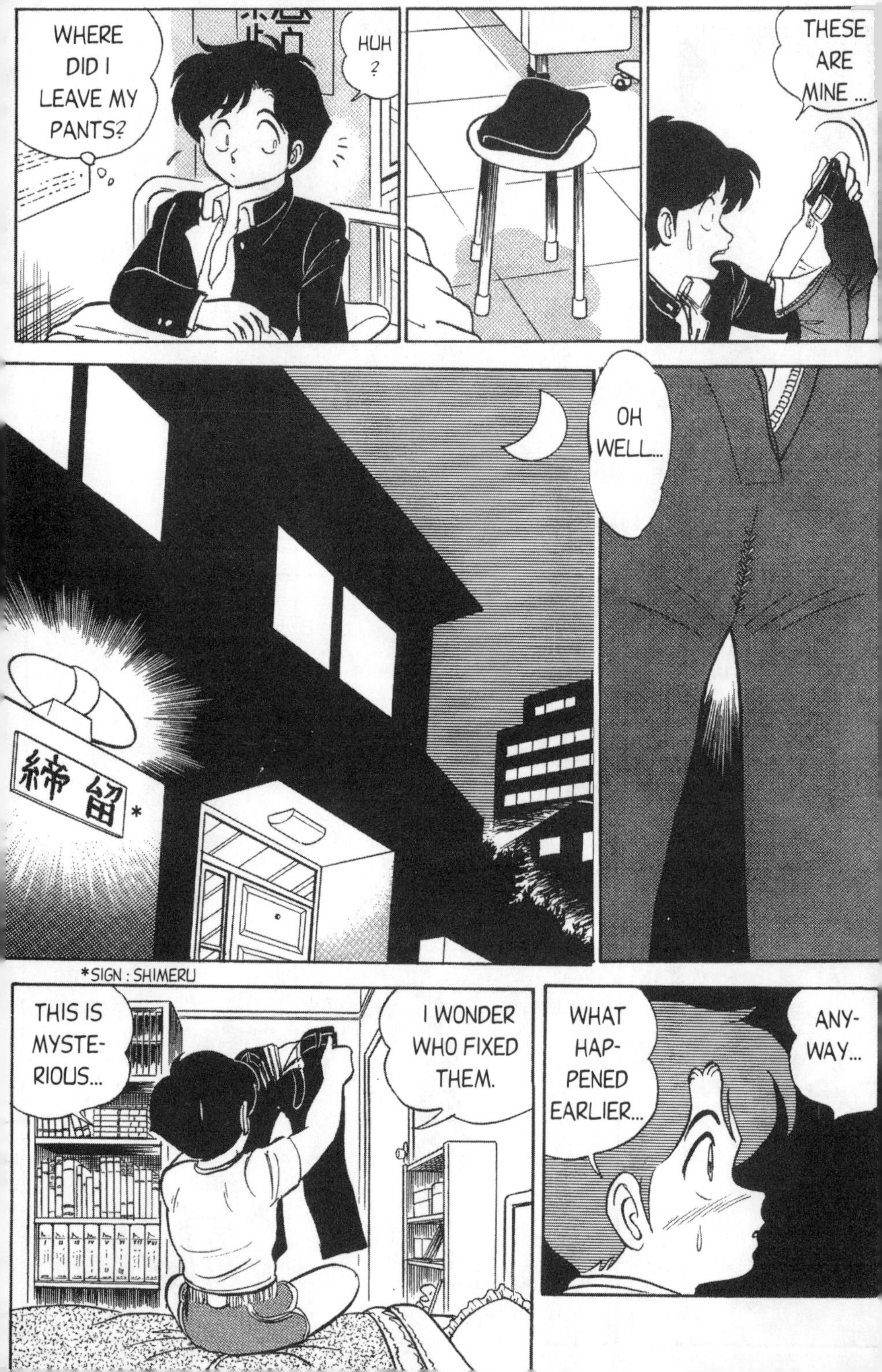
WHERE DID I LEAVE MY PANTS?
HUH ?
THESE ARE MINE ...
OH WELL...
締留*
*SIGN : SHIMERU
THIS IS MYSTE-RIOUS...
I WONDER WHO FIXED THEM.
WHAT HAP-PENED EARLIER...
ANY-WAY...

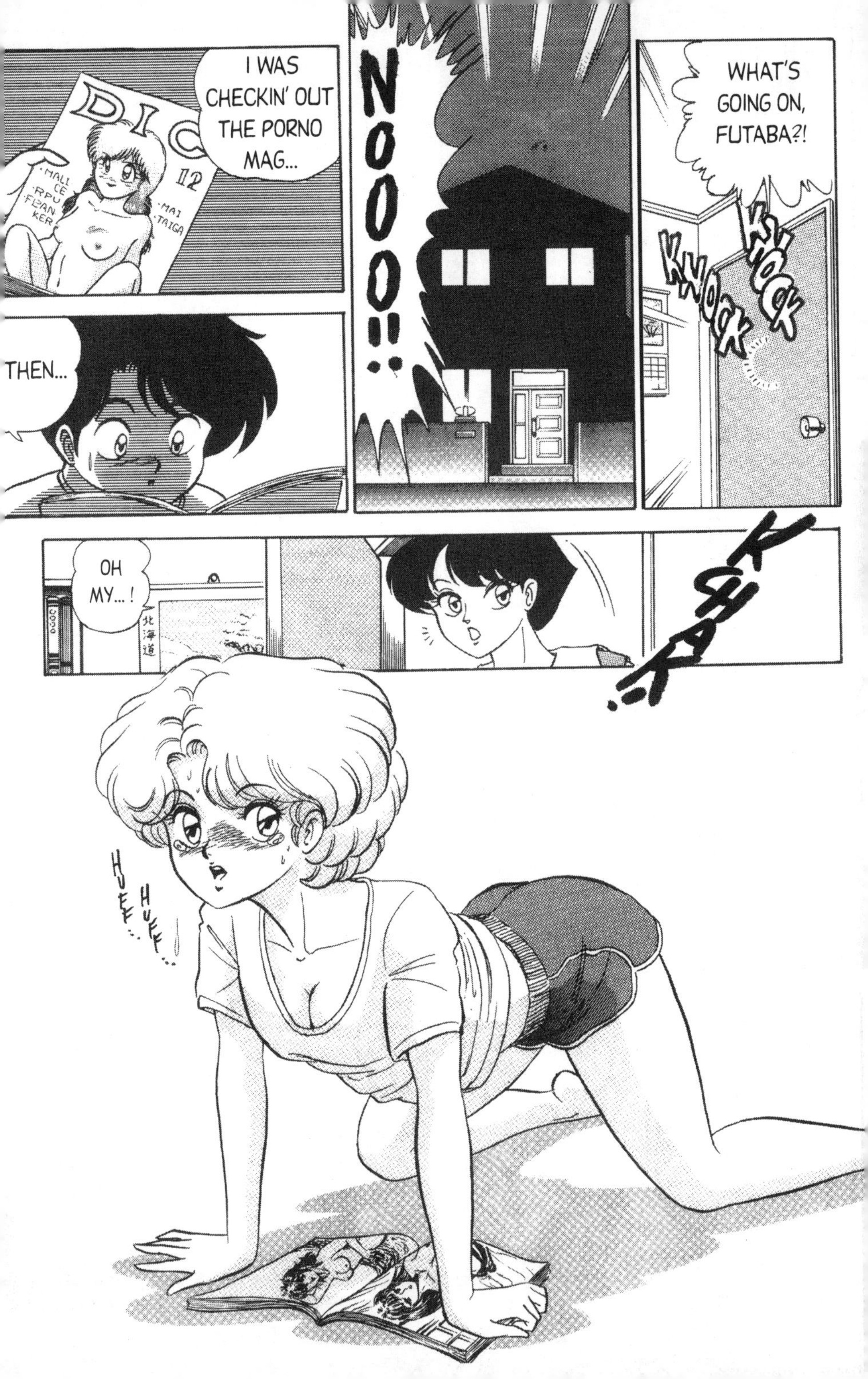

I WAS CHECKIN' OUT THE PORNO MAG...
THEN...
NOOOO!!
WHAT'S GOING ON, FUTABA?!
KNOCK KNOCK
OH MY...!
KSHAK!!
HUFF... HUFF...

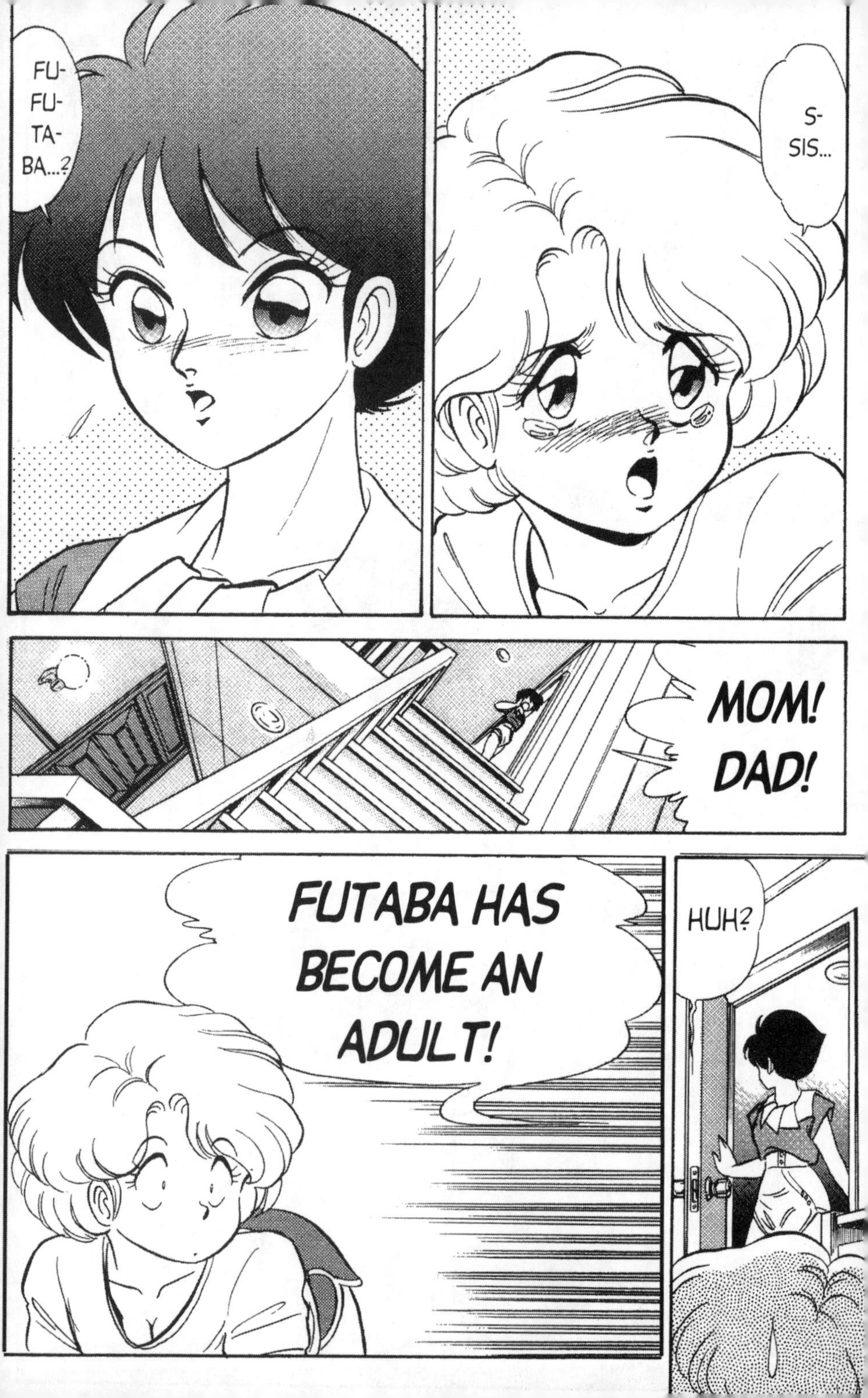
FU-FU-TA-BA...?
S-SIS...
MOM! DAD!
FUTABA HAS BECOME AN ADULT!
HUH?

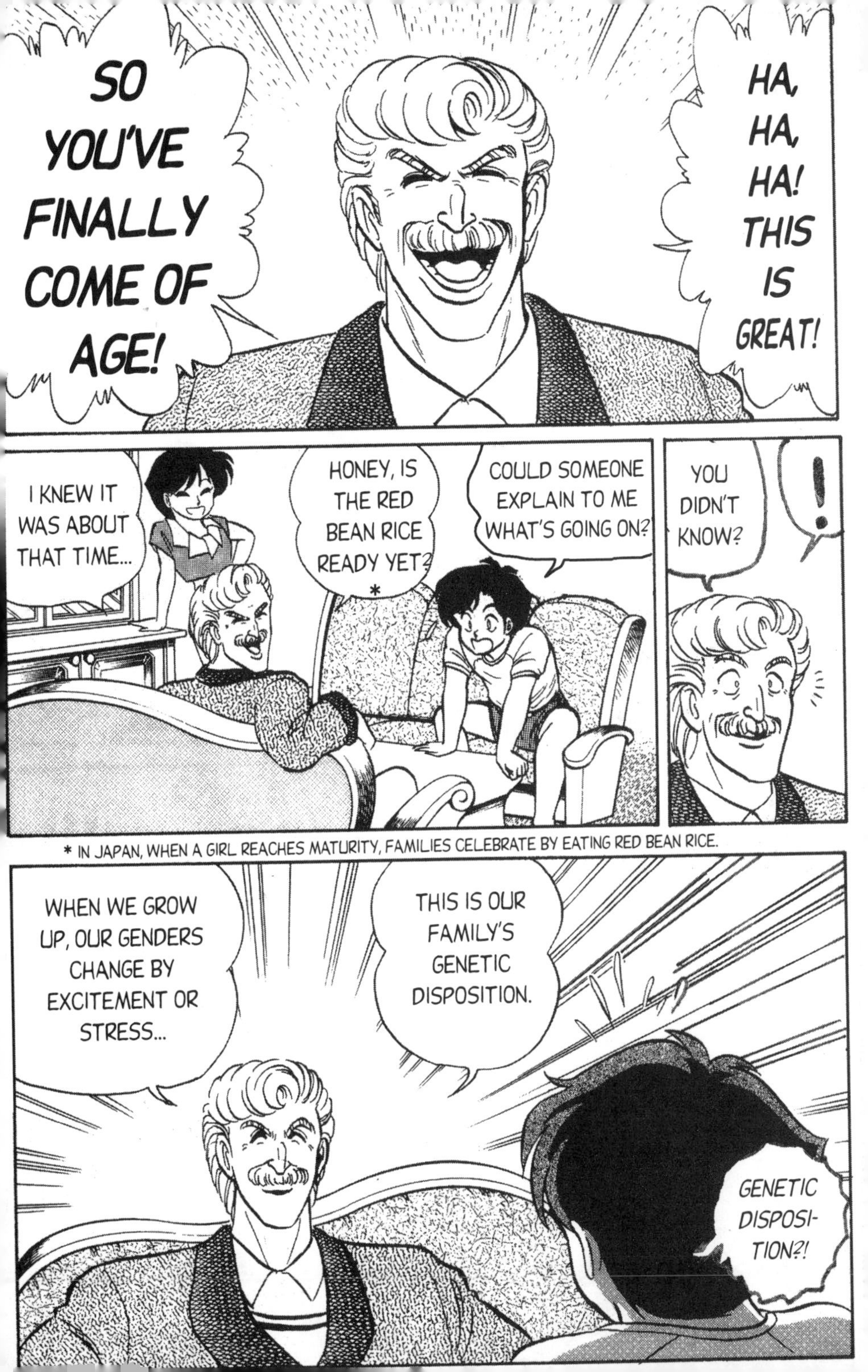
SO YOU'VE FINALLY COME OF AGE!
HA, HA, HA! THIS IS GREAT!
I KNEW IT WAS ABOUT THAT TIME...
HONEY, IS THE RED BEAN RICE READY YET? *
COULD SOMEONE EXPLAIN TO ME WHAT'S GOING ON?
YOU DIDN'T KNOW?
!
WHEN WE GROW UP, OUR GENDERS CHANGE BY EXCITEMENT OR STRESS...
THIS IS OUR FAMILY'S GENETIC DISPOSITION.
GENETIC DISPOSI-TION?!

* IN JAPAN, WHEN A GIRL REACHES MATURITY, FAMILIES CELEBRATE BY EATING RED BEAN RICE.

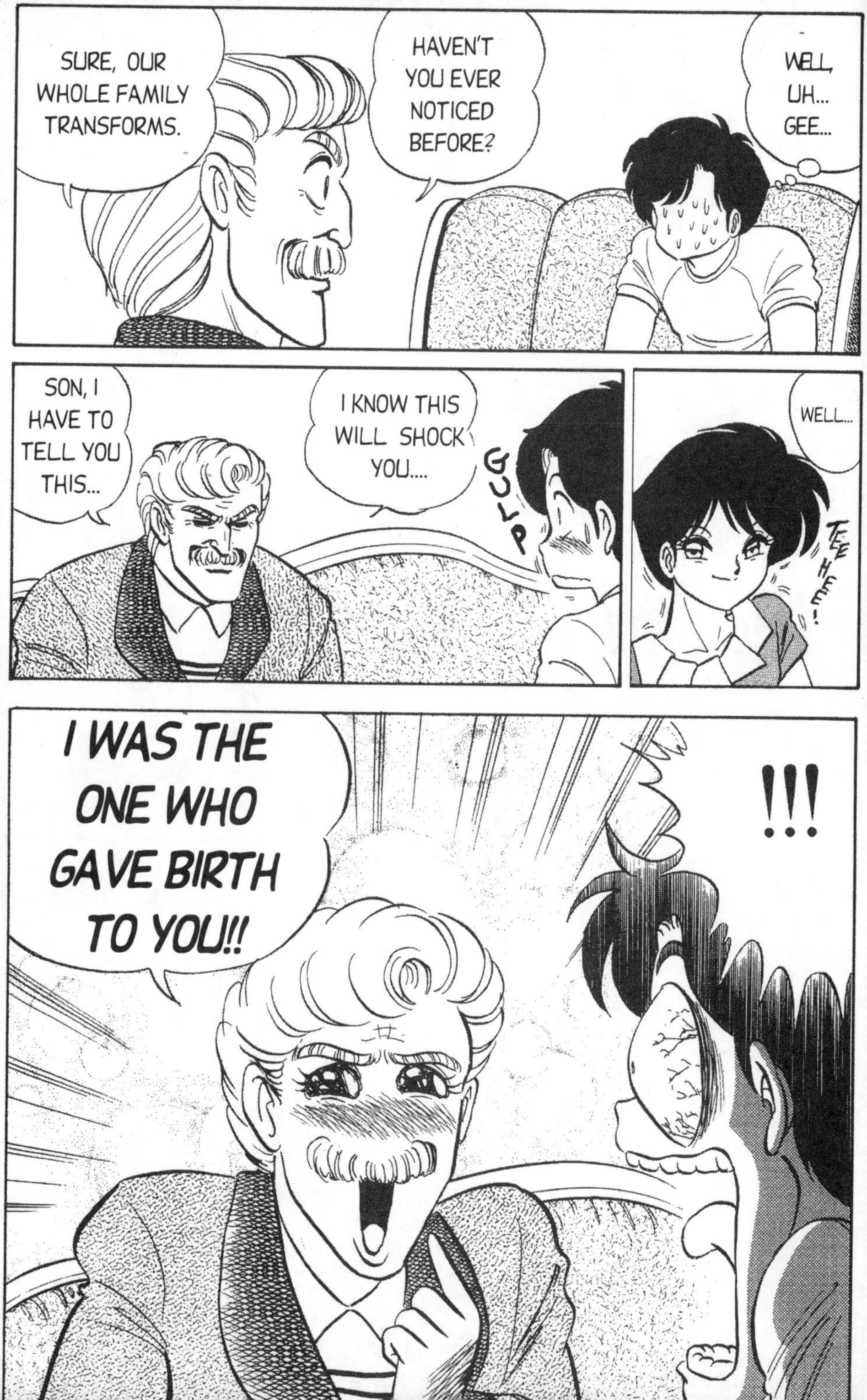
SURE, OUR WHOLE FAMILY TRANSFORMS.
HAVEN'T YOU EVER NOTICED BEFORE?
WELL, UH... GEE...
SON, I HAVE TO TELL YOU THIS...
I KNOW THIS WILL SHOCK YOU....
GULP
WELL...
TEE HEE!
I WAS THE ONE WHO GAVE BIRTH TO YOU!!
!!!

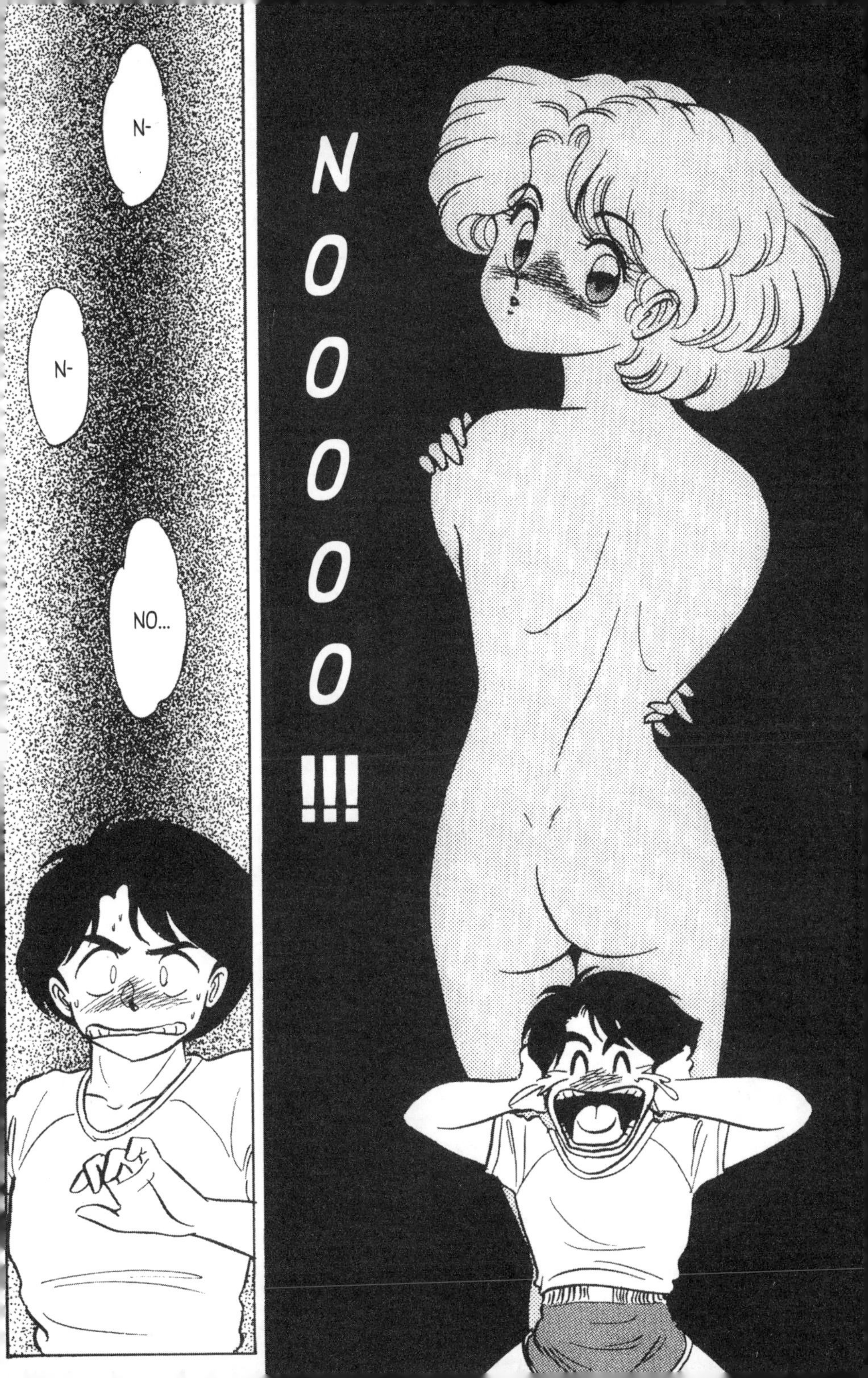
N-
N-
NO...
NOOOOOO!!!

MY WORKS LIST

I HAVE BEEN RECEIVING A LOT OF REQUESTS
FROM MY AMERICAN READERS FOR A LIST OF MY
WORKS, SO LET ME INDULGE THEM WITH A PAR-
TIAL LIST:

WORKS PUBLISHED BY SHUEISHA
BUGI UGI ALLIGATOR (BOOGIE WOOGIE ALLIGATOR), JUMP COMICS SELECTION
OMISORE! TORABURIKKO. (THE INVINCIBLE TROUBLE GIRL), JUMP SUPER COMICS
TOTTEMO SHONEN TANKENTAI (VERY BOYS EXPLORERS), JUMP SUPER COMICS
YUU AND MII (YOU AND ME) 8 VOLUMES TOTAL, JUMP COMICS
SHERIFF, 2 VOLUMES TOTAL , JUMP COMICS
PARANOIYA GEKIJOU (PARANOIA THEATER), JUMP COMICS DELUXE
FUTABA-KUN CHANGE 8 VOLUMES TOTAL, THIS IS IT!

TOKUMA PUBLISHING
MORUMO 1/10 2 VOLUMES TOTAL , SHONEN CAPTAIN COMICS
UNKAI NO TABIBITO (TRAVELERS OF CLOUD WORLD), ANIMAGE COMICS SPECIAL
WAKAOKUSAMA NO ABUNAI SHUMI (NEWLY WED MADAM'S PSYCHO HOBBY),
SHONEN CAPTAIN COMICS
SPECIAL

FUJIMI SHOBOU
TRICK STAR (FUJIMI FANTASIA COMICS)

THESE ARE THE BOOKS RELEASED AS OF 1991

IF YOU WANT TO SEE MORE OF MY WORKS TRANSLATED, WRITE TO THE IRONCAT GUYS AND TELL THEM!!

SASH: NICE TO MEET YOU!

Futaba's Locked Room Close Encounter!!

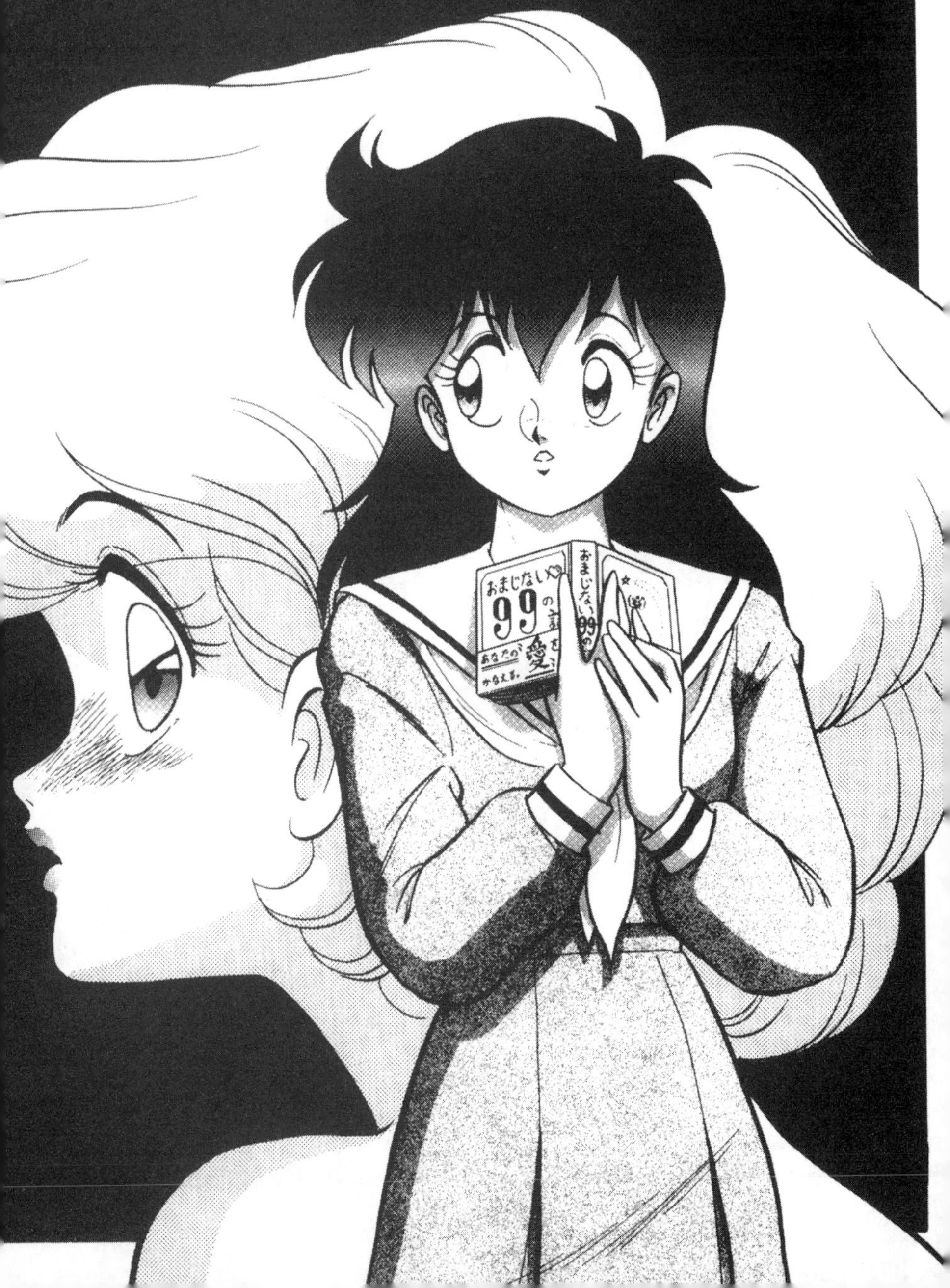
おまじない
99

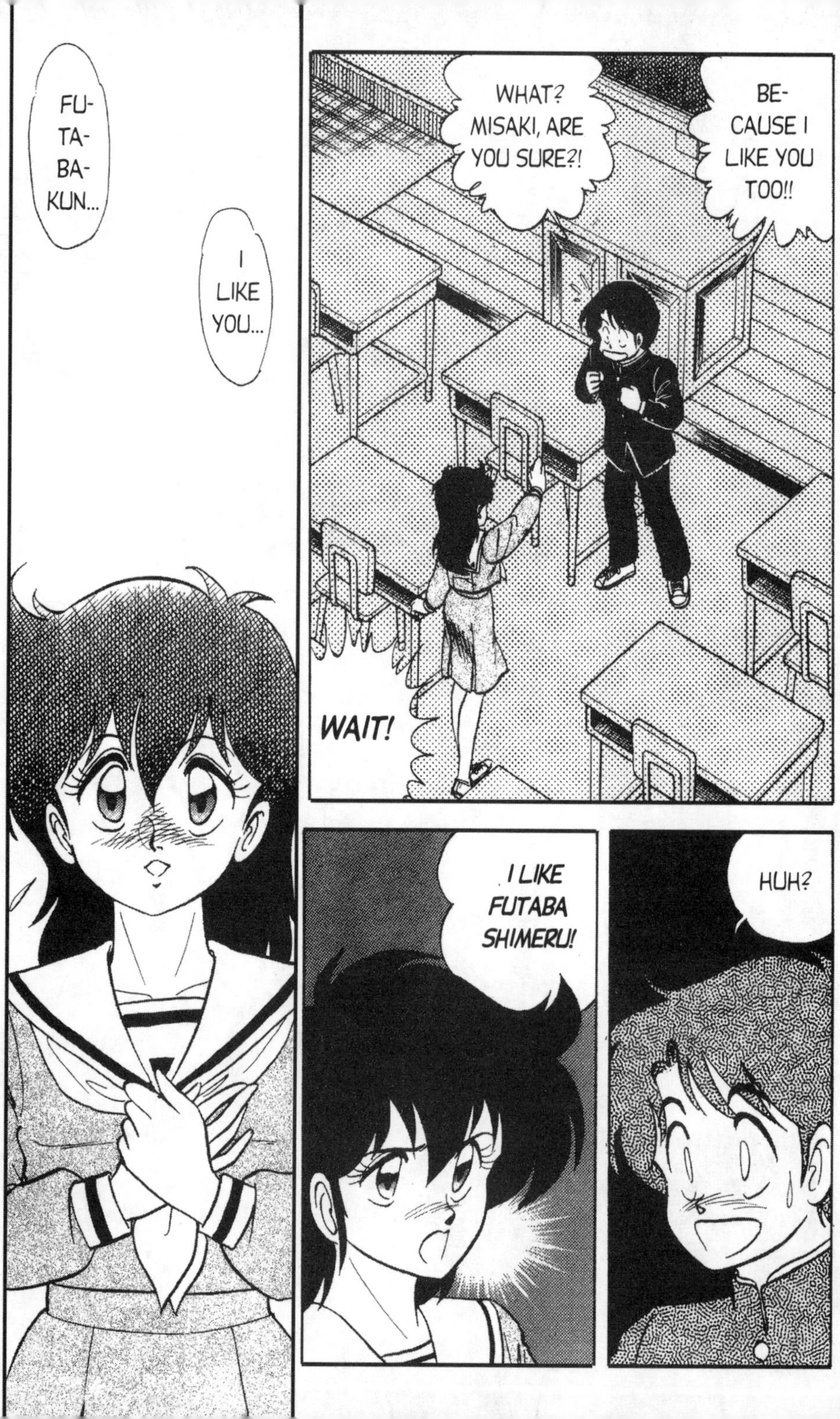
FU-TA-BA-KUN...
I LIKE YOU...
WAIT!
WHAT? MISAKI, ARE YOU SURE?!
BE-CAUSE I LIKE YOU TOO!!
I LIKE FUTABA SHIMERU!
HUH?

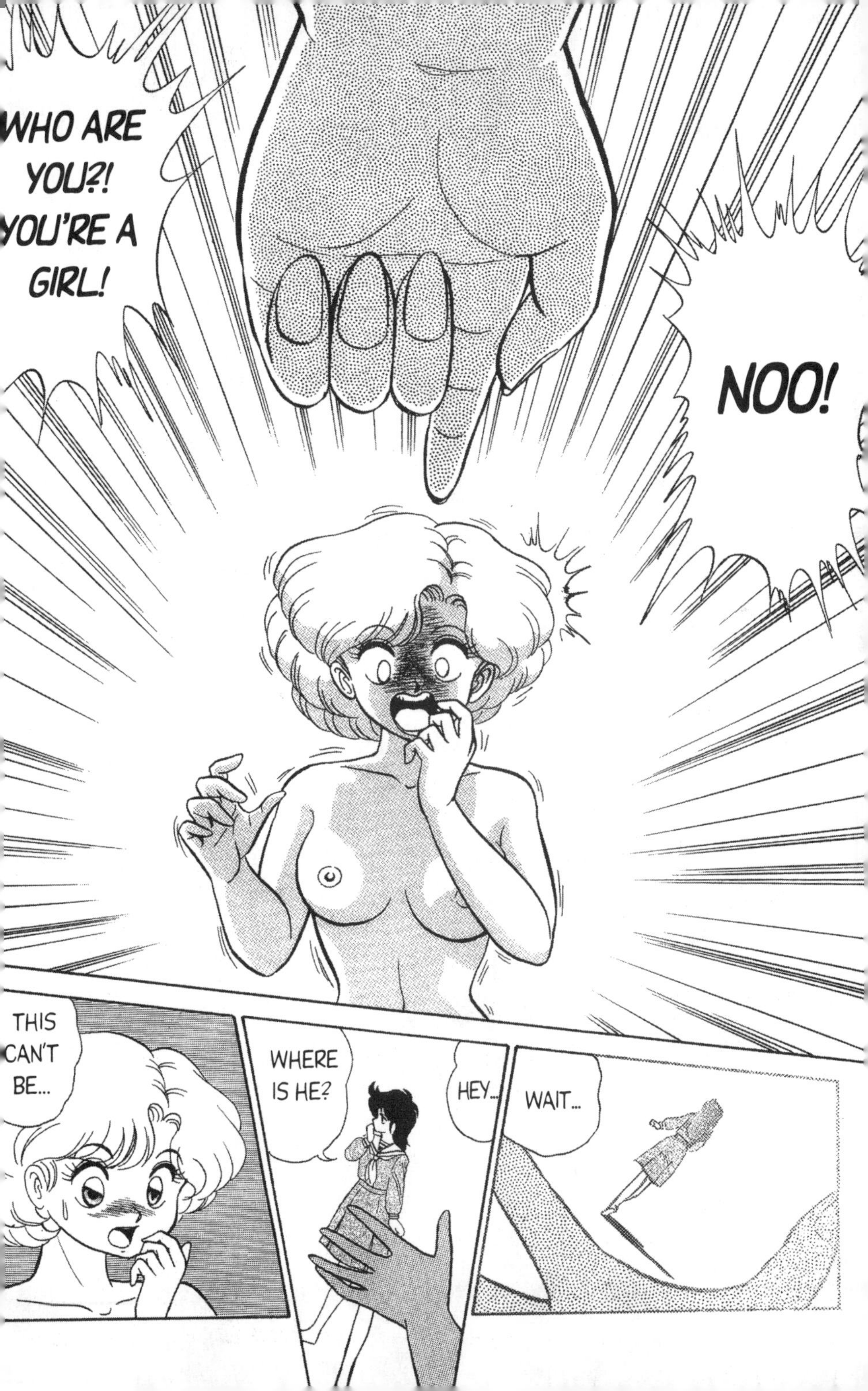
WHO ARE YOU?! YOU'RE A GIRL!
NOO!
THIS CAN'T BE...
WHERE IS HE?
HEY...
WAIT...

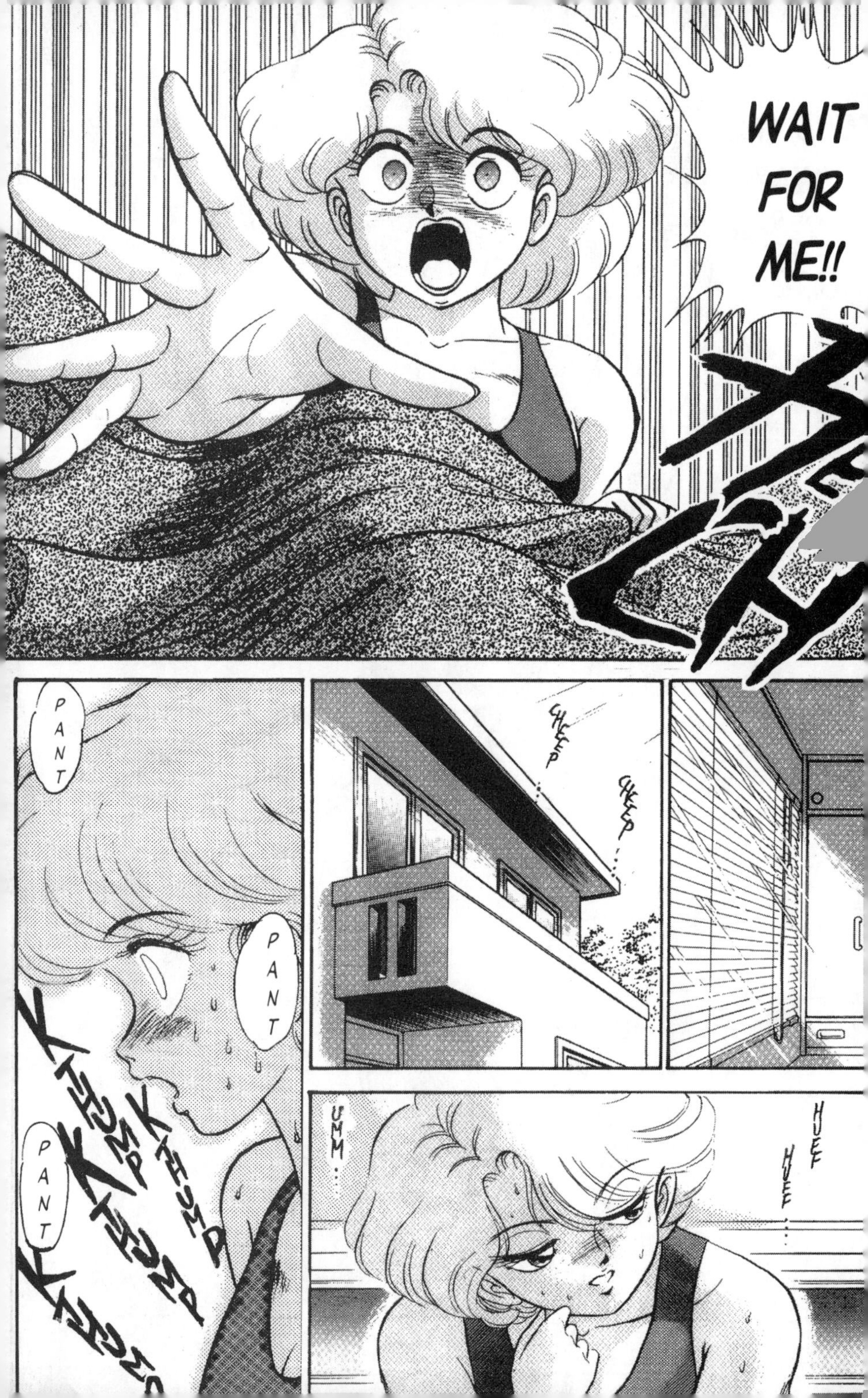

WAIT FOR ME!!
PANT
PANT
PANT
THUMP
THUMP
THUMP
THUMP
CHEEP...
CHEEP...
UMM...
HUFF
HUFF...

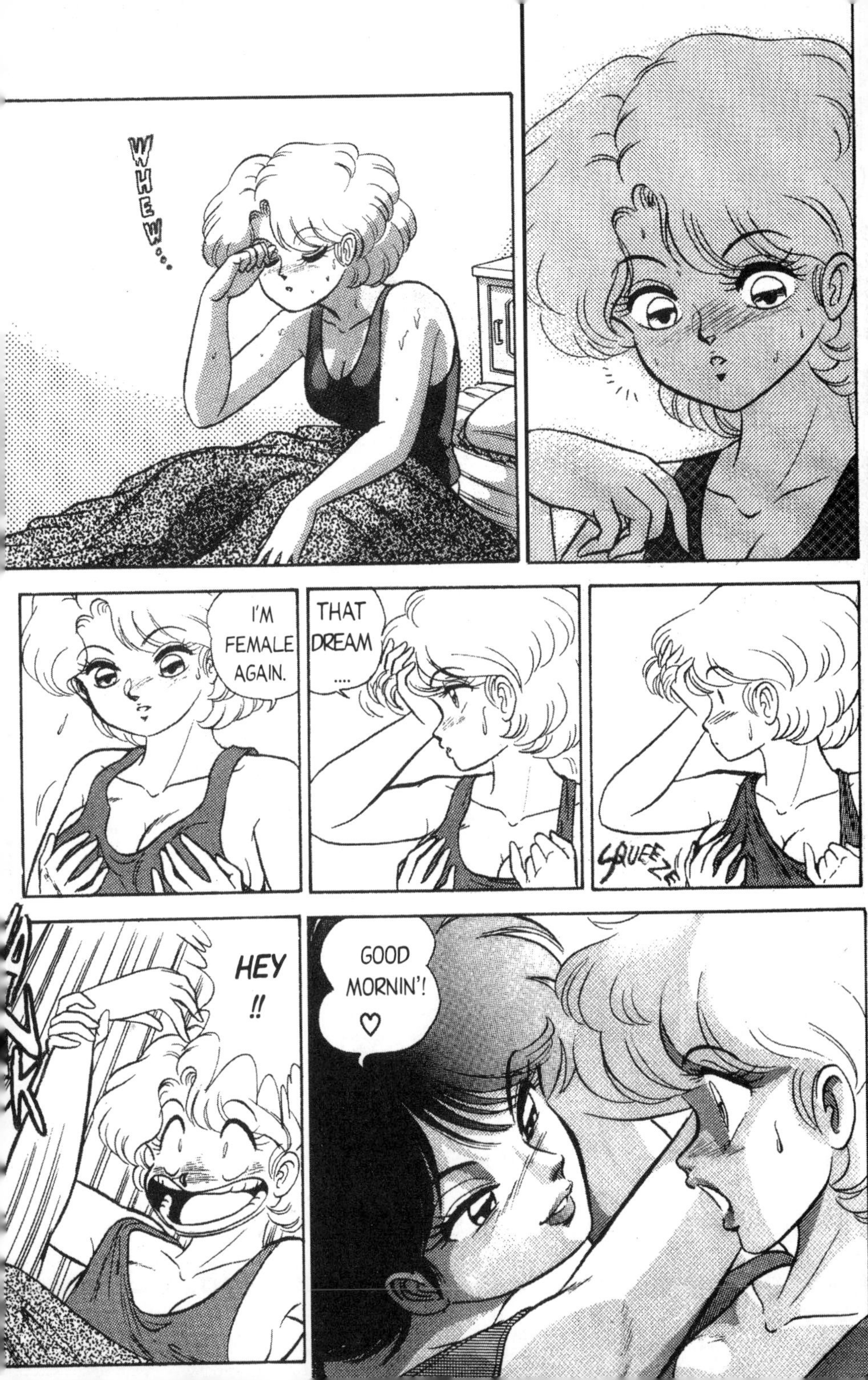
WHEW...
I'M FEMALE AGAIN.
THAT DREAM ....
SQUEEZE
HEY !!
GOOD MORNIN'! ♥

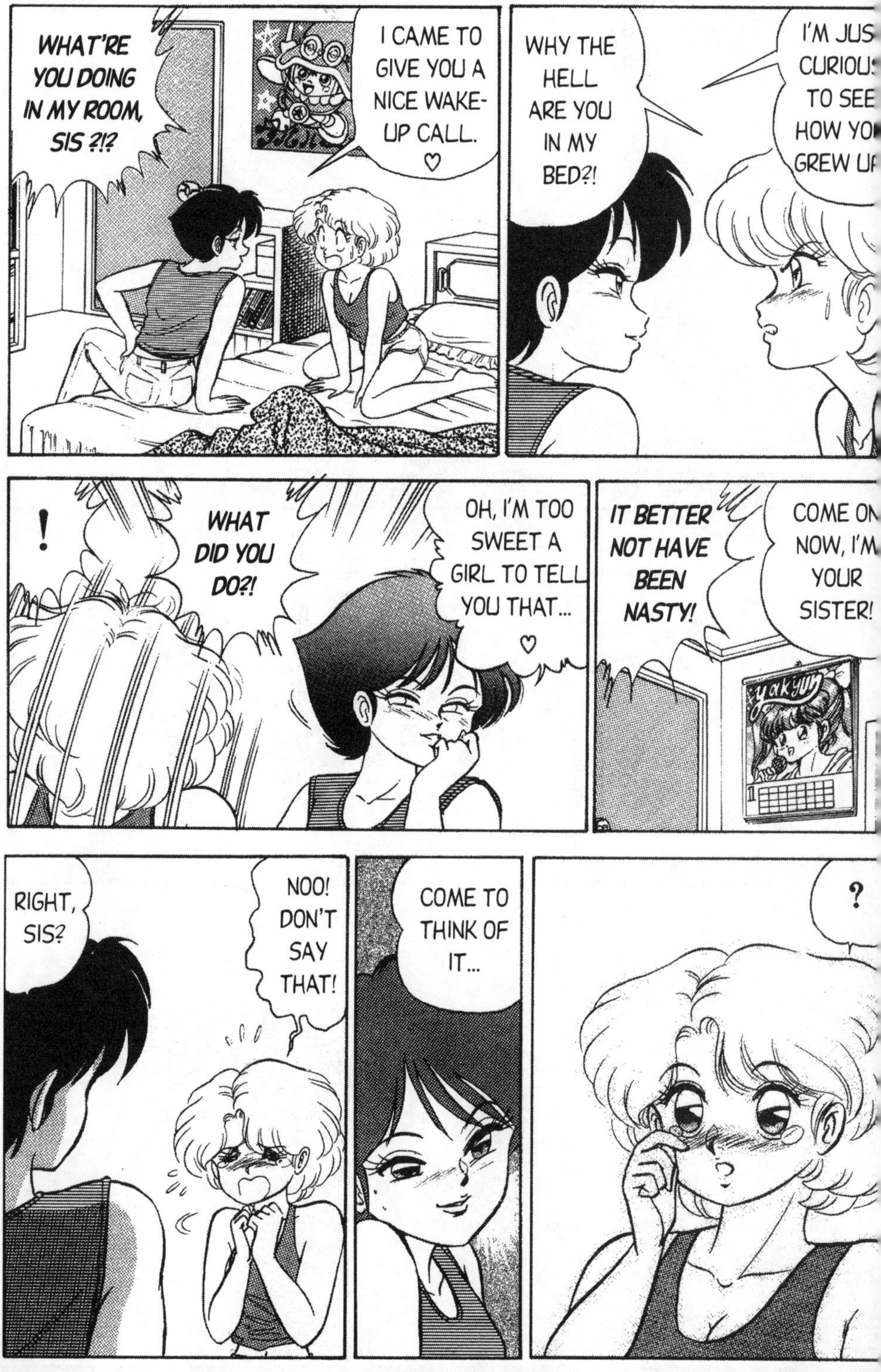
WHAT'RE YOU DOING IN MY ROOM, SIS ?!?
I CAME TO GIVE YOU A NICE WAKE-UP CALL. ♡
WHY THE HELL ARE YOU IN MY BED?!
I'M JUS CURIOU TO SEE HOW YO GREW U
!
WHAT DID YOU DO?!
OH, I'M TOO SWEET A GIRL TO TELL YOU THAT... ♡
IT BETTER NOT HAVE BEEN NASTY!
COME O NOW, I'M YOUR SISTER!
RIGHT, SIS?
NOO! DON'T SAY THAT!
COME TO THINK OF IT...
?

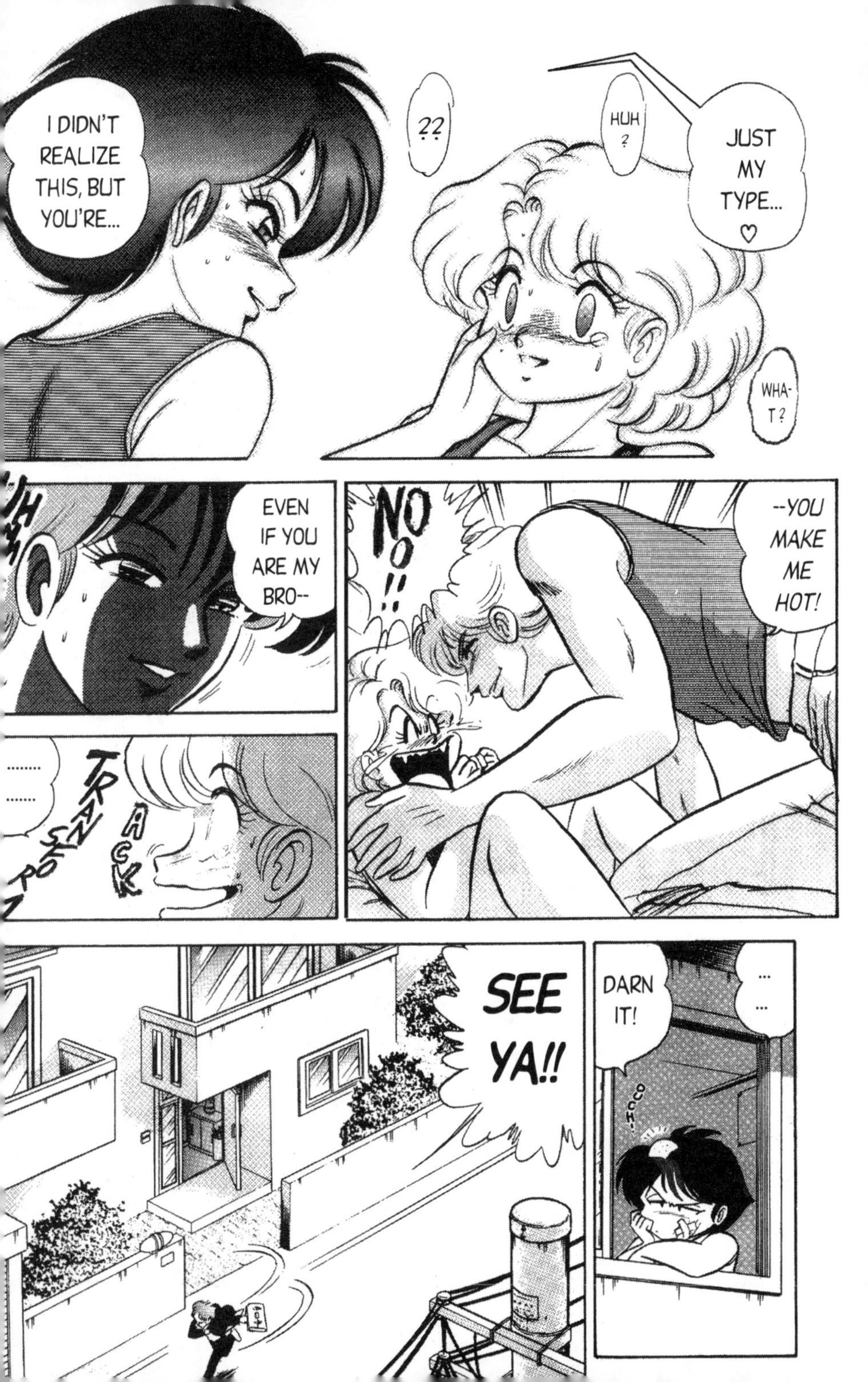
I DIDN'T REALIZE THIS, BUT YOU'RE...
??
HUH?
JUST MY TYPE... ♡
WHA-T?
EVEN IF YOU ARE MY BRO--
NOO!!
--YOU MAKE ME HOT!
....
TRANSFORM
ACK
SEE YA!!
DARN IT!
... ...
OOCH!

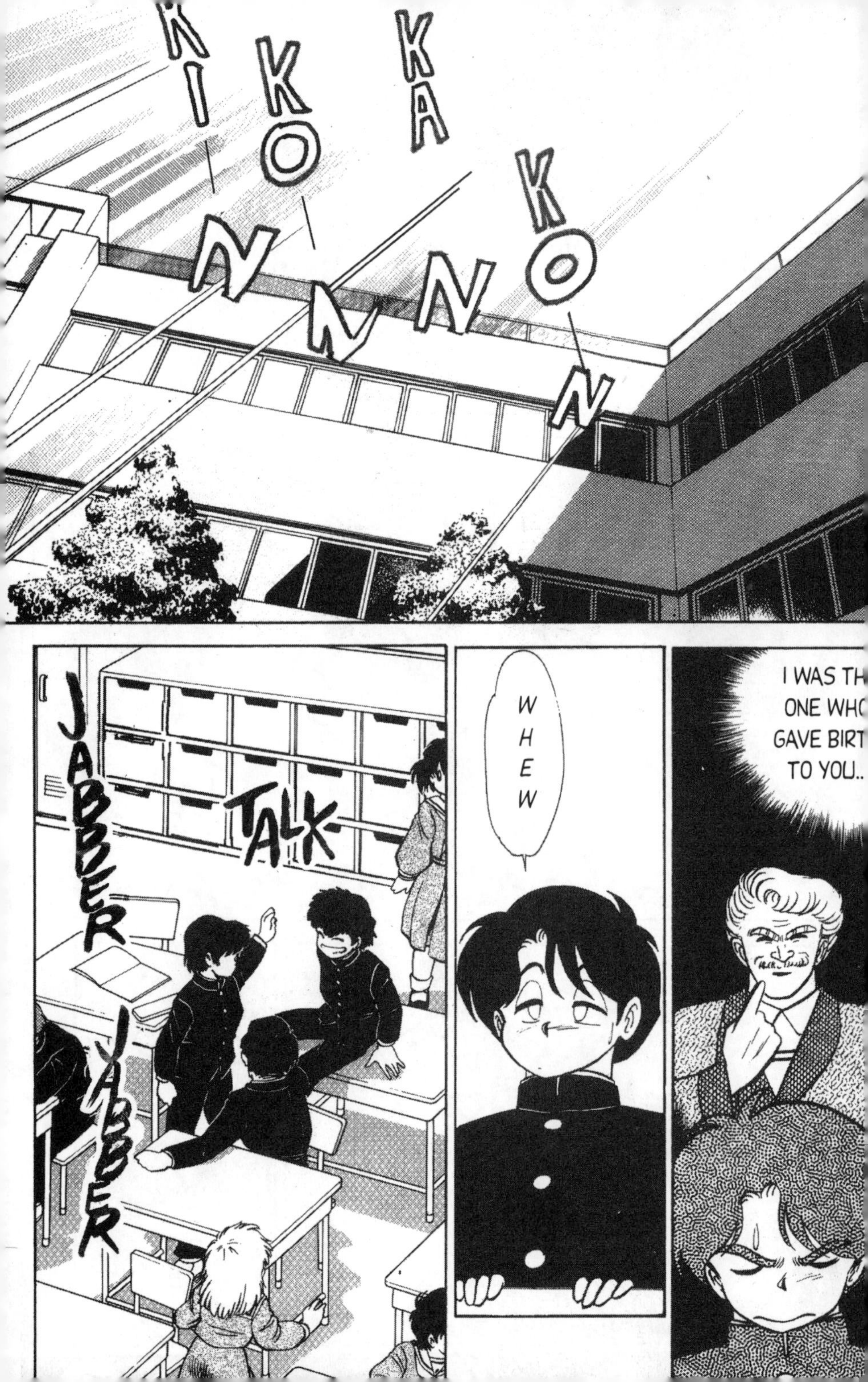

KI—N
KO—N
KA—N
KO—N
JABBER
TALK
JABBER
WHEW
I WAS TH
ONE WH
GAVE BIRT
TO YOU..

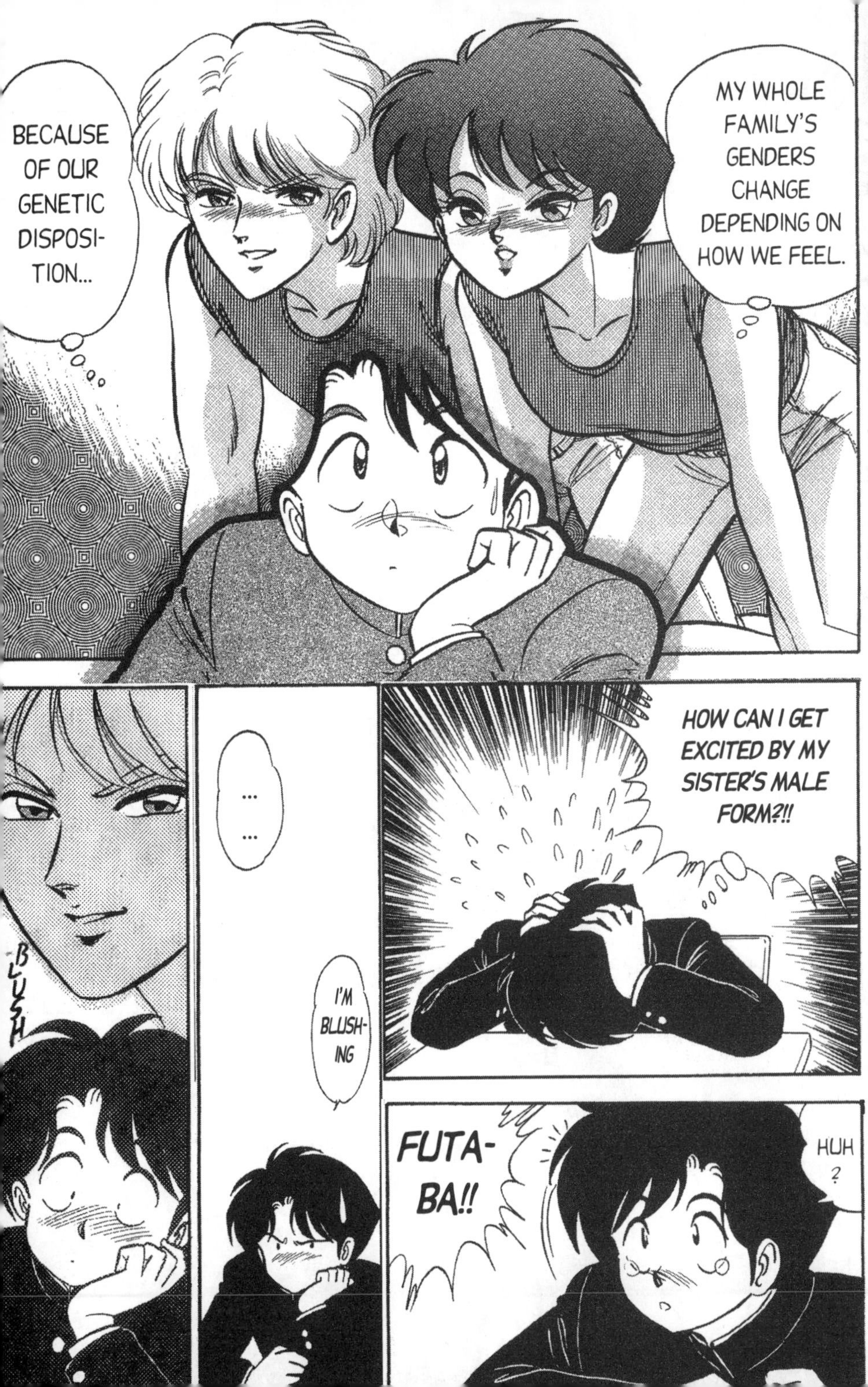
BECAUSE OF OUR GENETIC DISPOSI- TION...
MY WHOLE FAMILY'S GENDERS CHANGE DEPENDING ON HOW WE FEEL.
BLUSH
... ...
I'M BLUSH- ING
HOW CAN I GET EXCITED BY MY SISTER'S MALE FORM?!!
FUTA- BA!!
HUH ?

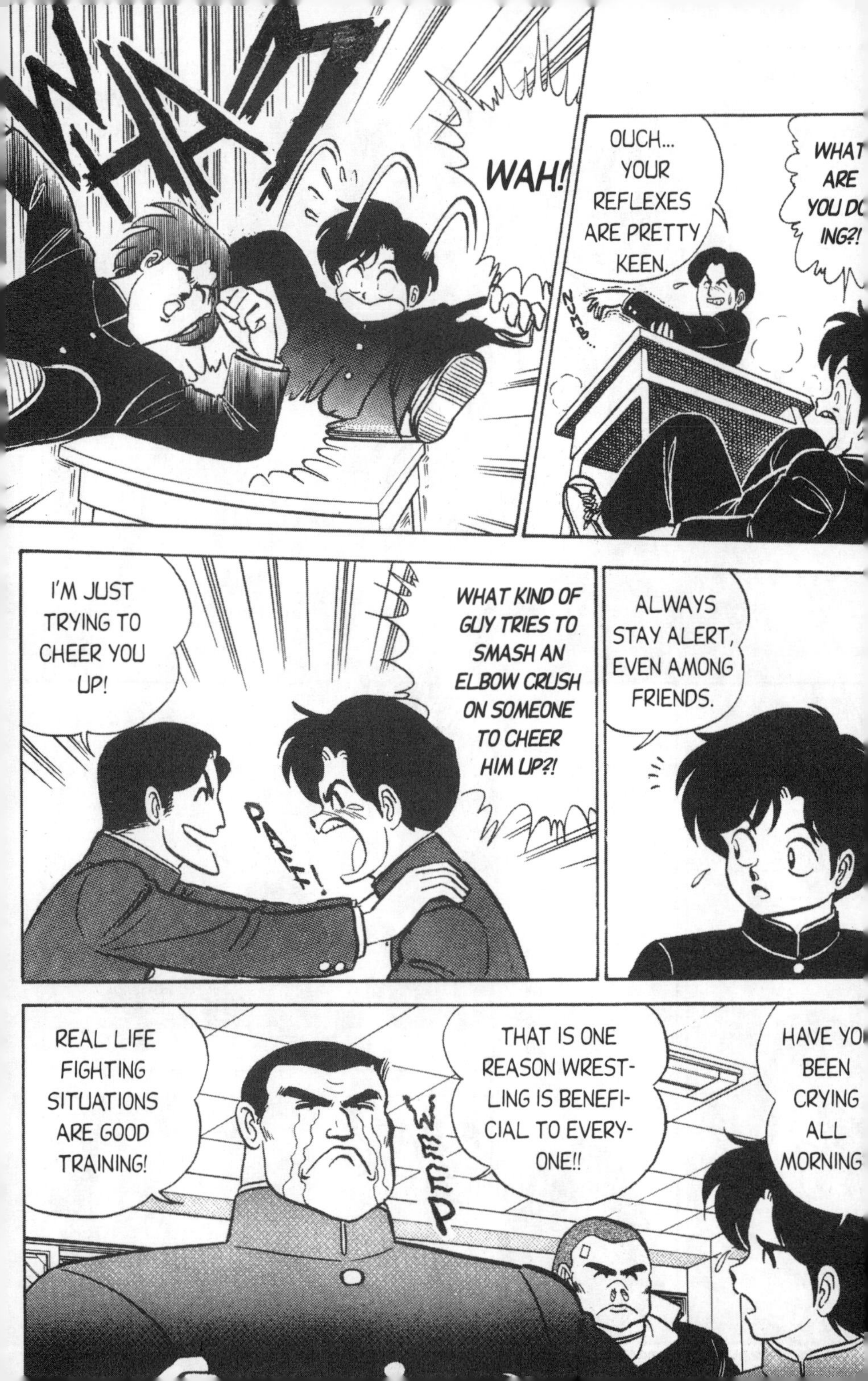
WHAM
WAH!
OUCH... YOUR REFLEXES ARE PRETTY KEEN.
NUMB...
WHAT ARE YOU DO ING?!
I'M JUST TRYING TO CHEER YOU UP!
WHAT KIND OF GUY TRIES TO SMASH AN ELBOW CRUSH ON SOMEONE TO CHEER HIM UP?!
ALWAYS STAY ALERT, EVEN AMONG FRIENDS.
REAL LIFE FIGHTING SITUATIONS ARE GOOD TRAINING!
WEEP
THAT IS ONE REASON WREST-LING IS BENEFI-CIAL TO EVERY-ONE!!
HAVE YO BEEN CRYING ALL MORNING

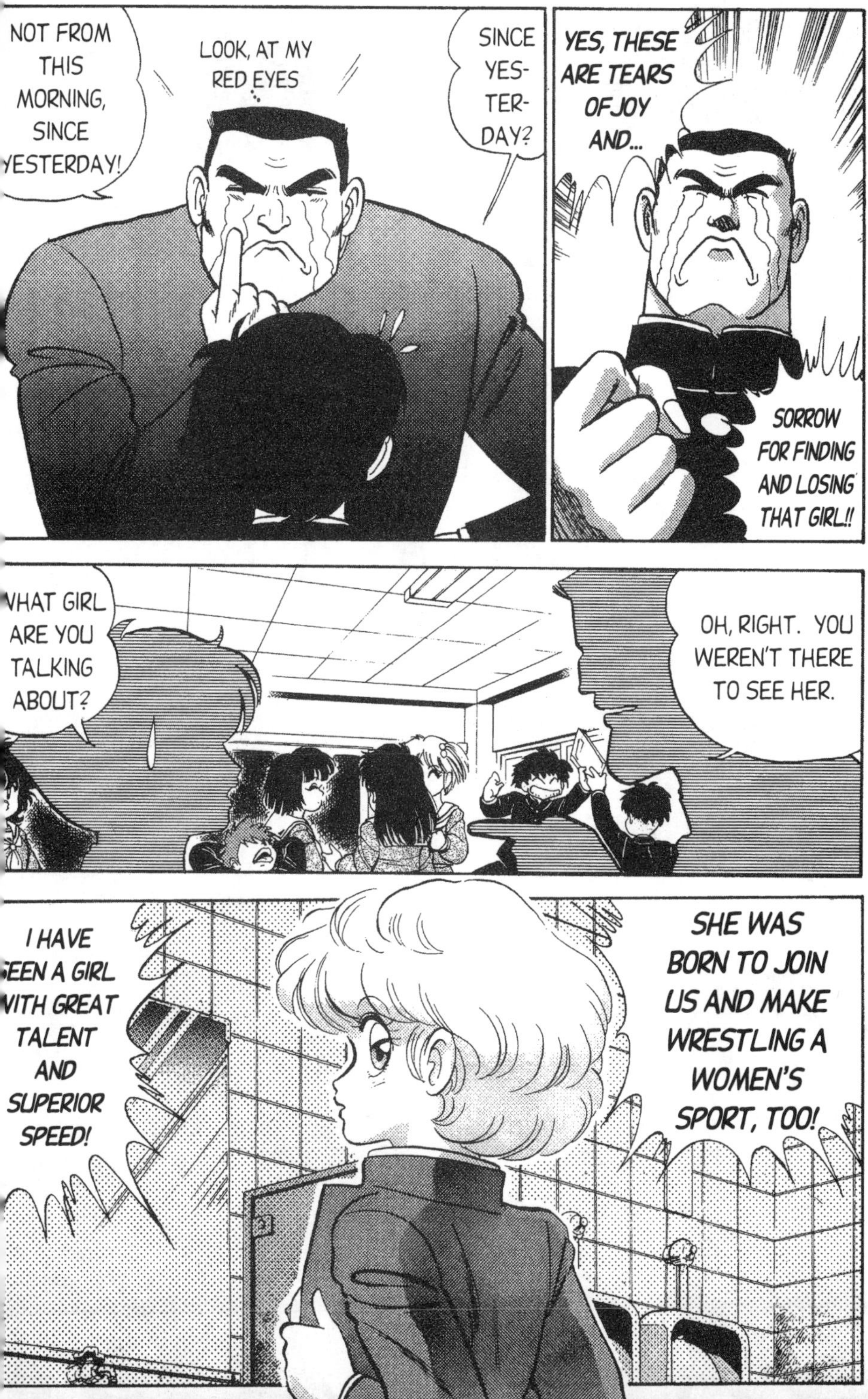
NOT FROM THIS MORNING, SINCE YESTERDAY!
LOOK, AT MY RED EYES
SINCE YES-TER-DAY?
YES, THESE ARE TEARS OF JOY AND...
SORROW FOR FINDING AND LOSING THAT GIRL!!
WHAT GIRL ARE YOU TALKING ABOUT?
OH, RIGHT. YOU WEREN'T THERE TO SEE HER.
I HAVE SEEN A GIRL WITH GREAT TALENT AND SUPERIOR SPEED!
SHE WAS BORN TO JOIN US AND MAKE WRESTLING A WOMEN'S SPORT, TOO!

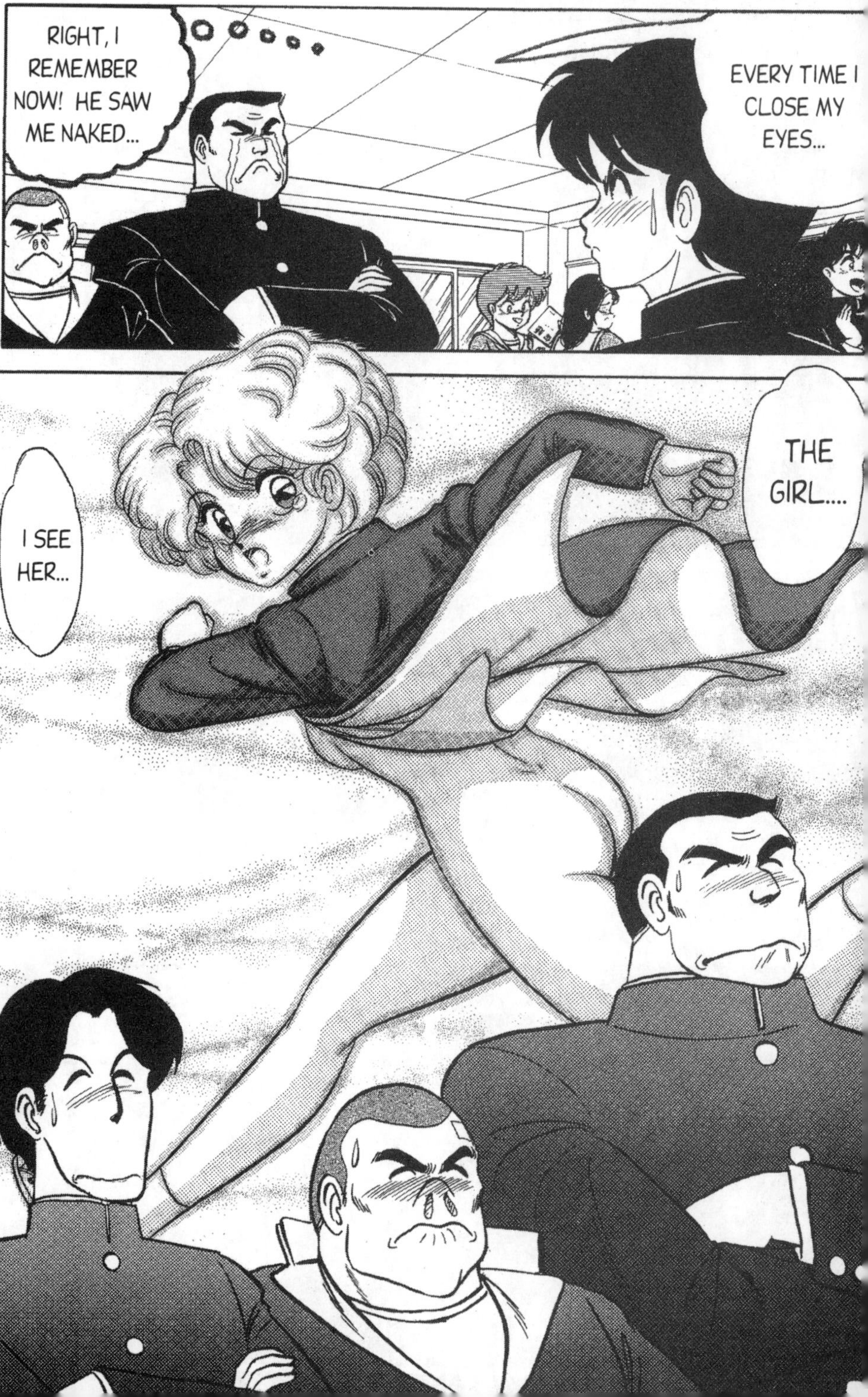
EVERY TIME I CLOSE MY EYES...
RIGHT, I REMEMBER NOW! HE SAW ME NAKED...
THE GIRL....
I SEE HER...

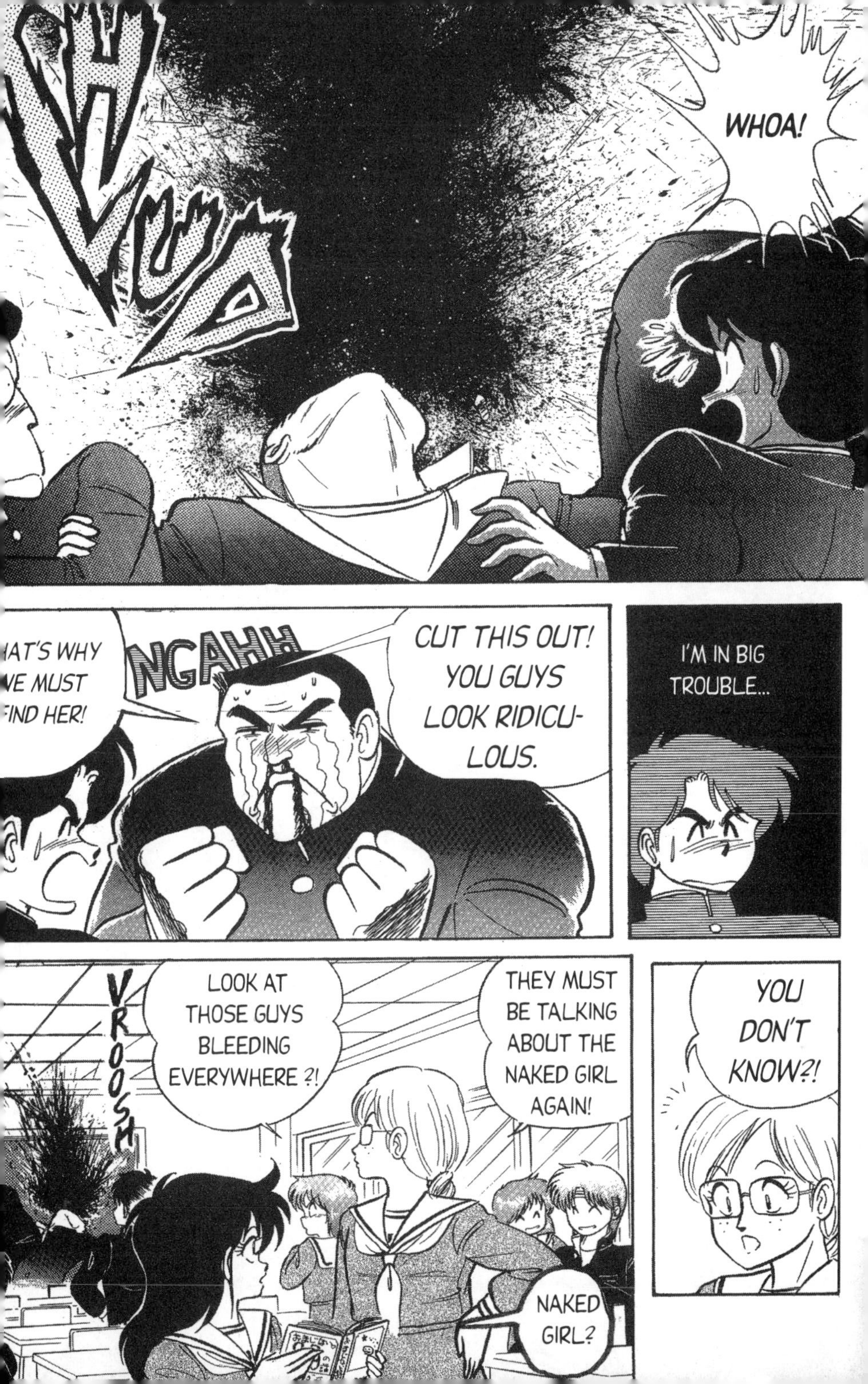
WHOA!
NGAHH
CUT THIS OUT! YOU GUYS LOOK RIDICU-LOUS.
HAT'S WHY VE MUST FIND HER!
I'M IN BIG TROUBLE...
VROOOSH
LOOK AT THOSE GUYS BLEEDING EVERYWHERE ?!
THEY MUST BE TALKING ABOUT THE NAKED GIRL AGAIN!
NAKED GIRL?
YOU DON'T KNOW?!

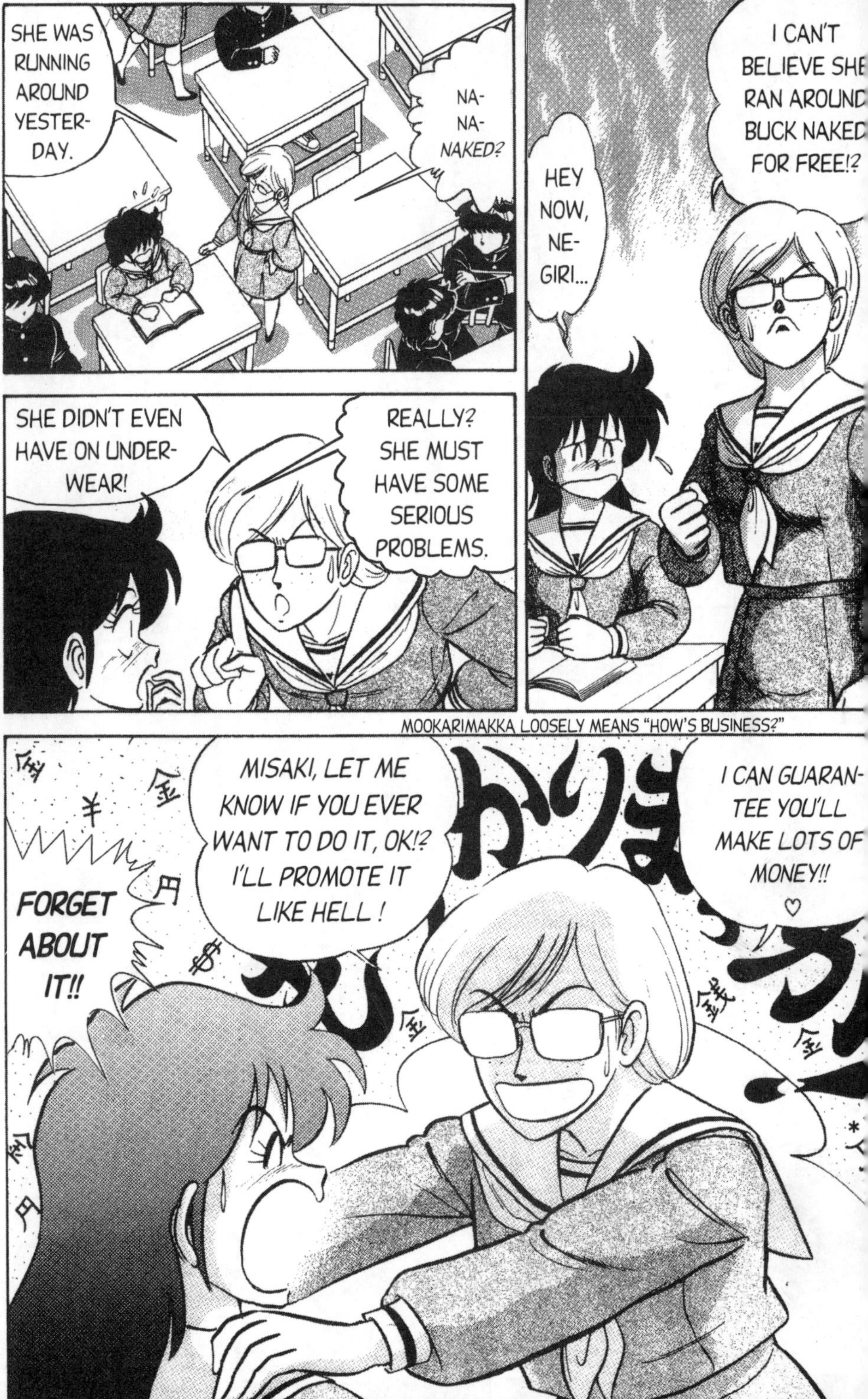

SHE WAS RUNNING AROUND YESTER-DAY.
NA-NA-NAKED?
SHE DIDN'T EVEN HAVE ON UNDER-WEAR!
REALLY? SHE MUST HAVE SOME SERIOUS PROBLEMS.
HEY NOW, NE-GIRI...
I CAN'T BELIEVE SHE RAN AROUND BUCK NAKED FOR FREE!?
MOOKARIMAKKA LOOSELY MEANS "HOW'S BUSINESS?"
MISAKI, LET ME KNOW IF YOU EVER WANT TO DO IT, OK!? I'LL PROMOTE IT LIKE HELL !
I CAN GUARAN-TEE YOU'LL MAKE LOTS OF MONEY!! ♡
FORGET ABOUT IT!!

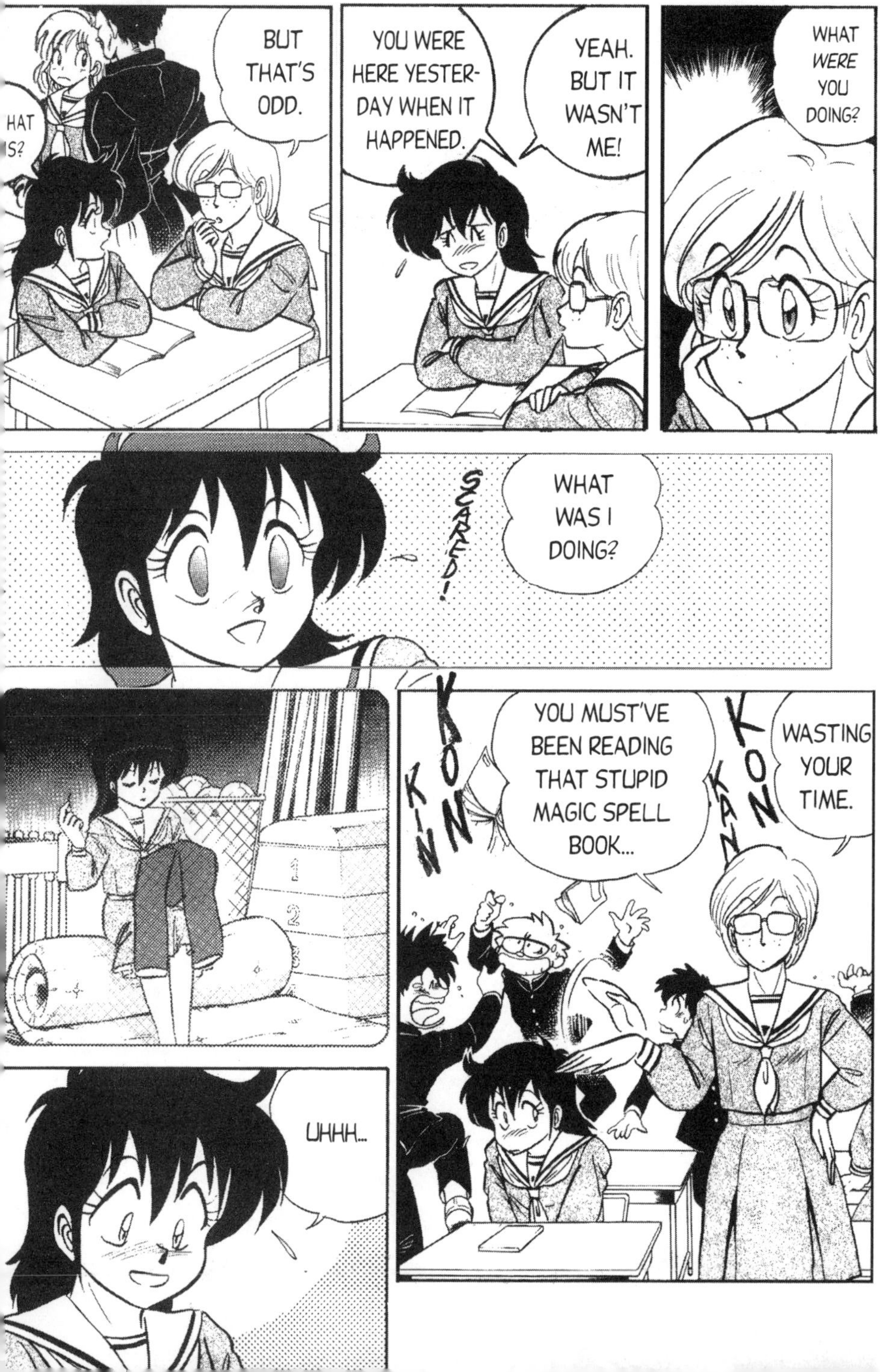
HAT S?
BUT THAT'S ODD.
YOU WERE HERE YESTER-DAY WHEN IT HAPPENED.
YEAH. BUT IT WASN'T ME!
WHAT WERE YOU DOING?
SCARED!
WHAT WAS I DOING?
KON
KIN
YOU MUST'VE BEEN READING THAT STUPID MAGIC SPELL BOOK...
KON
KAN
WASTING YOUR TIME.
UHHH...

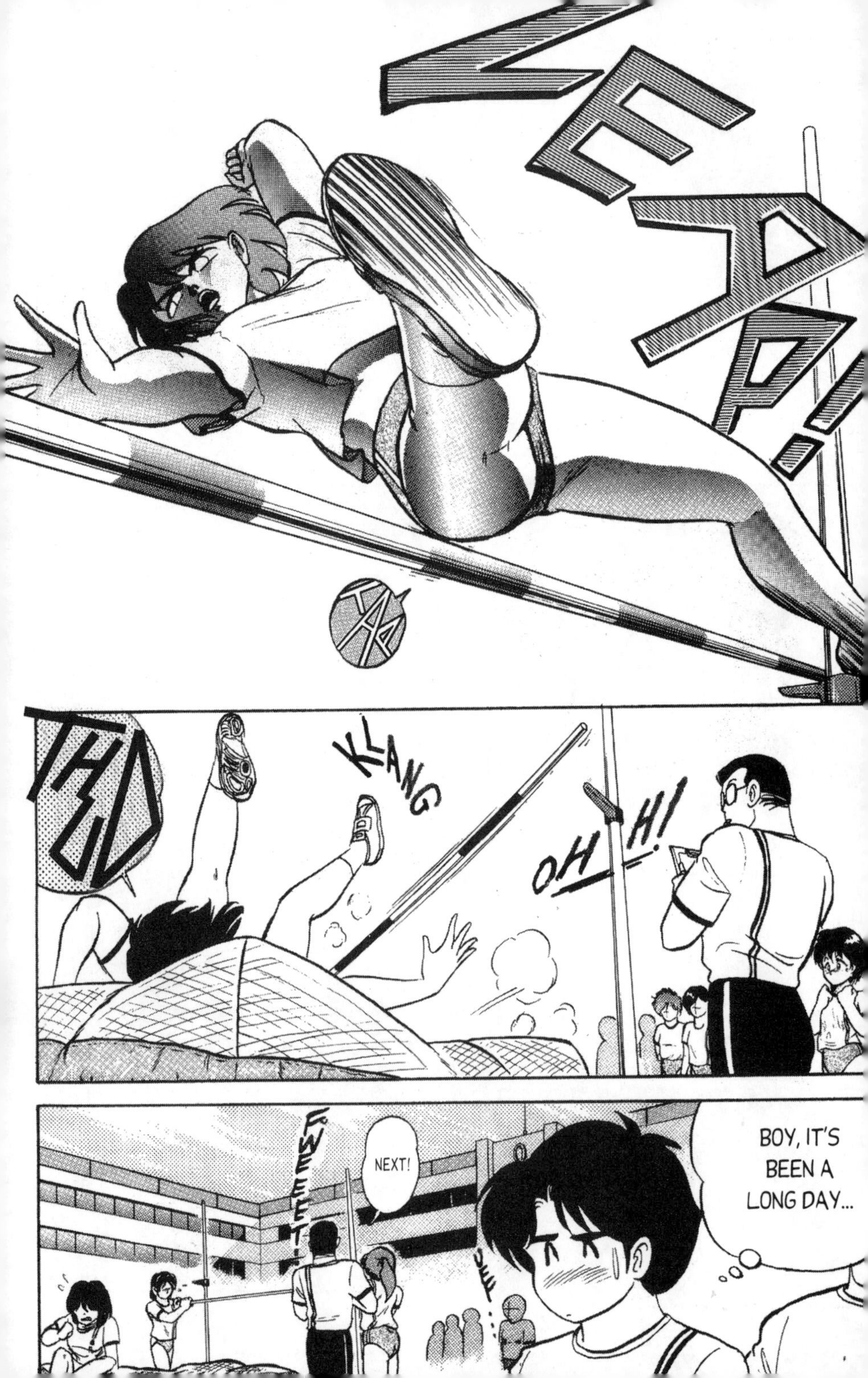
YEAP!!
KAA
THD
KLANG
OH HI!
FWEEET!
NEXT!
BOY, IT'S BEEN A LONG DAY...

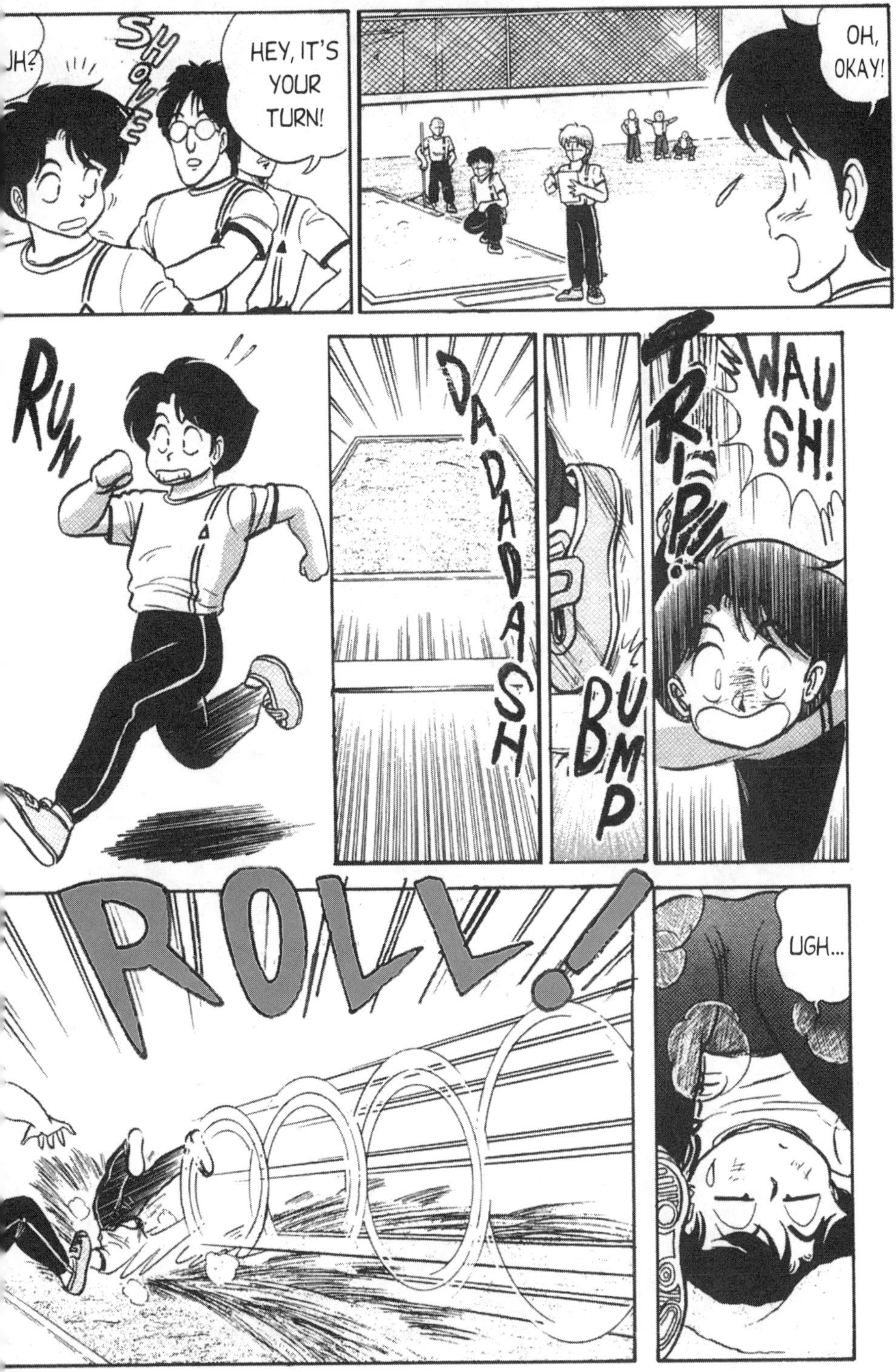

OH, OKAY!
HEY, IT'S YOUR TURN!
SHOVE
UH?
RUN
DADADASH
BUMP
TRIP
WAUGH!
ROLL!
UGH...

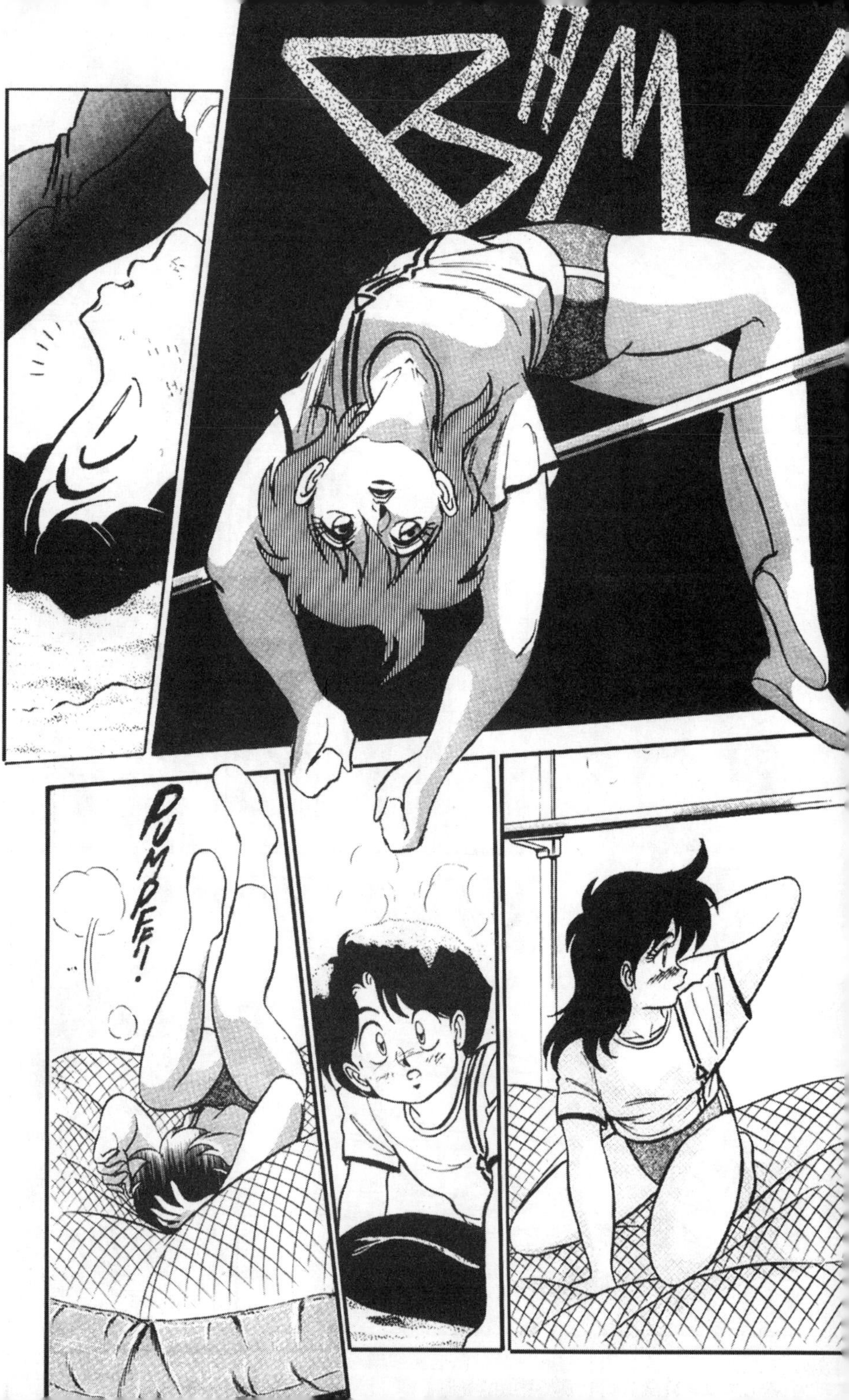
BAM!!
PUMPF!!
...

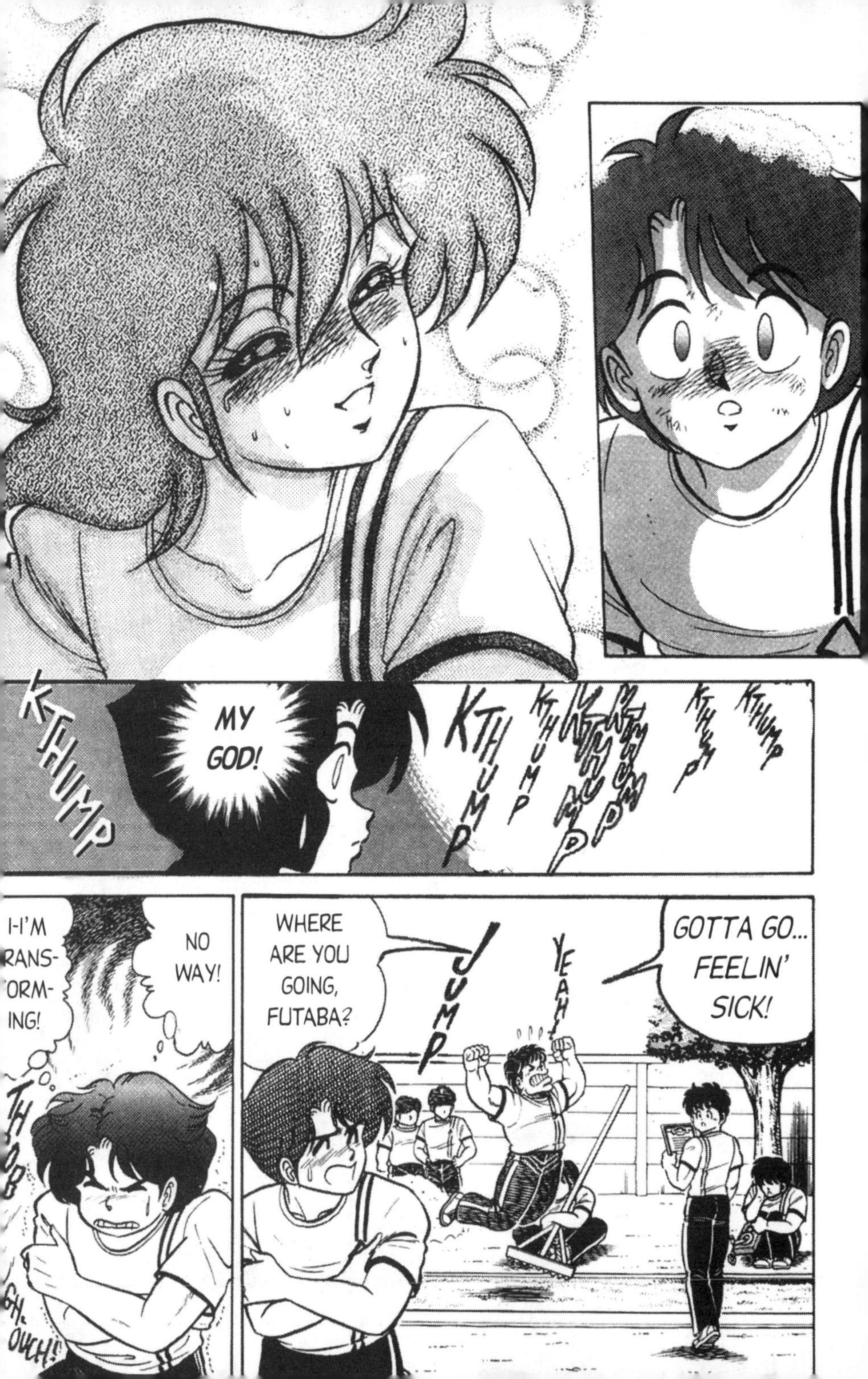

KTHUMP
KTHUMP
KTHUMP
MY GOD!
KTHUMP
GOTTA GO... FEELIN' SICK!
YEAH!
JUMP
WHERE ARE YOU GOING, FUTABA?
NO WAY!
I-I'M RANS-ORM-ING!
OUCH!

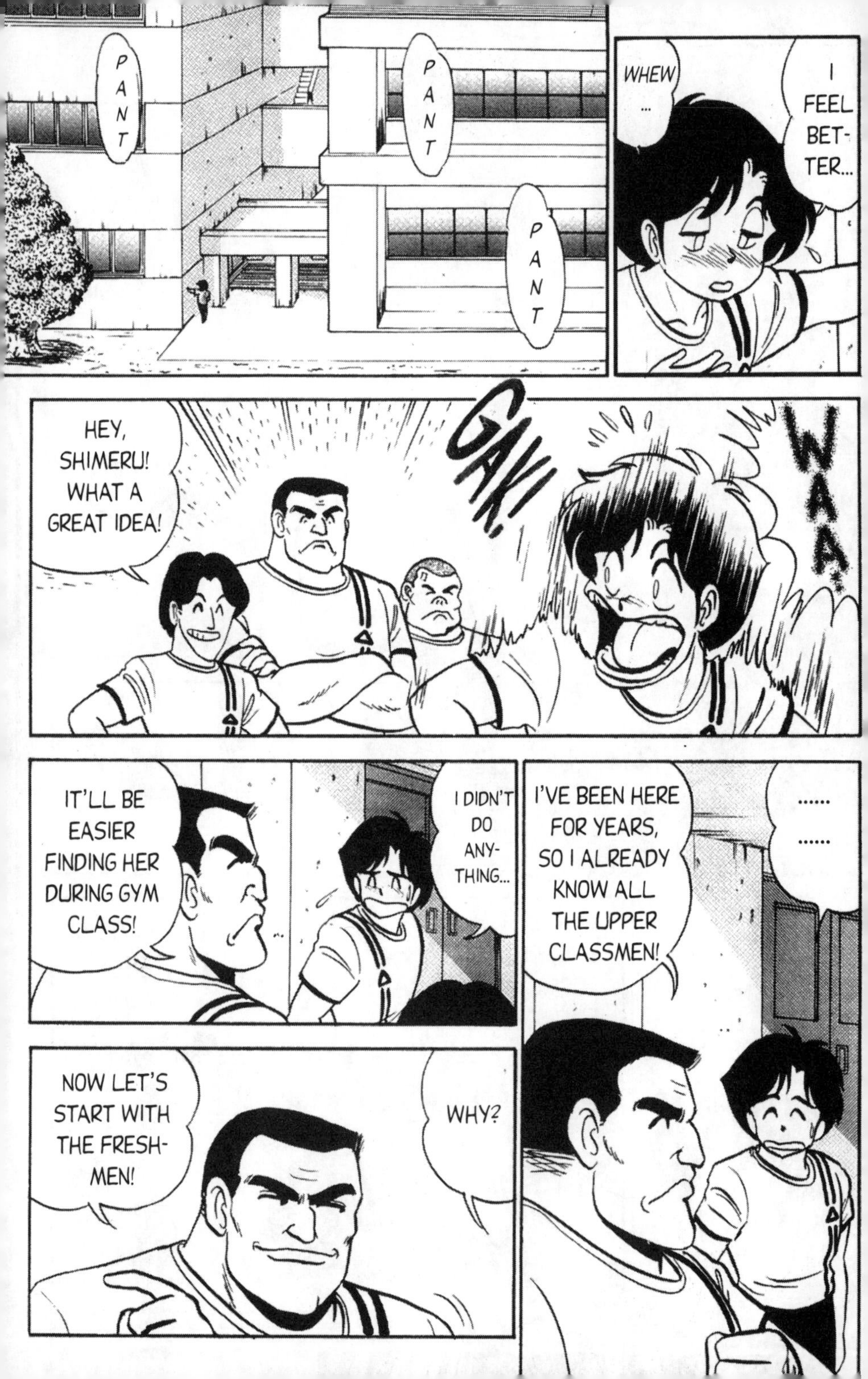
PANT
PANT
PANT
WHEW...
I FEEL BETTER...
HEY, SHIMERU! WHAT A GREAT IDEA!
GAK!
WAAA!
IT'LL BE EASIER FINDING HER DURING GYM CLASS!
I DIDN'T DO ANYTHING...
I'VE BEEN HERE FOR YEARS, SO I ALREADY KNOW ALL THE UPPER CLASSMEN!
......
......
NOW LET'S START WITH THE FRESHMEN!
WHY?

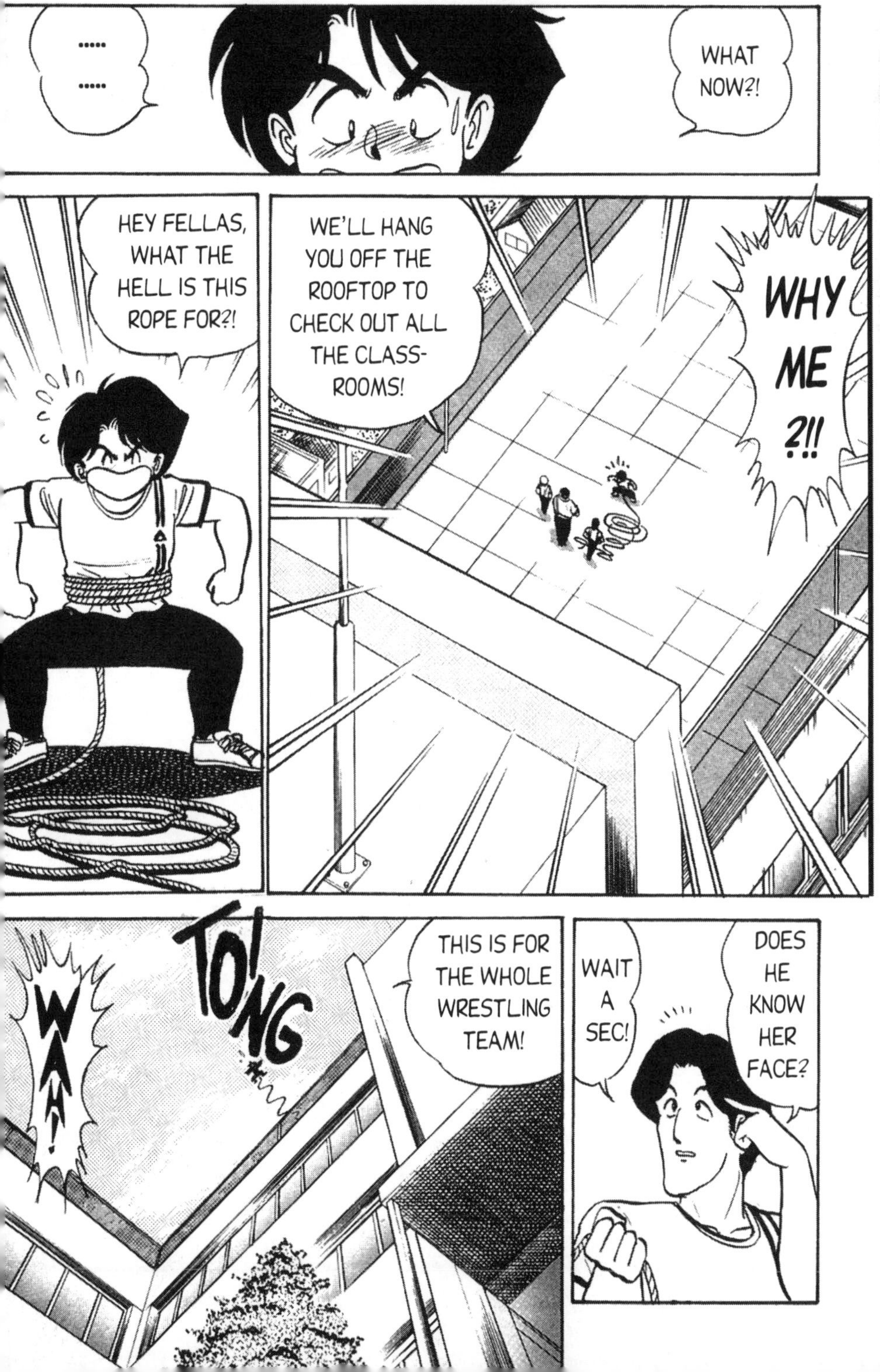
WHAT NOW?!
.....
.....
WHY ME ?!!
WE'LL HANG YOU OFF THE ROOFTOP TO CHECK OUT ALL THE CLASS-ROOMS!
HEY FELLAS, WHAT THE HELL IS THIS ROPE FOR?!
DOES HE KNOW HER FACE?
WAIT A SEC!
THIS IS FOR THE WHOLE WRESTLING TEAM!
TONG
WAH!

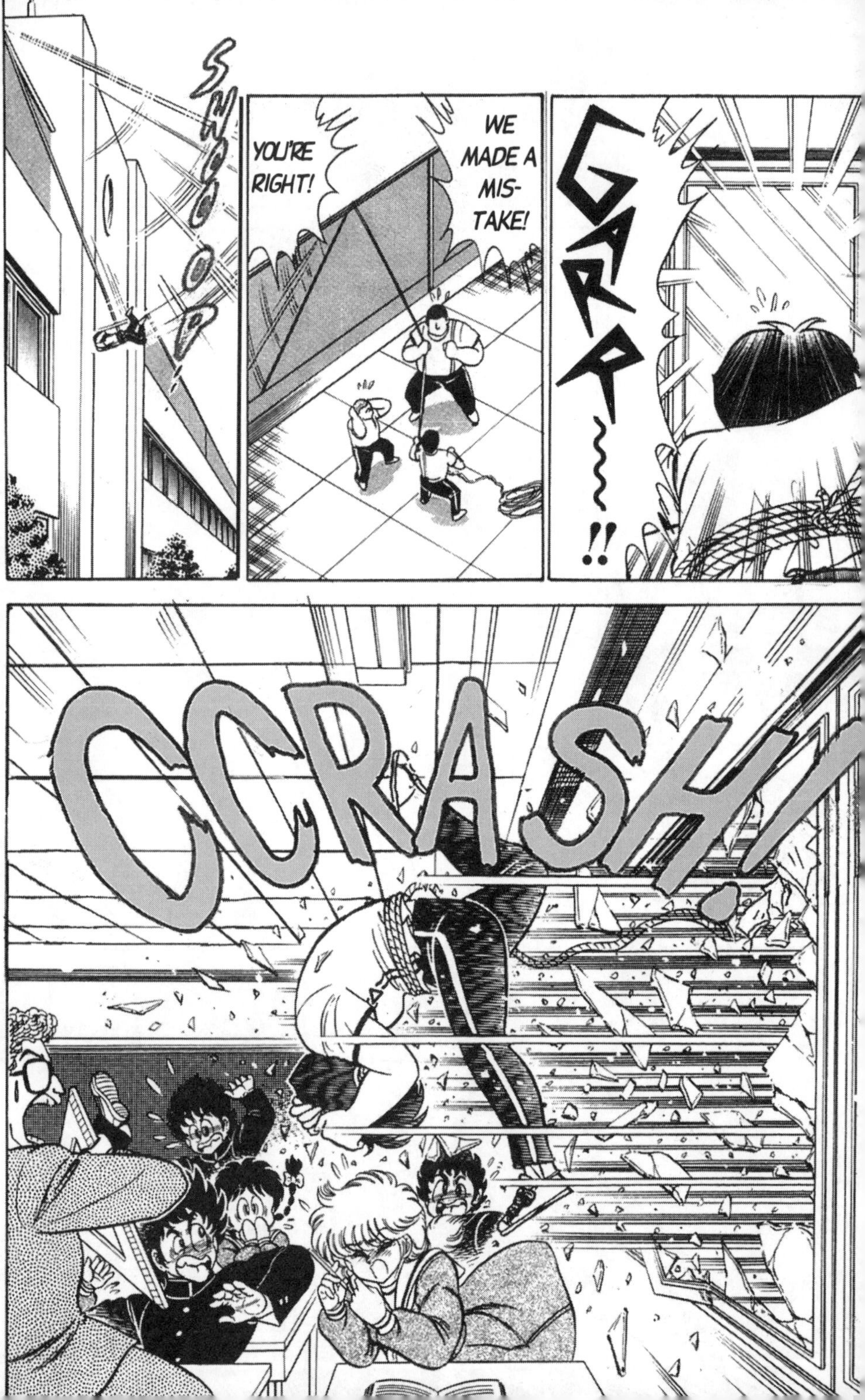
SHOOOP!
WE MADE A MIS-TAKE!
YOU'RE RIGHT!
GARR~!!
CCRASH!

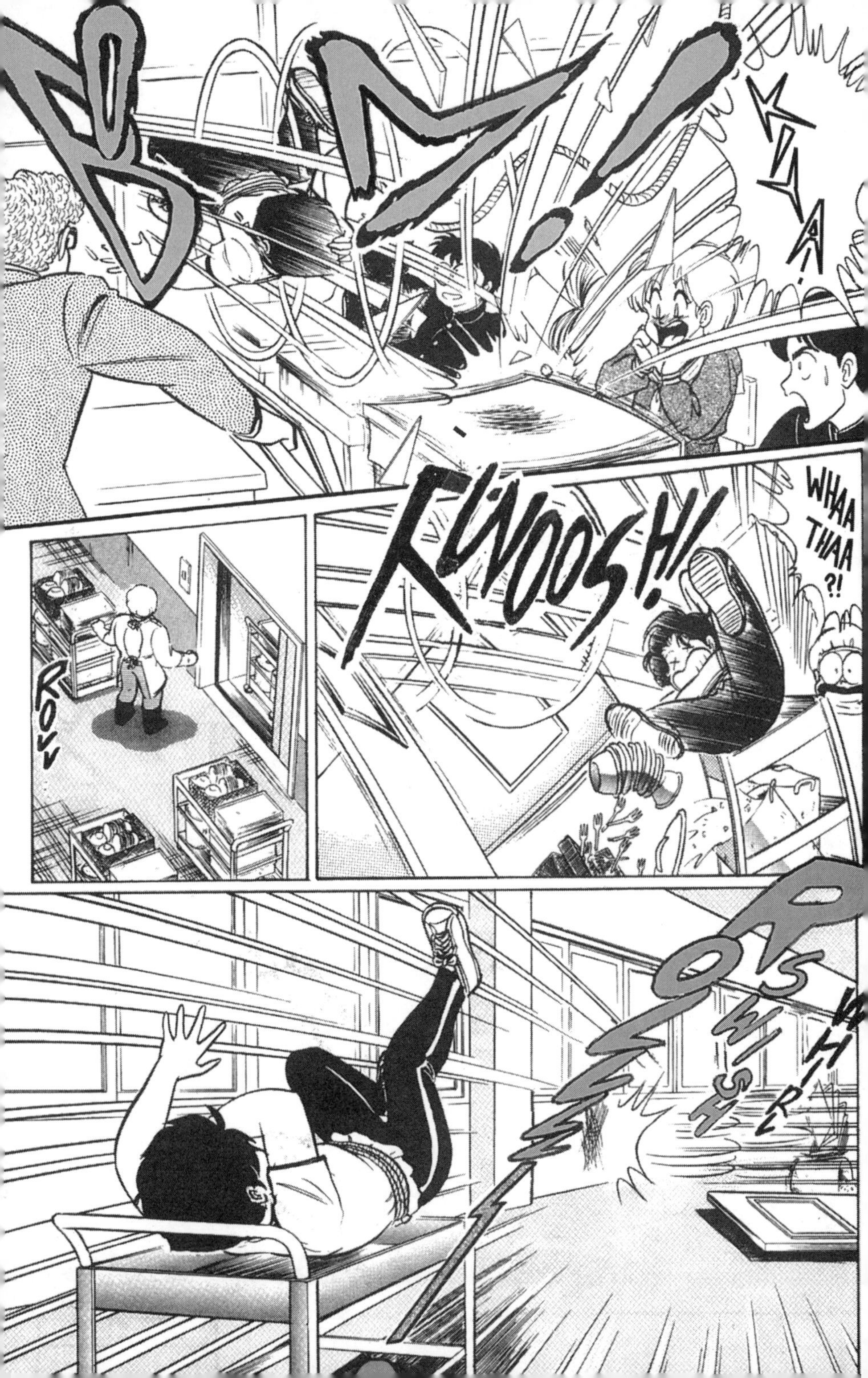
KYAA!
KWOOSH!!
WHAA THAA ?!
SWISH
WHIRL

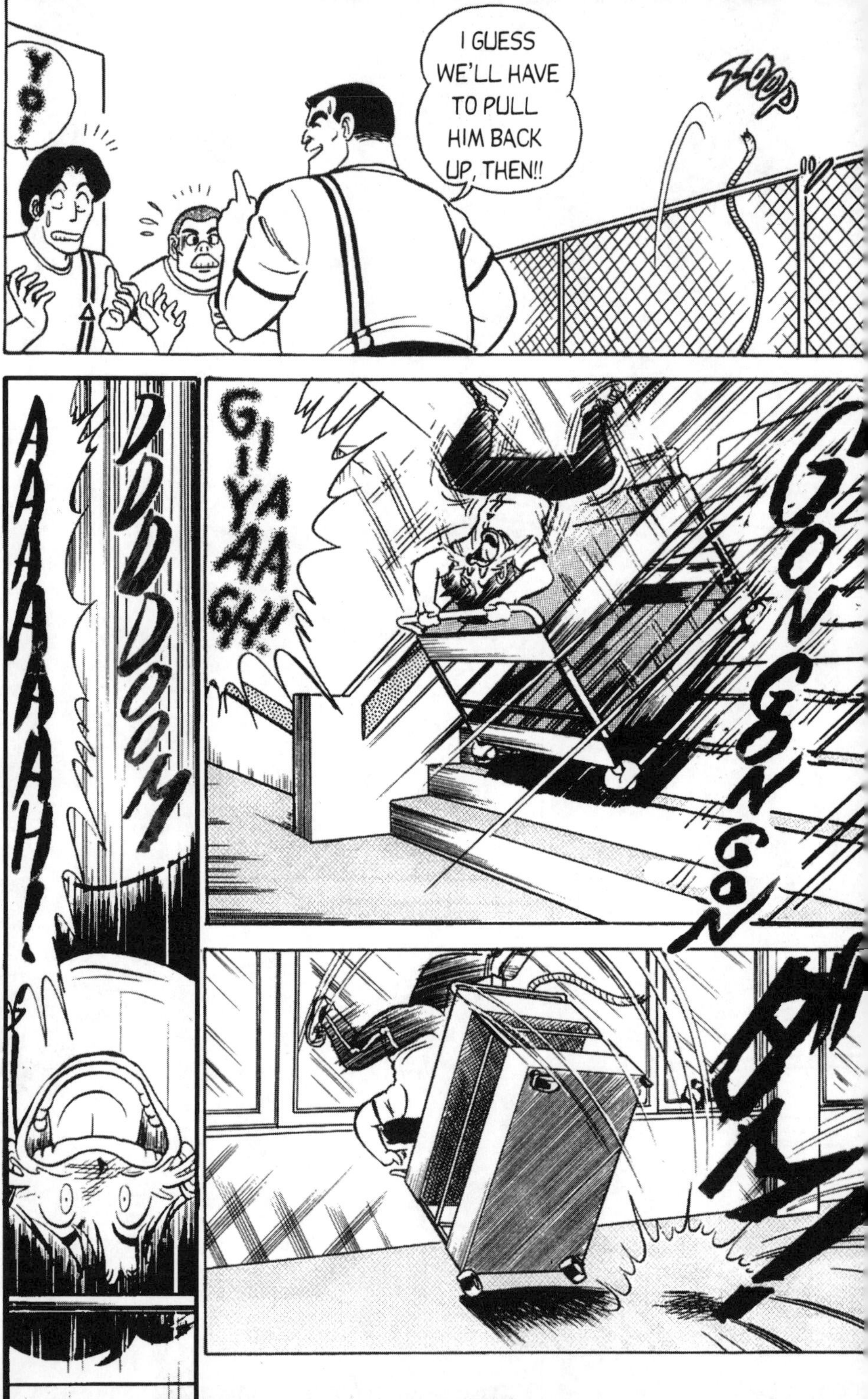
YO!
I GUESS WE'LL HAVE TO PULL HIM BACK UP, THEN!!
ZOOP
GIYAAAGH!!
GONGONGONGON
DDDDOOOM
AAAAAAAH!

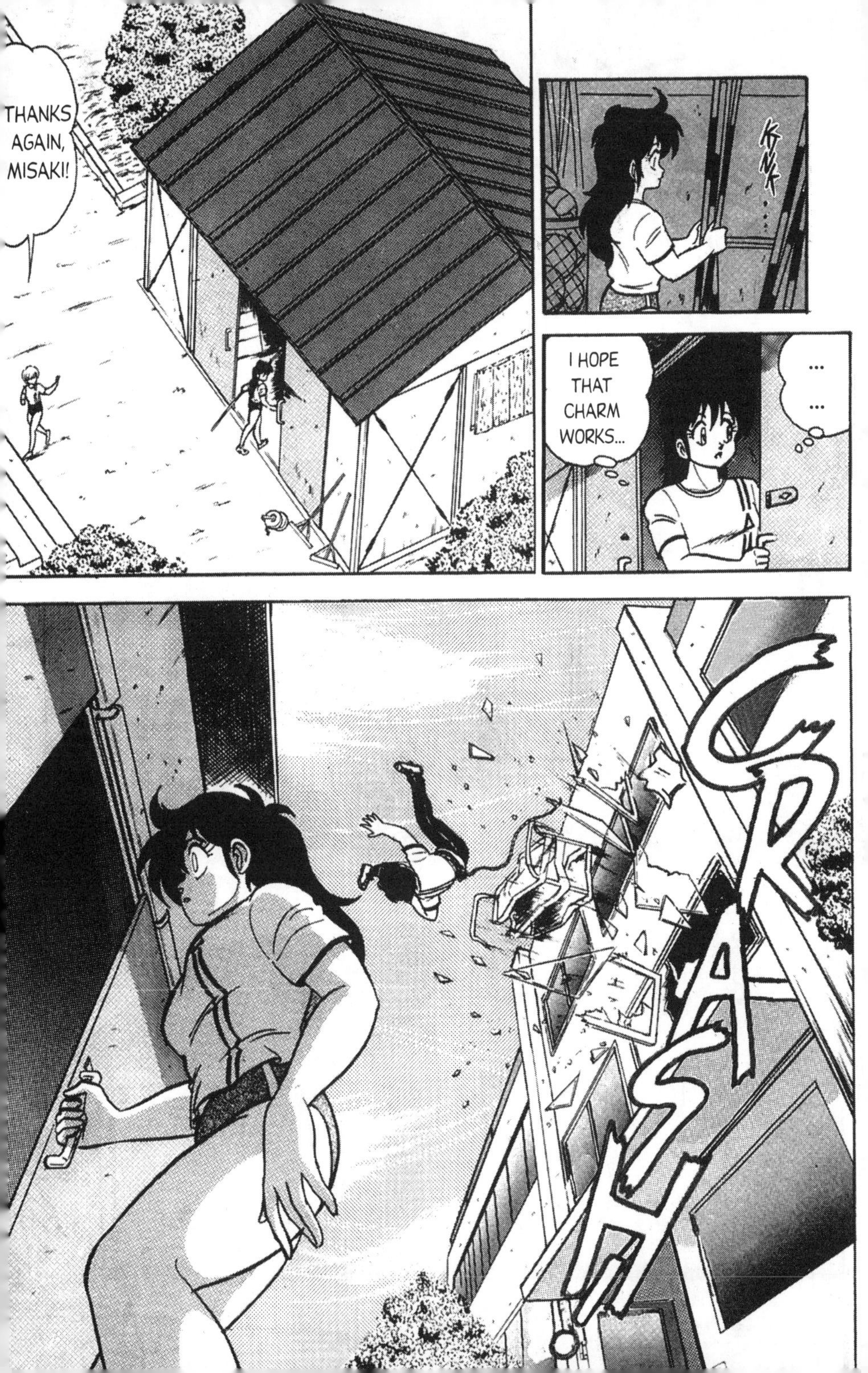
THANKS AGAIN, MISAKI!
KTNK
I HOPE THAT CHARM WORKS...
... ...
CRASH

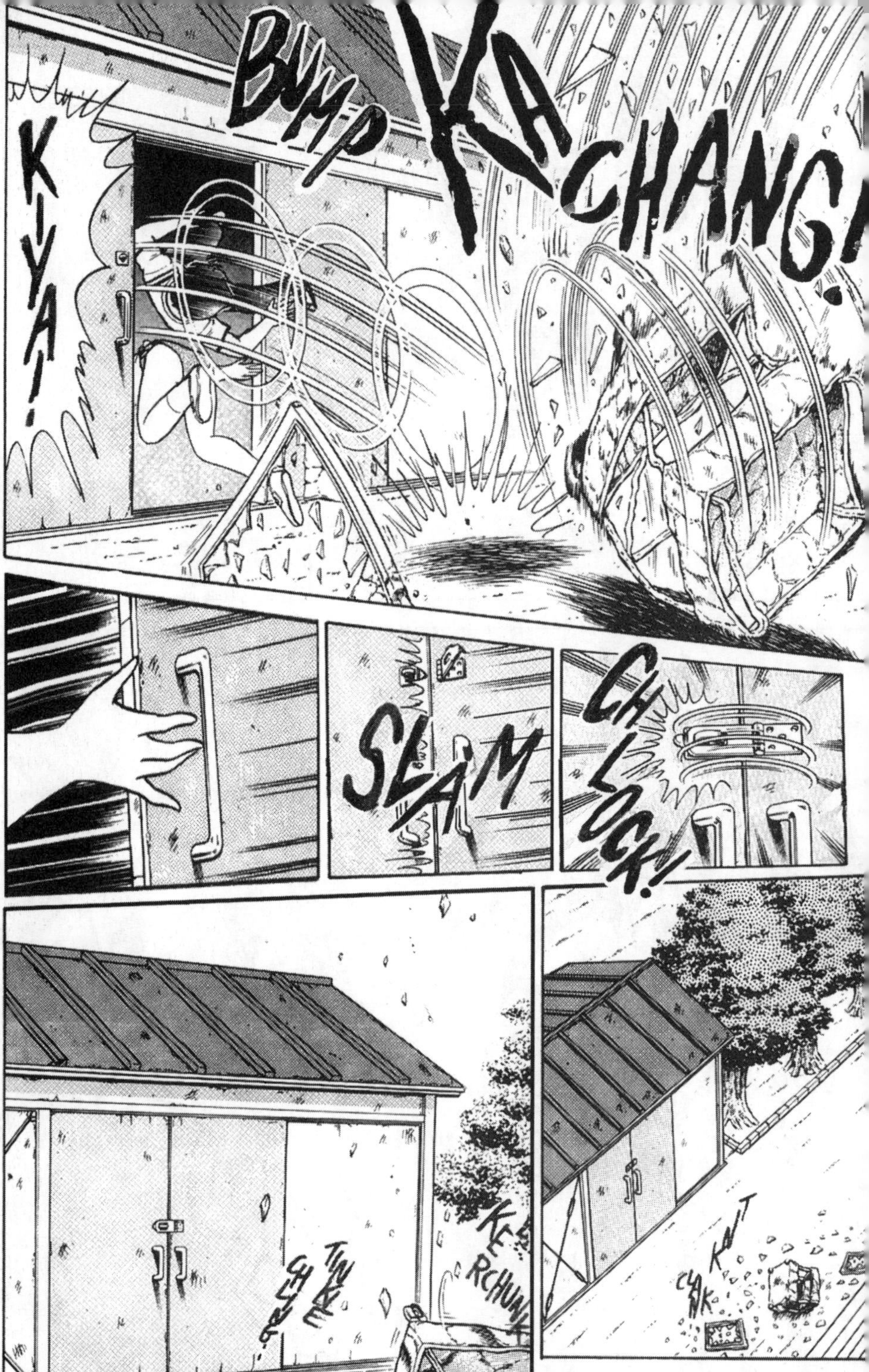
KA CHANG!
BUMP
KIYA!
CHI LOCK!
SLAM
CLANK
KE RCHUN
TINKLE

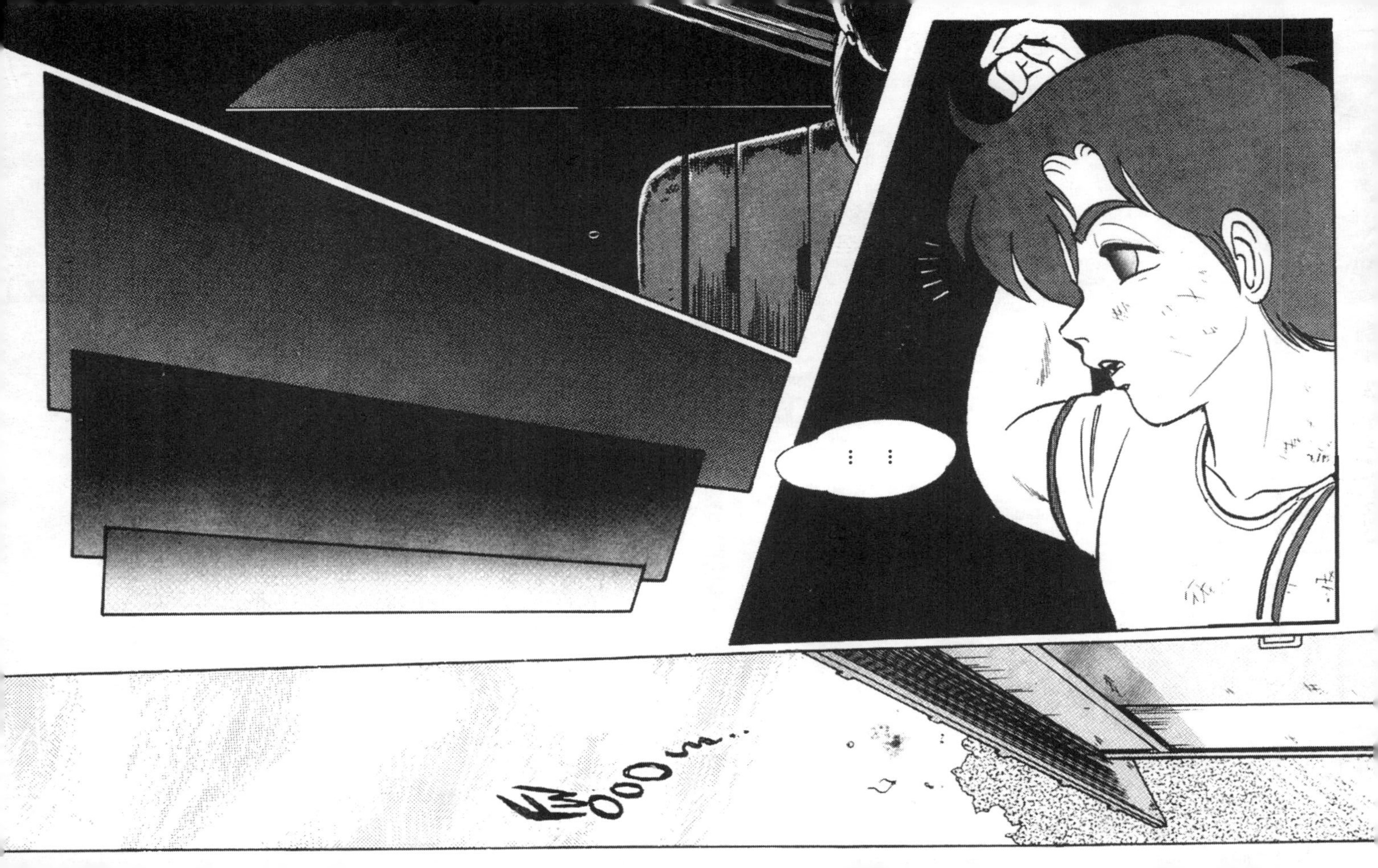
……
FWOOO...

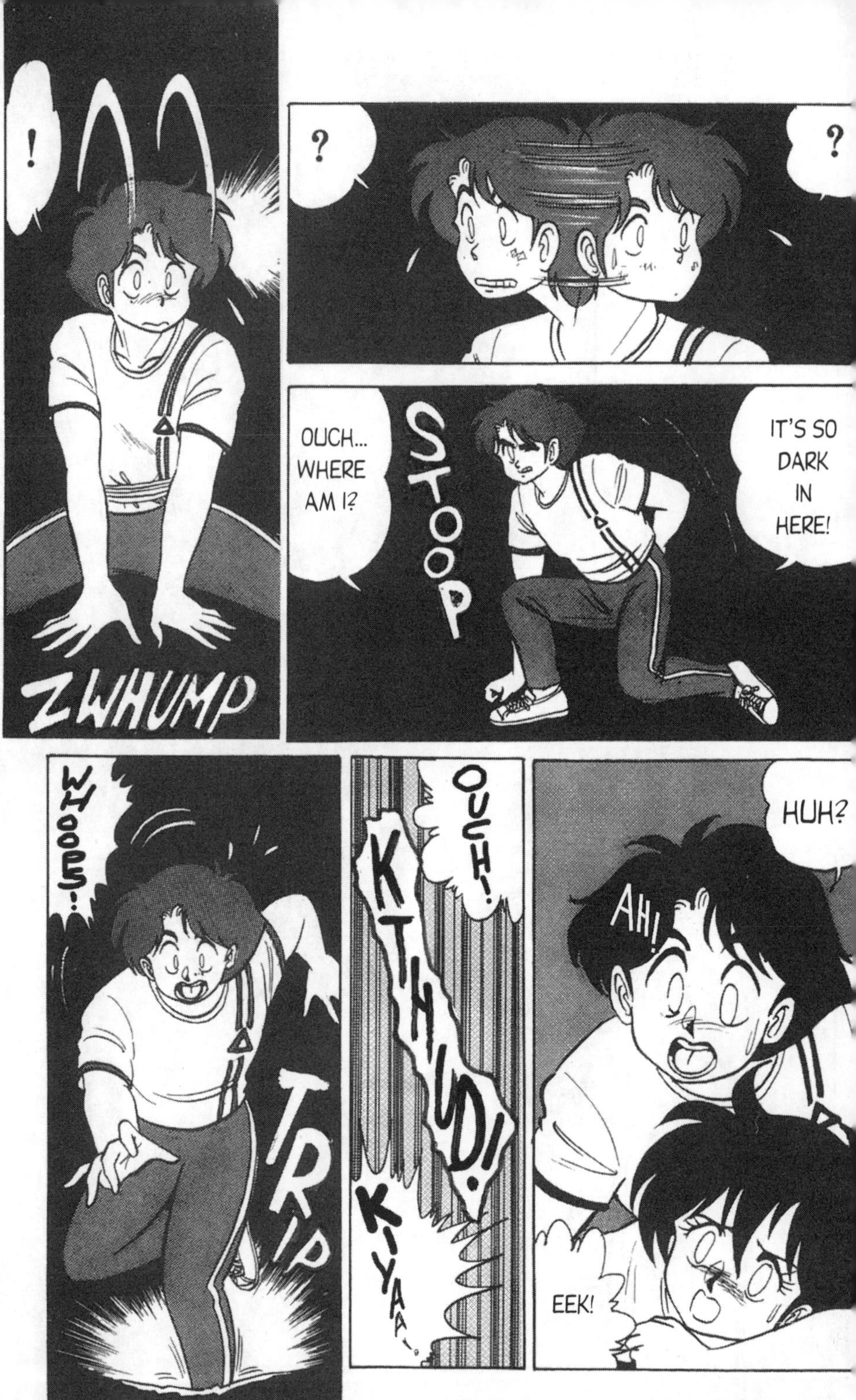
!
ZWHUMP
?
?
OUCH... WHERE AM I?
STOOP
IT'S SO DARK IN HERE!
WHOOPS!
TRIP
OUCH!
KTHUD!
KIYAA
HUH?
AH!
EEK!

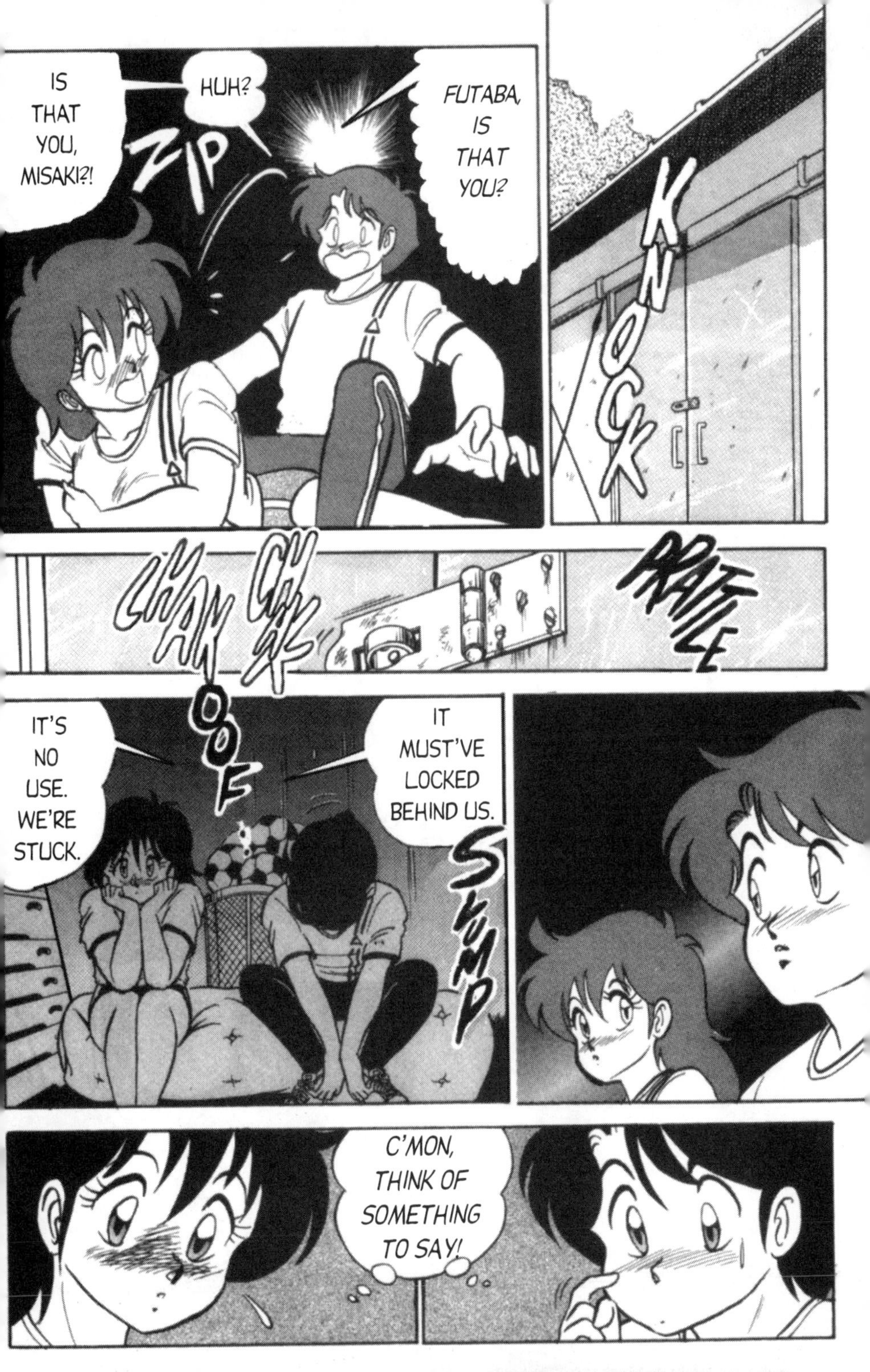
KNOCK
FUTABA, IS THAT YOU?
HUH?
ZIP
IS THAT YOU, MISAKI?!
RATTLE
CHAK
CHAK
IT MUST'VE LOCKED BEHIND US.
SLUMP
OOF
IT'S NO USE. WE'RE STUCK.
C'MON, THINK OF SOMETHING TO SAY!

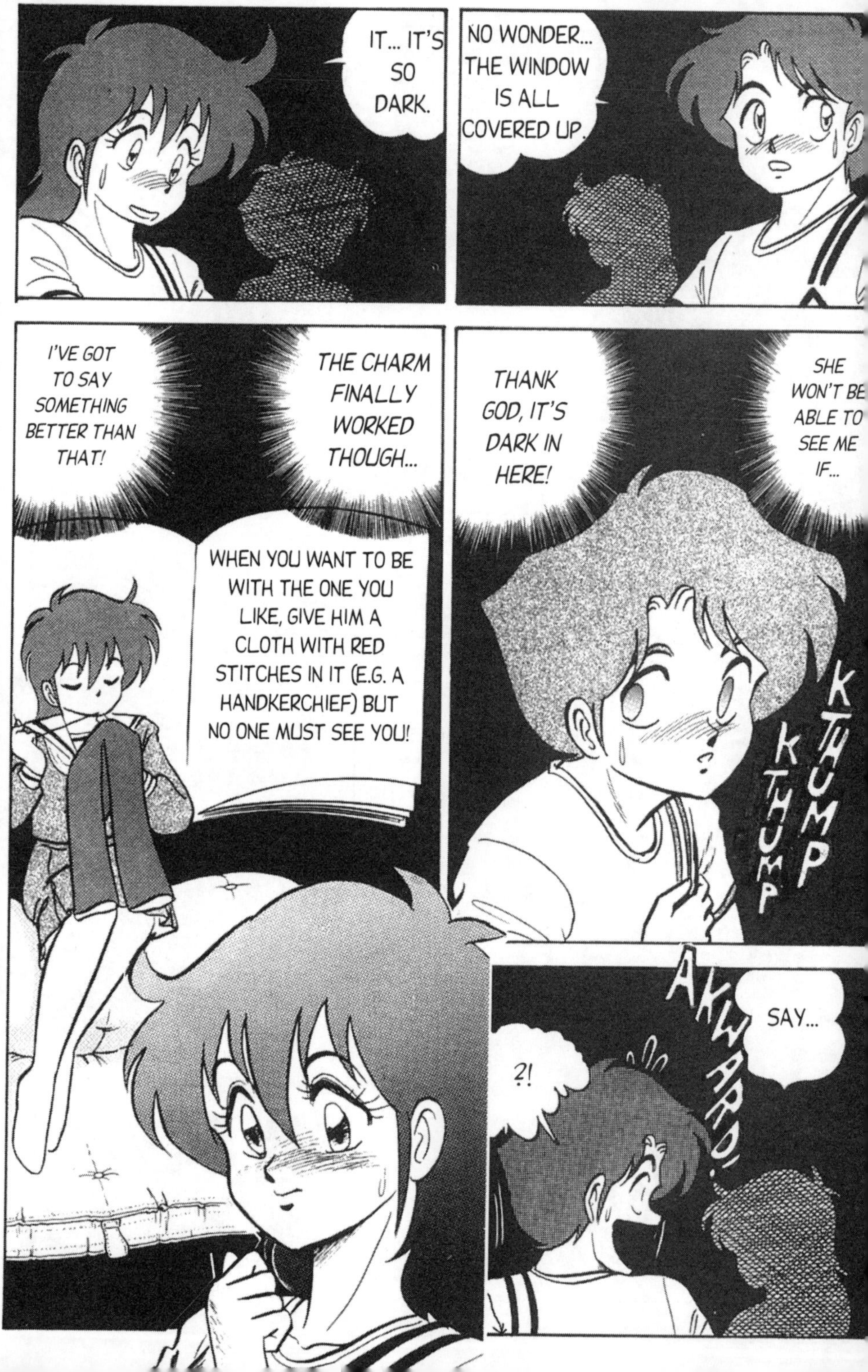
IT... IT'S SO DARK.
NO WONDER... THE WINDOW IS ALL COVERED UP.
I'VE GOT TO SAY SOMETHING BETTER THAN THAT!
THE CHARM FINALLY WORKED THOUGH...
THANK GOD, IT'S DARK IN HERE!
SHE WON'T BE ABLE TO SEE ME IF...
WHEN YOU WANT TO BE WITH THE ONE YOU LIKE, GIVE HIM A CLOTH WITH RED STITCHES IN IT (E.G. A HANDKERCHIEF) BUT NO ONE MUST SEE YOU!
KTHUMP KTHUMP
SAY...
?!
AKWARD!

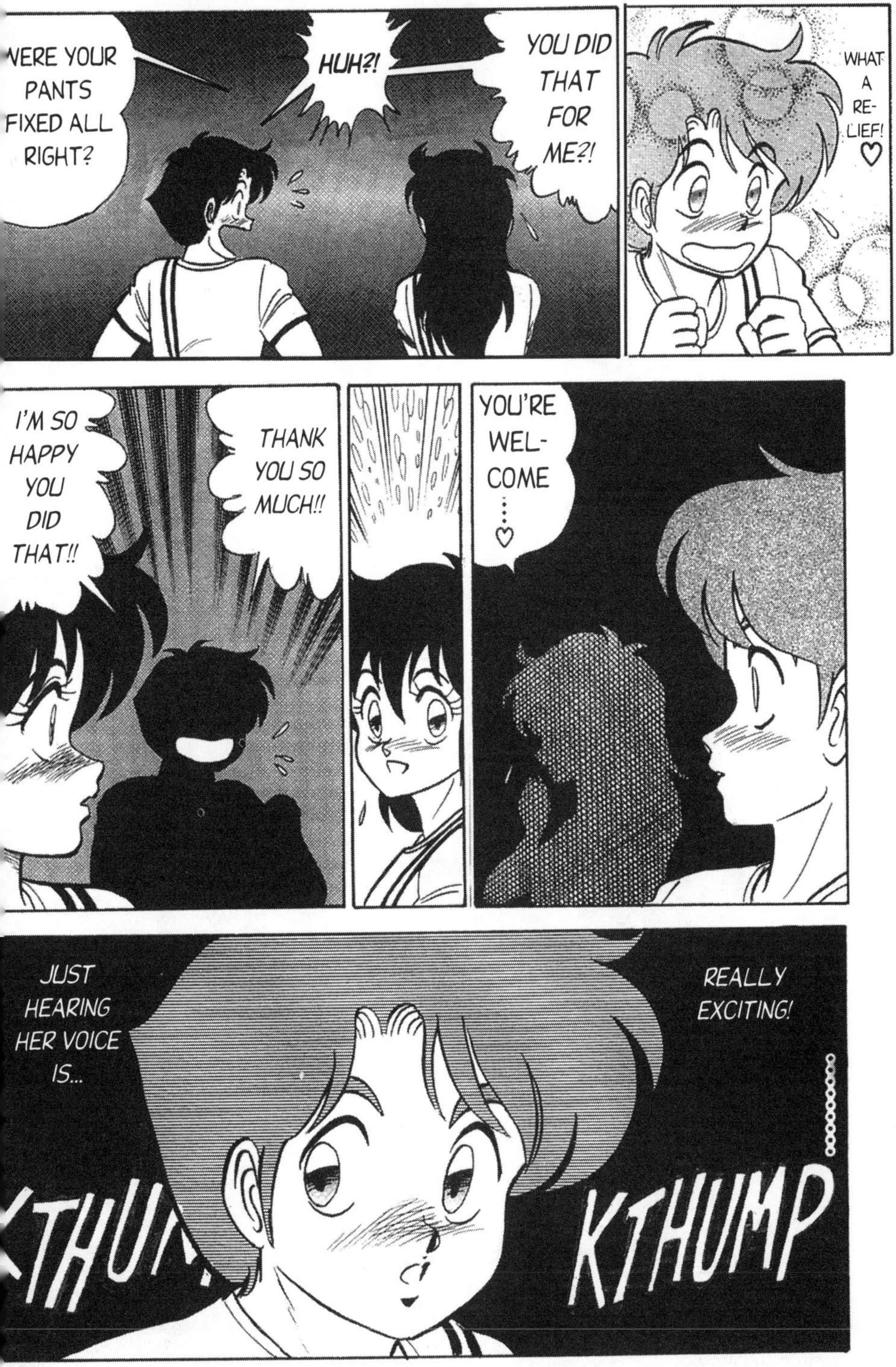
WERE YOUR PANTS FIXED ALL RIGHT?
HUH?!
YOU DID THAT FOR ME?!
WHAT A RE-LIEF! ♡
I'M SO HAPPY YOU DID THAT!!
THANK YOU SO MUCH!!
YOU'RE WEL-COME ♡
JUST HEARING HER VOICE IS...
REALLY EXCITING!
KTHUMP
KTHUMP

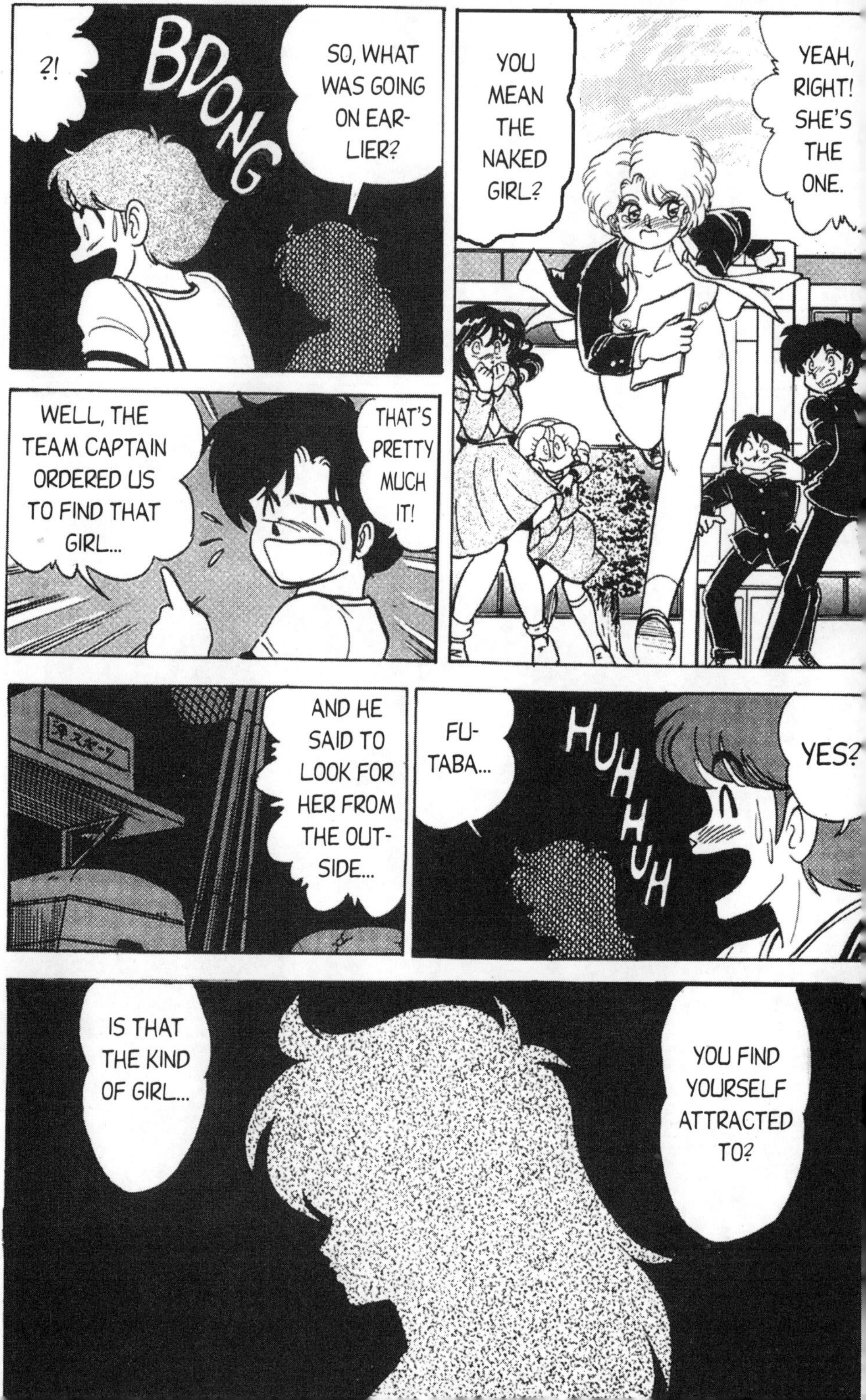
?!
BDONG
SO, WHAT WAS GOING ON EAR-LIER?
YOU MEAN THE NAKED GIRL?
YEAH, RIGHT! SHE'S THE ONE.
WELL, THE TEAM CAPTAIN ORDERED US TO FIND THAT GIRL...
THAT'S PRETTY MUCH IT!
AND HE SAID TO LOOK FOR HER FROM THE OUT-SIDE...
FU-TABA...
HUHHUH
YES?
IS THAT THE KIND OF GIRL...
YOU FIND YOURSELF ATTRACTED TO?

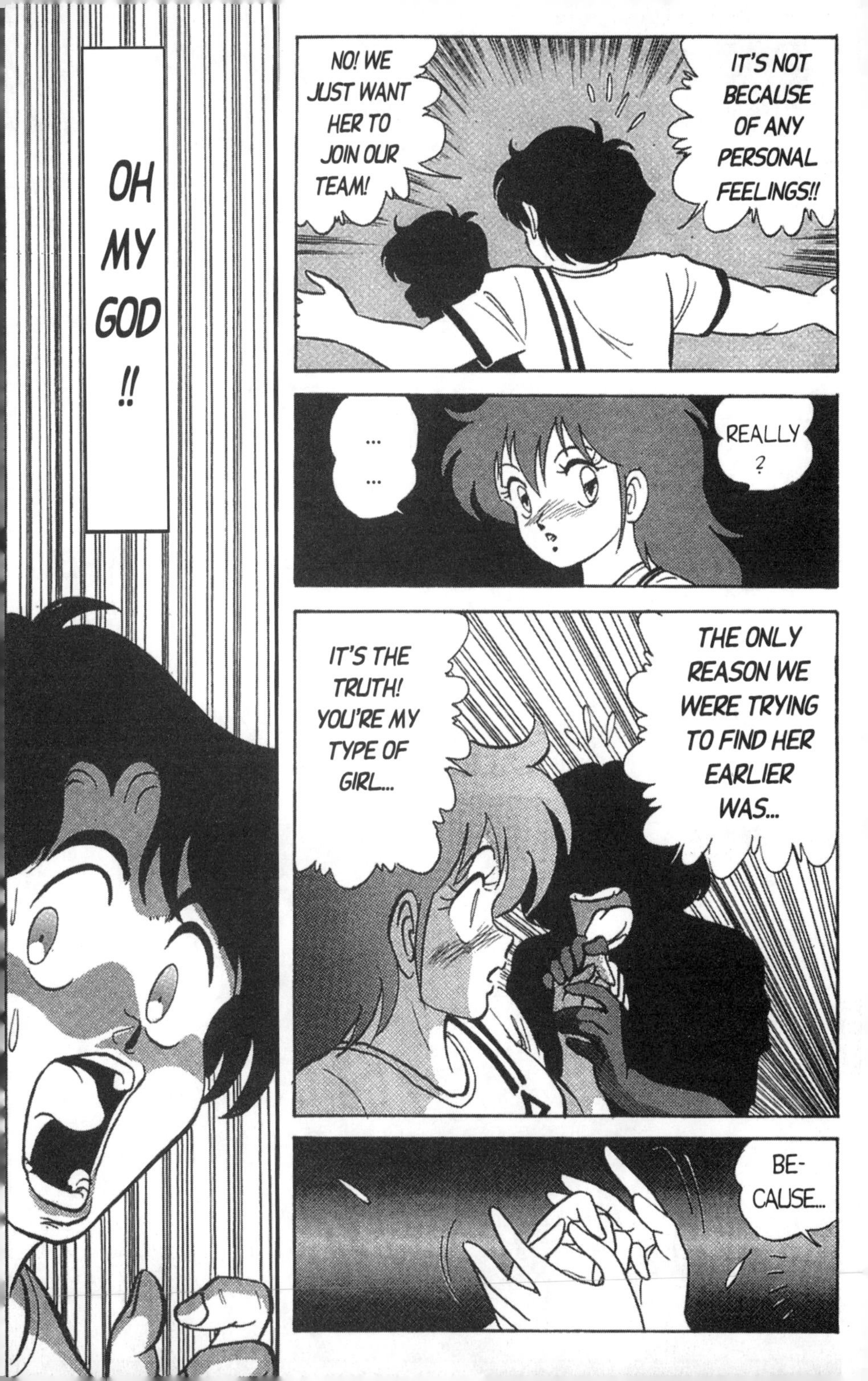
NO! WE JUST WANT HER TO JOIN OUR TEAM!
IT'S NOT BECAUSE OF ANY PERSONAL FEELINGS!!
REALLY?
......
IT'S THE TRUTH! YOU'RE MY TYPE OF GIRL...
THE ONLY REASON WE WERE TRYING TO FIND HER EARLIER WAS...
BE-CAUSE...
OH MY GOD!!

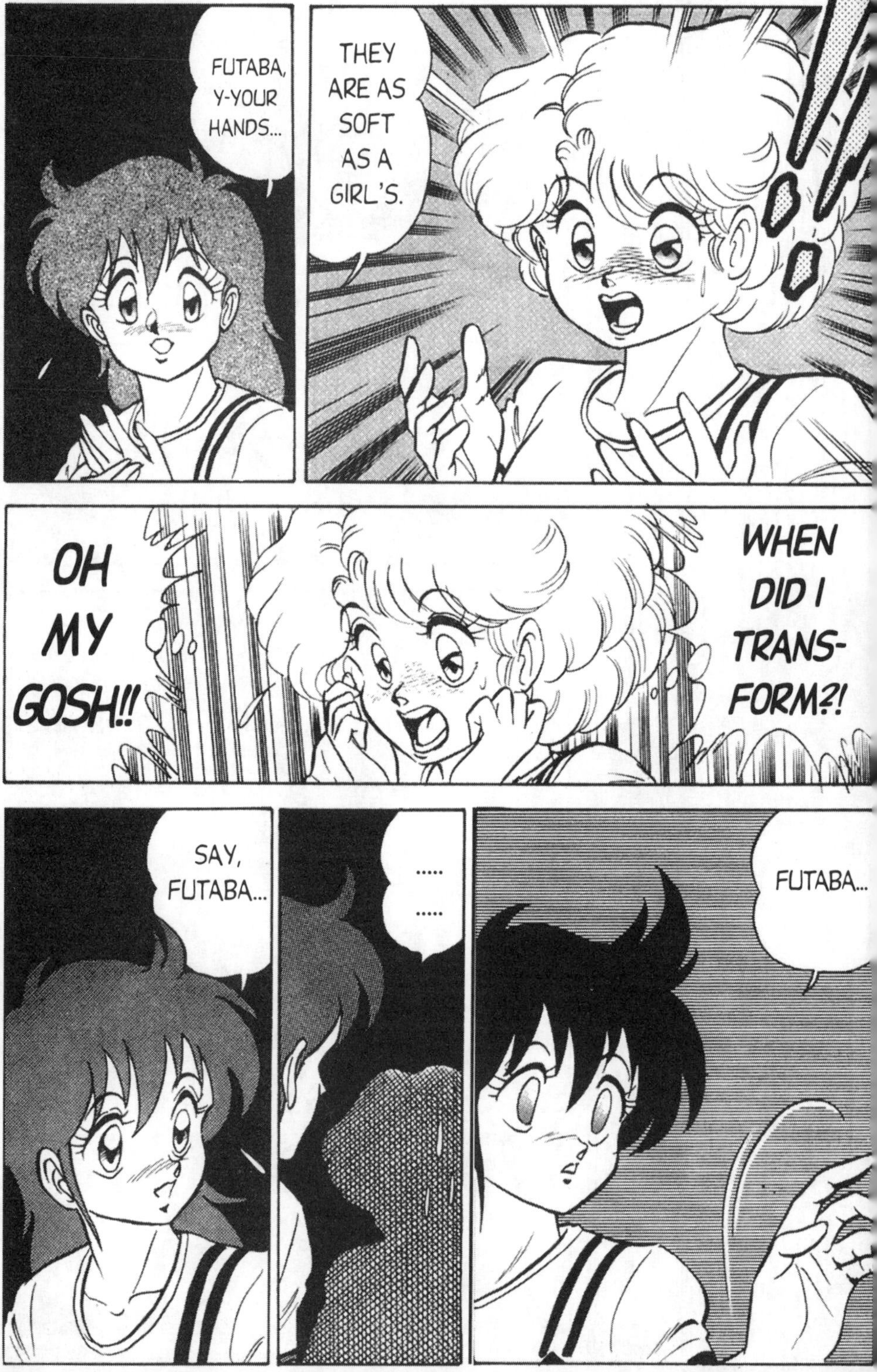
FUTABA, Y-YOUR HANDS...
THEY ARE AS SOFT AS A GIRL'S.
!!
WHEN DID I TRANS-FORM?!
OH MY GOSH!!
SAY, FUTABA...
.....
.....
FUTABA...

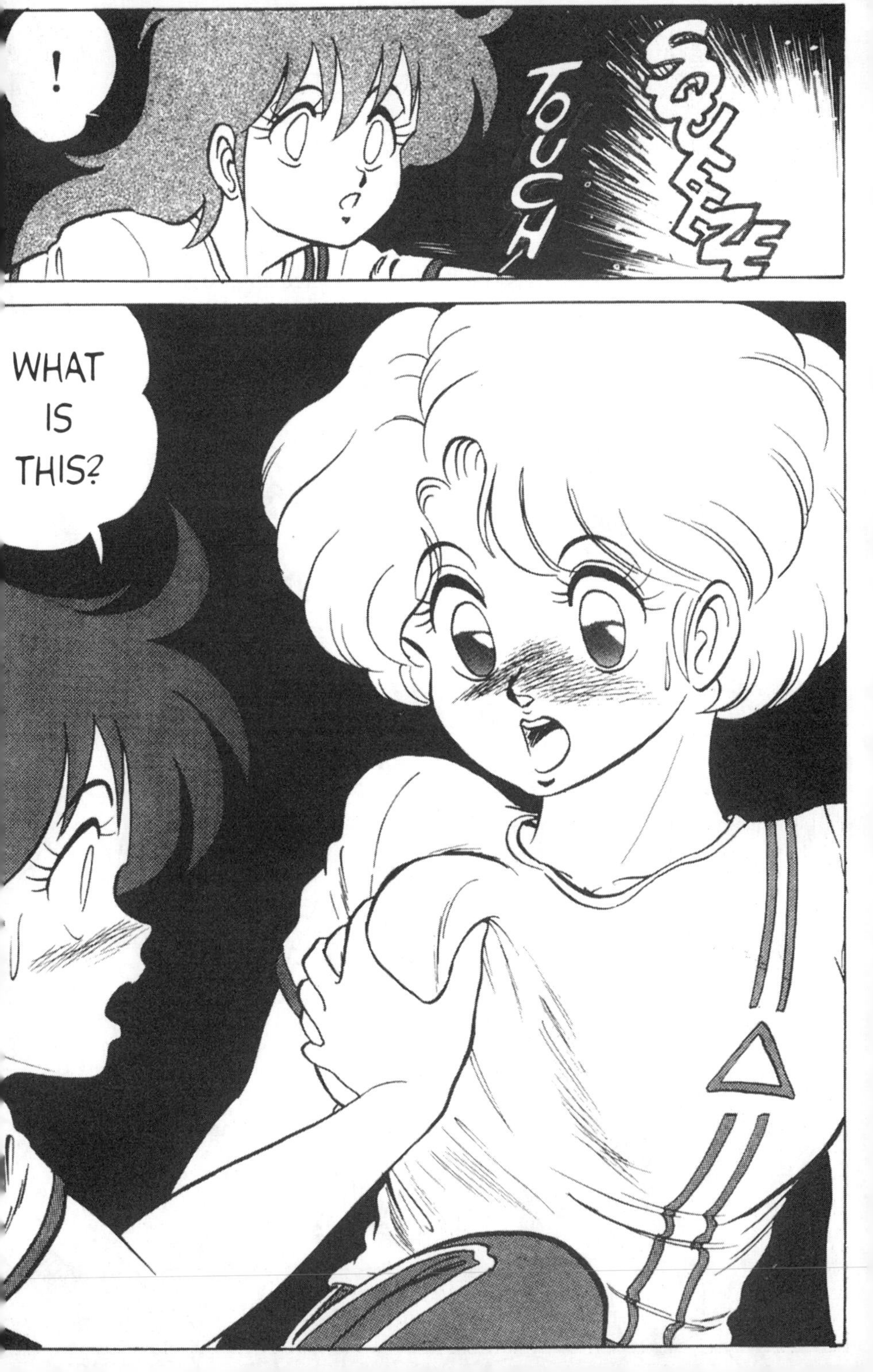
SQUEEZE
TOUCH
!
WHAT IS THIS?

Introducing my staff members who helped produce ***Futaba-kun Change!***

Koji Sugitani

He is the youngest of all. he's a video game otaku and his favorites are RPG's. He is a great guy who loves pro wrestling, Sake, karaoke, and dirty jokes."Huh? works that I want to work on? Well, I should challenge anything while I'm still young!" (but he hasn't created any works yet...).

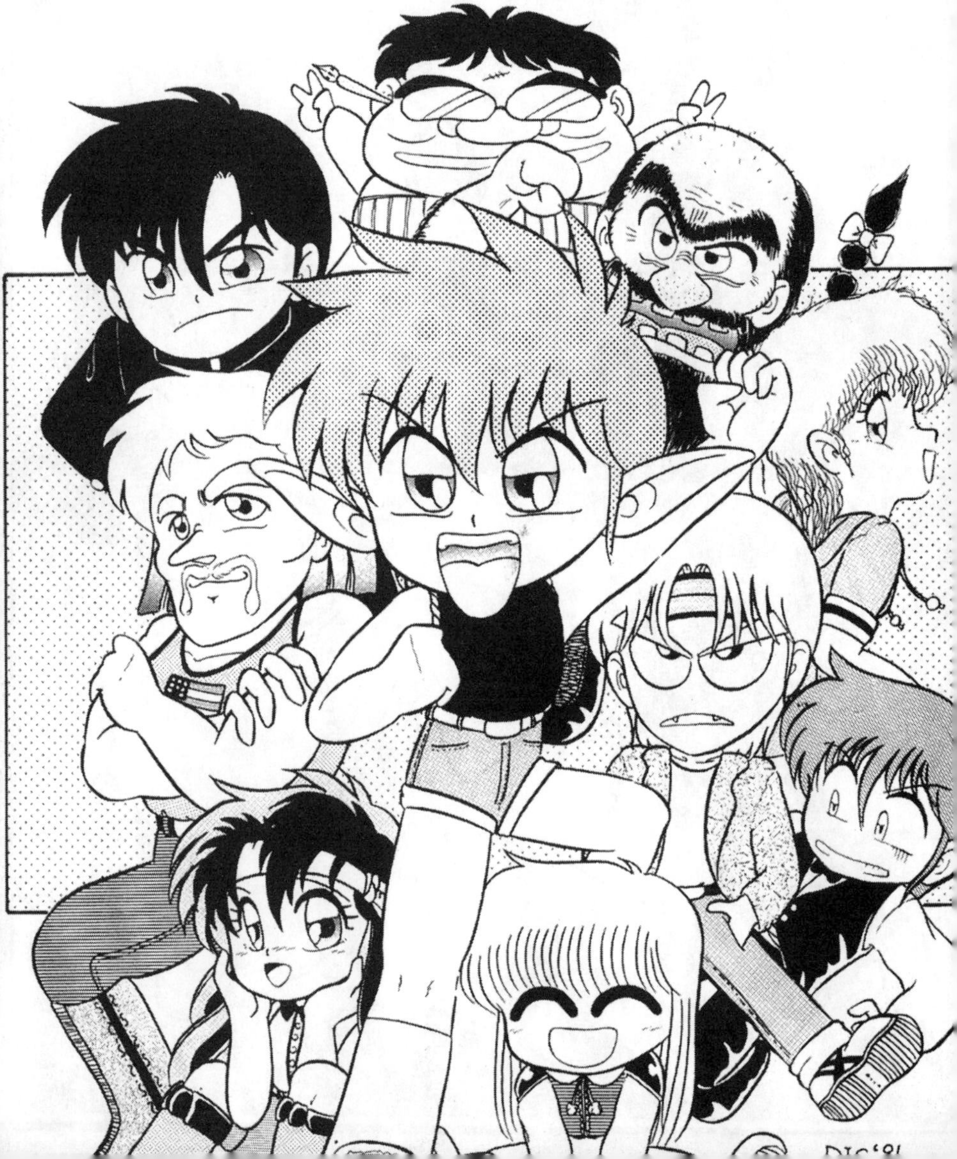

Futaba Escapes!!

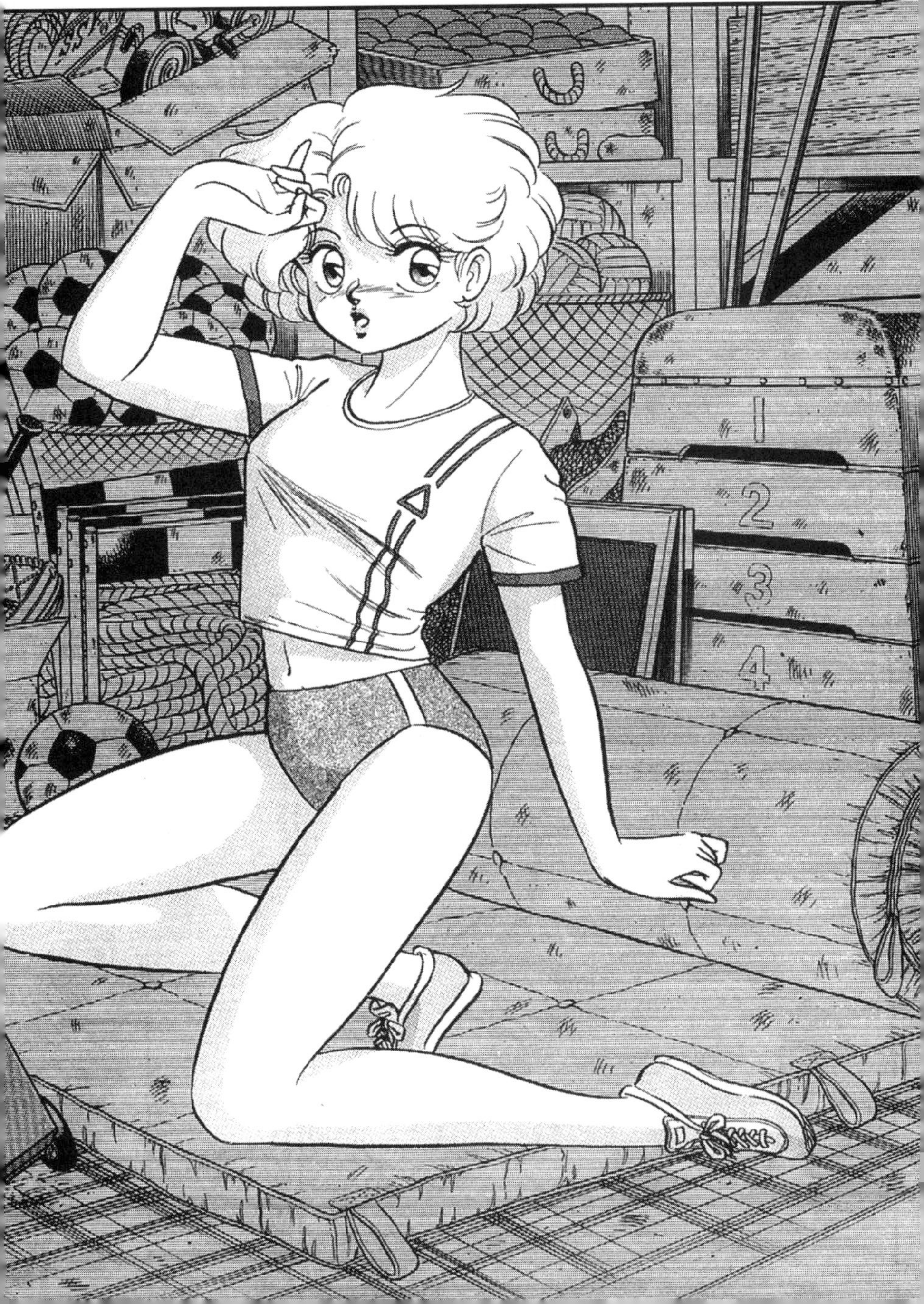

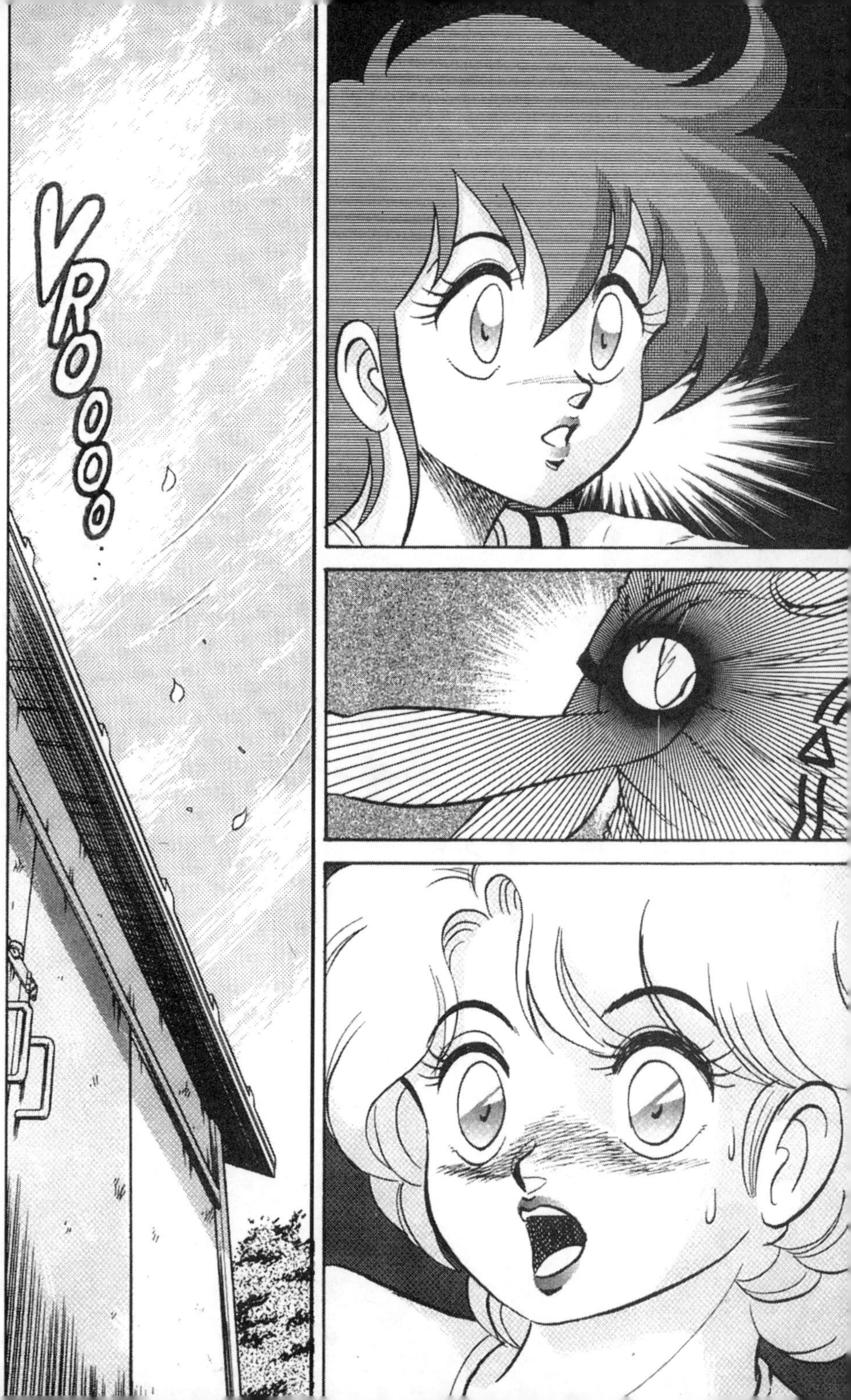
VROOOO...

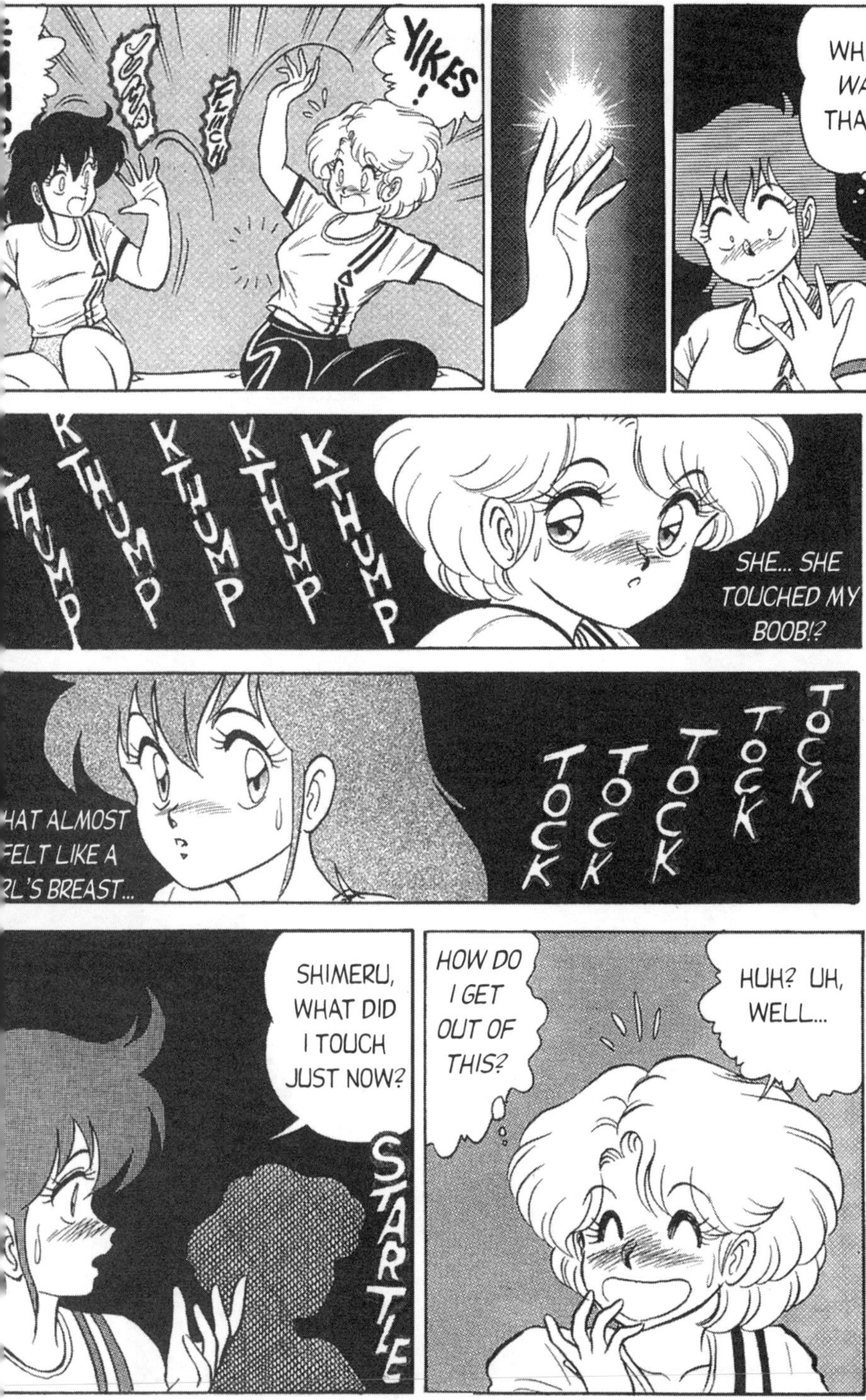
YIKES!
FLINCH
WHAT WAS THAT?!
KTHUMP KTHUMP KTHUMP KTHUMP
SHE... SHE TOUCHED MY BOOB!?
HAT ALMOST FELT LIKE A RL'S BREAST...
TOCK TOCK TOCK TOCK TOCK
SHIMERU, WHAT DID I TOUCH JUST NOW?
STARTLE
HOW DO I GET OUT OF THIS?
HUH? UH, WELL...

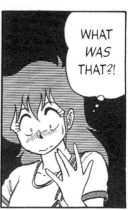

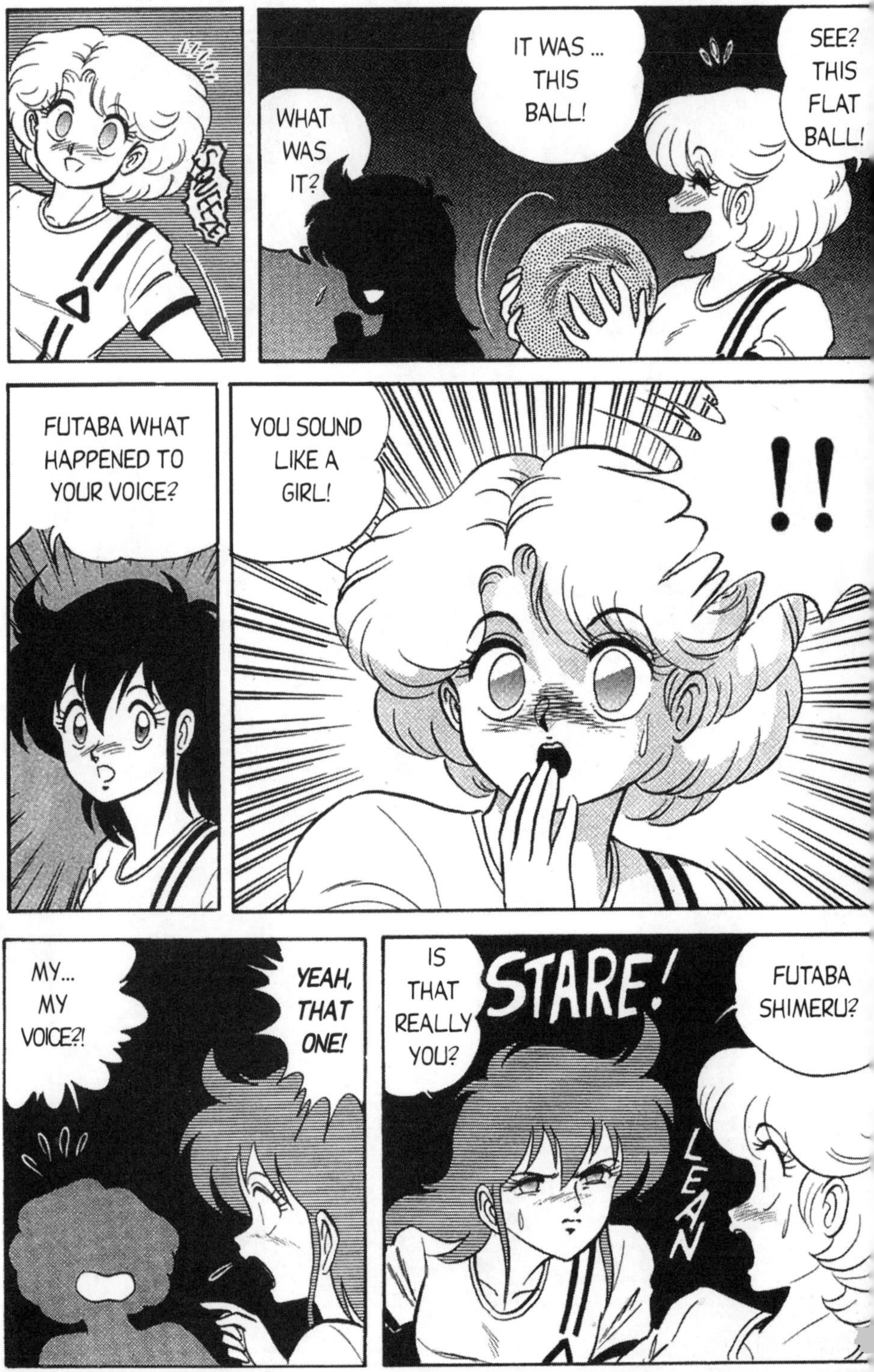
SQUEEZE
WHAT WAS IT?
IT WAS ... THIS BALL!
SEE? THIS FLAT BALL!
FUTABA WHAT HAPPENED TO YOUR VOICE?
YOU SOUND LIKE A GIRL!
!!
MY... MY VOICE?!
YEAH, THAT ONE!
IS THAT REALLY YOU?
STARE!
FUTABA SHIMERU?
LEAN

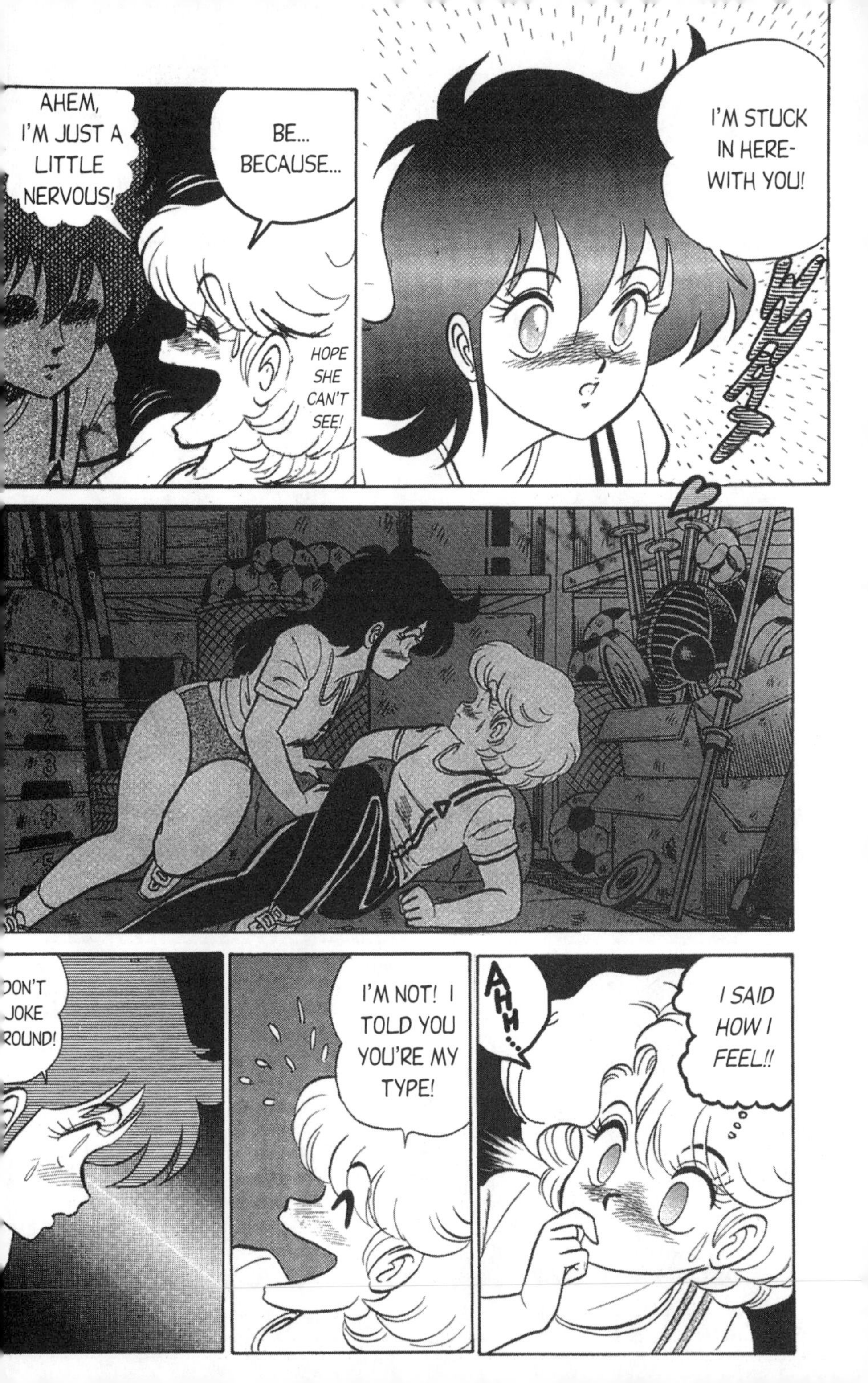
BE... BECAUSE...
AHEM, I'M JUST A LITTLE NERVOUS!
HOPE SHE CAN'T SEE!
I'M STUCK IN HERE- WITH YOU!
DON'T JOKE ROUND!
I'M NOT! I TOLD YOU YOU'RE MY TYPE!
AHH...
I SAID HOW I FEEL!!

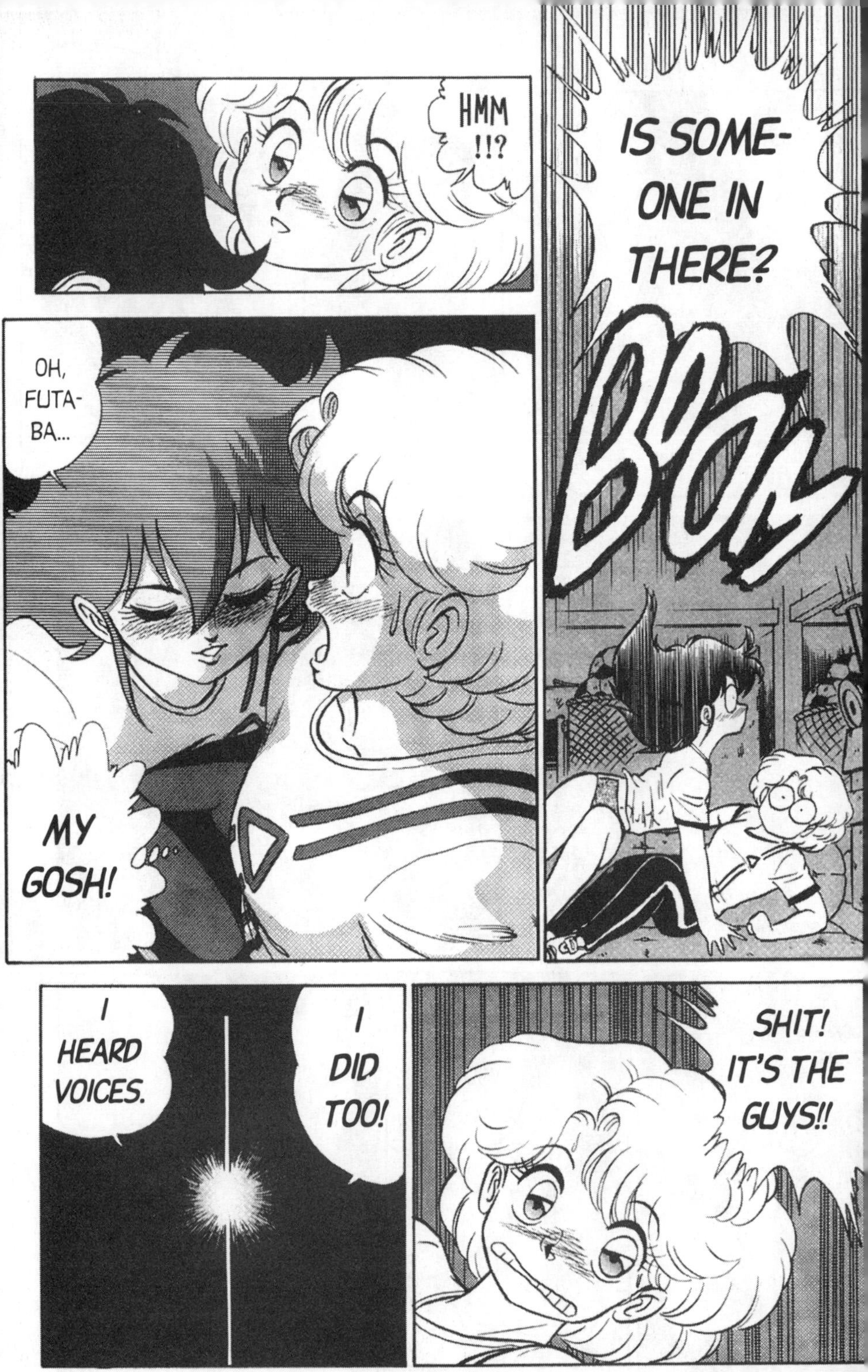
HMM !!?
OH, FUTA-BA...
MY GOSH!
IS SOME-ONE IN THERE?
BOOM
I HEARD VOICES.
I DID TOO!
SHIT! IT'S THE GUYS!!

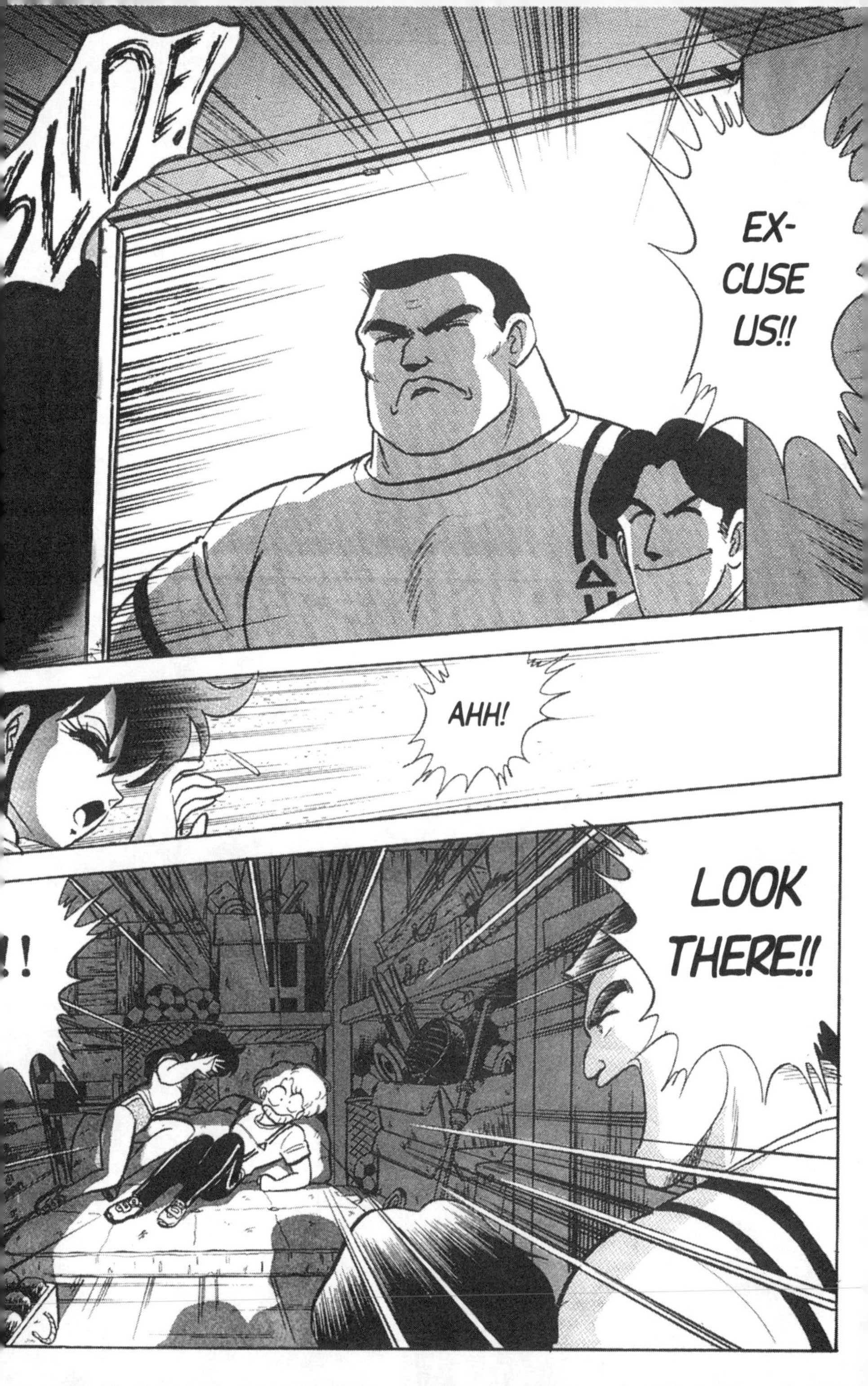
SLIDE!
EX-
CUSE
US!!
AHH!
LOOK
THERE!!
!!

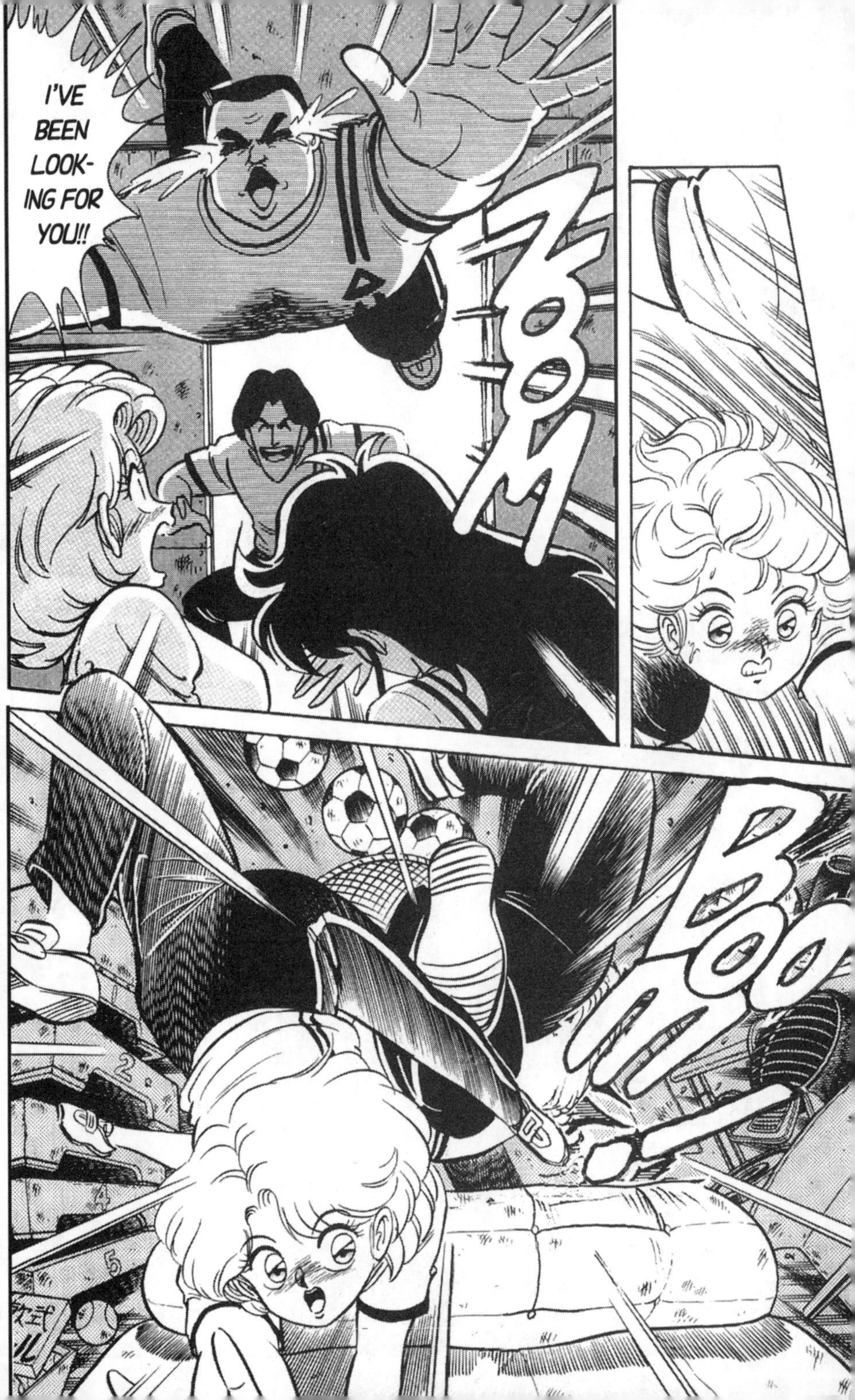
I'VE BEEN LOOKING FOR YOU!!
ZOOM
BOOM

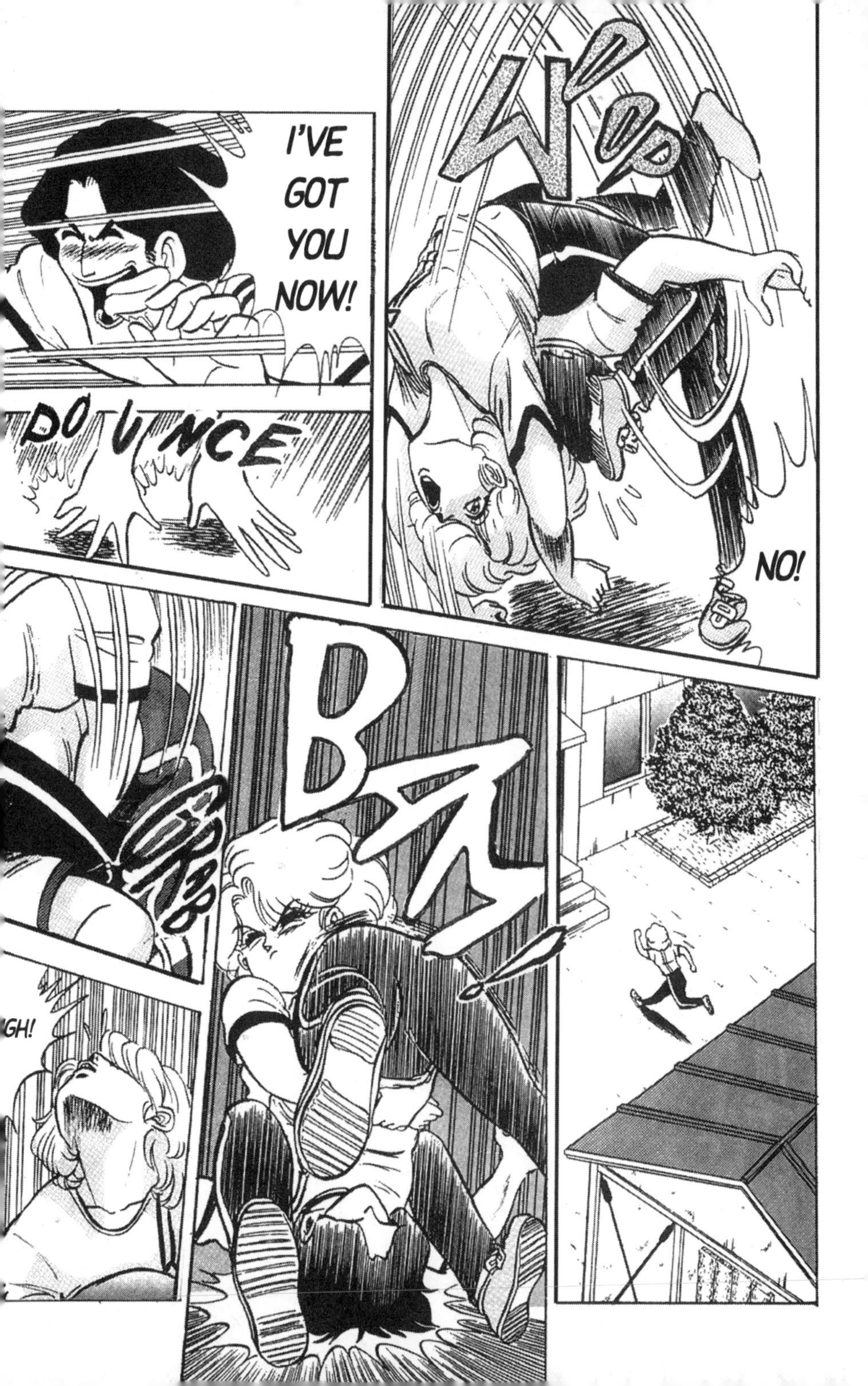
WOOP
I'VE GOT YOU NOW!
POUNCE
NO!
GRAB
BAM!
GH!

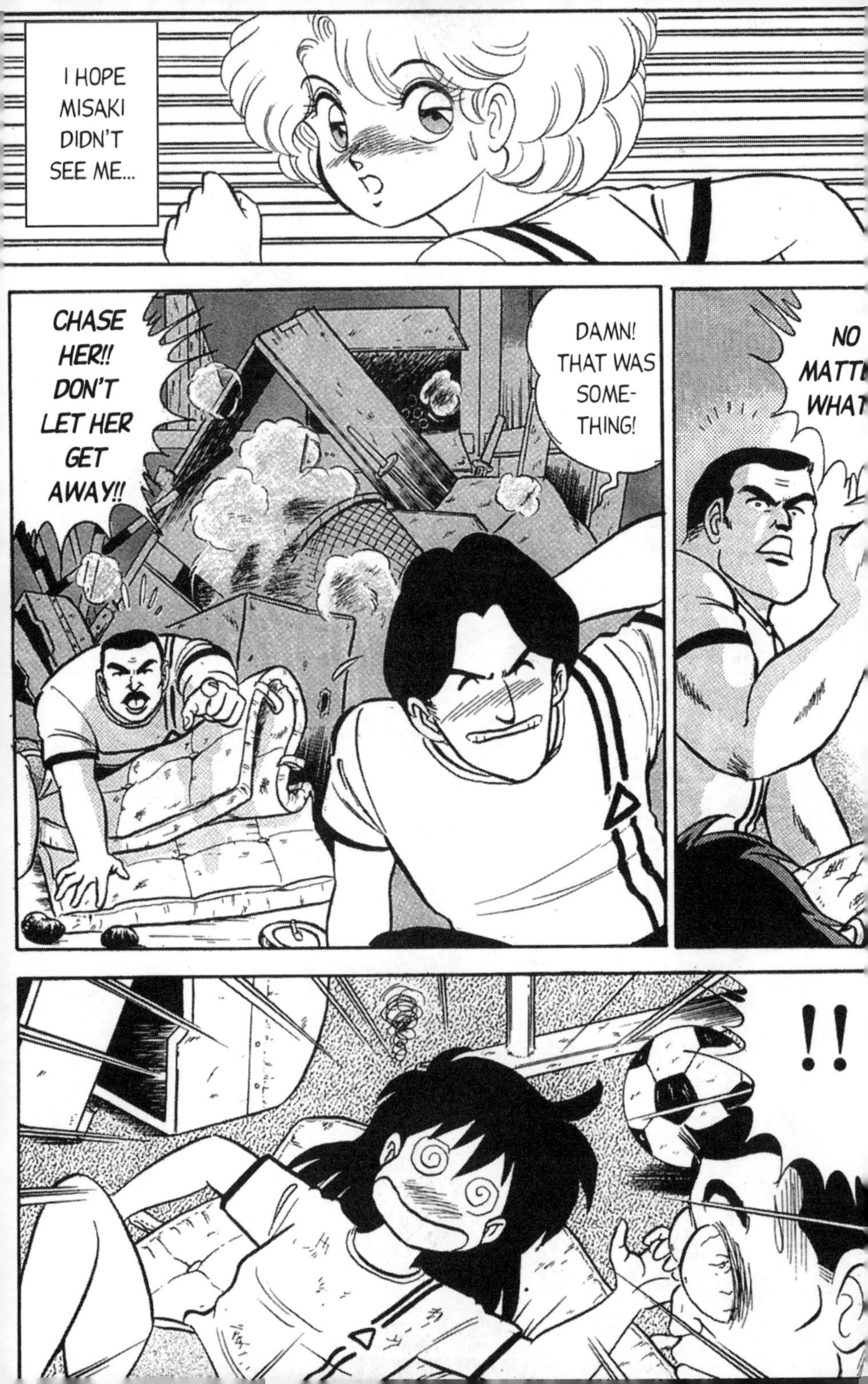
I HOPE MISAKI DIDN'T SEE ME...
NO MATT WHAT
DAMN! THAT WAS SOME-THING!
CHASE HER!! DON'T LET HER GET AWAY!!
!!

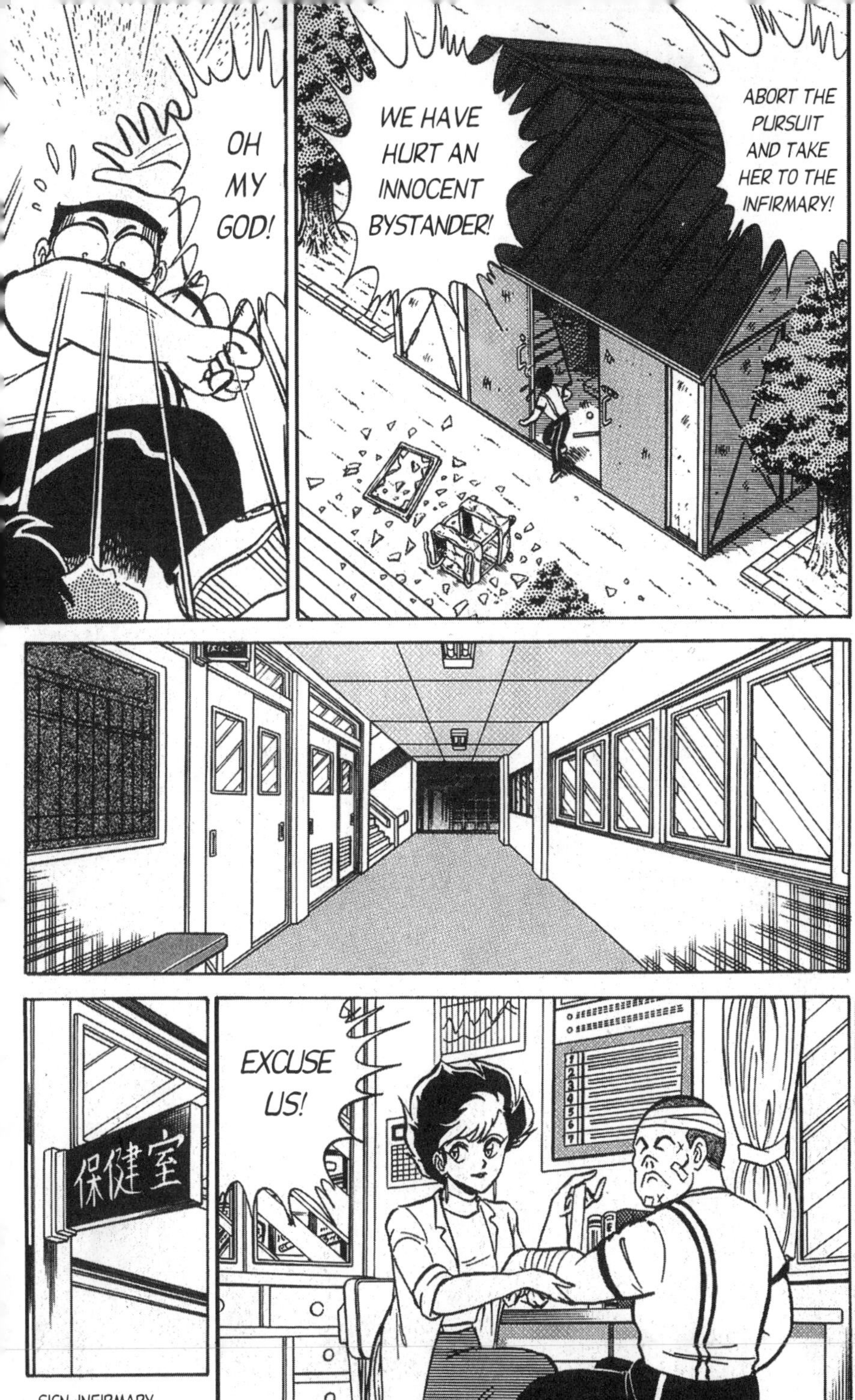
OH MY GOD!
WE HAVE HURT AN INNOCENT BYSTANDER!
ABORT THE PURSUIT AND TAKE HER TO THE INFIRMARY!
保健室
EXCUSE US!

SIGN :INFIRMARY

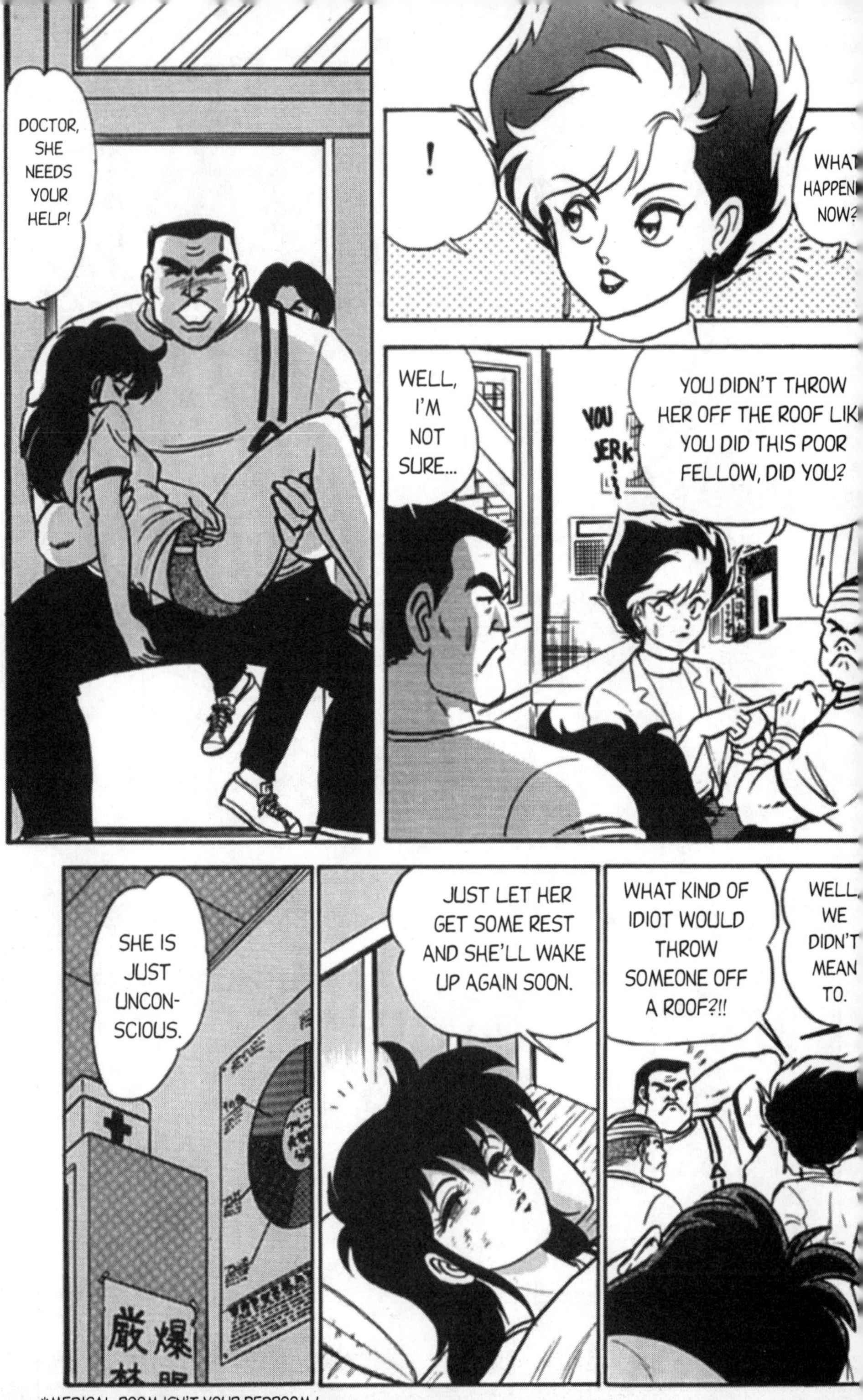
DOCTOR, SHE NEEDS YOUR HELP!
!
WHAT HAPPEN NOW?
WELL, I'M NOT SURE...
YOU JERK
YOU DIDN'T THROW HER OFF THE ROOF LIK YOU DID THIS POOR FELLOW, DID YOU?
SHE IS JUST UNCON-SCIOUS.
JUST LET HER GET SOME REST AND SHE'LL WAKE UP AGAIN SOON.
WHAT KIND OF IDIOT WOULD THROW SOMEONE OFF A ROOF?!!
WELL, WE DIDN'T MEAN TO.

*MEDICAL ROOM ISN'T YOUR BEDROOM !

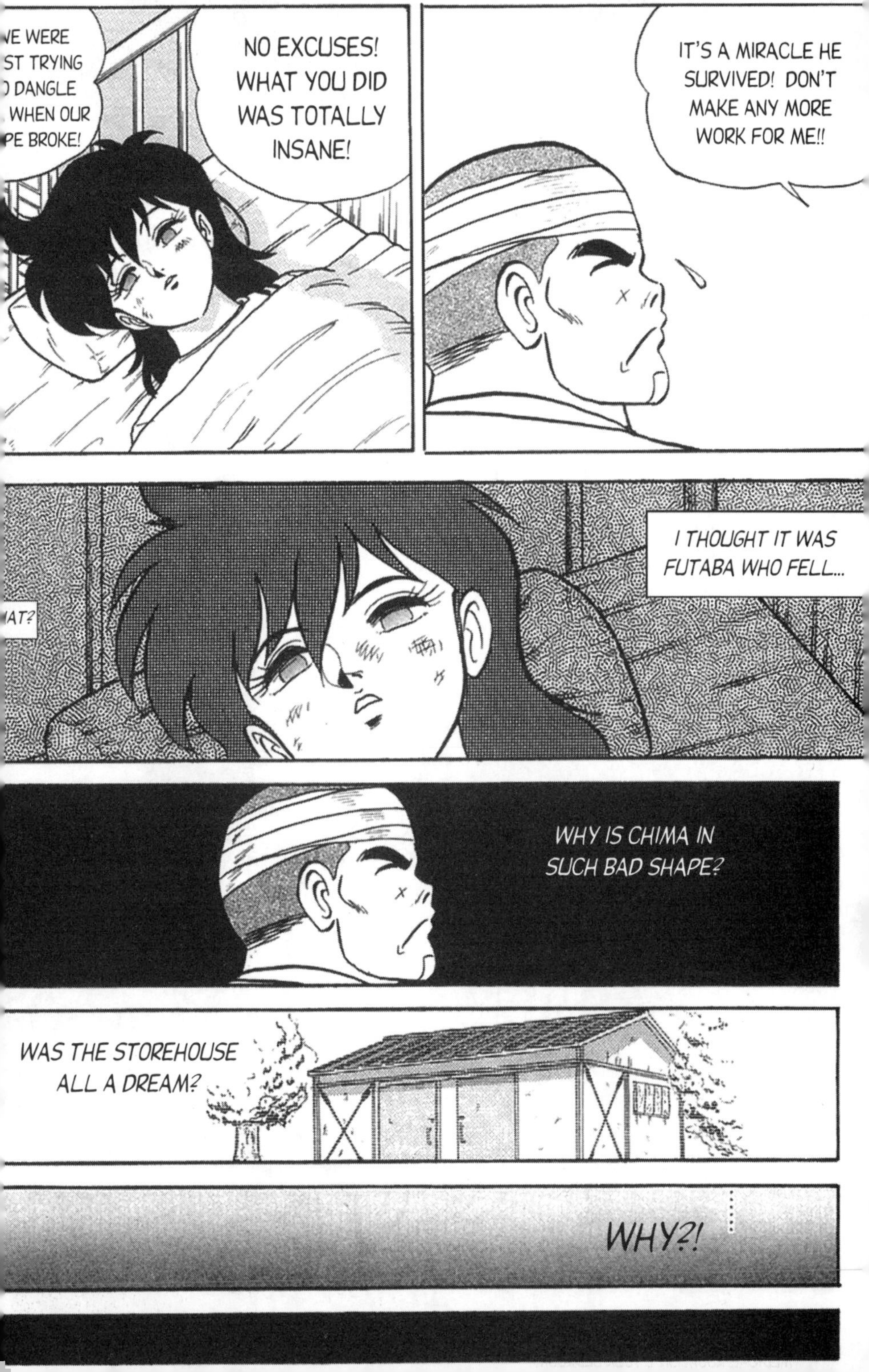

VE WERE
ST TRYING
) DANGLE
WHEN OUR
PE BROKE!
NO EXCUSES! WHAT YOU DID WAS TOTALLY INSANE!
IT'S A MIRACLE HE SURVIVED! DON'T MAKE ANY MORE WORK FOR ME!!
AT?
I THOUGHT IT WAS FUTABA WHO FELL...
WHY IS CHIMA IN SUCH BAD SHAPE?
WAS THE STOREHOUSE ALL A DREAM?
WHY?!
......

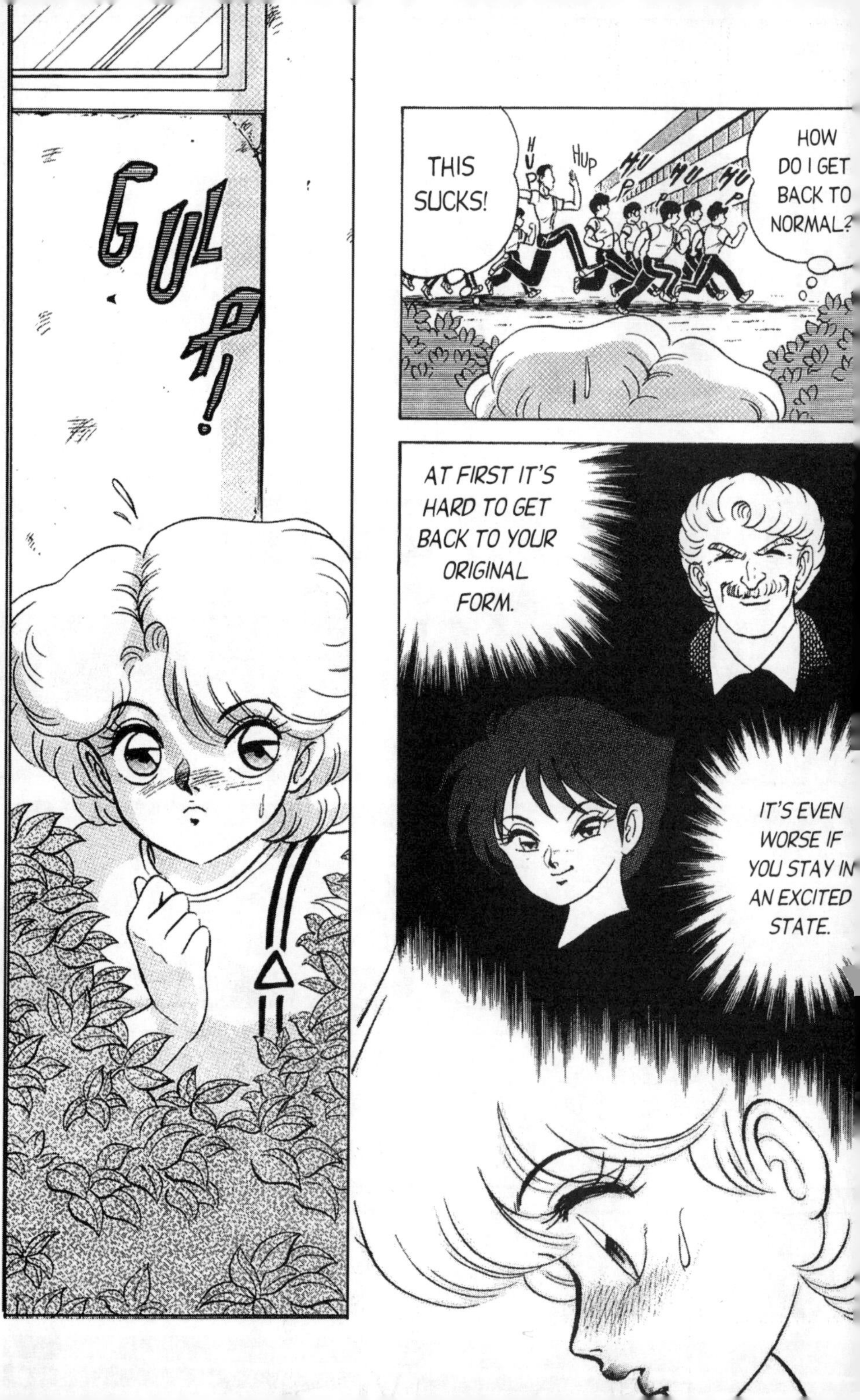
GULP!
THIS SUCKS!
HUP
HUP
HOW DO I GET BACK TO NORMAL?
AT FIRST IT'S HARD TO GET BACK TO YOUR ORIGINAL FORM.
IT'S EVEN WORSE IF YOU STAY IN AN EXCITED STATE.

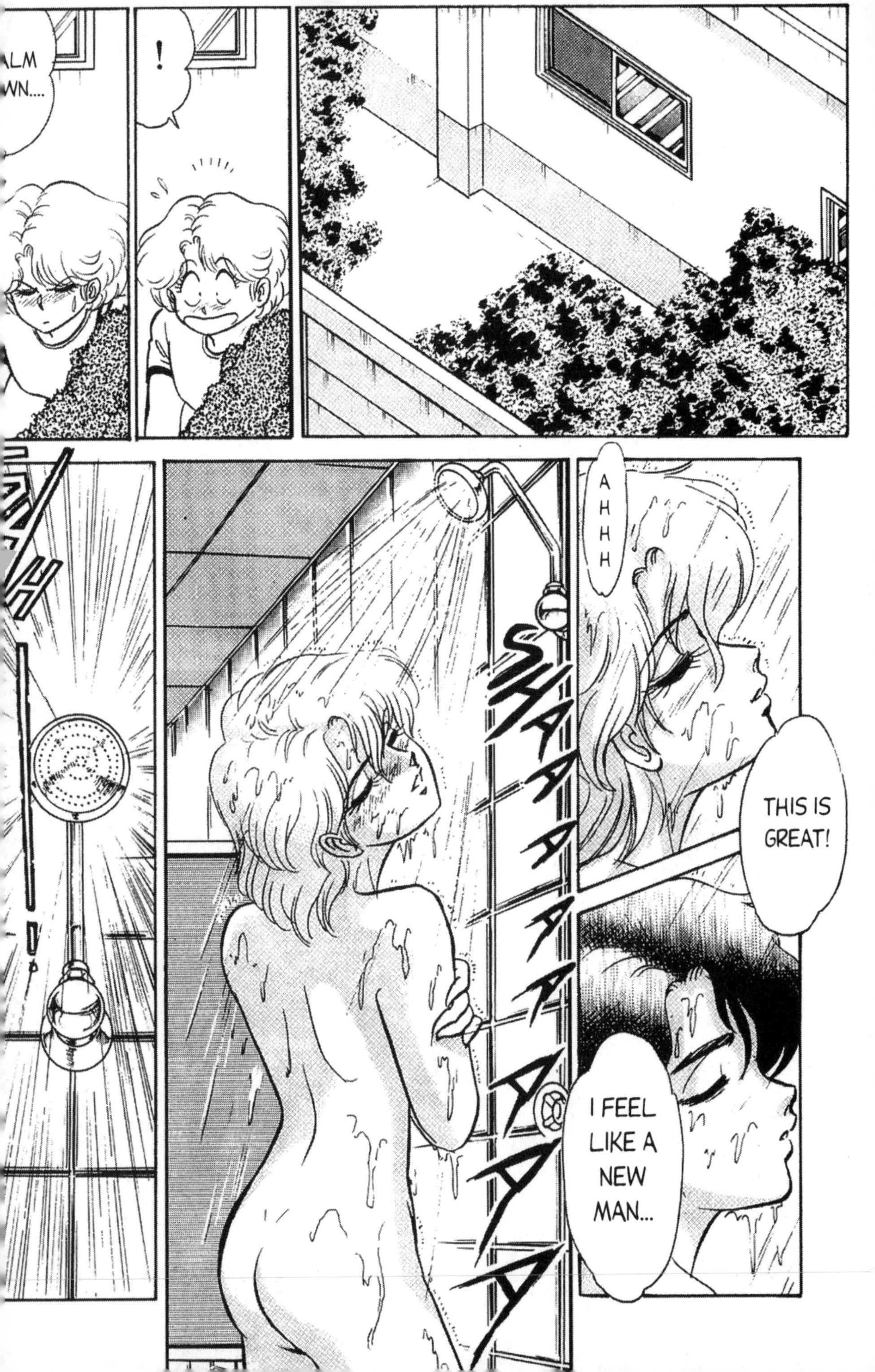
ALM
WN....
!
AHHH
SHAAAAAAAA
THIS IS GREAT!
I FEEL LIKE A NEW MAN...

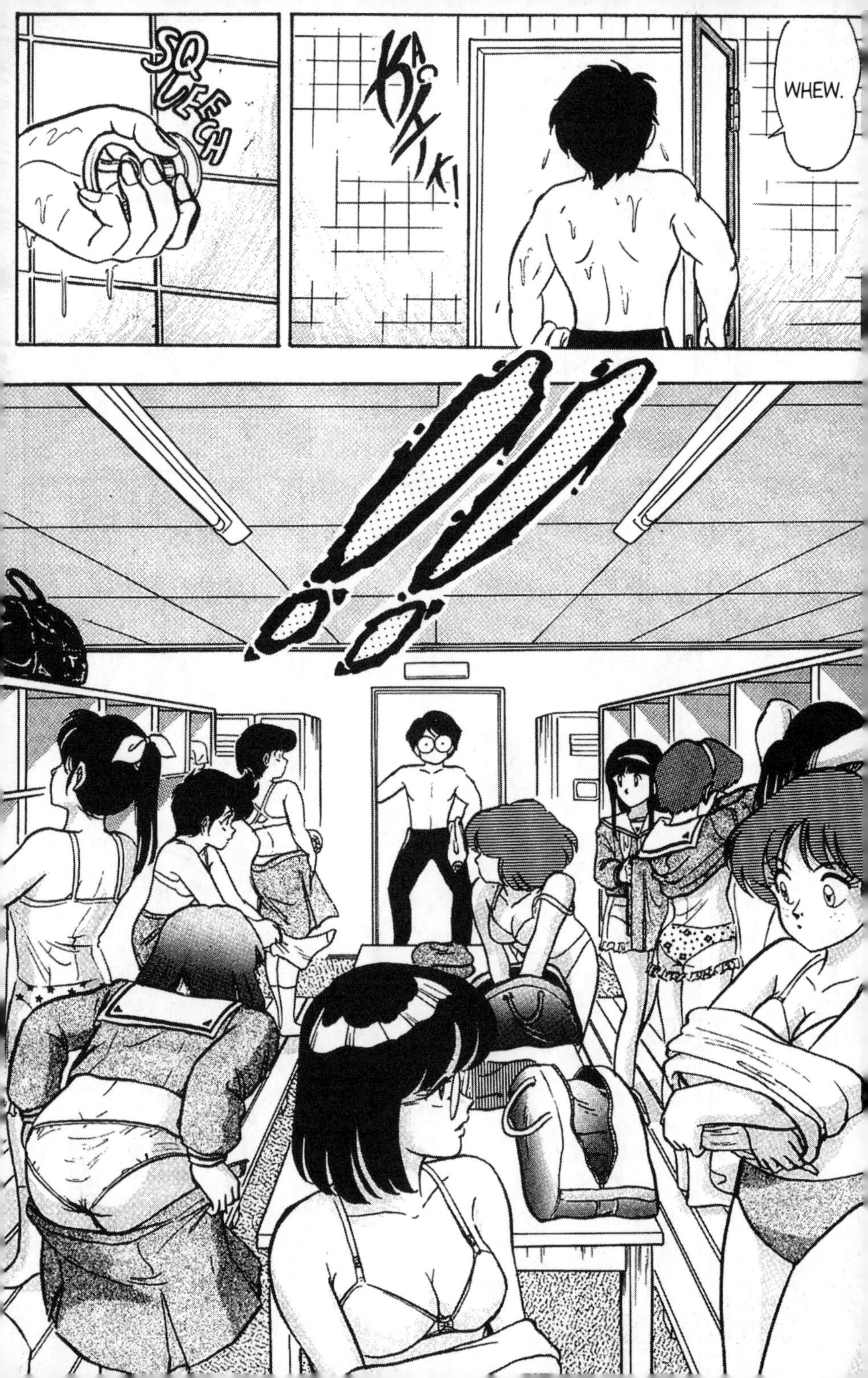
WHEW.
KACHIK!
SQUEECH

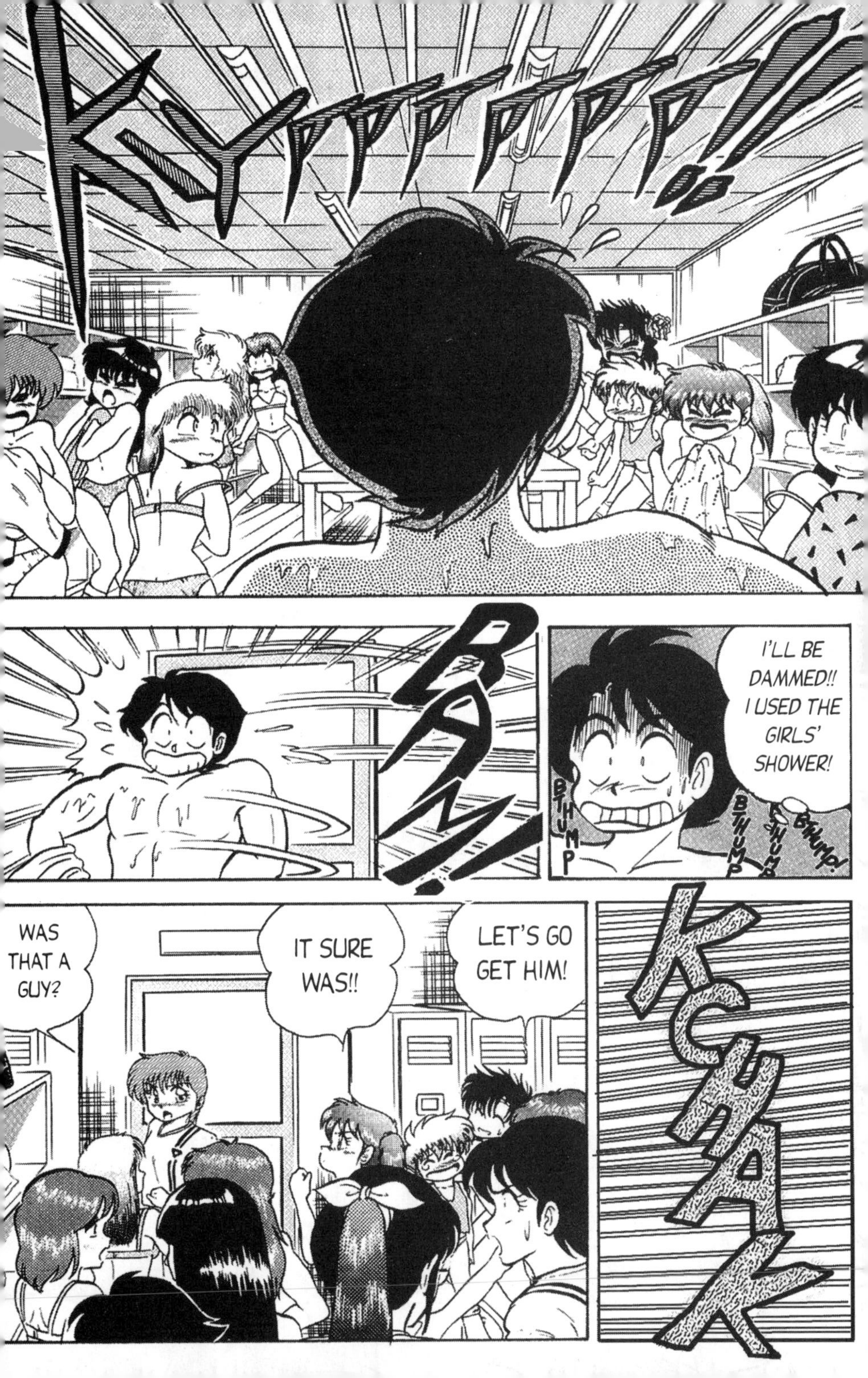

BAM!!
I'LL BE DAMMED!! I USED THE GIRLS' SHOWER!
BTHUMP
BTHUMP
BTHUMP!
WAS THAT A GUY?
IT SURE WAS!!
LET'S GO GET HIM!
KCHAK

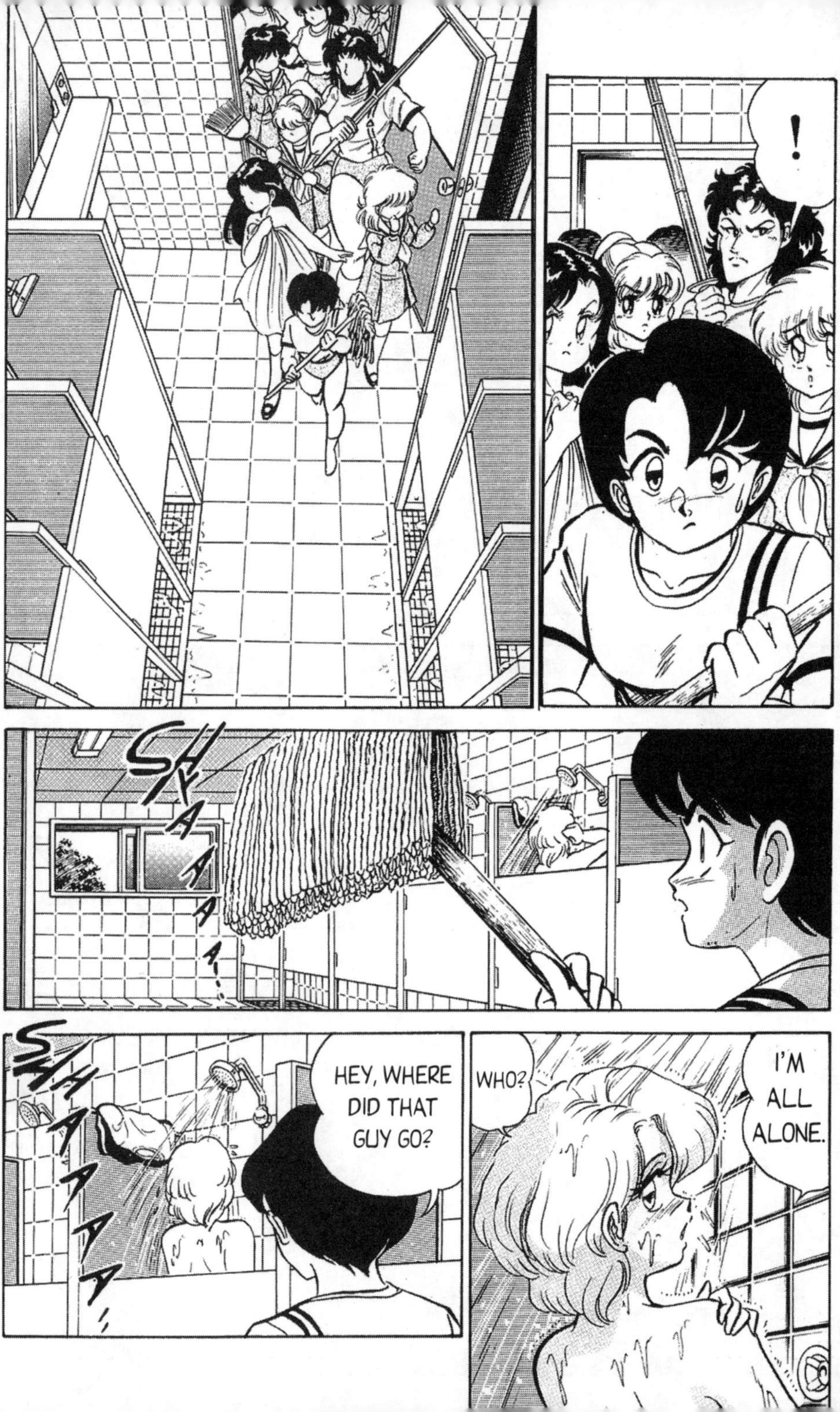
!
SHAAAAA...
SHAAAAAA
HEY, WHERE DID THAT GUY GO?
WHO?
I'M ALL ALONE.

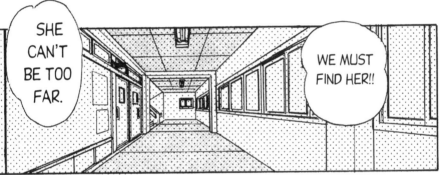

SHE CAN'T BE TOO FAR.

WE MUST FIND HER!!

WHAT ABOUT SHIMERU? WE HAVEN'T SEEN HIM EITHER.

OH YES, OUR COMRADE SHIMERU...

WEEEP WEE P!!

WE SHALL NEVER FORGET HIS SACRIFICE!

HUH?!

KYAAA!

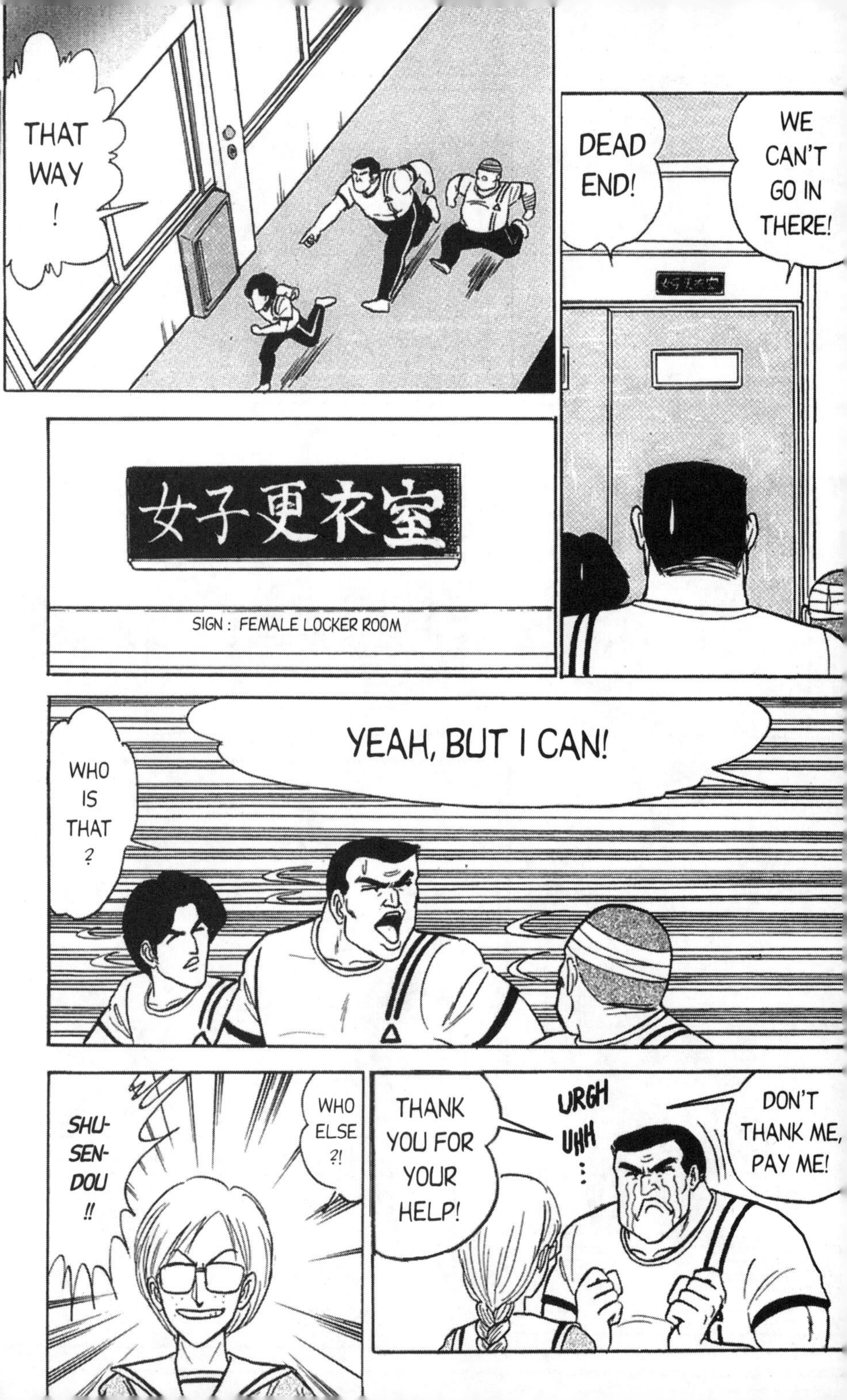
THAT WAY!
DEAD END!
WE CAN'T GO IN THERE!
女子更衣室
SIGN : FEMALE LOCKER ROOM
YEAH, BUT I CAN!
WHO IS THAT?
SHU-SEN-DOU!!
WHO ELSE?!
THANK YOU FOR YOUR HELP!
URGH UHH...
DON'T THANK ME, PAY ME!

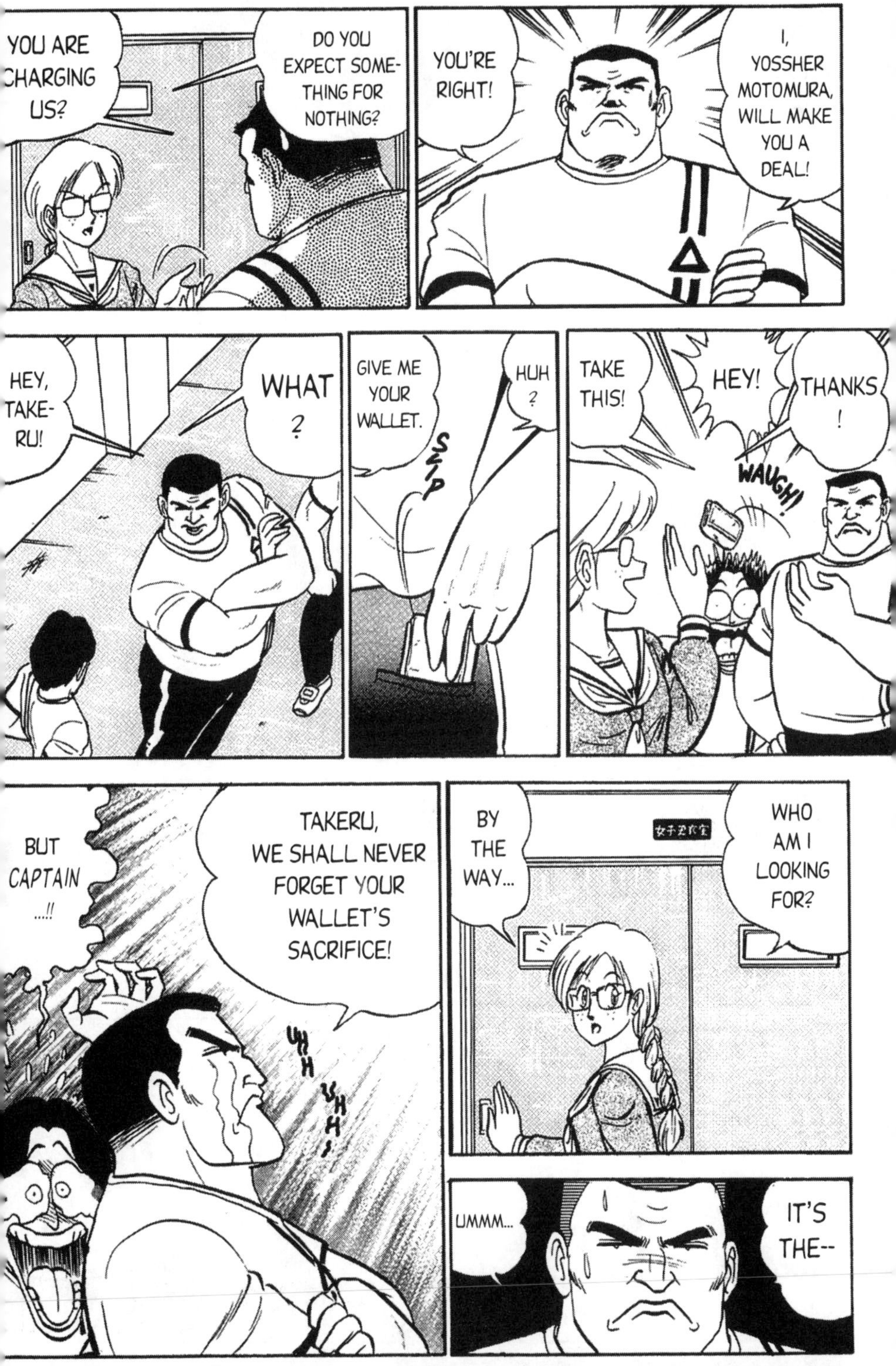
YOU ARE CHARGING US?
DO YOU EXPECT SOME-THING FOR NOTHING?
YOU'RE RIGHT!
I, YOSSHER MOTOMURA, WILL MAKE YOU A DEAL!
HEY, TAKE-RU!
WHAT?
GIVE ME YOUR WALLET.
SLIP
HUH?
TAKE THIS!
HEY!
THANKS!
WAUGH!
BUT CAPTAIN ...!!
TAKERU, WE SHALL NEVER FORGET YOUR WALLET'S SACRIFICE!
UHH UHH
BY THE WAY...
WHO AM I LOOKING FOR?
UMMM...
IT'S THE--

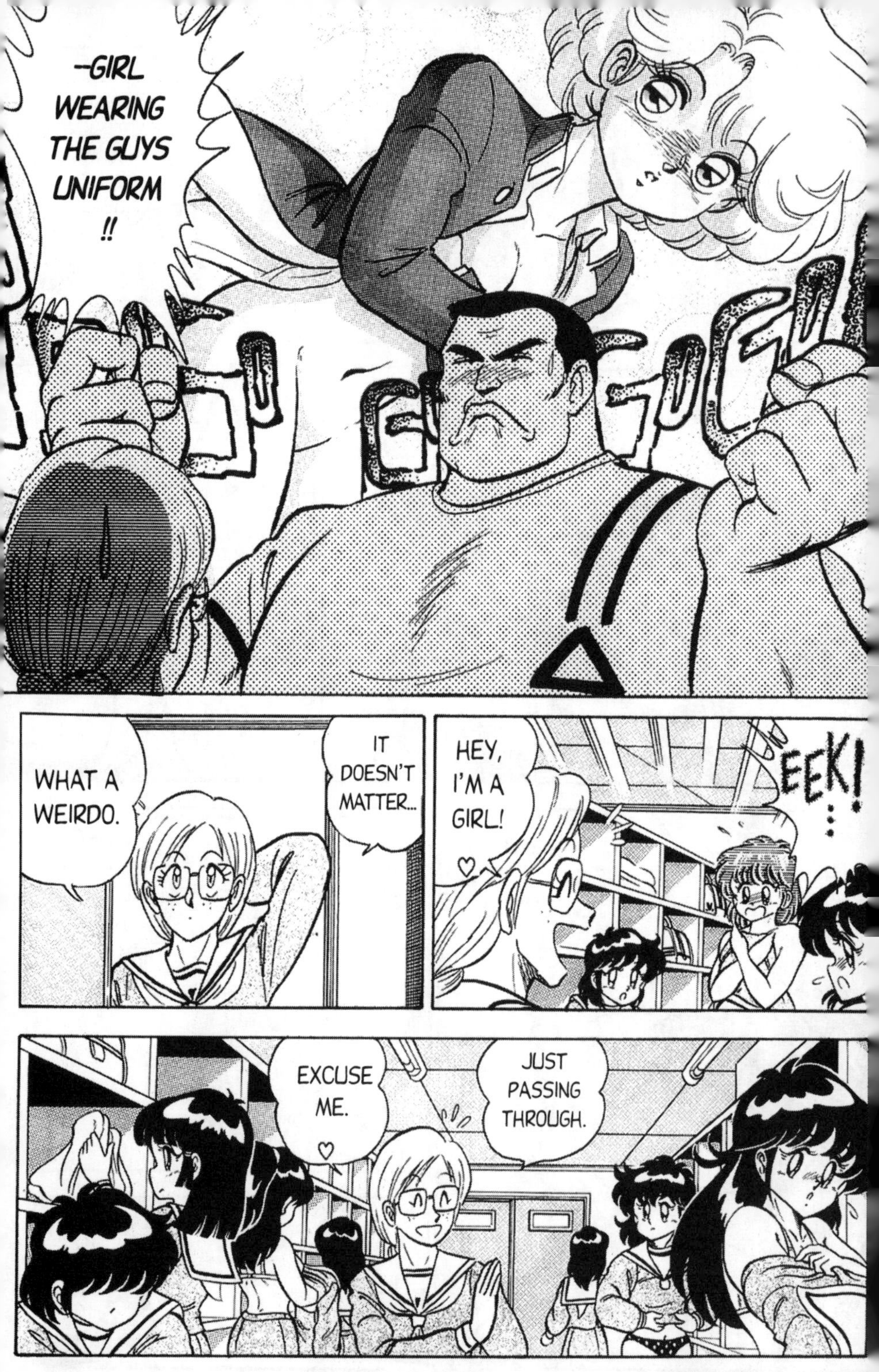
—GIRL WEARING THE GUYS UNIFORM !!
WHAT A WEIRDO.
IT DOESN'T MATTER...
HEY, I'M A GIRL! ♡
EEK!
EXCUSE ME. ♡
JUST PASSING THROUGH.

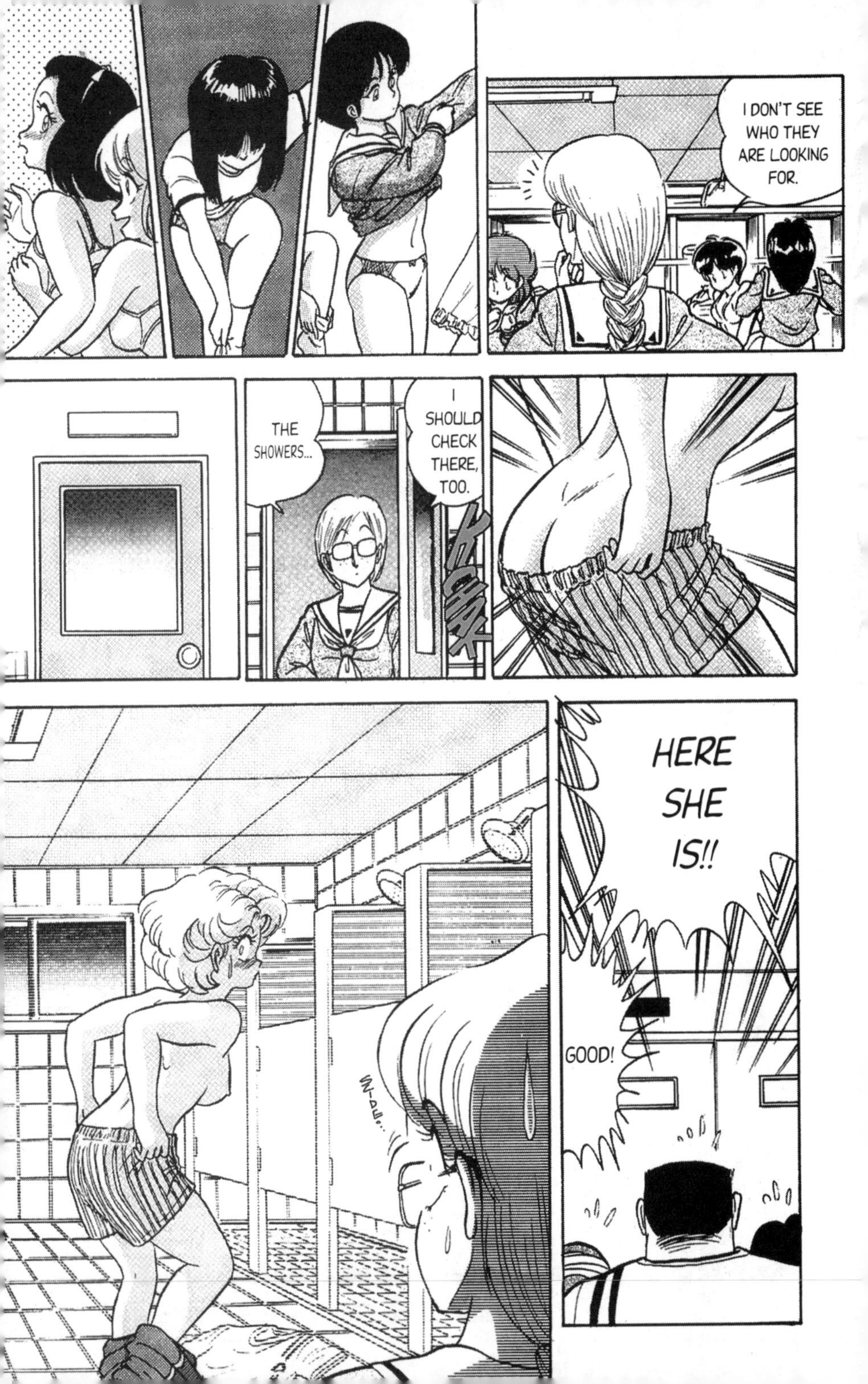

I DON'T SEE WHO THEY ARE LOOKING FOR.
THE SHOWERS...
I SHOULD CHECK THERE, TOO.
CLACK
HERE SHE IS!!
GOOD!
W-well...

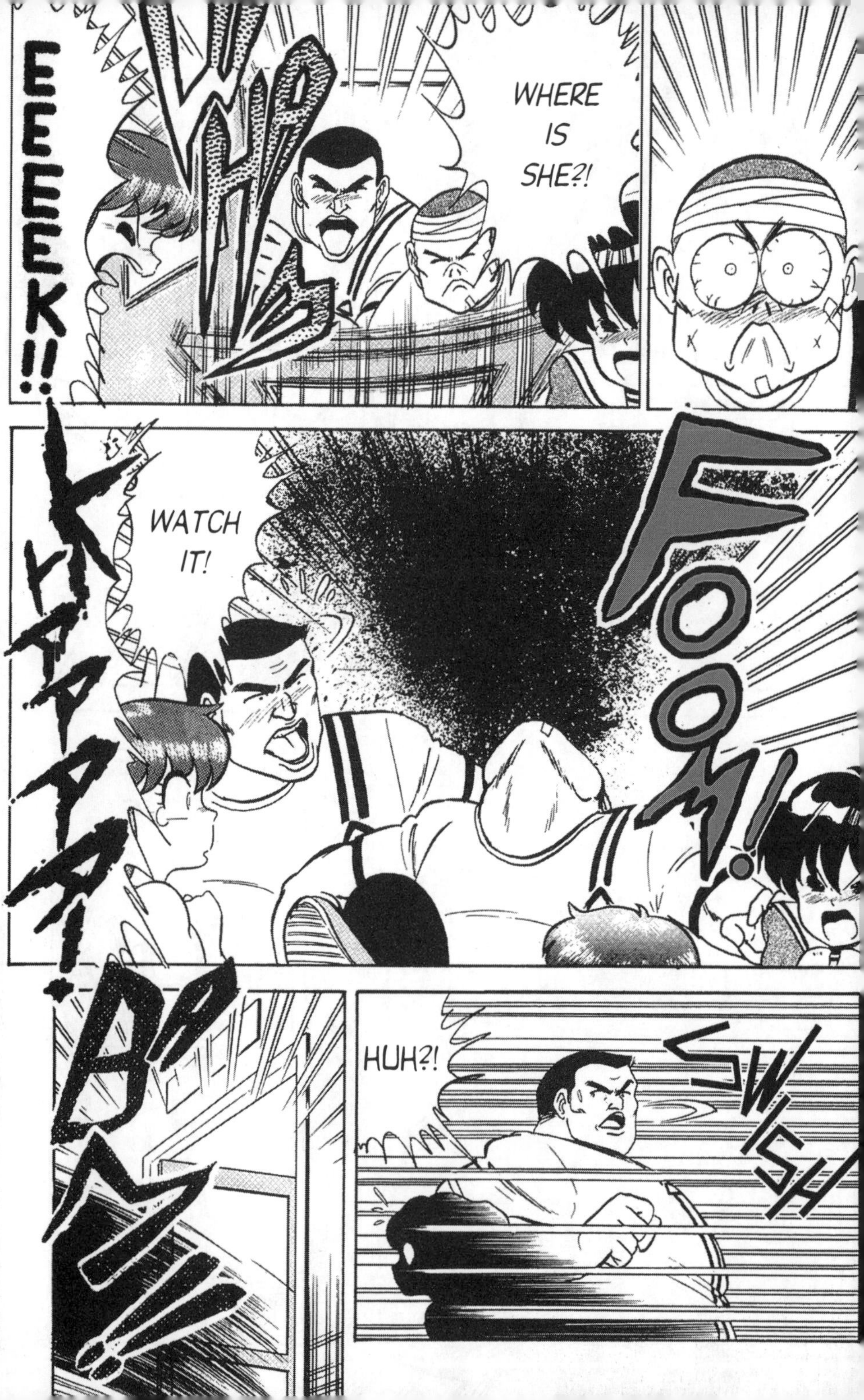
WHERE IS SHE?!
WHAP
EEEEEK!!
FOOM!
WATCH IT!
KYAAAA!!
SWISH
HUH?!
BAM!!

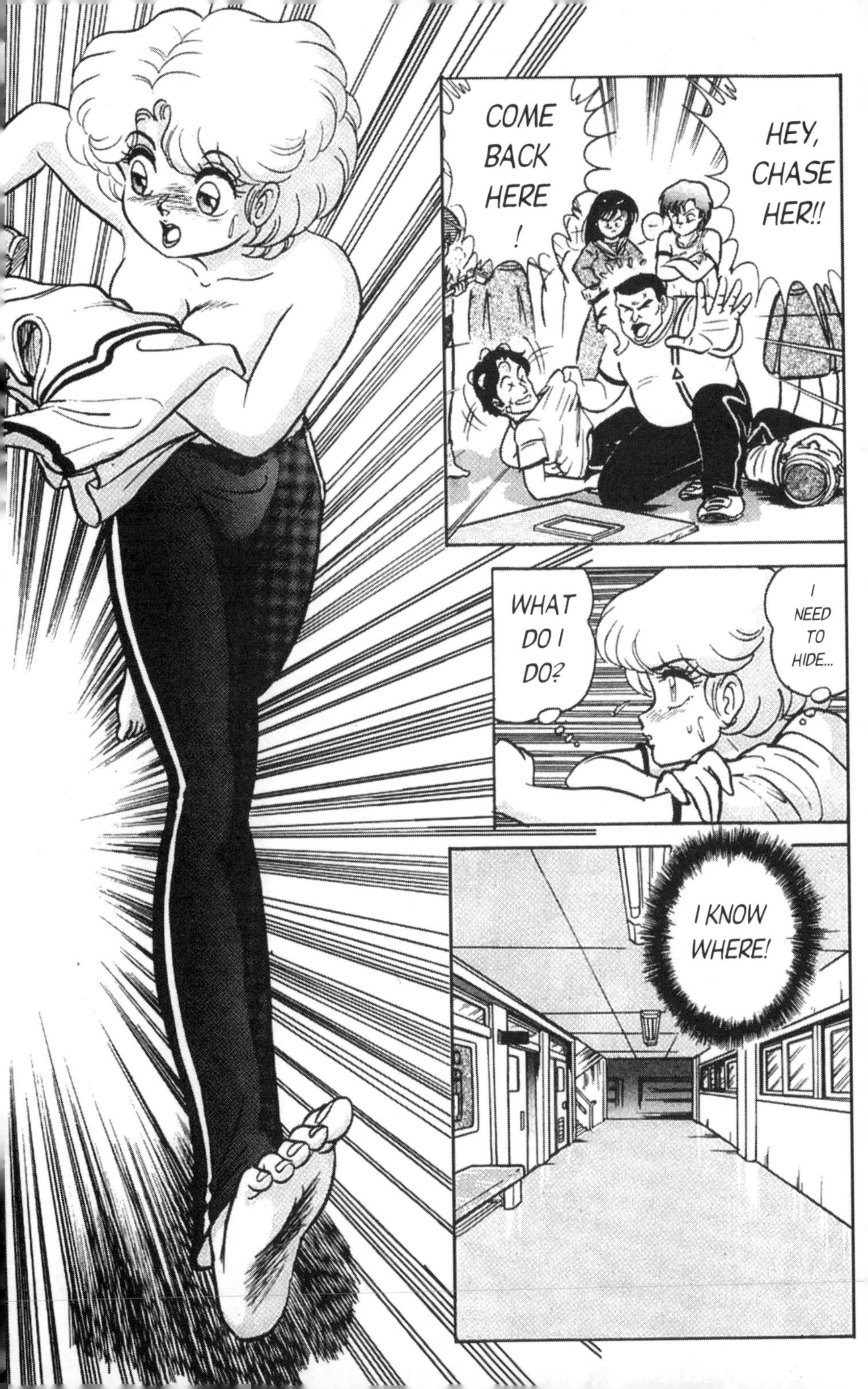
HEY, CHASE HER!!
COME BACK HERE!
I NEED TO HIDE...
WHAT DO I DO?
I KNOW WHERE!

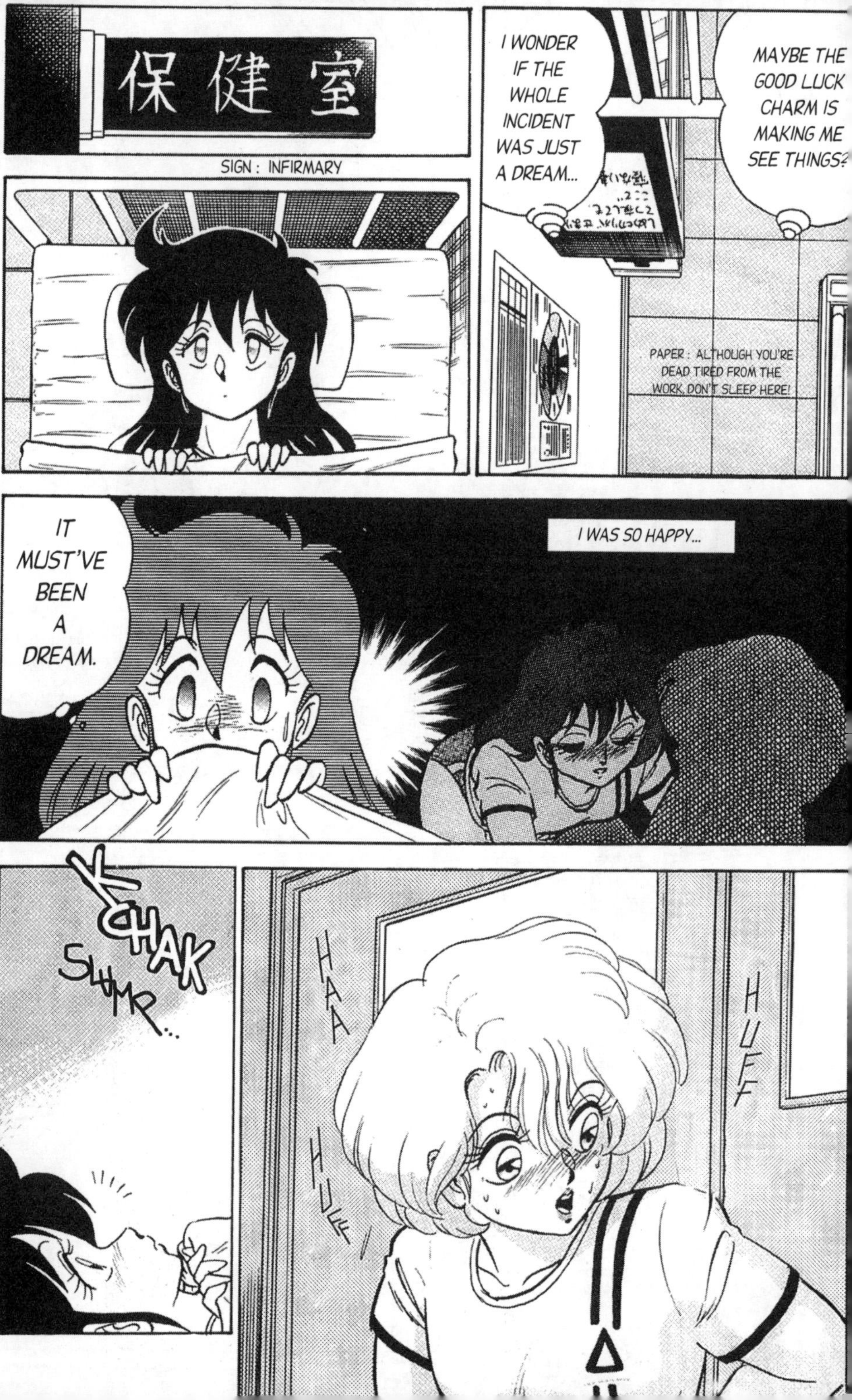
保健室
SIGN : INFIRMARY
I WONDER IF THE WHOLE INCIDENT WAS JUST A DREAM...
MAYBE THE GOOD LUCK CHARM IS MAKING ME SEE THINGS?
PAPER : ALTHOUGH YOU'RE DEAD TIRED FROM THE WORK, DON'T SLEEP HERE!
IT MUST'VE BEEN A DREAM.
I WAS SO HAPPY...
KCHAK
SLUMP...
HAA
HUFF
HUFF

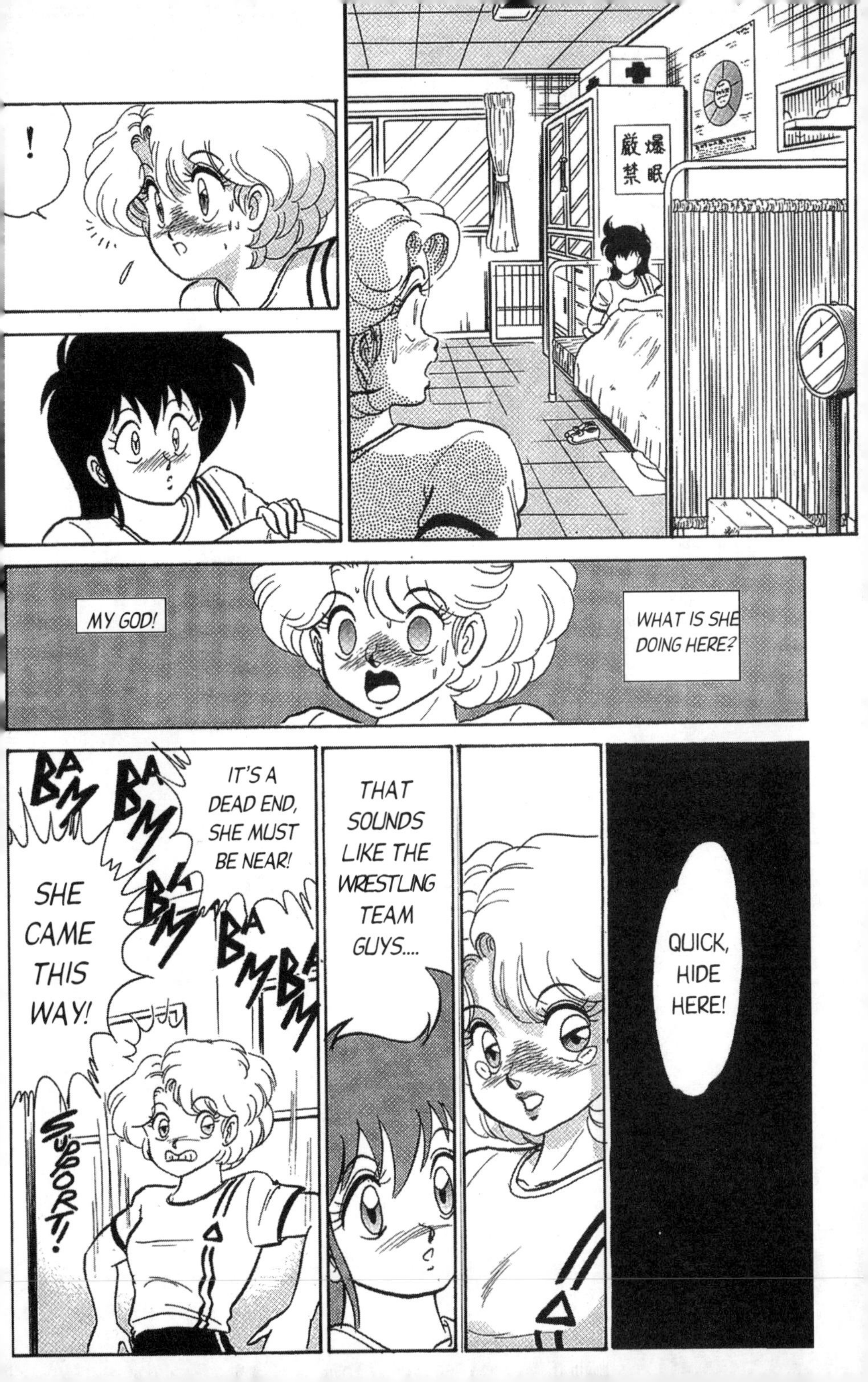
!
爆眠
厳禁
MY GOD!
WHAT IS SHE DOING HERE?
BABM
BABM
BABM
BABMBABM
SHE CAME THIS WAY!
IT'S A DEAD END, SHE MUST BE NEAR!
SUPPORT!!
THAT SOUNDS LIKE THE WRESTLING TEAM GUYS....
QUICK, HIDE HERE!

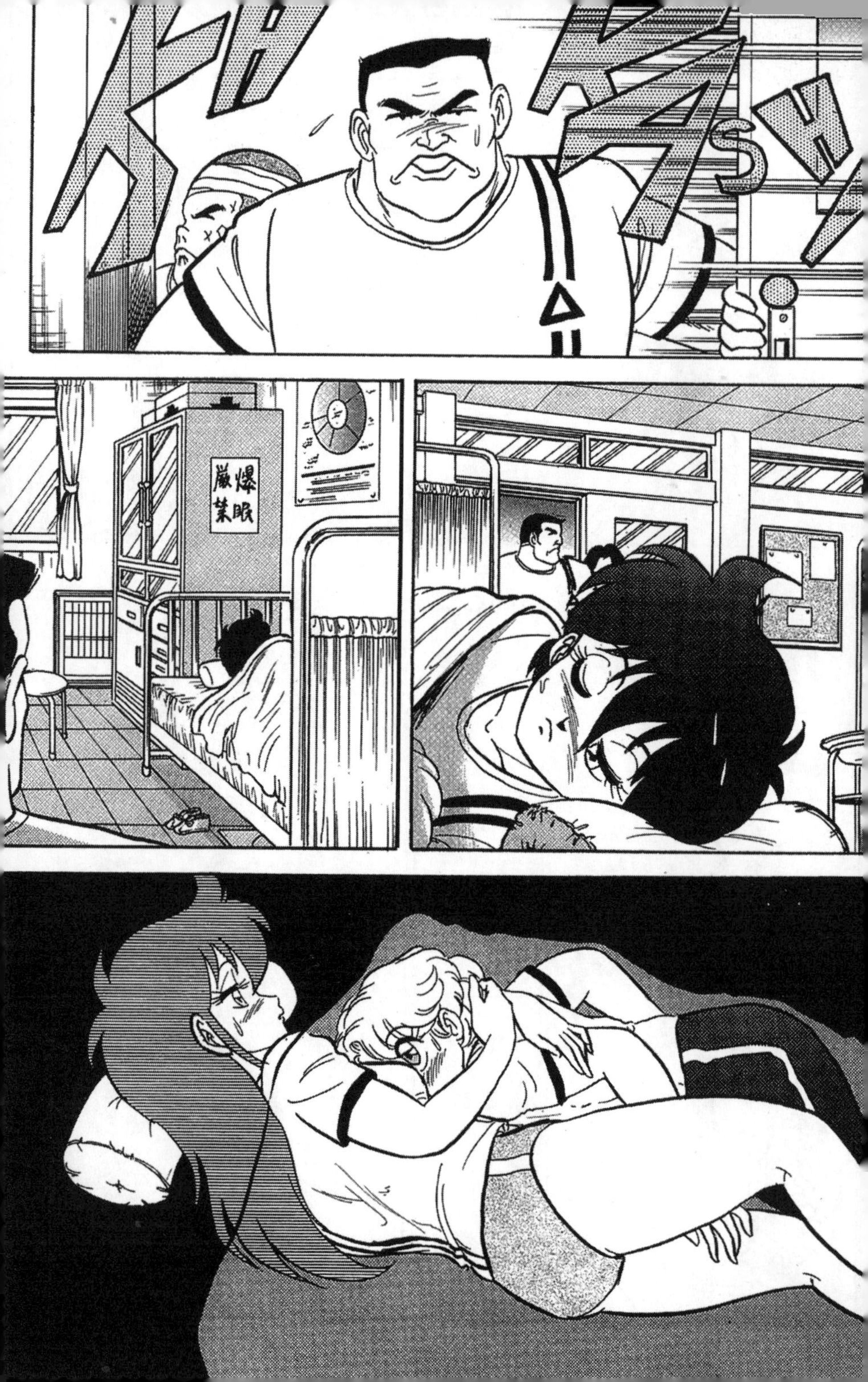
爆眠厳禁

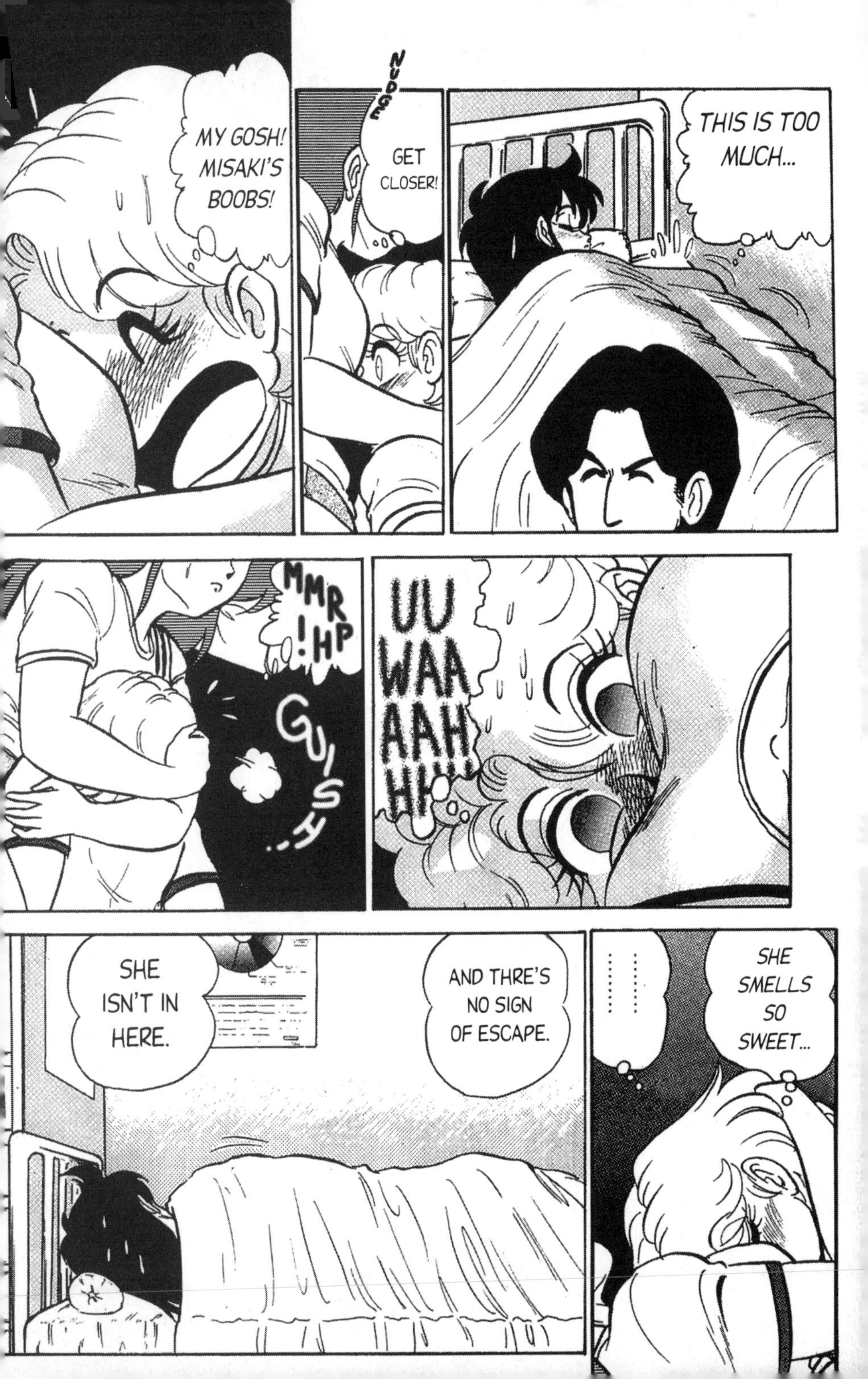
MY GOSH! MISAKI'S BOOBS!
NUDGE
GET CLOSER!
THIS IS TOO MUCH...
MMRHP!!
GUISH..
UUWAAAAHH!!
SHE ISN'T IN HERE.
AND THRE'S NO SIGN OF ESCAPE.
......
SHE SMELLS SO SWEET...

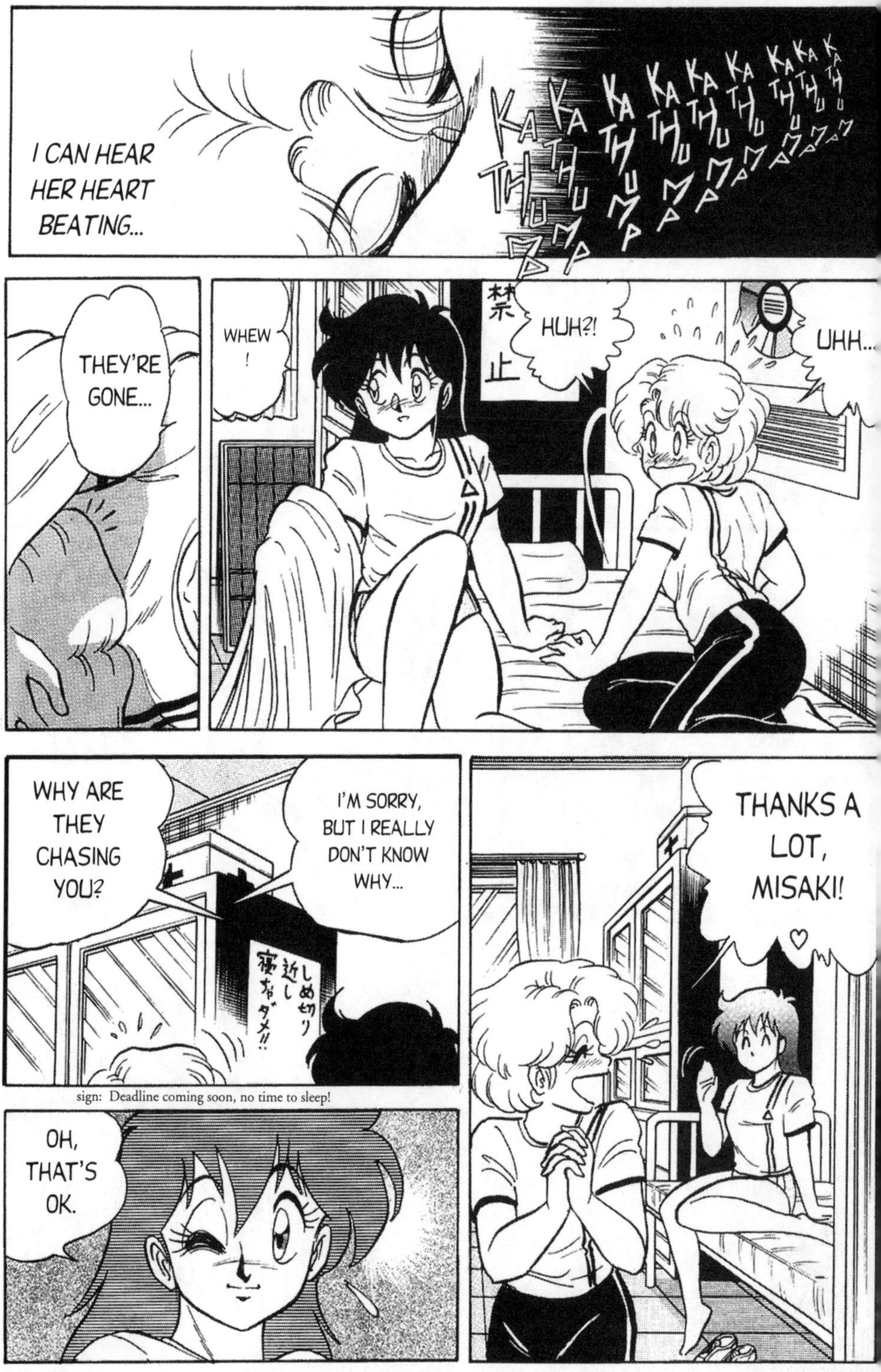
I CAN HEAR HER HEART BEATING...
KA THUMP KA THUMP KA THUMP KA THUMP KA THUMP KA THUMP KA THUMP KA THUMP
THEY'RE GONE...
WHEW!
HUH?!
UHH...
WHY ARE THEY CHASING YOU?
I'M SORRY, BUT I REALLY DON'T KNOW WHY...
しめ切り近し寝ちゃダメ!!
THANKS A LOT, MISAKI! ♡
OH, THAT'S OK.

sign: Deadline coming soon, no time to sleep!

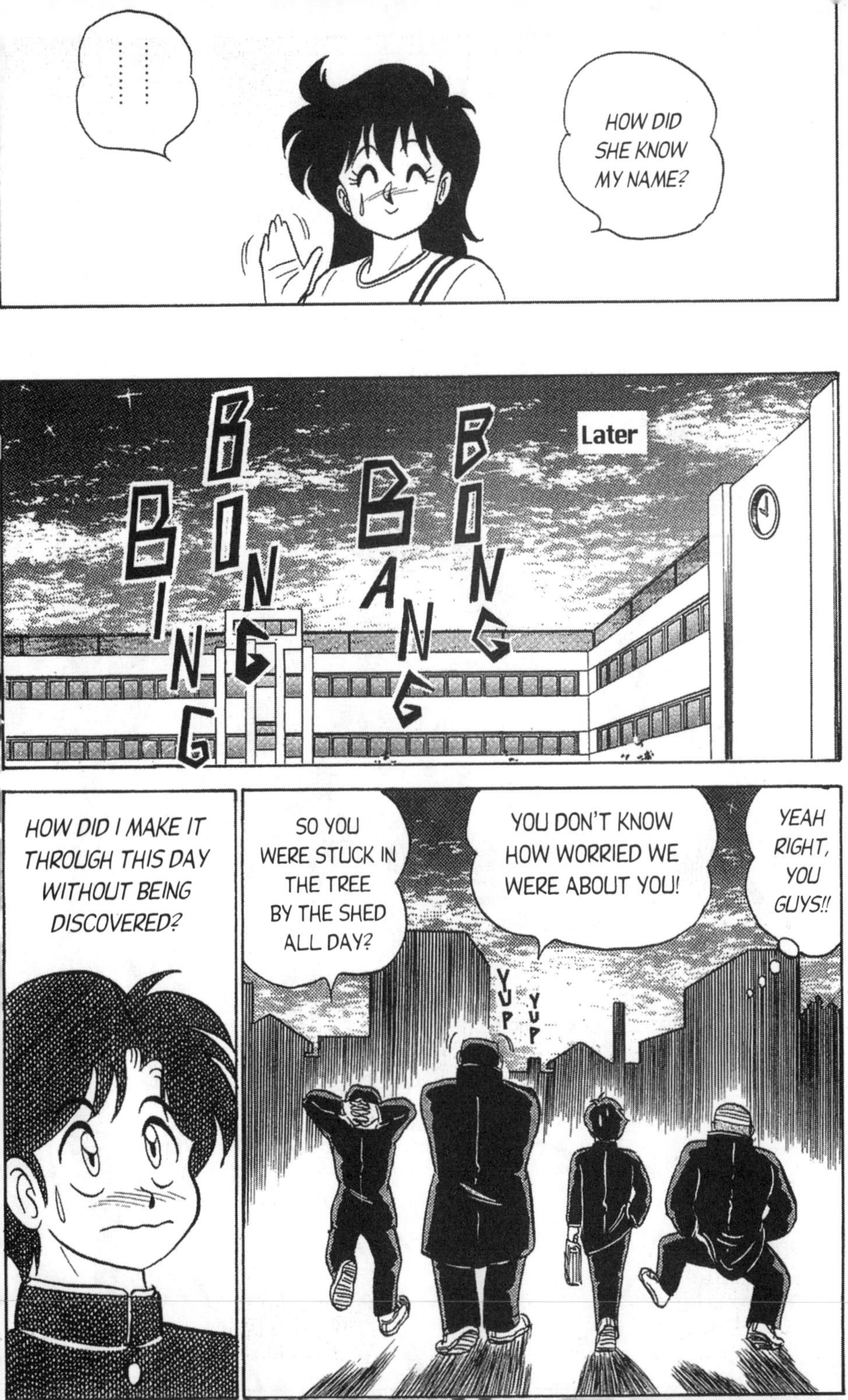

......
HOW DID SHE KNOW MY NAME?
BING BING BANG BING
Later
HOW DID I MAKE IT THROUGH THIS DAY WITHOUT BEING DISCOVERED?
SO YOU WERE STUCK IN THE TREE BY THE SHED ALL DAY?
YUP YUP
YOU DON'T KNOW HOW WORRIED WE WERE ABOUT YOU!
YEAH RIGHT, YOU GUYS!!

Introducing my staff members who helped produce ***Futaba-kun Change!***

Ami Kyomoto

He used to be an assistant to Mr. Osamu Akimoto* just like I used to be. He referes to himself as the "shy guy who loves wrestling, Hissatsu series and fitness".

*The longest running Manga ever "Kochira Katsushika-ku Kameari Koenmae Hashutsujo"'s creator. He is also matchmaker of Ippongi Bang wedding!

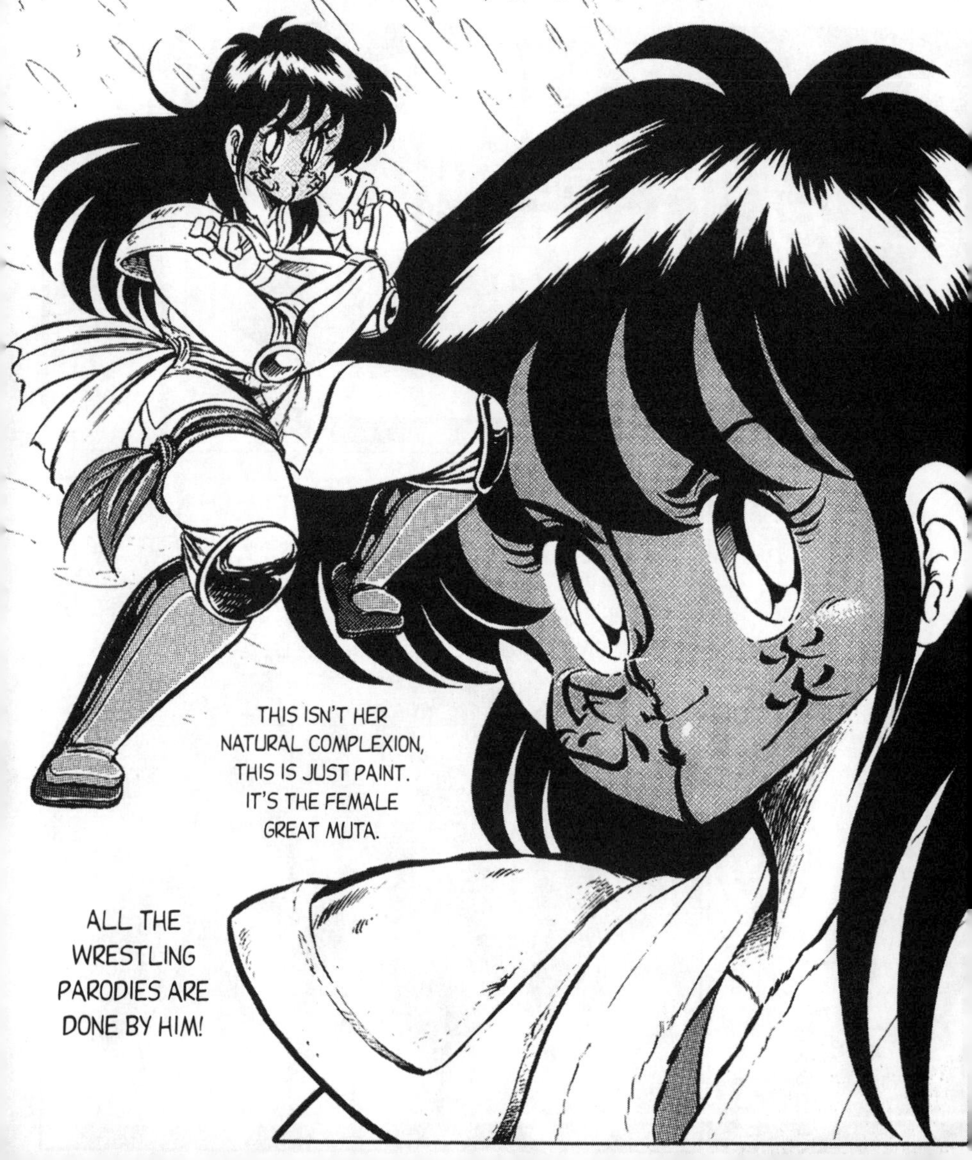
THIS ISN'T HER NATURAL COMPLEXION, THIS IS JUST PAINT. IT'S THE FEMALE GREAT MUTA.
ALL THE WRESTLING PARODIES ARE DONE BY HIM!

Futaba-chan, the New Transfer Student!!

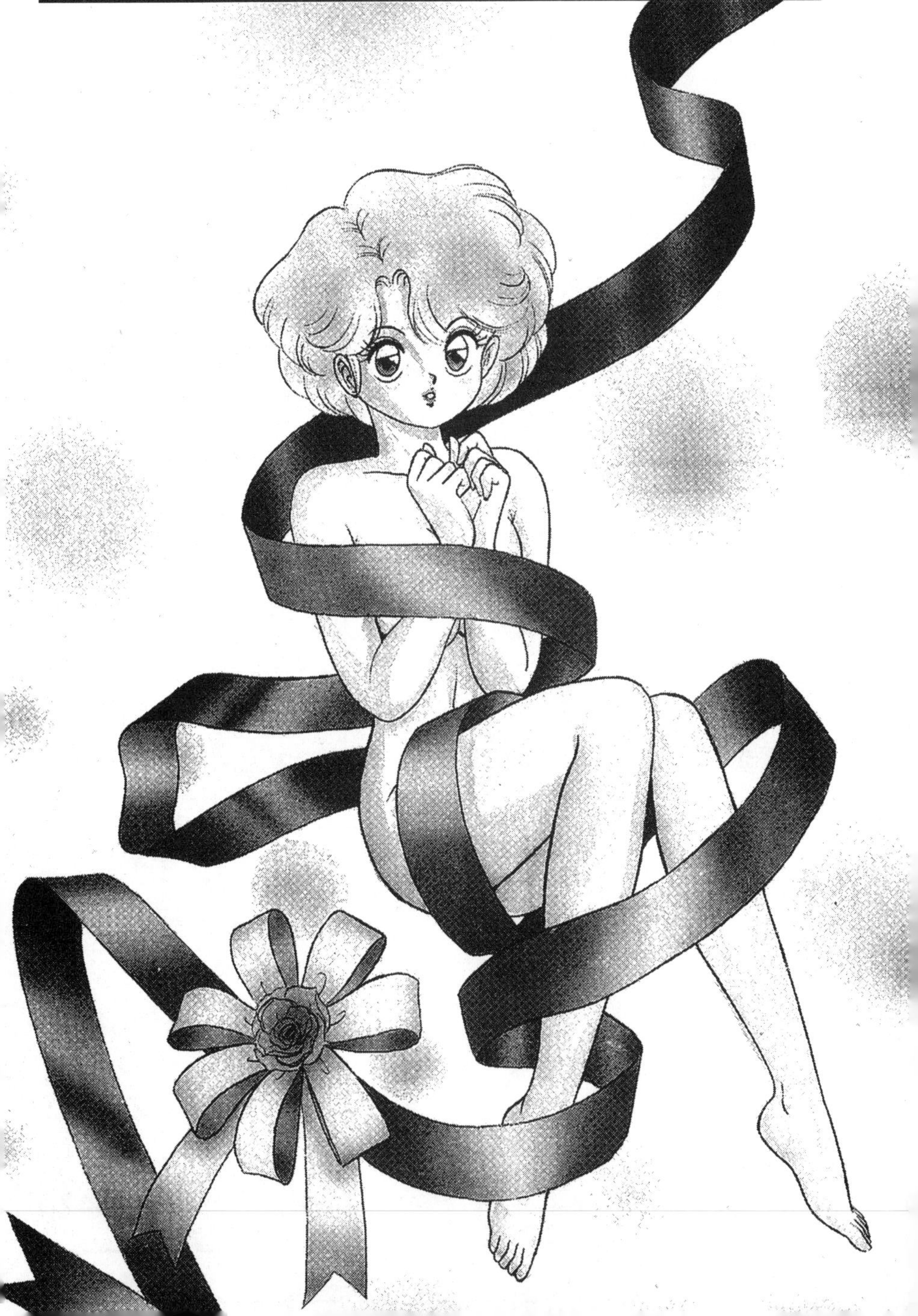

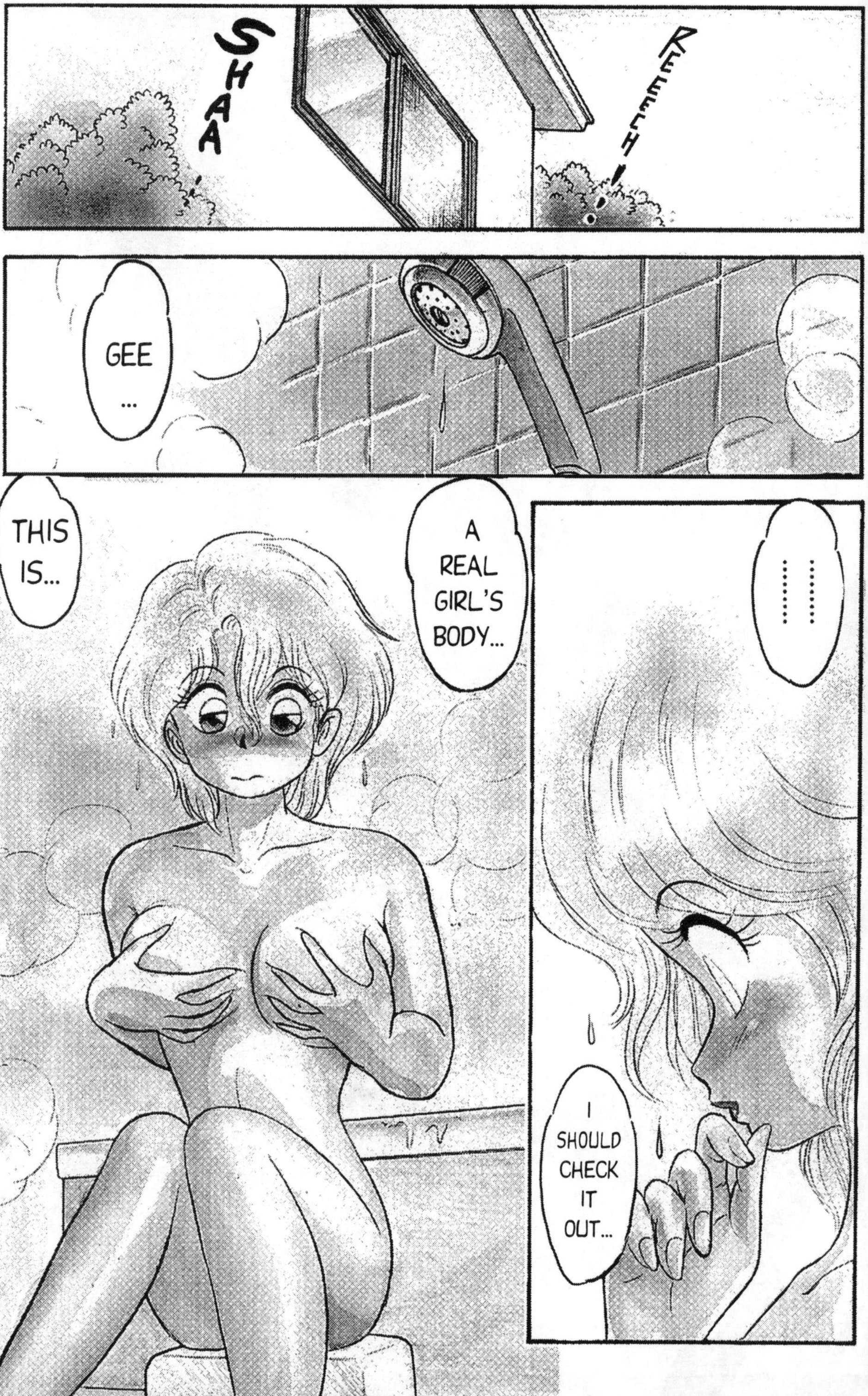
SHAA
REEECH
GEE ...
THIS IS...
A REAL GIRL'S BODY...
......
I SHOULD CHECK IT OUT...

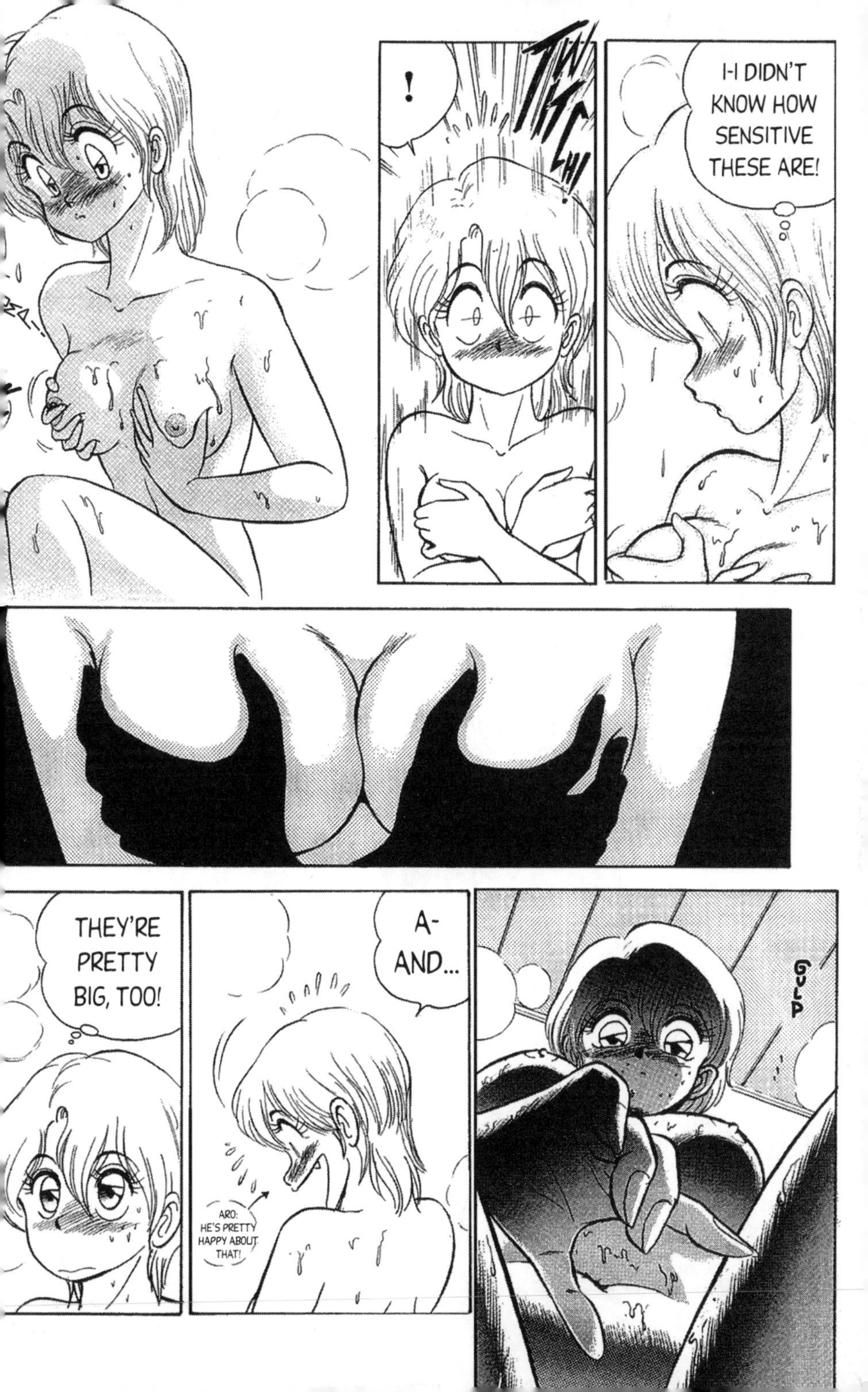
!
TWITCH!
I-I DIDN'T KNOW HOW SENSITIVE THESE ARE!
THEY'RE PRETTY BIG, TOO!
A- AND...
ARO: HE'S PRETTY HAPPY ABOUT THAT!
GULP

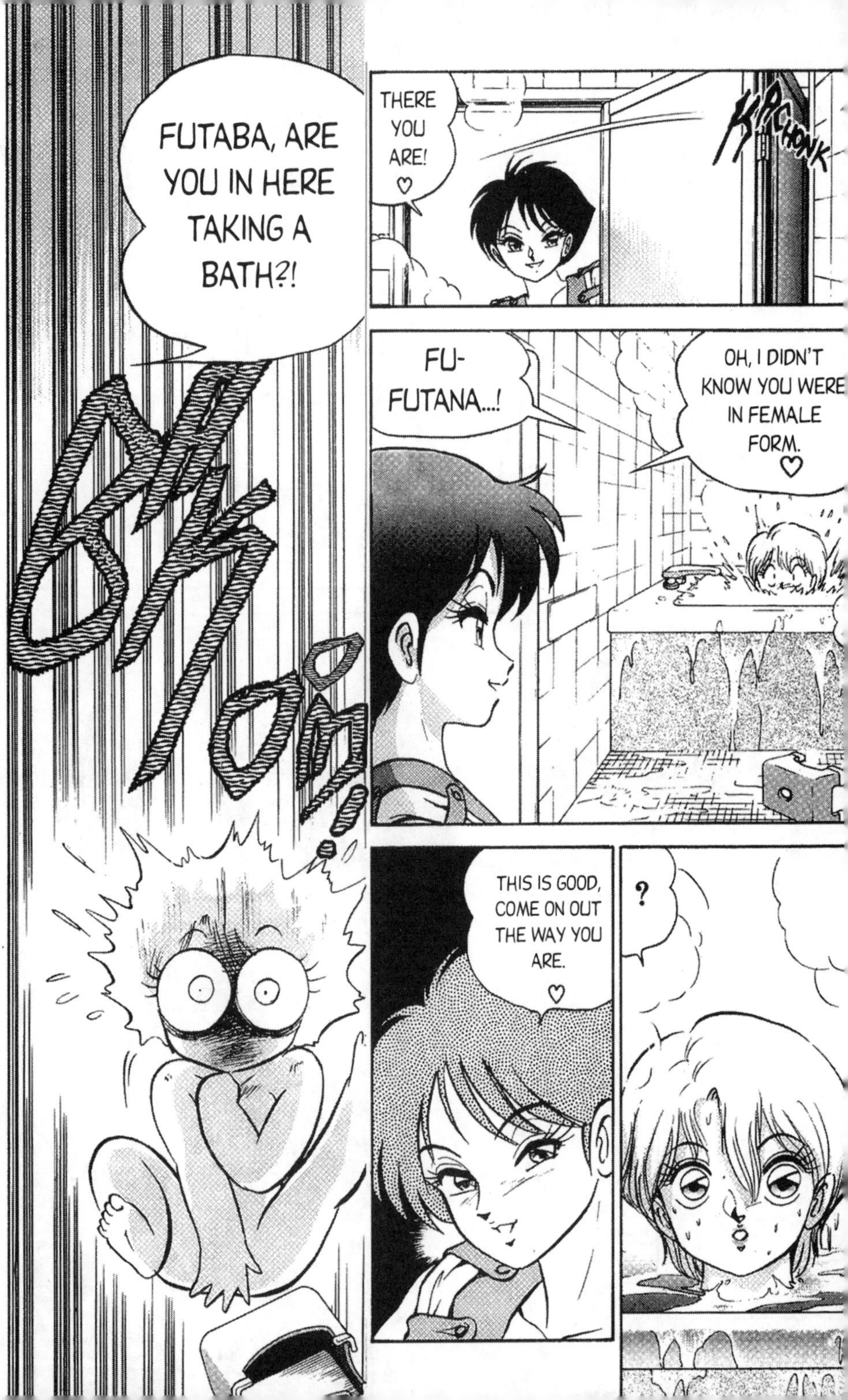

FUTABA, ARE YOU IN HERE TAKING A BATH?!
THERE YOU ARE! ♡
KACHONK
FU- FUTANA...!
OH, I DIDN'T KNOW YOU WERE IN FEMALE FORM. ♡
THIS IS GOOD, COME ON OUT THE WAY YOU ARE. ♡
?

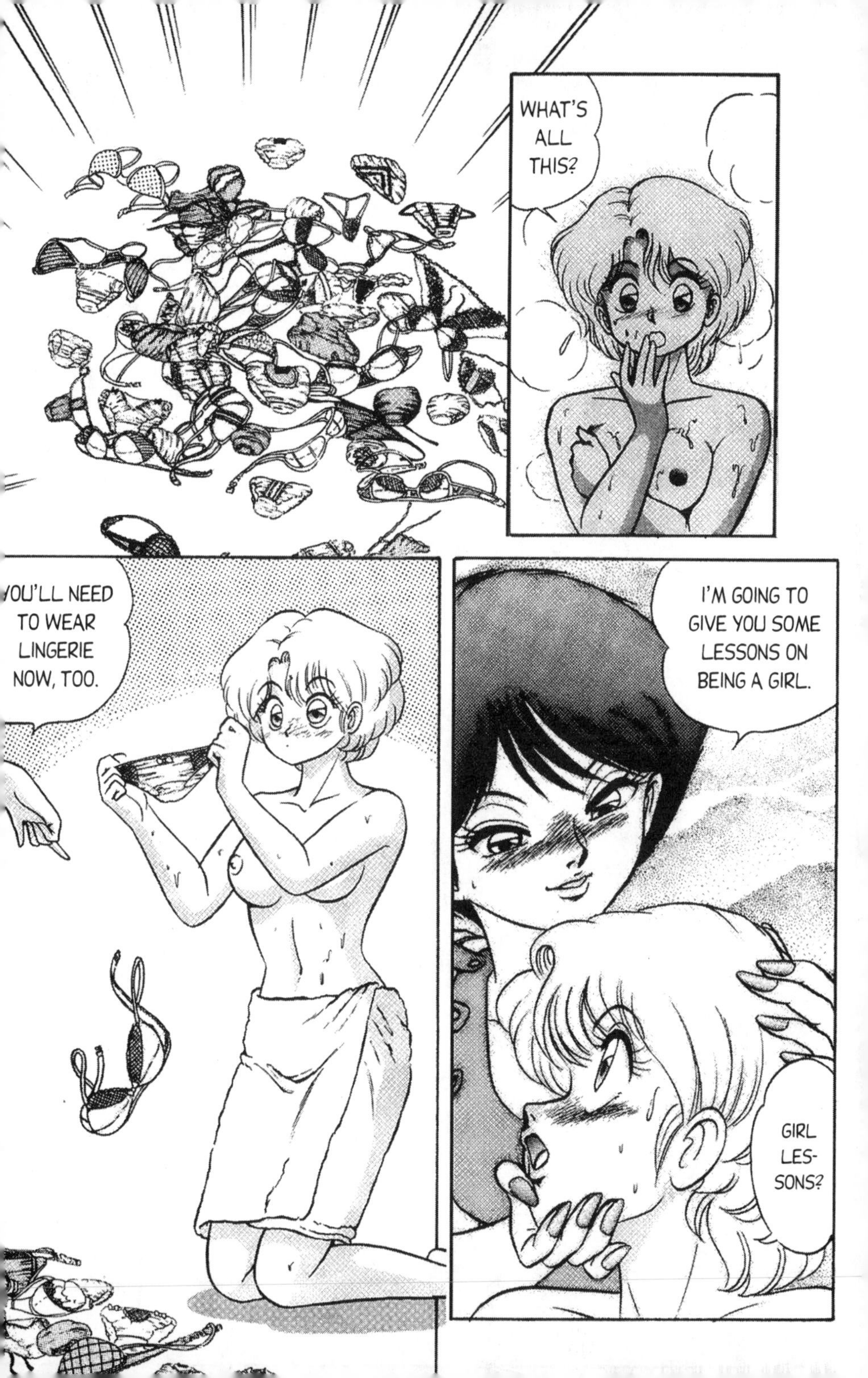
WHAT'S ALL THIS?
YOU'LL NEED TO WEAR LINGERIE NOW, TOO.
I'M GOING TO GIVE YOU SOME LESSONS ON BEING A GIRL.
GIRL LES-SONS?

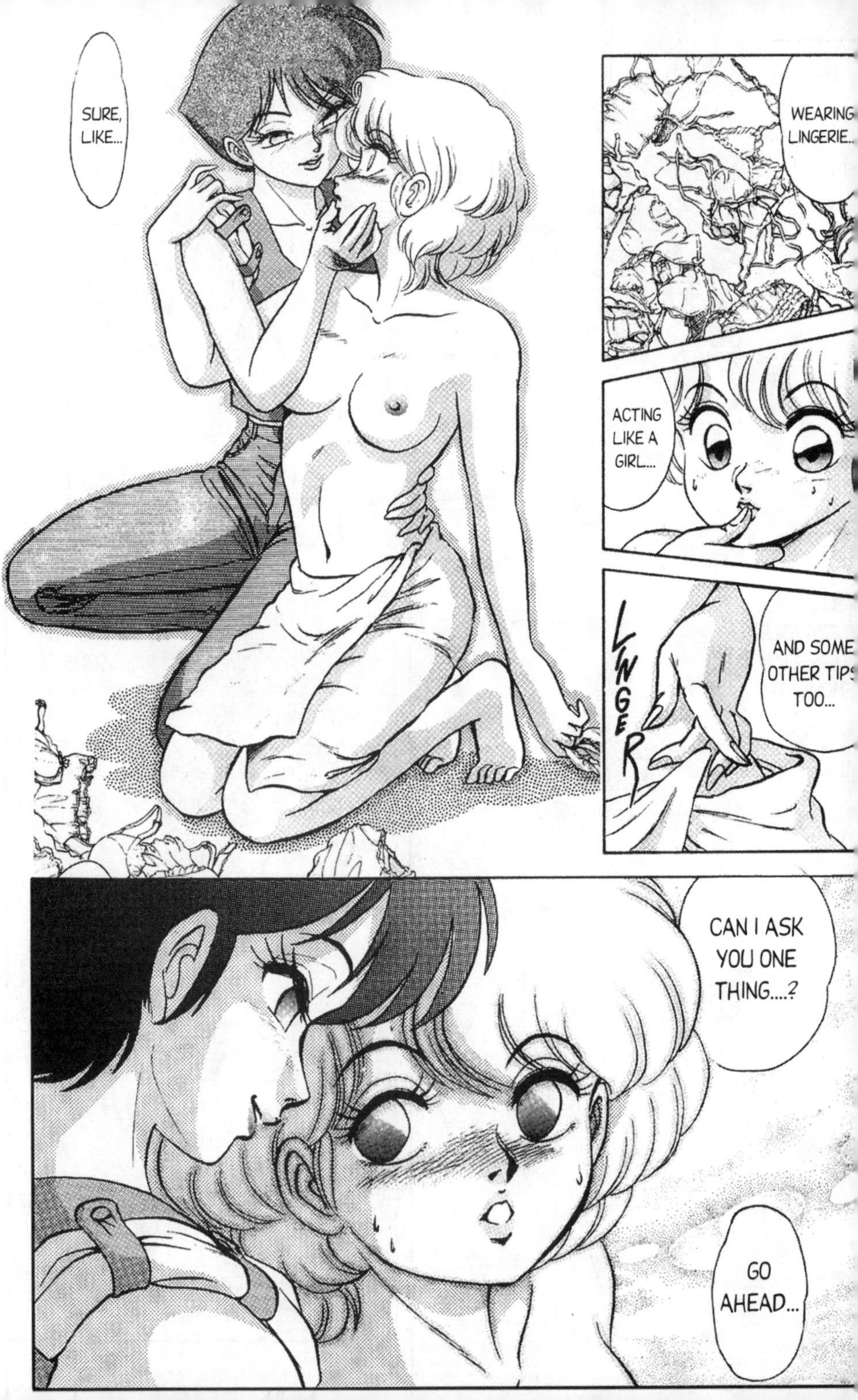
SURE, LIKE...
WEARING LINGERIE..
ACTING LIKE A GIRL...
LINGER
AND SOME OTHER TIPS TOO...
CAN I ASK YOU ONE THING....?
GO AHEAD...

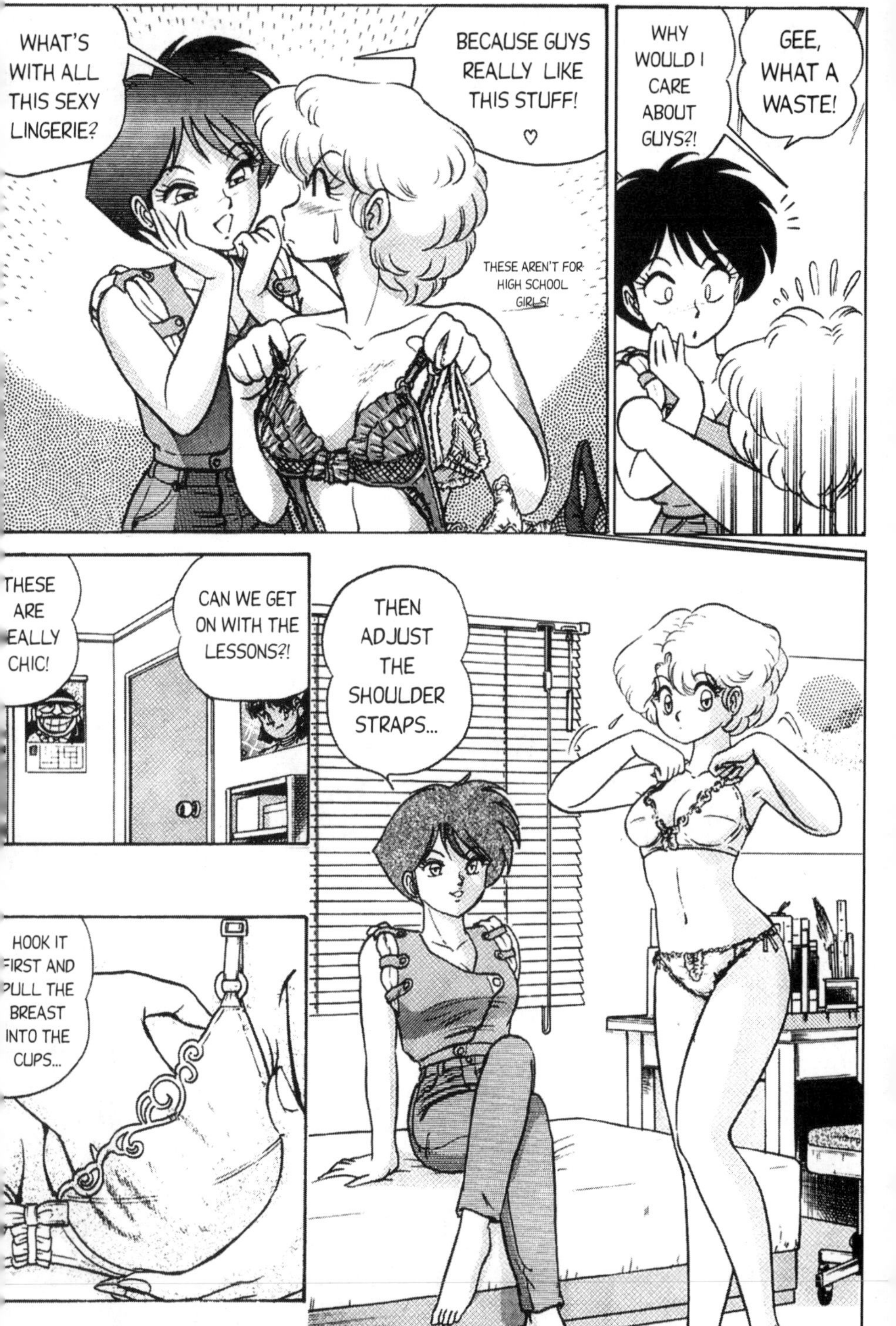
WHAT'S WITH ALL THIS SEXY LINGERIE?
BECAUSE GUYS REALLY LIKE THIS STUFF! ♡
THESE AREN'T FOR HIGH SCHOOL GIRLS!
WHY WOULD I CARE ABOUT GUYS?!
GEE, WHAT A WASTE!
THESE ARE EALLY CHIC!
CAN WE GET ON WITH THE LESSONS?!
THEN ADJUST THE SHOULDER STRAPS...
HOOK IT IRST AND ULL THE BREAST INTO THE CUPS...

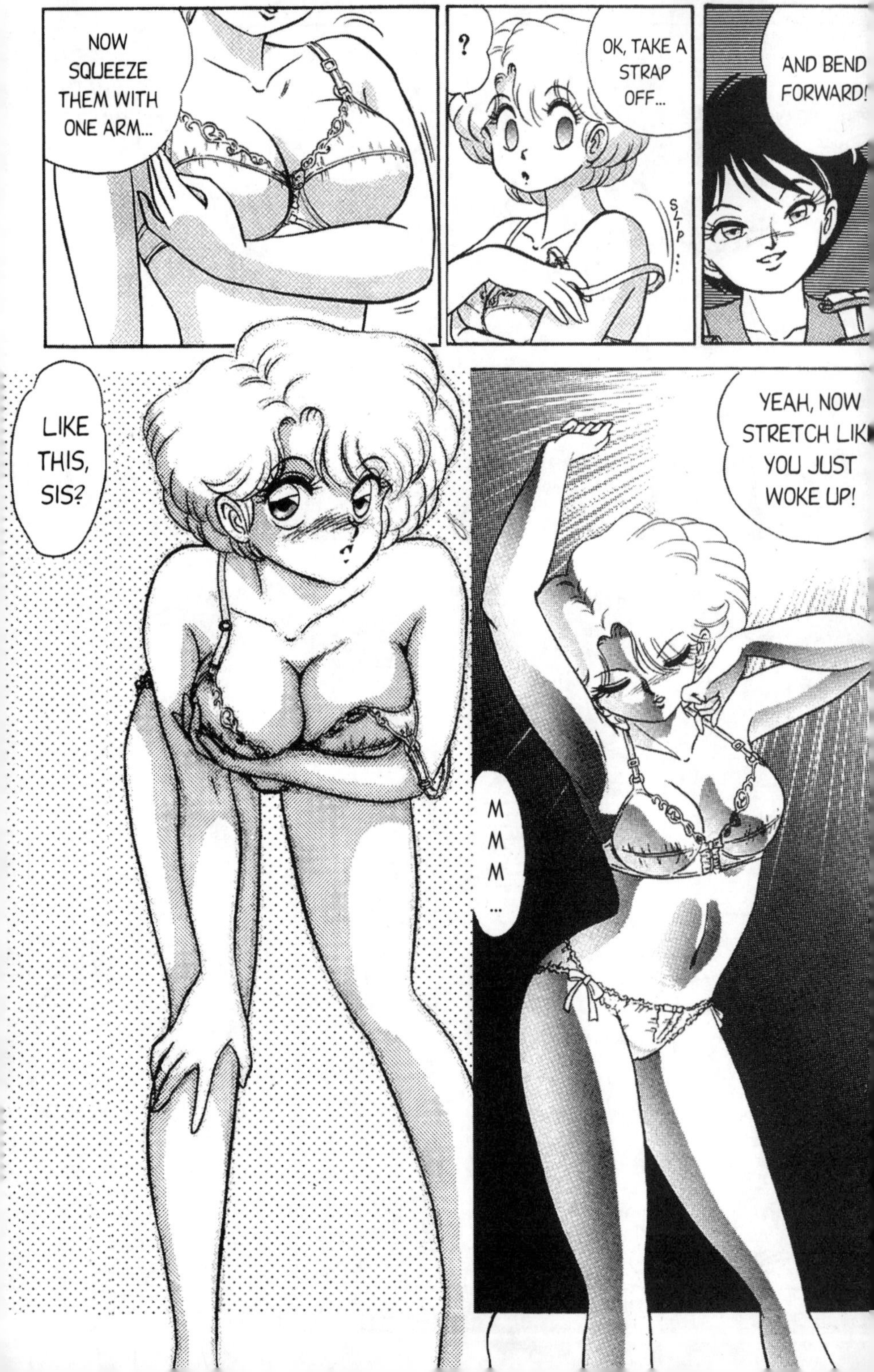
NOW SQUEEZE THEM WITH ONE ARM...
?
OK, TAKE A STRAP OFF...
SLIP...
AND BEND FORWARD!
LIKE THIS, SIS?
YEAH, NOW STRETCH LIK
YOU JUST WOKE UP!
MMM...

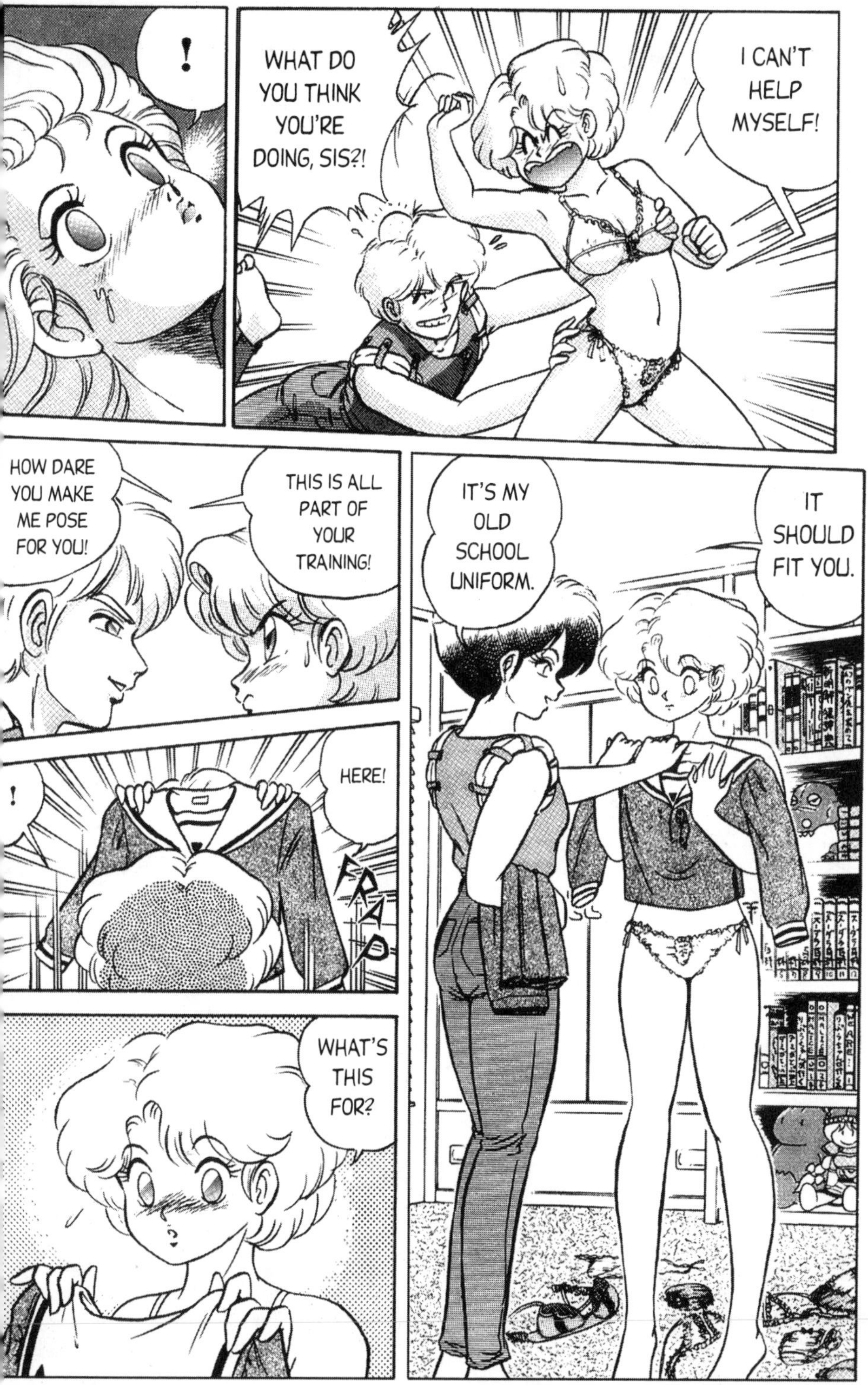
!
WHAT DO YOU THINK YOU'RE DOING, SIS?!
I CAN'T HELP MYSELF!
HOW DARE YOU MAKE ME POSE FOR YOU!
THIS IS ALL PART OF YOUR TRAINING!
!
HERE!
FRAP
WHAT'S THIS FOR?
IT'S MY OLD SCHOOL UNIFORM.
IT SHOULD FIT YOU.

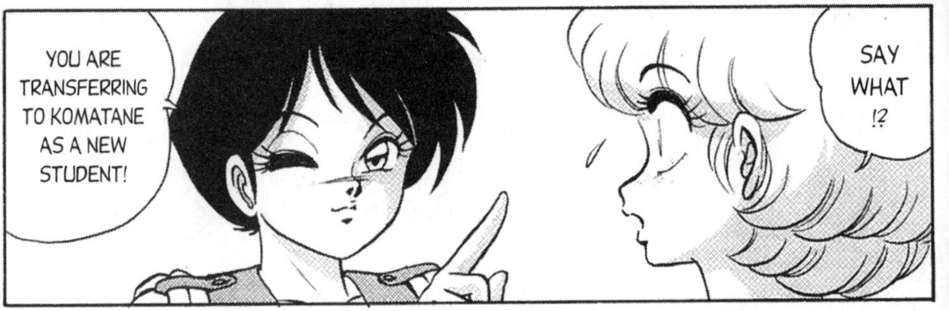
YOU ARE TRANSFERRING TO KOMATANE AS A NEW STUDENT!
SAY WHAT !?

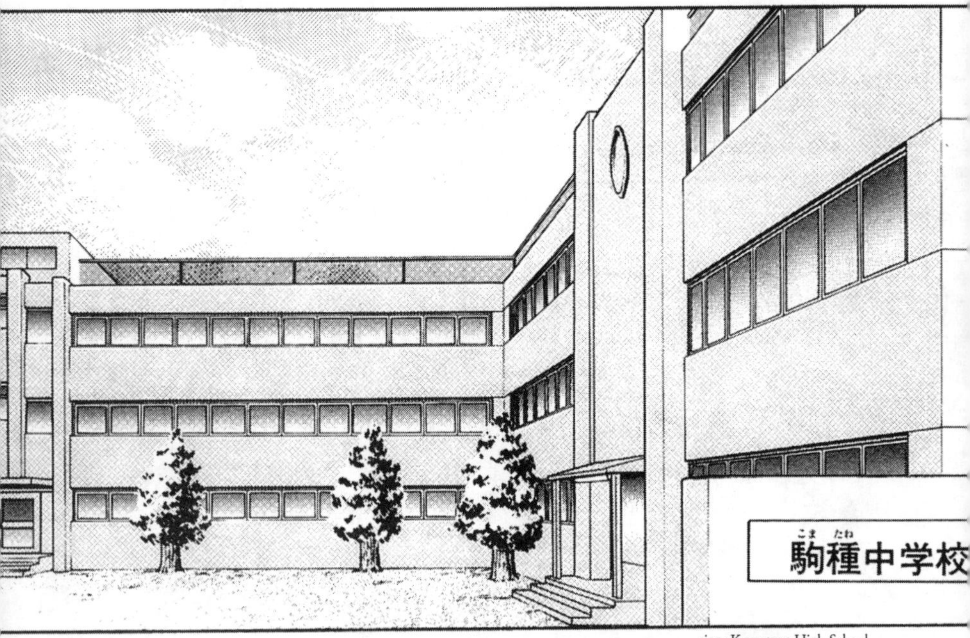
こま たね
駒種中学校

sign: Komatane High School

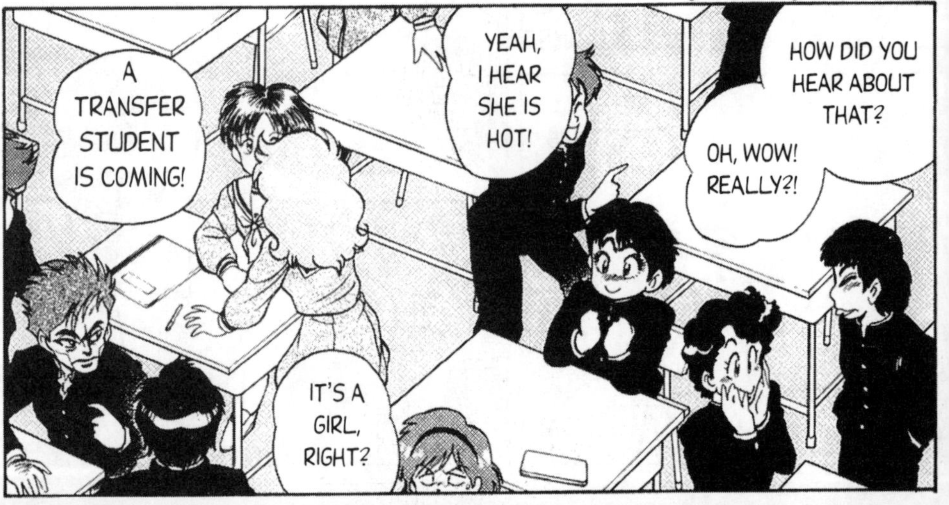
A TRANSFER STUDENT IS COMING!
YEAH, I HEAR SHE IS HOT!
HOW DID YOU HEAR ABOUT THAT?
OH, WOW! REALLY?!
IT'S A GIRL, RIGHT?

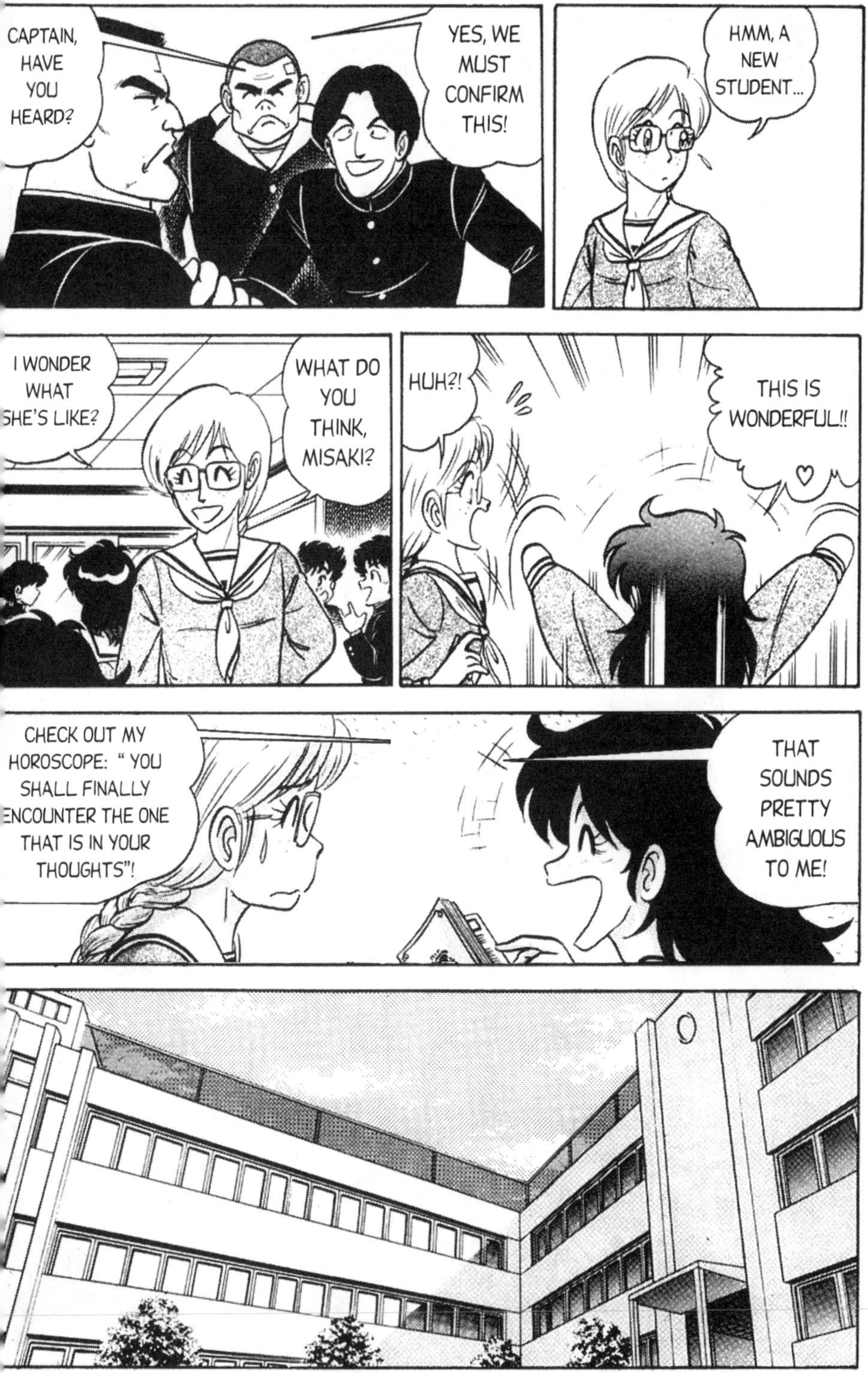
CAPTAIN, HAVE YOU HEARD?
YES, WE MUST CONFIRM THIS!
HMM, A NEW STUDENT...
I WONDER WHAT SHE'S LIKE?
WHAT DO YOU THINK, MISAKI?
HUH?!
THIS IS WONDERFUL!!
CHECK OUT MY HOROSCOPE: " YOU SHALL FINALLY ENCOUNTER THE ONE THAT IS IN YOUR THOUGHTS"!
THAT SOUNDS PRETTY AMBIGUOUS TO ME!

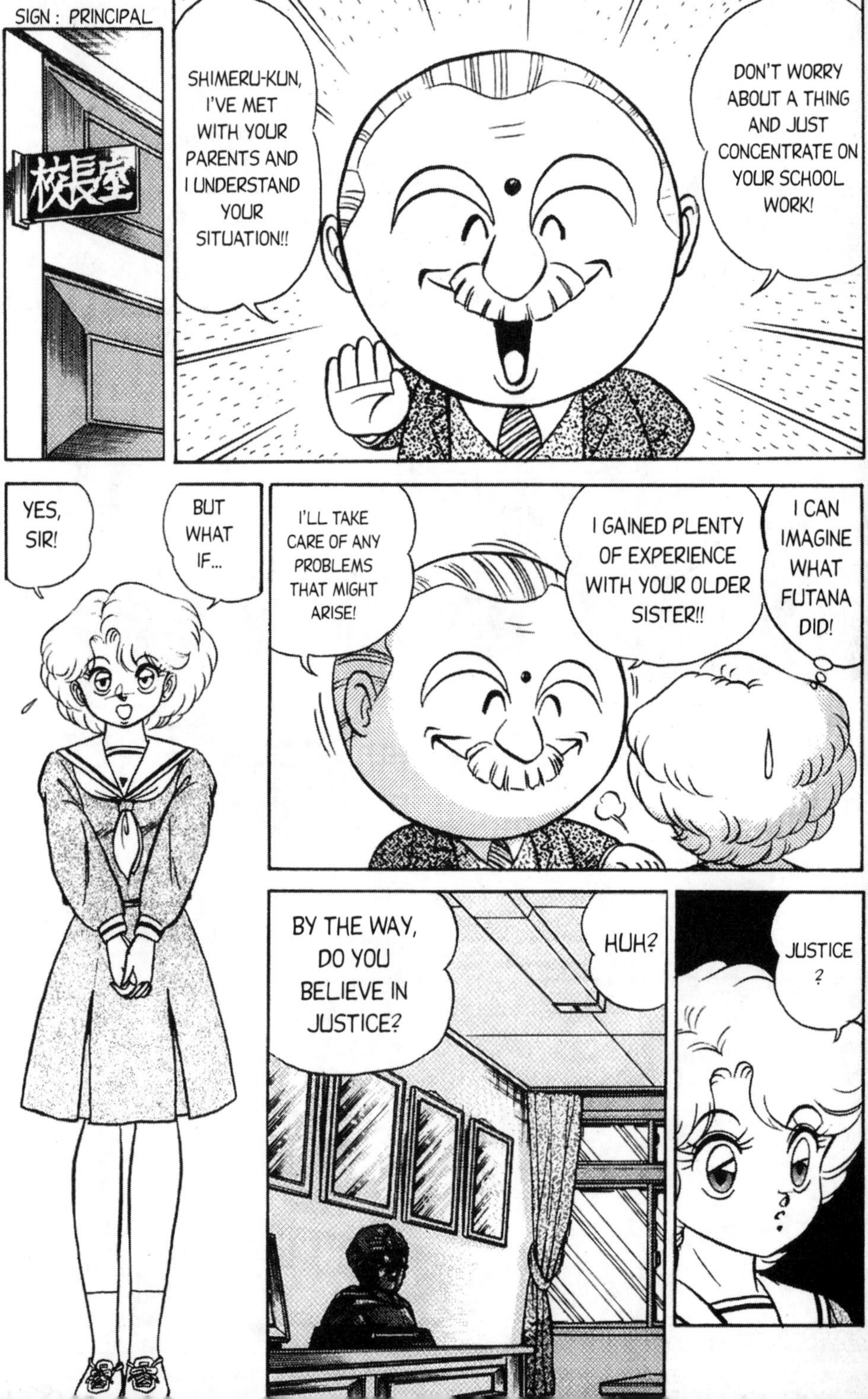
SIGN : PRINCIPAL
校長室
SHIMERU-KUN, I'VE MET WITH YOUR PARENTS AND I UNDERSTAND YOUR SITUATION!!
DON'T WORRY ABOUT A THING AND JUST CONCENTRATE ON YOUR SCHOOL WORK!
YES, SIR!
BUT WHAT IF...
I'LL TAKE CARE OF ANY PROBLEMS THAT MIGHT ARISE!
I GAINED PLENTY OF EXPERIENCE WITH YOUR OLDER SISTER!!
I CAN IMAGINE WHAT FUTANA DID!
BY THE WAY, DO YOU BELIEVE IN JUSTICE?
HUH?
JUSTICE ?

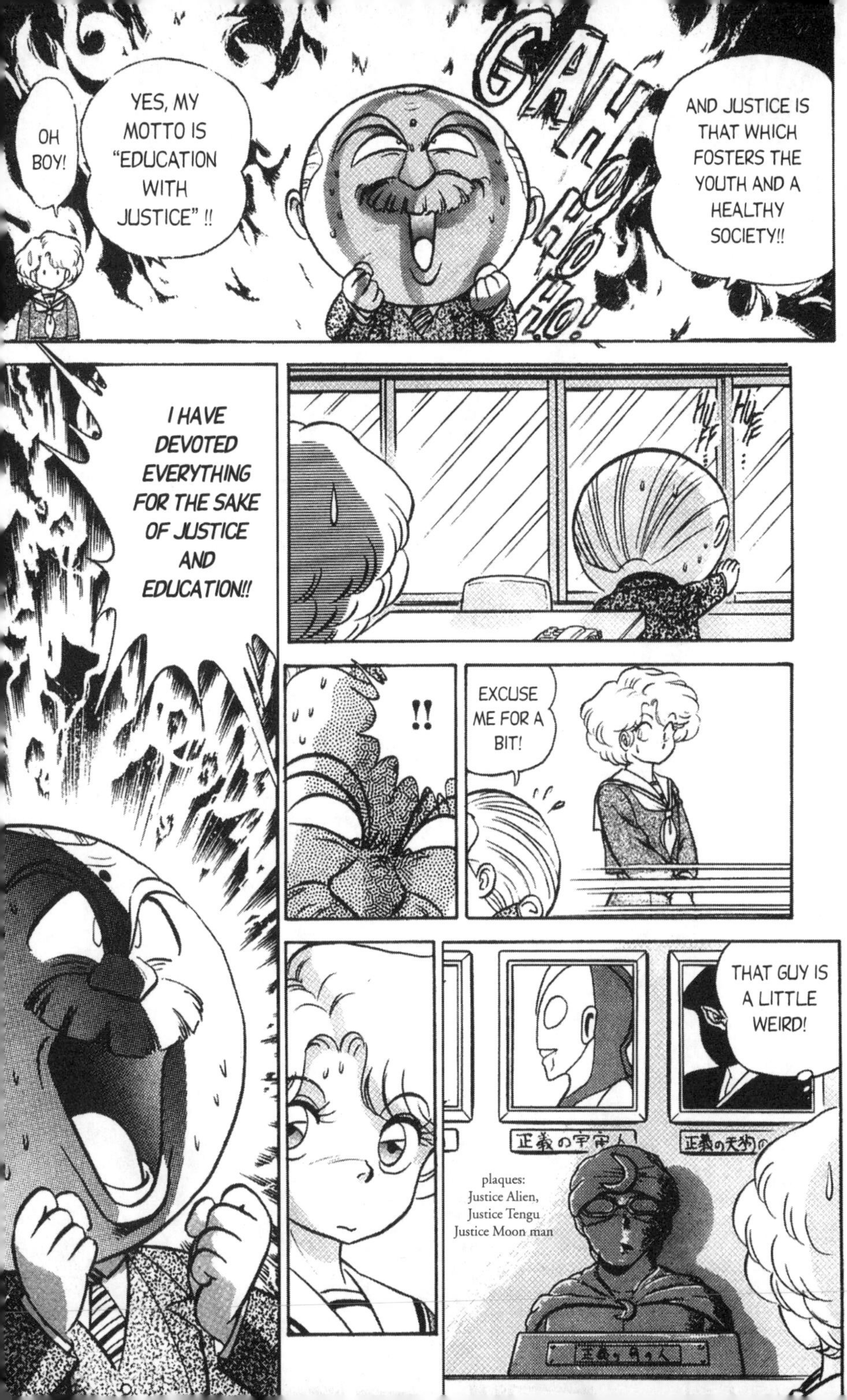
YES, MY MOTTO IS "EDUCATION WITH JUSTICE" !!
AND JUSTICE IS THAT WHICH FOSTERS THE YOUTH AND A HEALTHY SOCIETY!!
GAHOHOHO!
OH BOY!
I HAVE DEVOTED EVERYTHING FOR THE SAKE OF JUSTICE AND EDUCATION!!
HUFF HUFF
!!
EXCUSE ME FOR A BIT!
THAT GUY IS A LITTLE WEIRD!
正義の宇宙人
plaques: Justice Alien, Justice Tengu Justice Moon man

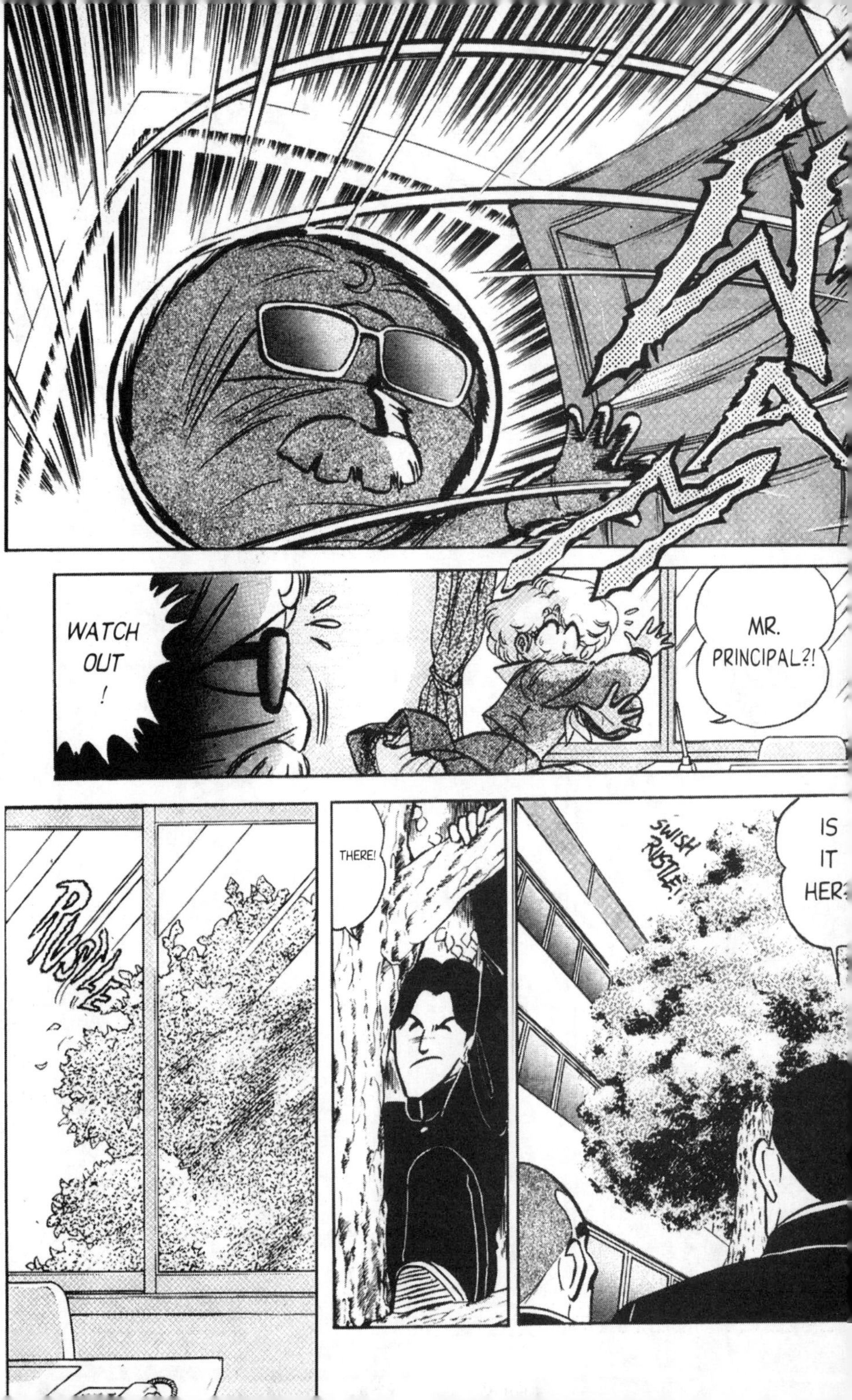

MR. PRINCIPAL?!
WATCH OUT !
IS IT HER
SWISH RUSTLE!
THERE!
RUSTLE

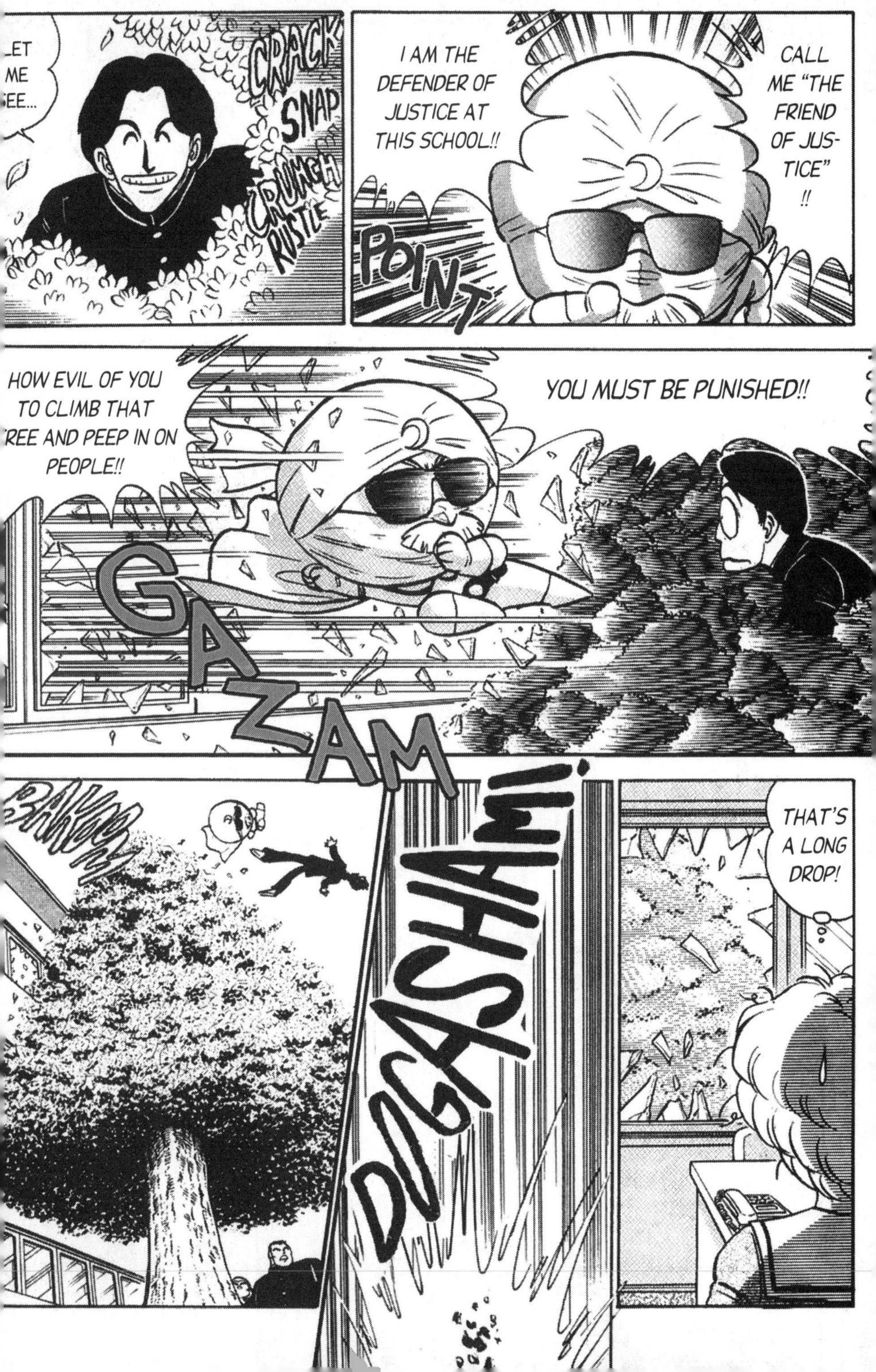
LET ME SEE...
CRACK
SNAP
CRUNCH
RUSTLE
I AM THE DEFENDER OF JUSTICE AT THIS SCHOOL!!
CALL ME "THE FRIEND OF JUSTICE"!!
POINT
HOW EVIL OF YOU TO CLIMB THAT TREE AND PEEP IN ON PEOPLE!!
YOU MUST BE PUNISHED!!
GAZAM
DOGASHAM!
THAT'S A LONG DROP!

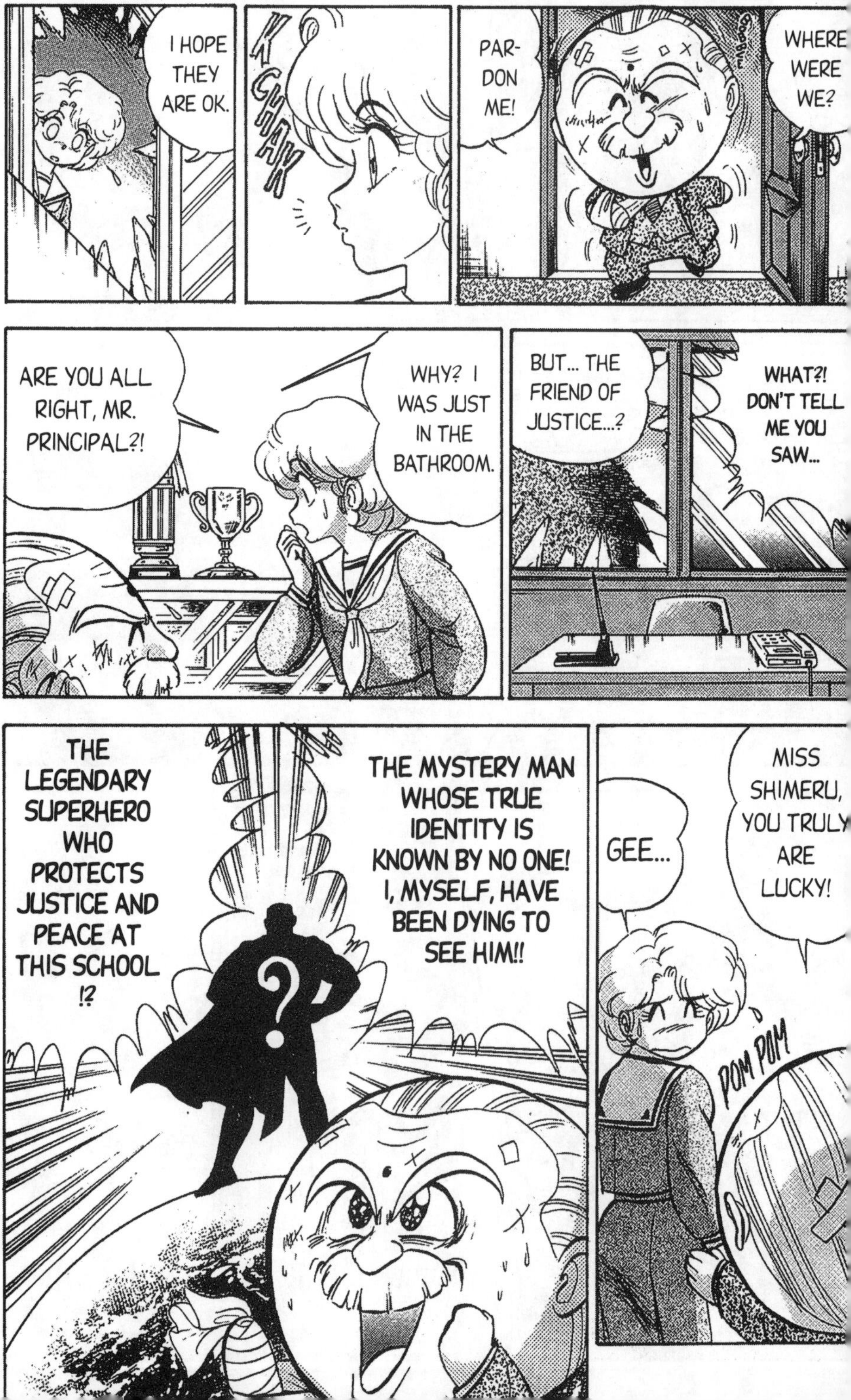
I HOPE THEY ARE OK.
KCHAK
PAR- DON ME!
WHERE WERE WE?
ARE YOU ALL RIGHT, MR. PRINCIPAL?!
WHY? I WAS JUST IN THE BATHROOM.
BUT... THE FRIEND OF JUSTICE...?
WHAT?! DON'T TELL ME YOU SAW...
THE LEGENDARY SUPERHERO WHO PROTECTS JUSTICE AND PEACE AT THIS SCHOOL !?
THE MYSTERY MAN WHOSE TRUE IDENTITY IS KNOWN BY NO ONE! I, MYSELF, HAVE BEEN DYING TO SEE HIM!!
GEE...
MISS SHIMERU, YOU TRULY ARE LUCKY!
POM POM

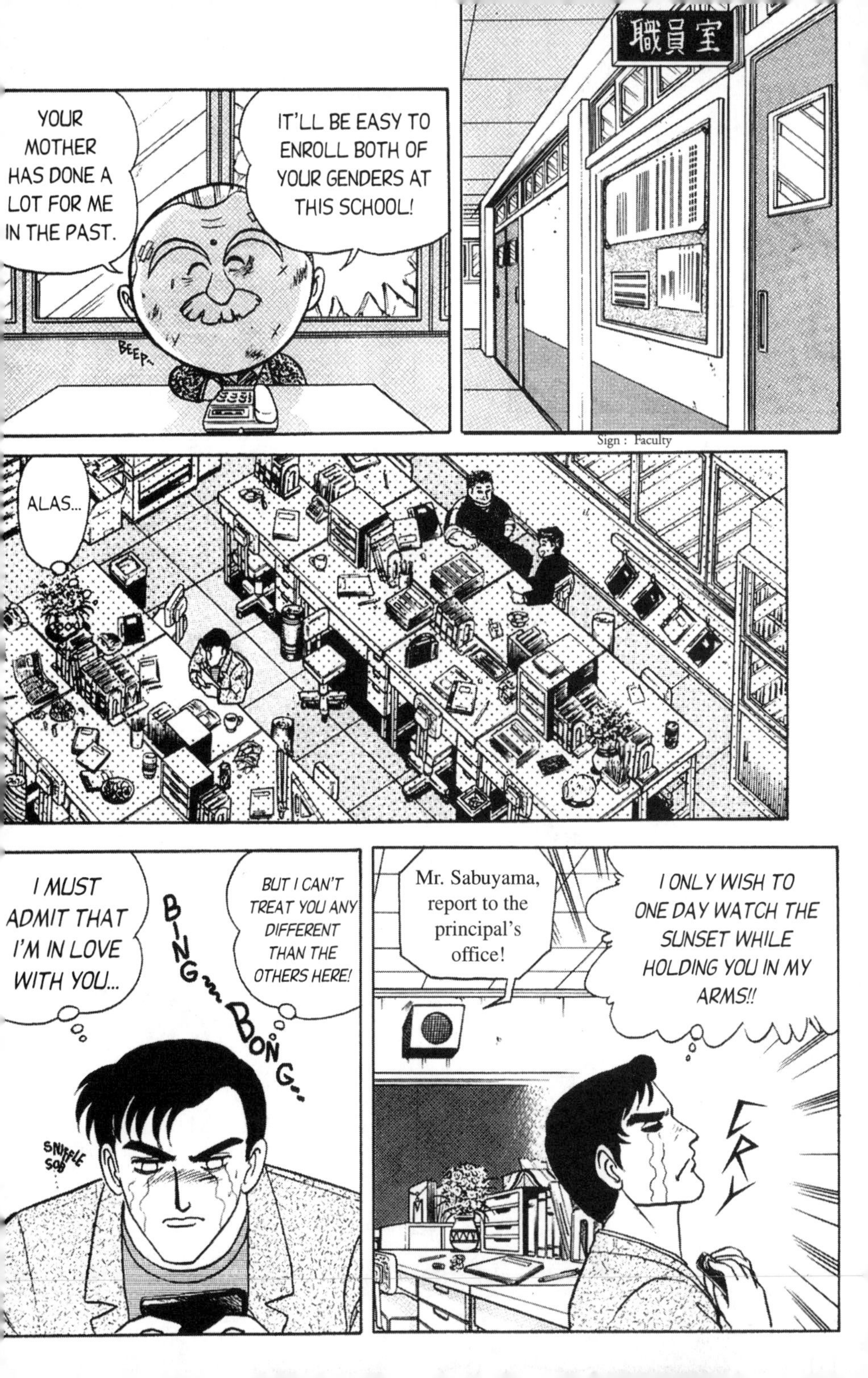

YOUR MOTHER HAS DONE A LOT FOR ME IN THE PAST.
IT'LL BE EASY TO ENROLL BOTH OF YOUR GENDERS AT THIS SCHOOL!
BEEP..
職員室
Sign : Faculty
ALAS...
I MUST ADMIT THAT I'M IN LOVE WITH YOU...
BUT I CAN'T TREAT YOU ANY DIFFERENT THAN THE OTHERS HERE!
BING.. BONG..
SNIFFLE SOB
Mr. Sabuyama, report to the principal's office!
I ONLY WISH TO ONE DAY WATCH THE SUNSET WHILE HOLDING YOU IN MY ARMS!!
CRY

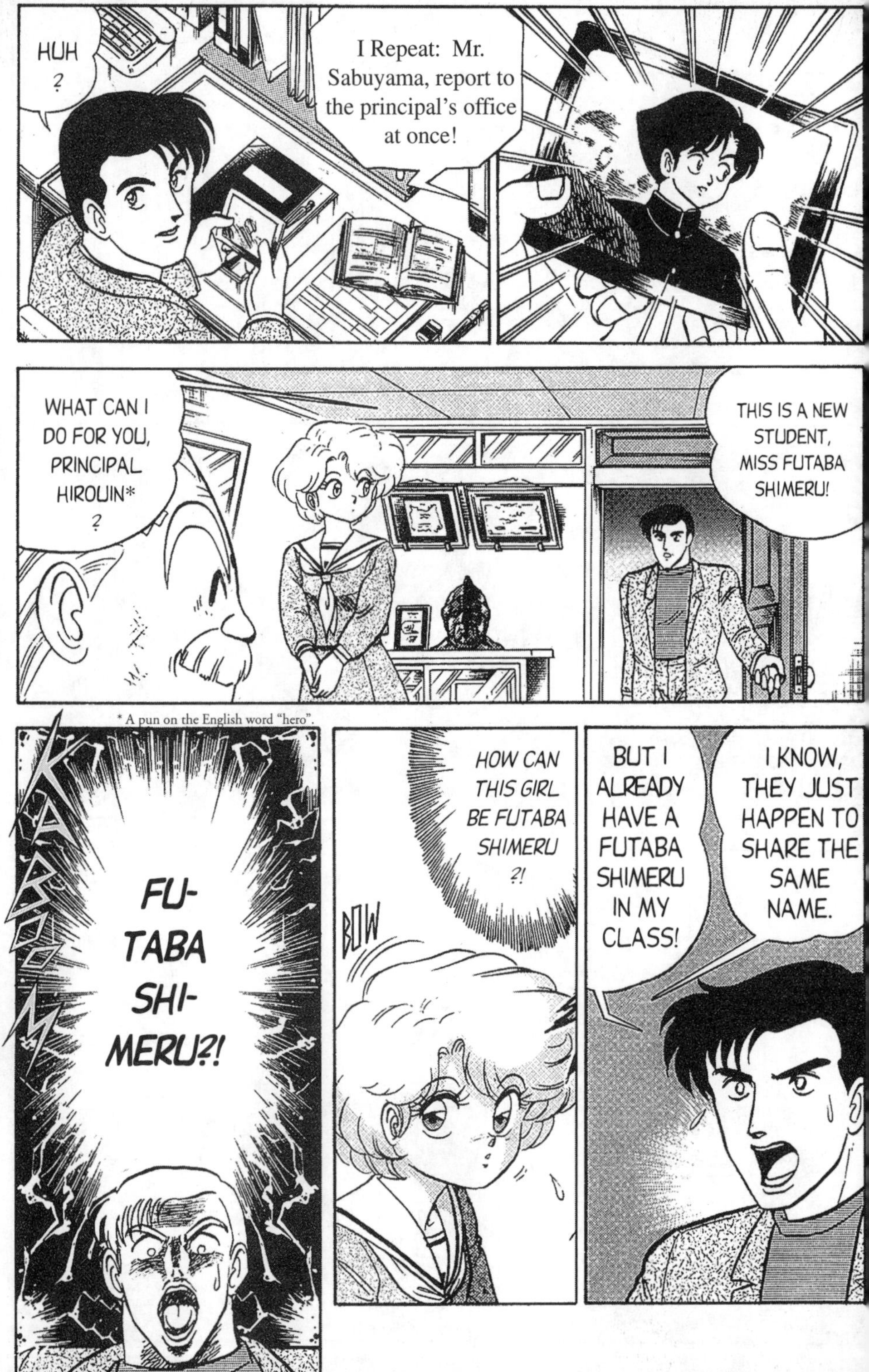
HUH?
I Repeat: Mr. Sabuyama, report to the principal's office at once!
WHAT CAN I DO FOR YOU, PRINCIPAL HIROUIN*?
THIS IS A NEW STUDENT, MISS FUTABA SHIMERU!
KABOOM
FU-TABA SHI-MERU?!
HOW CAN THIS GIRL BE FUTABA SHIMERU?!
BOW
BUT I ALREADY HAVE A FUTABA SHIMERU IN MY CLASS!
I KNOW, THEY JUST HAPPEN TO SHARE THE SAME NAME.

* A pun on the English word "hero".

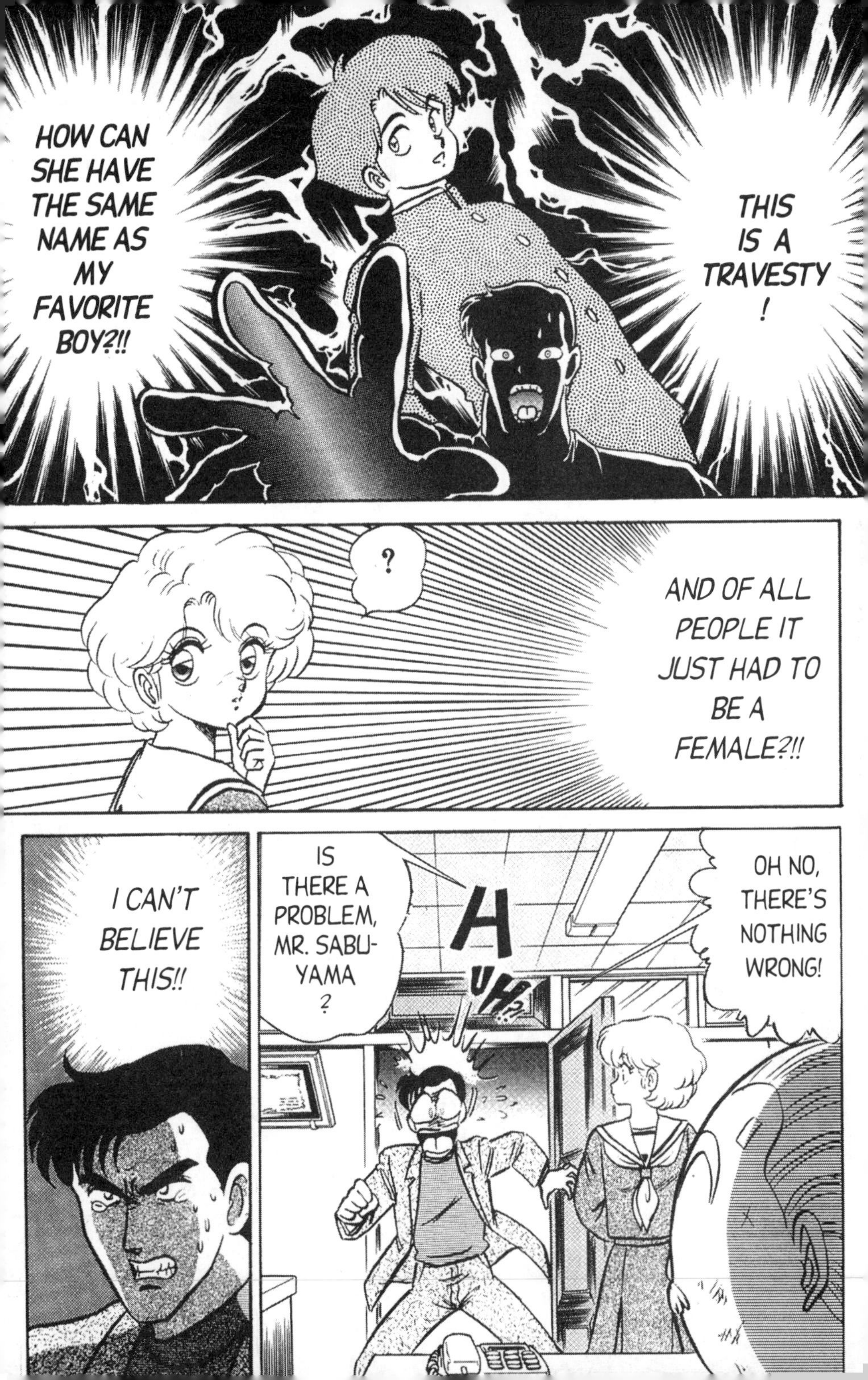
HOW CAN SHE HAVE THE SAME NAME AS MY FAVORITE BOY?!!
THIS IS A TRAVESTY!
?
AND OF ALL PEOPLE IT JUST HAD TO BE A FEMALE?!!
I CAN'T BELIEVE THIS!!
IS THERE A PROBLEM, MR. SABU-YAMA?
HUH?!
OH NO, THERE'S NOTHING WRONG!

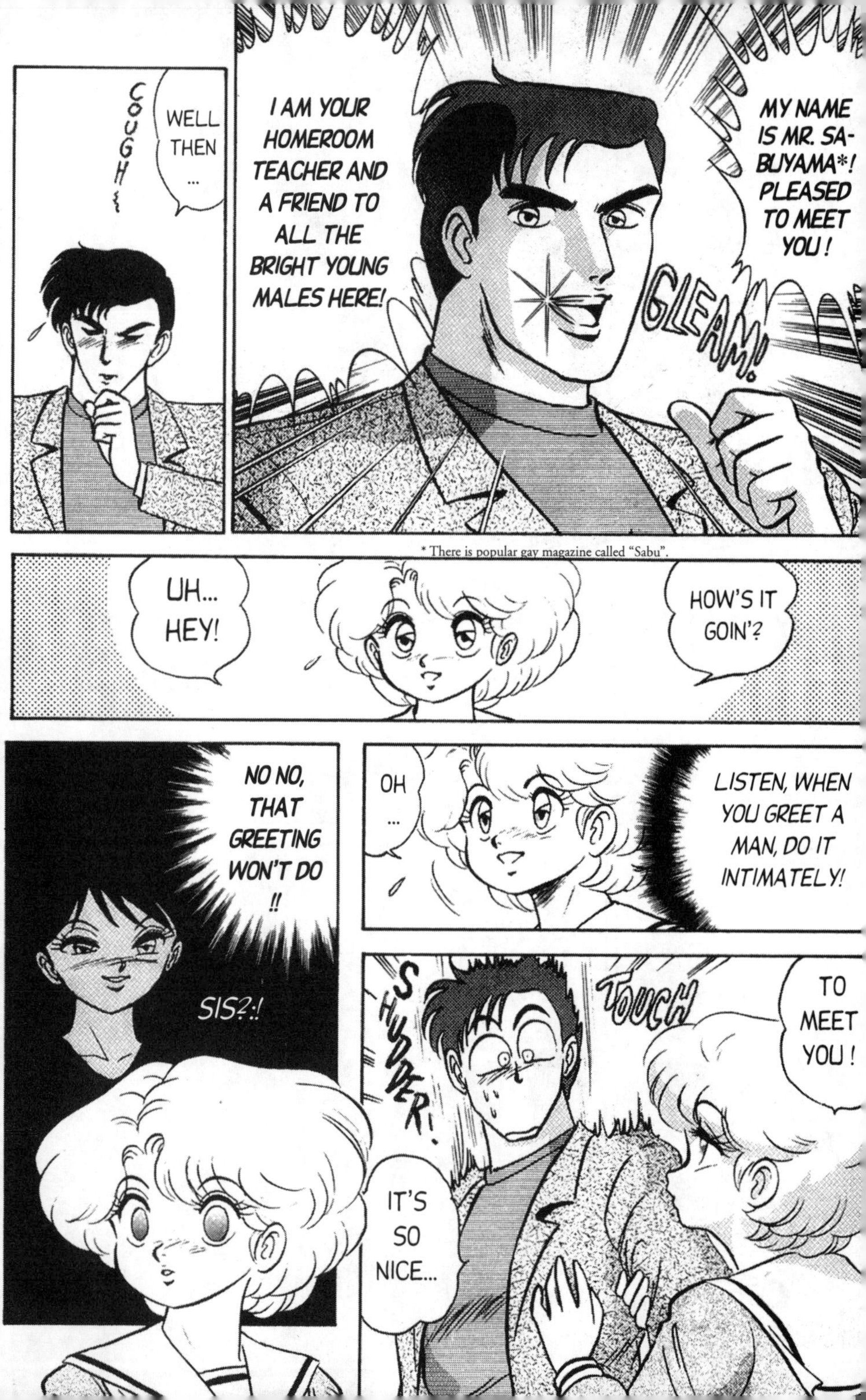
COUGH
WELL THEN ...
I AM YOUR HOMEROOM TEACHER AND A FRIEND TO ALL THE BRIGHT YOUNG MALES HERE!
MY NAME IS MR. SA-BUYAMA*! PLEASED TO MEET YOU!
GLEAM!
UH... HEY!
HOW'S IT GOIN'?
NO NO, THAT GREETING WON'T DO !!
SIS?:!
OH ...
LISTEN, WHEN YOU GREET A MAN, DO IT INTIMATELY!
SHUDDER!
TOUCH
TO MEET YOU!
IT'S SO NICE...

* There is popular gay magazine called "Sabu".

HEY, LET GO OF ME!!

DON'T GET SO CLOSE!!

HA, HA, LOOKS LIKE YOU TWO WILL GET ALONG GREAT!

FUTANA MUST'VE TAUGHT ME WRONG!

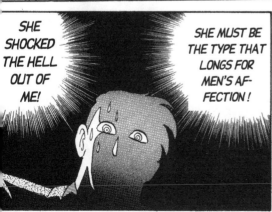

SHE SHOCKED THE HELL OUT OF ME!

SHE MUST BE THE TYPE THAT LONGS FOR MEN'S AFFECTION!

THIS GIRL WILL THREATEN THE TIES I HAVE WITH MY FAVORITE GUYS!!

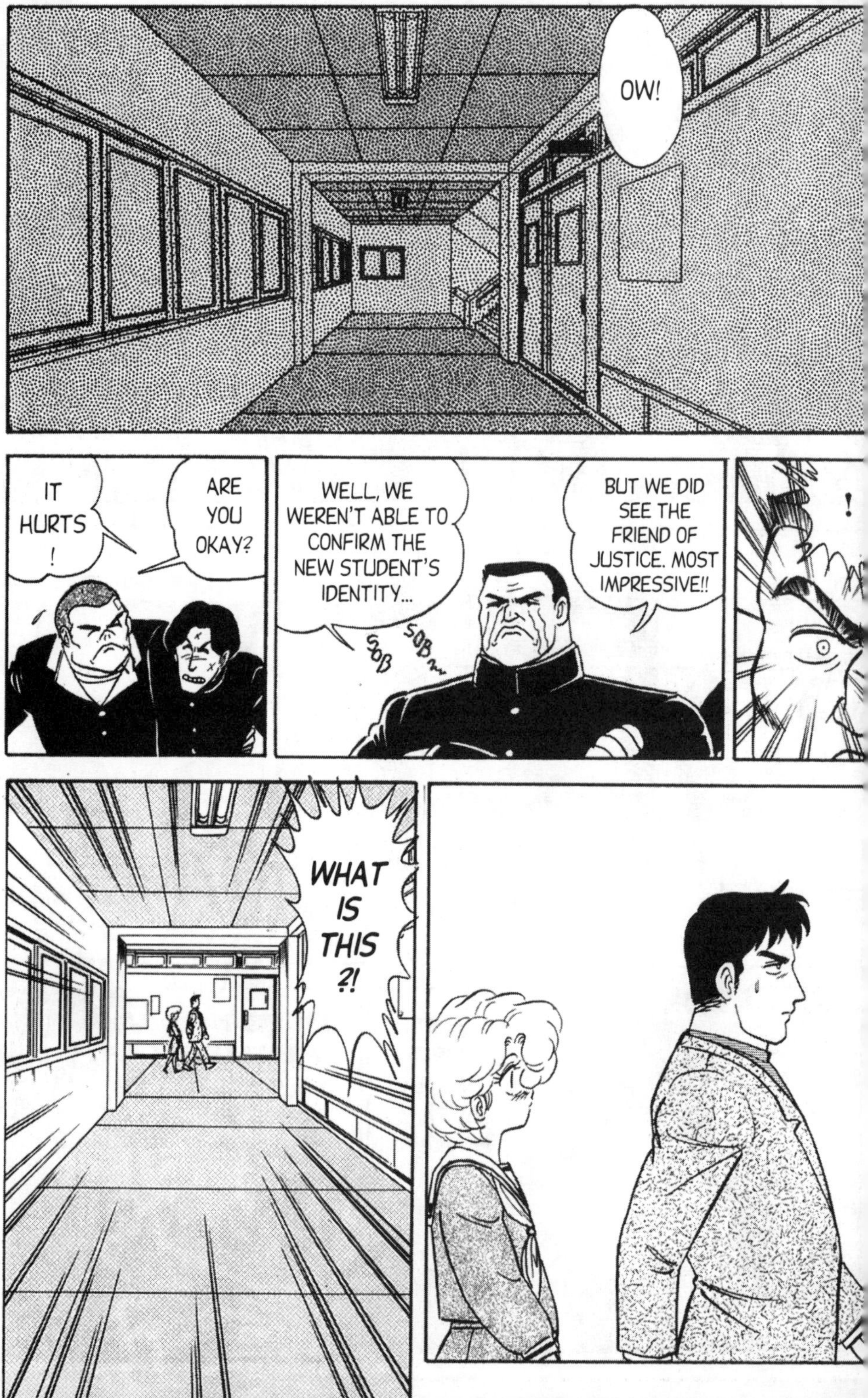

OW!
IT HURTS!
ARE YOU OKAY?
WELL, WE WEREN'T ABLE TO CONFIRM THE NEW STUDENT'S IDENTITY...
SOB
SOB
BUT WE DID SEE THE FRIEND OF JUSTICE. MOST IMPRESSIVE!!
!
WHAT IS THIS ?!

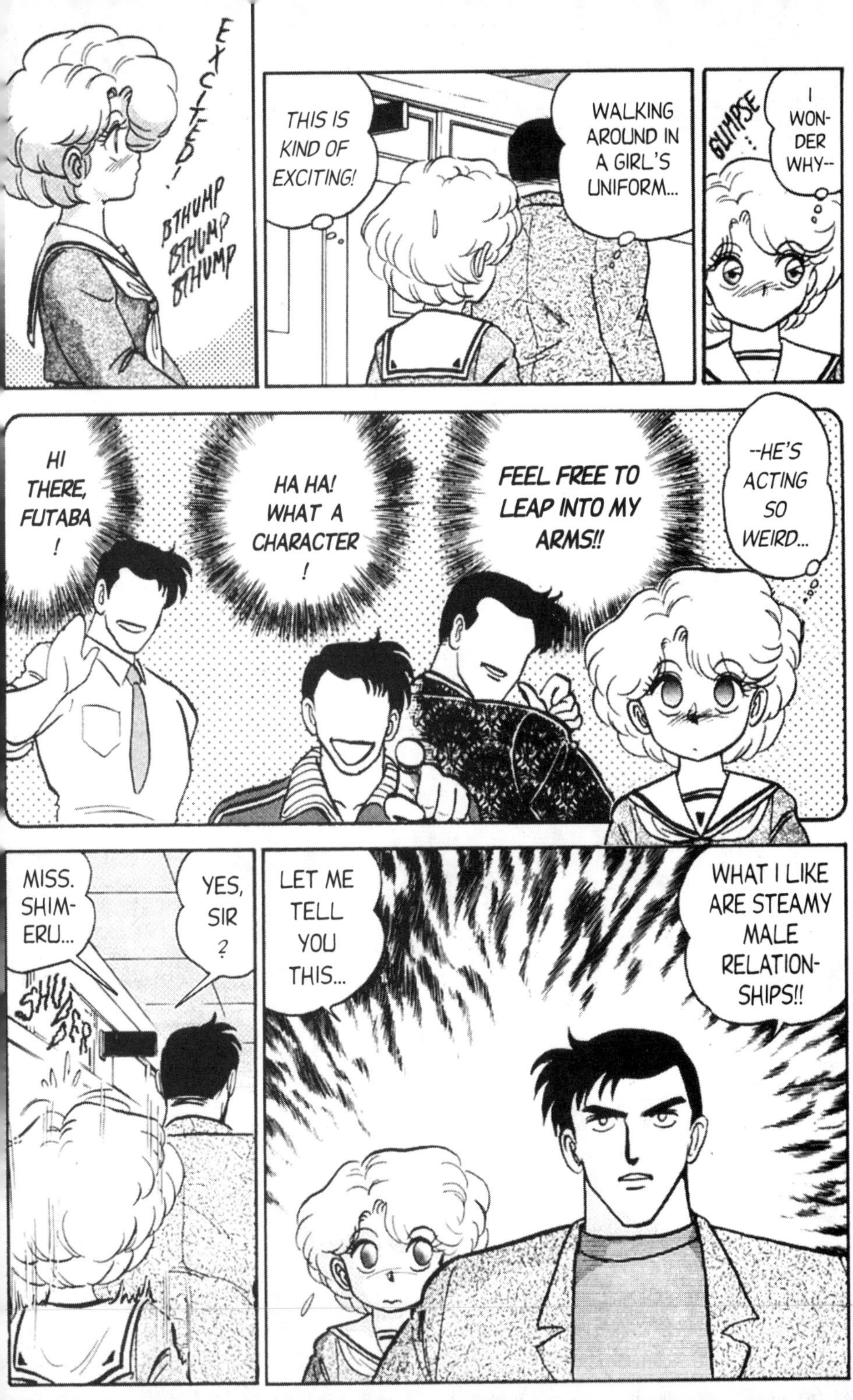
EXCITED!
BTHUMP BTHUMP BTHUMP
THIS IS KIND OF EXCITING!
WALKING AROUND IN A GIRL'S UNIFORM...
GLIMPSE...
I WONDER WHY--
HI THERE, FUTABA!
HA HA! WHAT A CHARACTER!
FEEL FREE TO LEAP INTO MY ARMS!!
--HE'S ACTING SO WEIRD...
MISS. SHIMERU...
YES, SIR?
SHUDDER
LET ME TELL YOU THIS...
WHAT I LIKE ARE STEAMY MALE RELATIONSHIPS!!

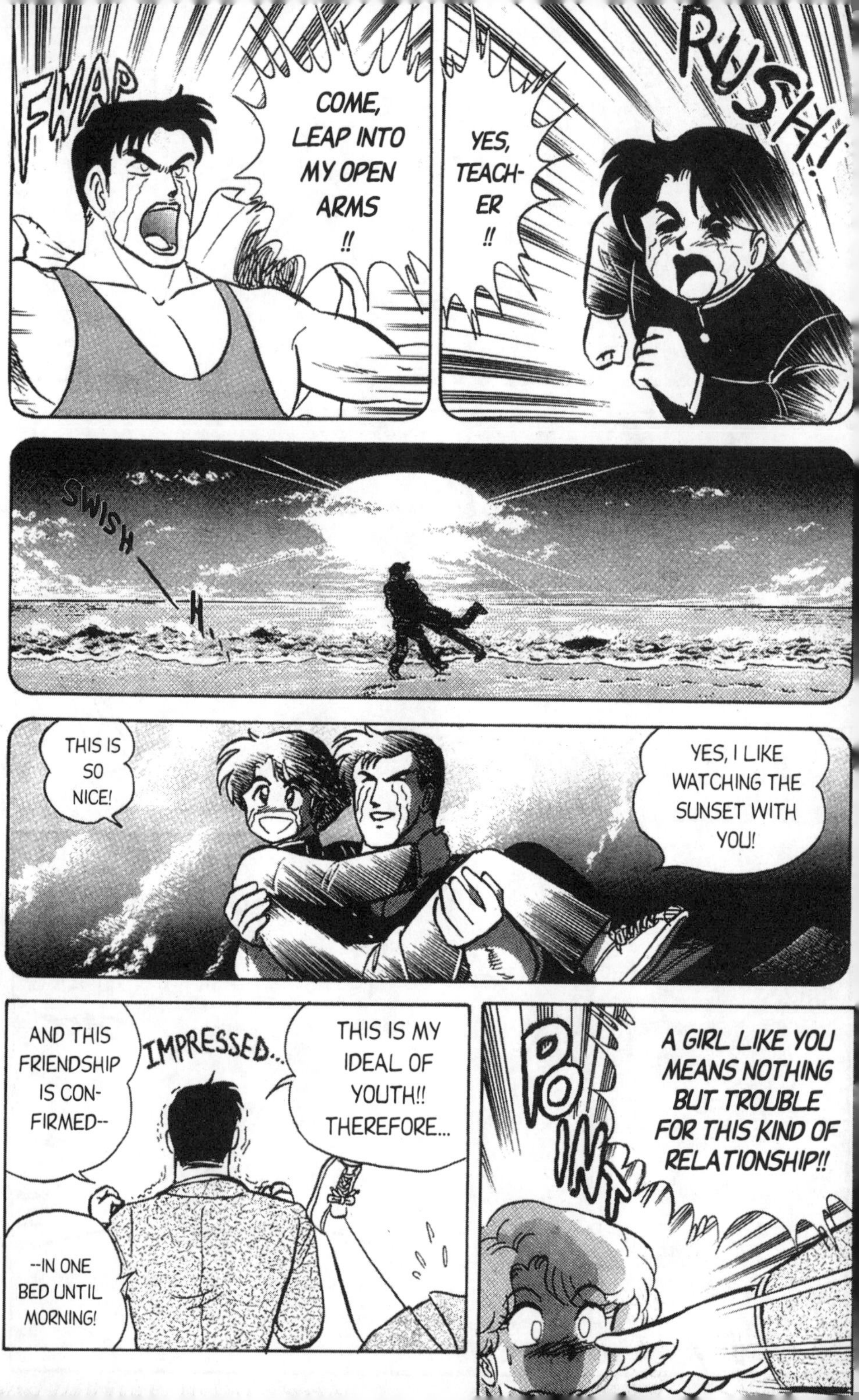

FWAP
COME, LEAP INTO MY OPEN ARMS !!
YES, TEACHER !!
RUSH!!
SWISH H
THIS IS SO NICE!
YES, I LIKE WATCHING THE SUNSET WITH YOU!
AND THIS FRIENDSHIP IS CONFIRMED--
IMPRESSED...
THIS IS MY IDEAL OF YOUTH!! THEREFORE...
--IN ONE BED UNTIL MORNING!
POINT
A GIRL LIKE YOU MEANS NOTHING BUT TROUBLE FOR THIS KIND OF RELATIONSHIP!!

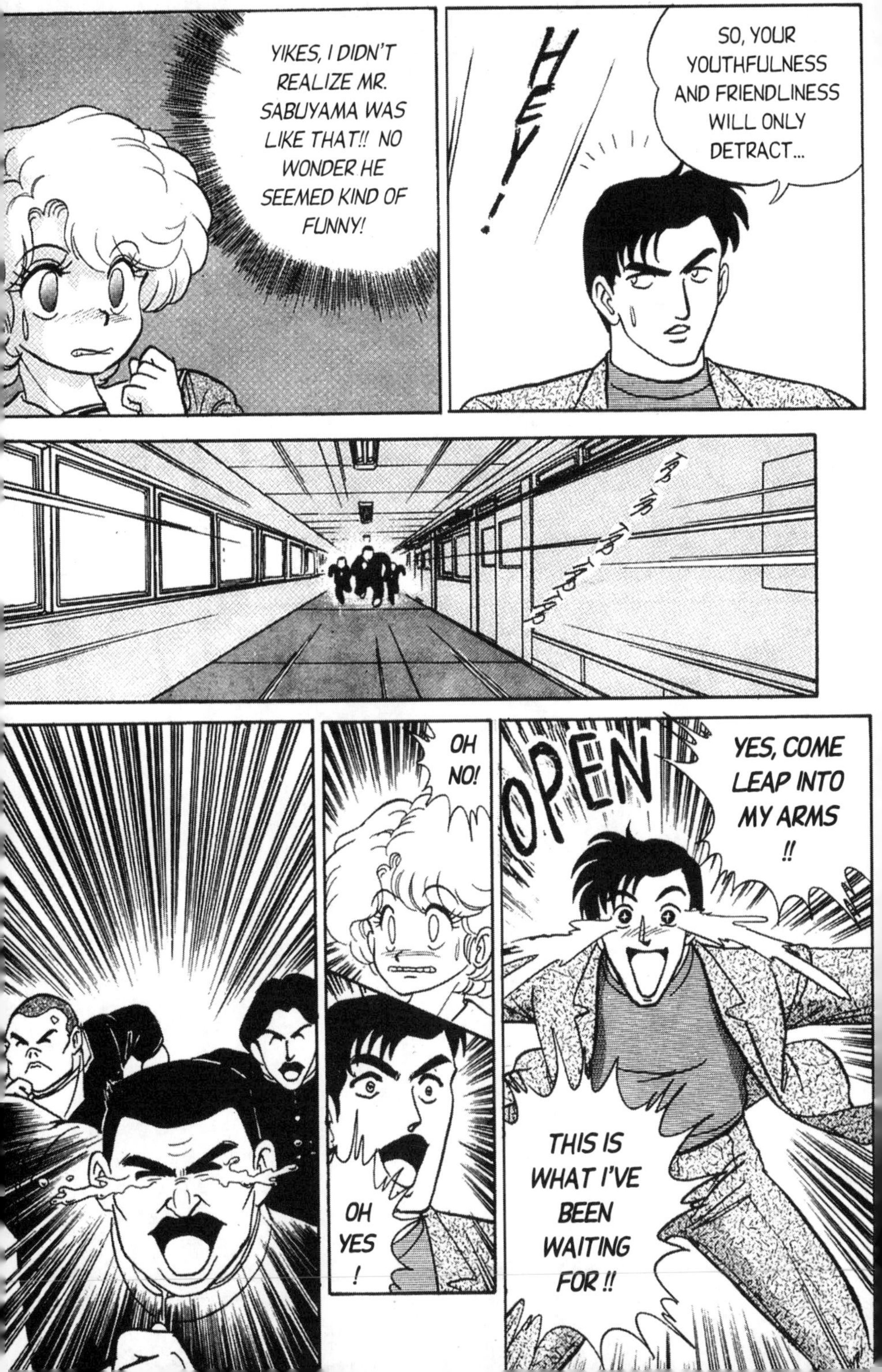

YIKES, I DIDN'T REALIZE MR. SABUYAMA WAS LIKE THAT!! NO WONDER HE SEEMED KIND OF FUNNY!
HEY!
SO, YOUR YOUTHFULNESS AND FRIENDLINESS WILL ONLY DETRACT...
TAP TAP TAP TAP TAP
OPEN
YES, COME LEAP INTO MY ARMS !!
THIS IS WHAT I'VE BEEN WAITING FOR !!
OH NO!
OH YES !

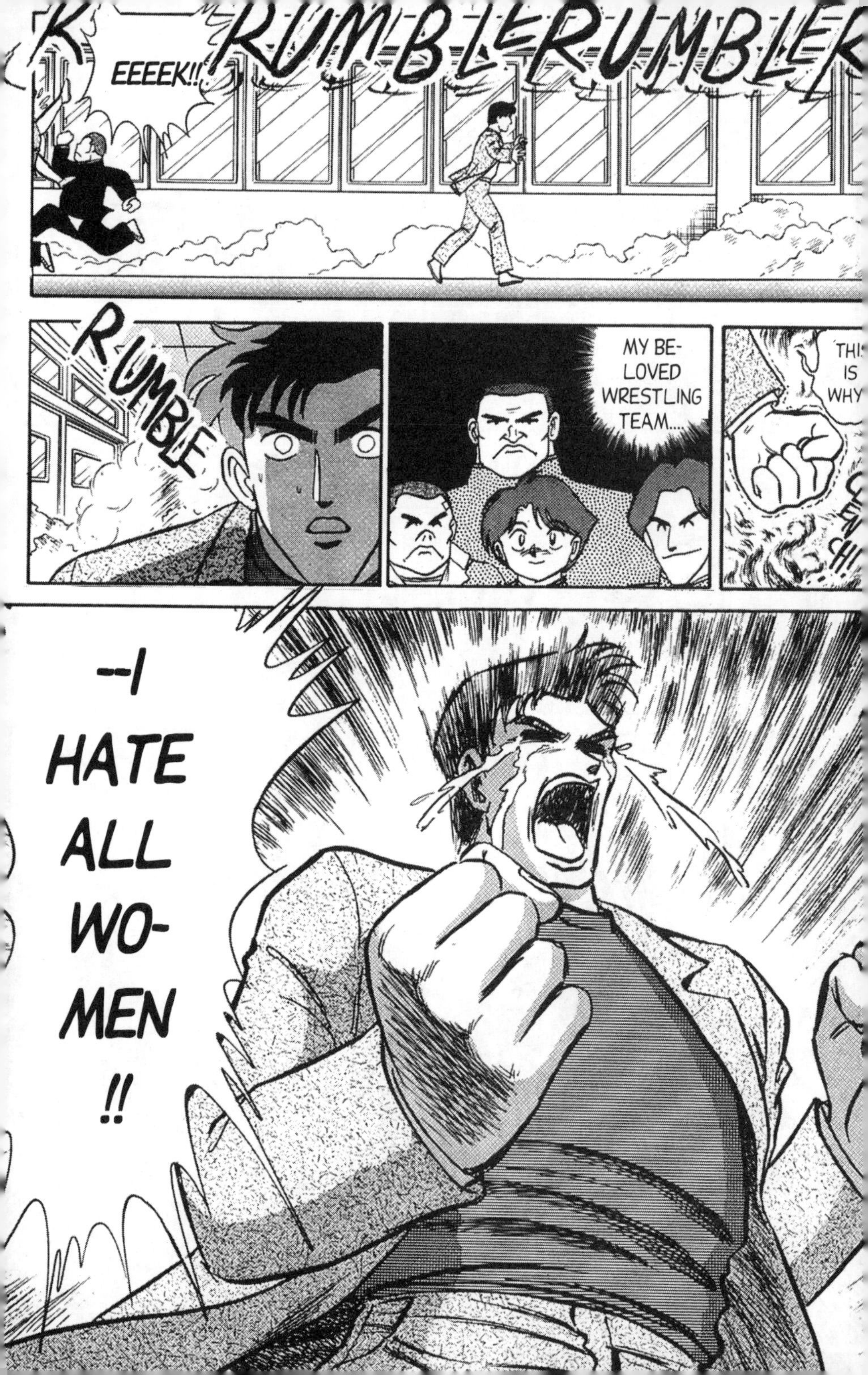
K
RUMBLE RUMBLE
EEEEK!!
RUMBLE
MY BE-LOVED WRESTLING TEAM....
THIS IS WHY
--I HATE ALL WO-MEN !!

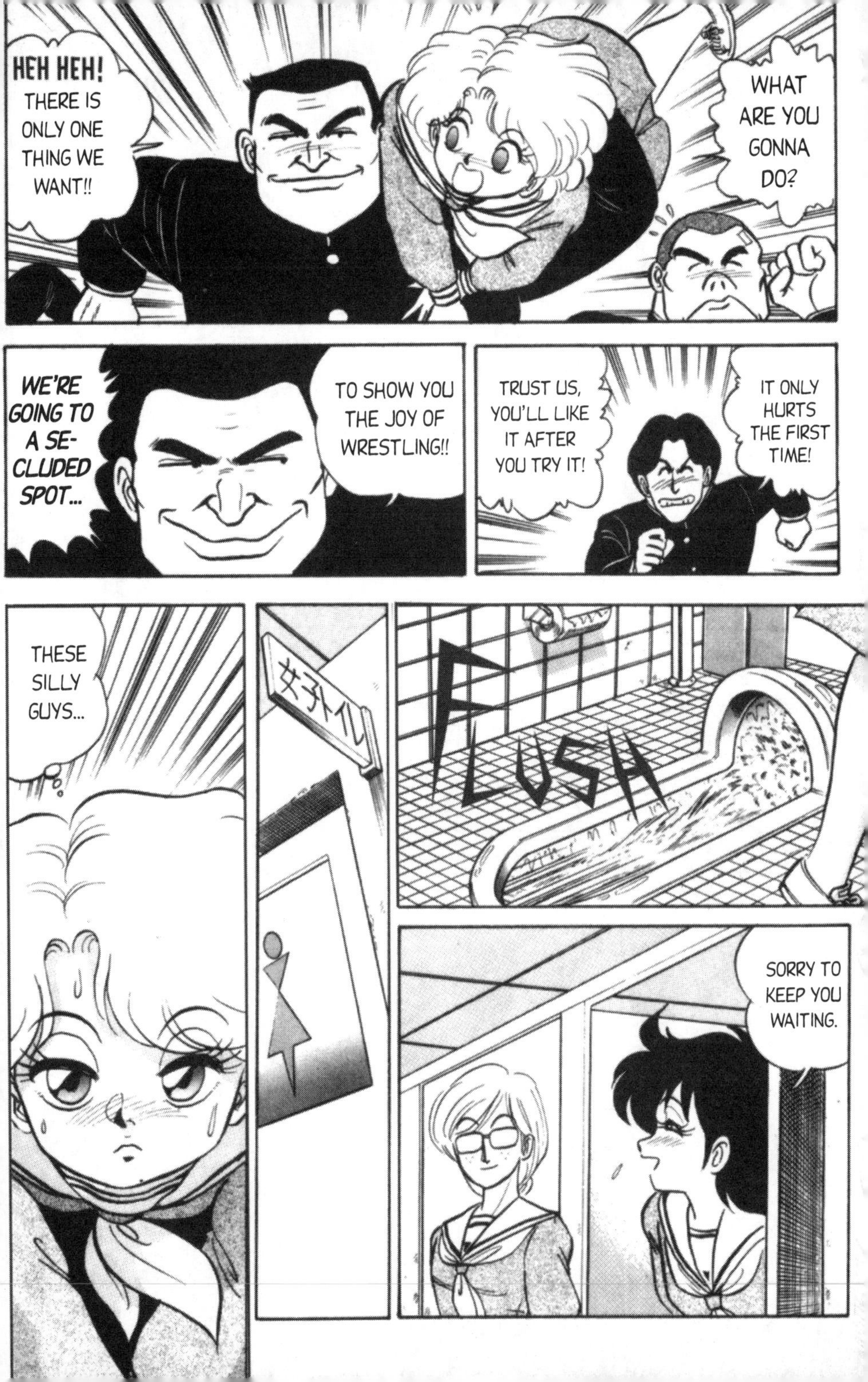
WHAT ARE YOU GONNA DO?
HEH HEH! THERE IS ONLY ONE THING WE WANT!!
WE'RE GOING TO A SE- CLUDED SPOT...
TO SHOW YOU THE JOY OF WRESTLING!!
TRUST US, YOU'LL LIKE IT AFTER YOU TRY IT!
IT ONLY HURTS THE FIRST TIME!
THESE SILLY GUYS...
女子トイレ
FLUSH
SORRY TO KEEP YOU WAITING.

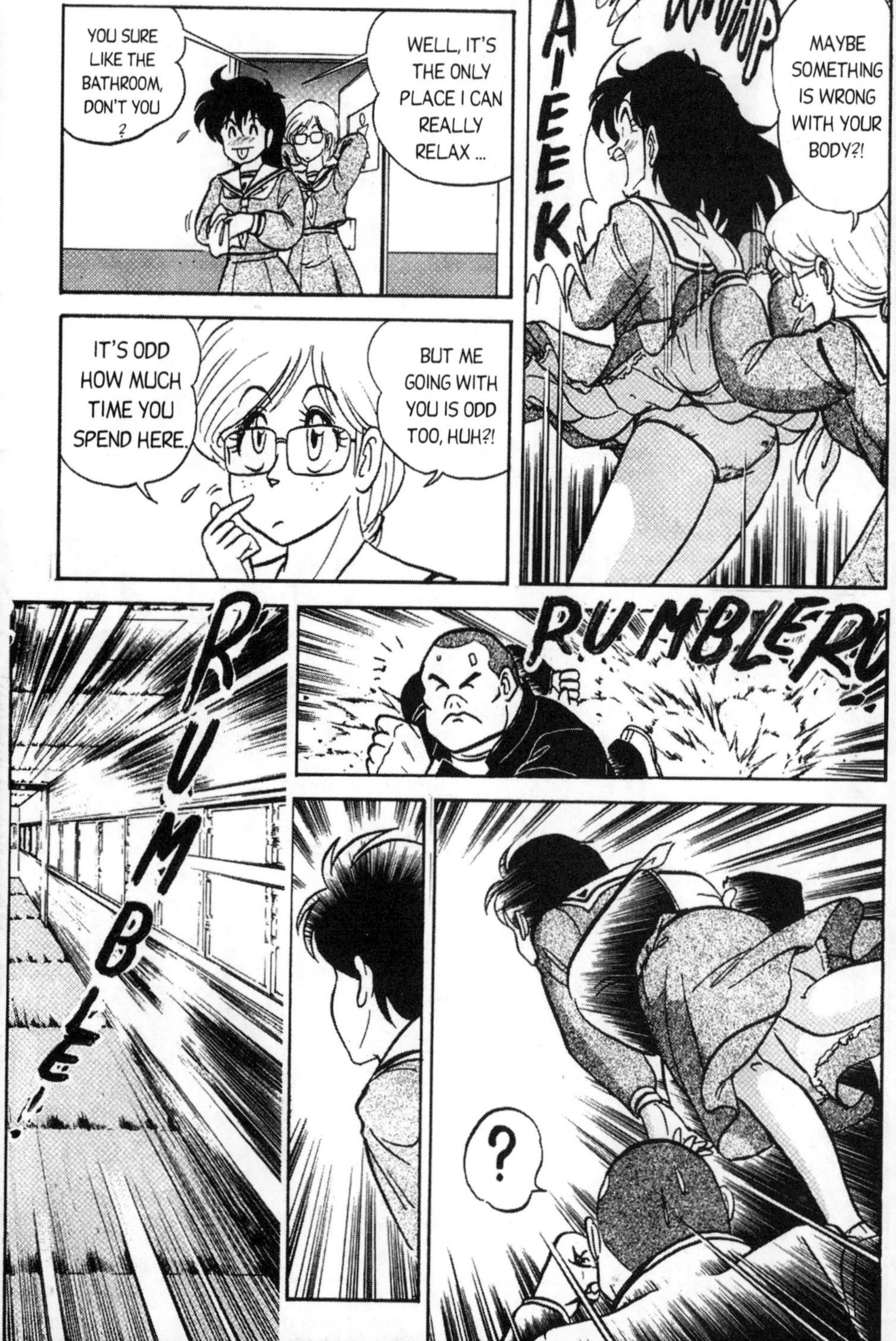

YOU SURE LIKE THE BATHROOM, DON'T YOU?
WELL, IT'S THE ONLY PLACE I CAN REALLY RELAX ...
IT'S ODD HOW MUCH TIME YOU SPEND HERE.
BUT ME GOING WITH YOU IS ODD TOO, HUH?!
WHAP
AIEEK
MAYBE SOMETHING IS WRONG WITH YOUR BODY?!
RUMBLE!!
RUMBLERU
?

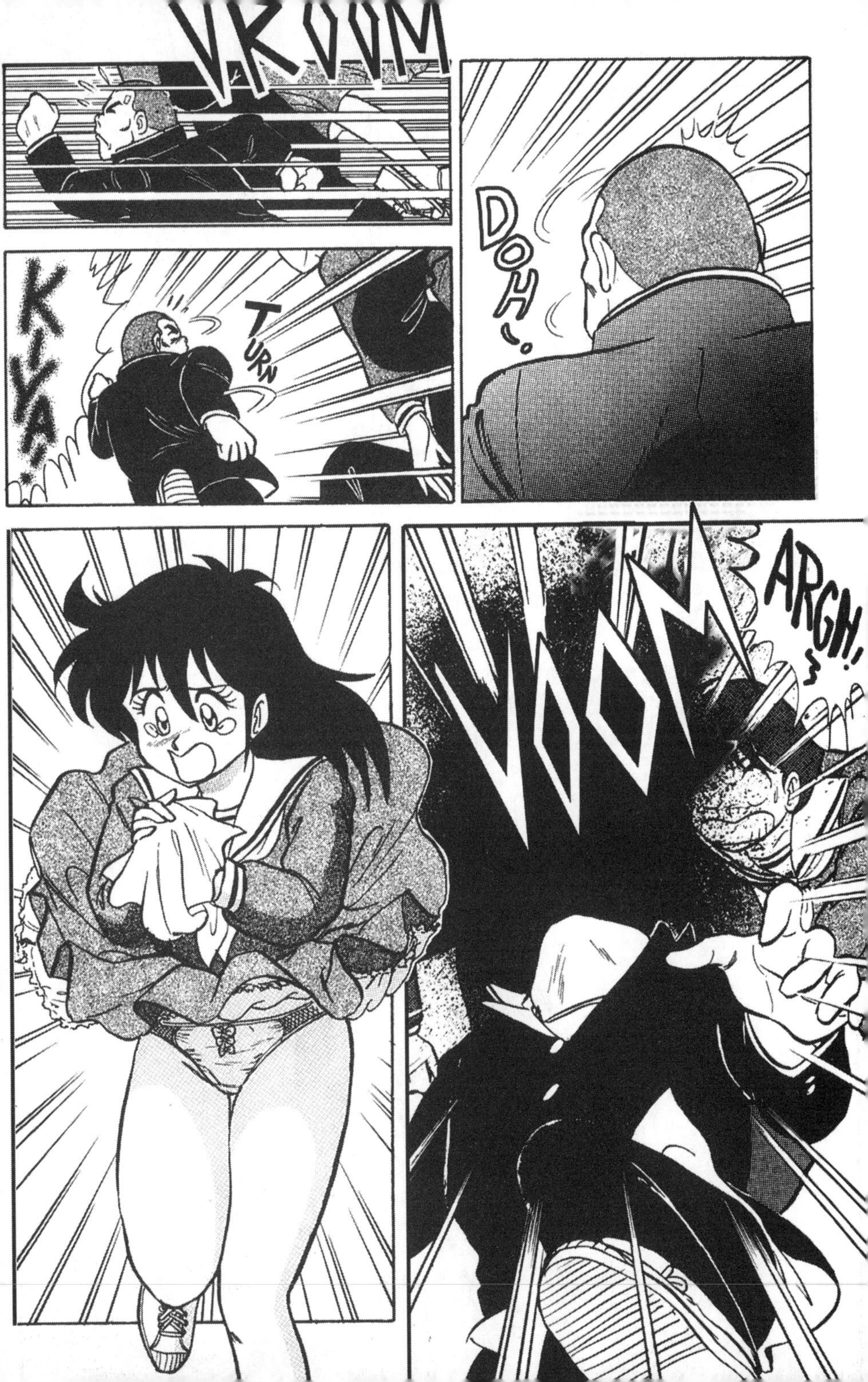
VROOM
KIYA!
TURN
DOH
VOOM
ARGH!!

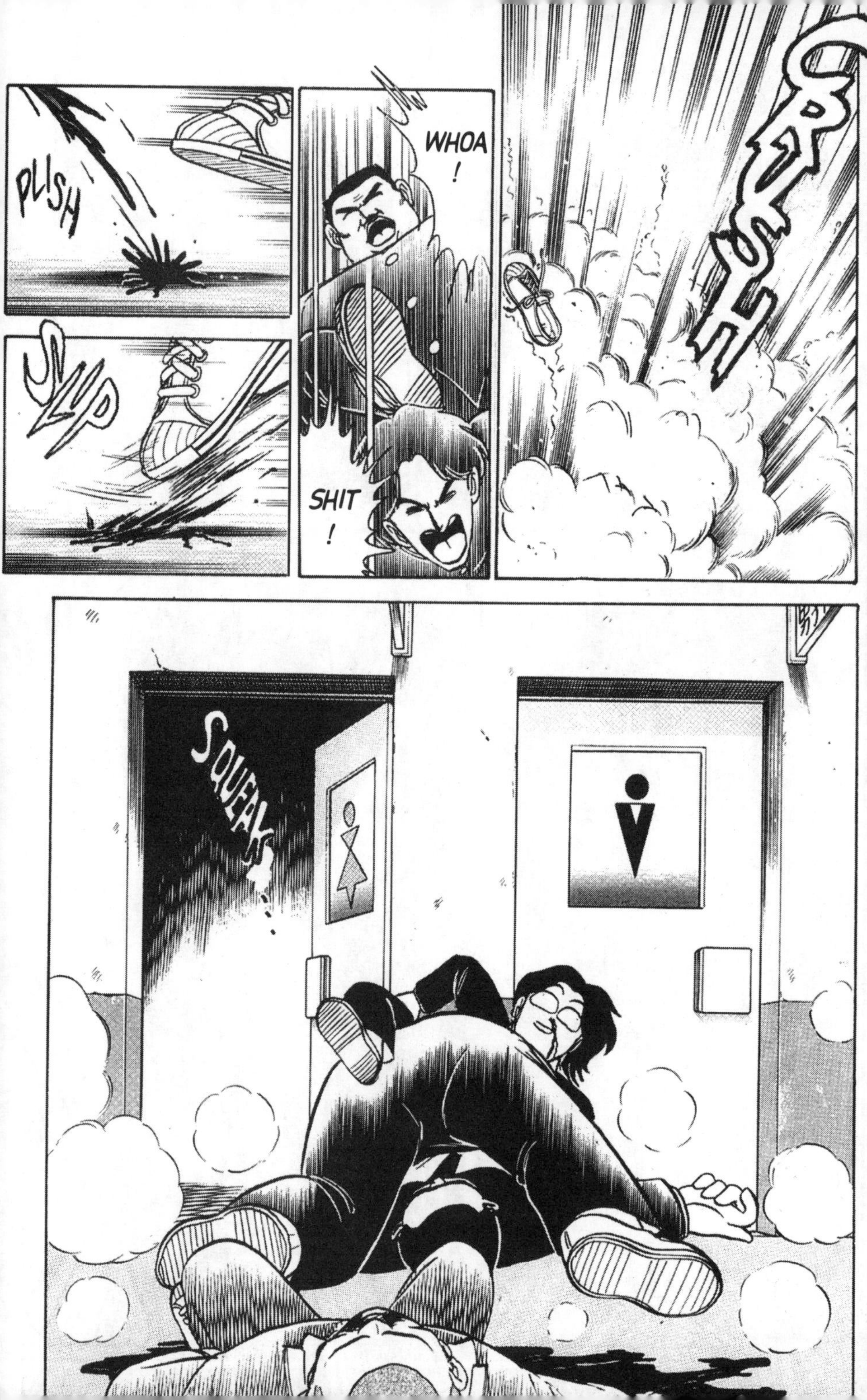
CRUSH
WHOA
!
SHIT
!
PLISH
SLIP
SQUEAK
...

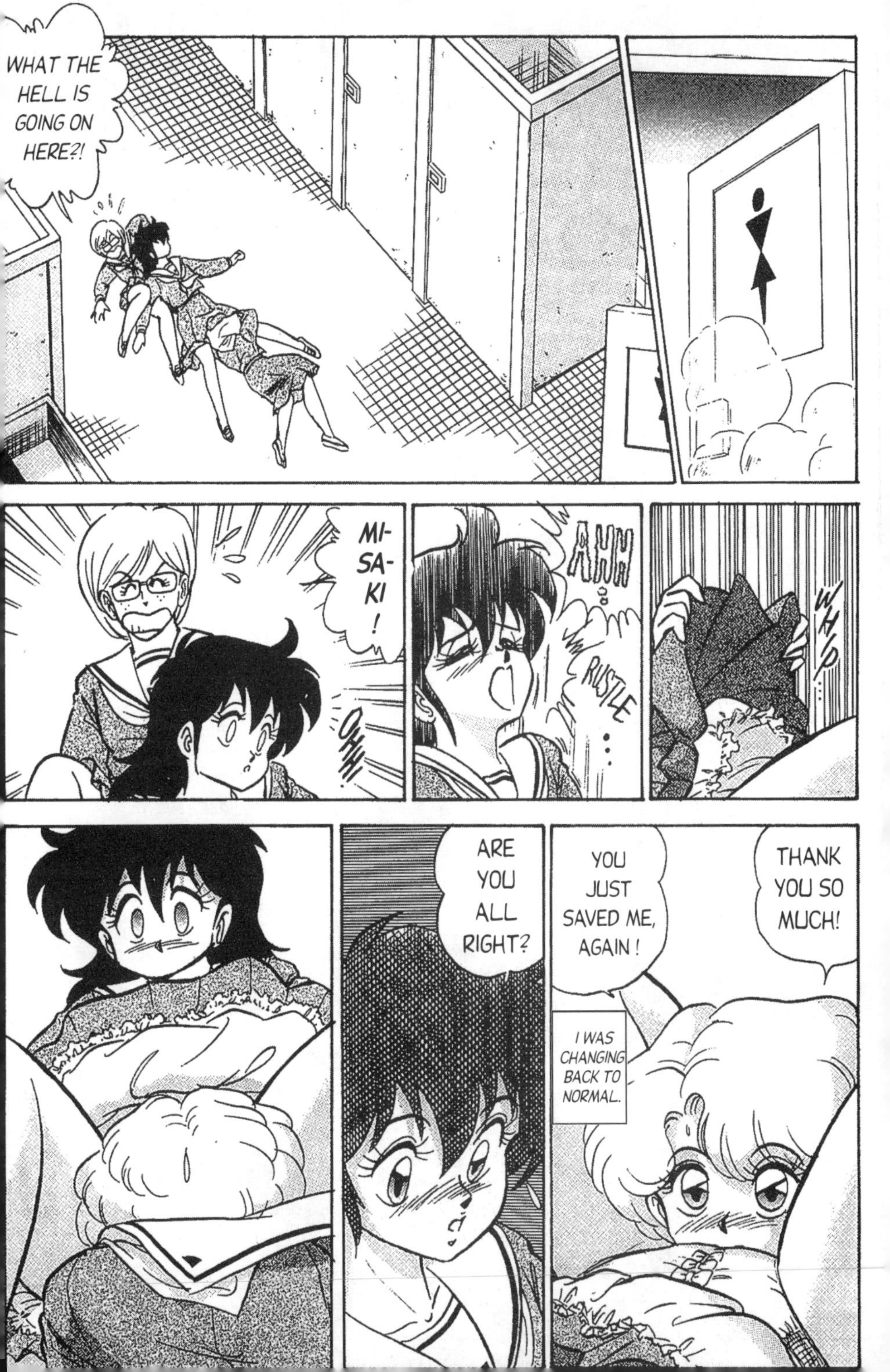
WHAT THE HELL IS GOING ON HERE?!
MI-SA-KI!
OHH
AHH
RUSTLE
WHIP
ARE YOU ALL RIGHT?
YOU JUST SAVED ME, AGAIN!
I WAS CHANGING BACK TO NORMAL.
THANK YOU SO MUCH!

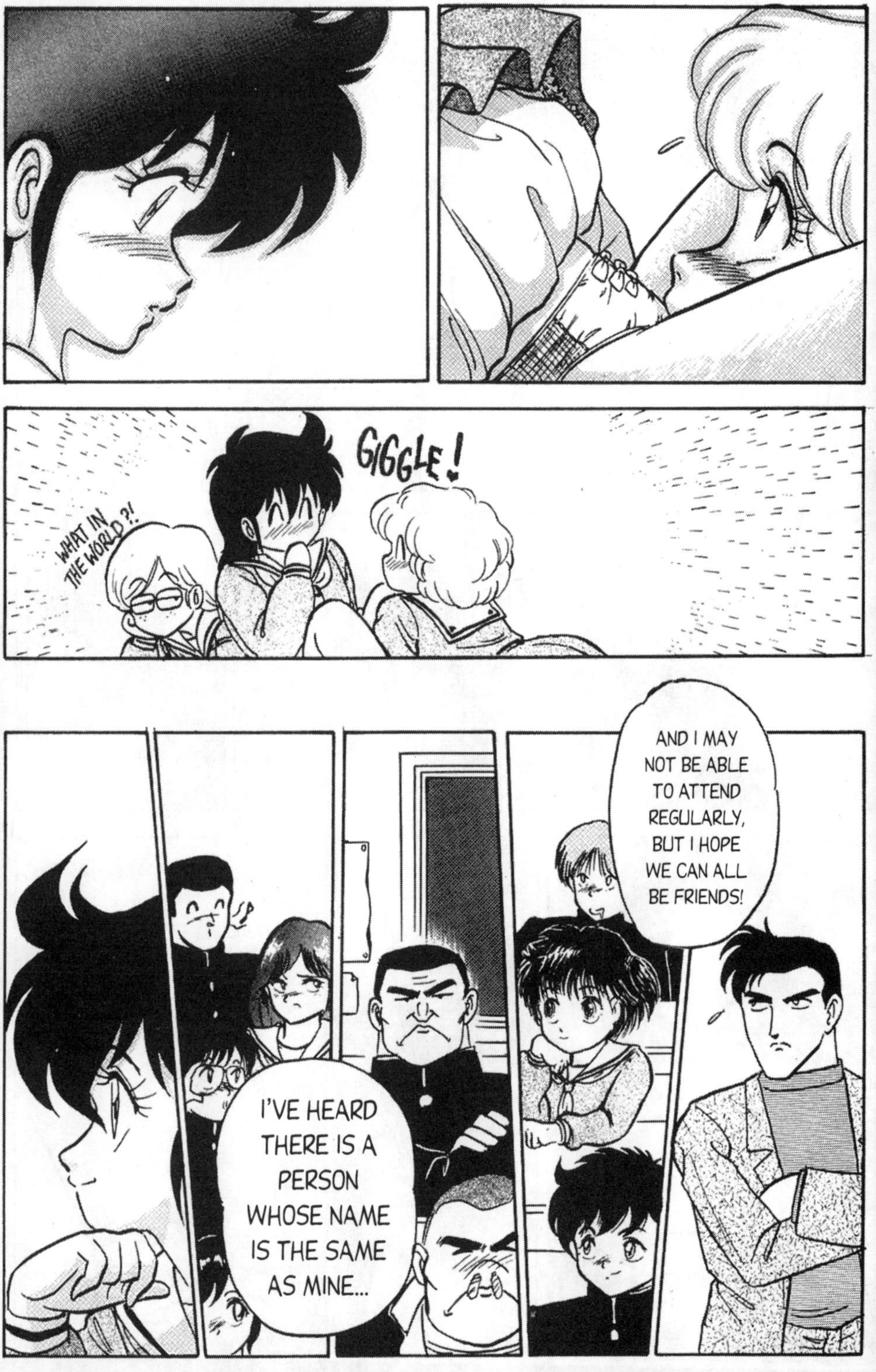
GIGGLE!
WHAT IN THE WORLD?!
AND I MAY NOT BE ABLE TO ATTEND REGULARLY, BUT I HOPE WE CAN ALL BE FRIENDS!
I'VE HEARD THERE IS A PERSON WHOSE NAME IS THE SAME AS MINE...

BLACKBOARD: FUTABA SHIMERU

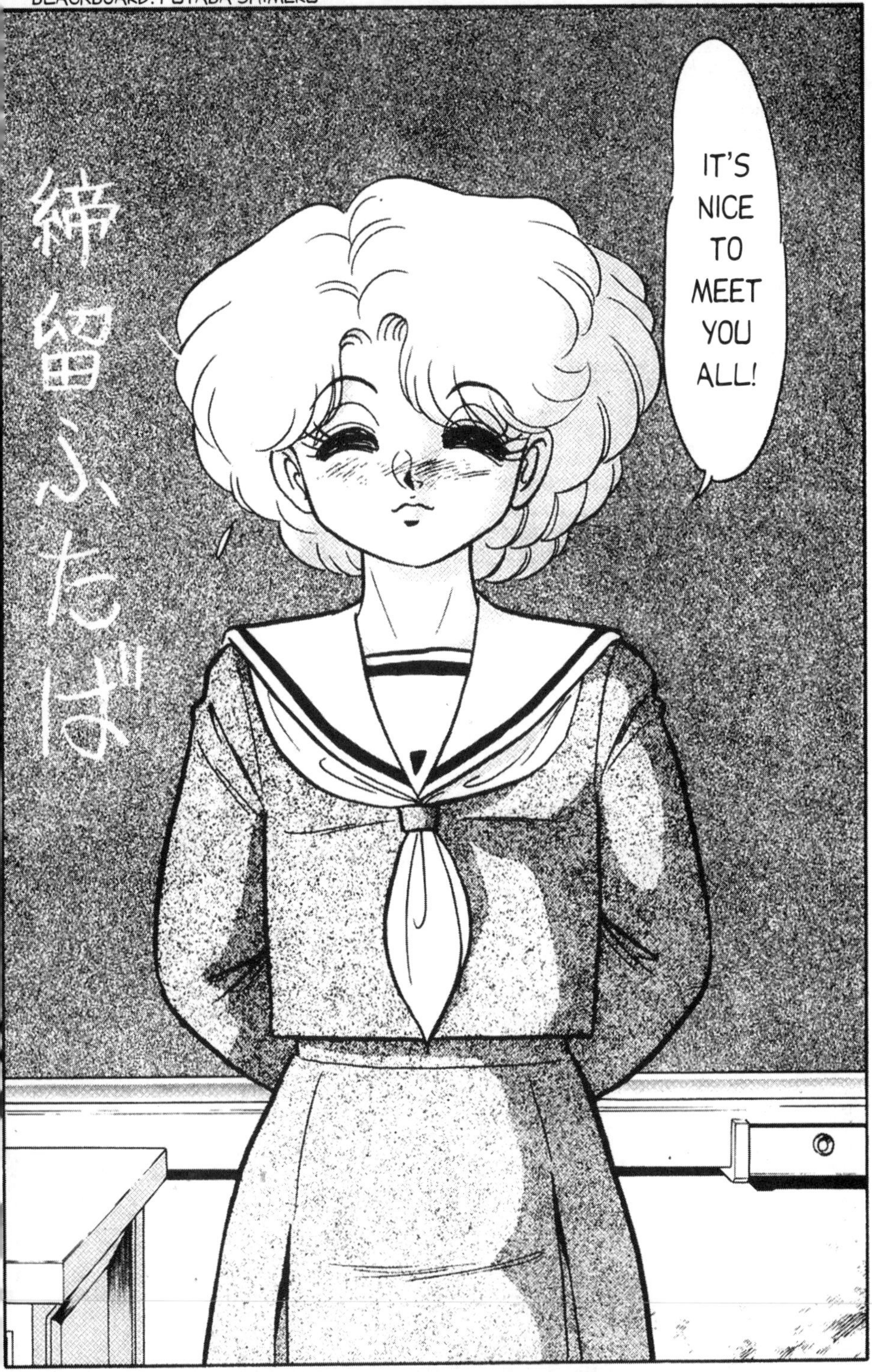
IT'S NICE TO MEET YOU ALL!
締留ふたば

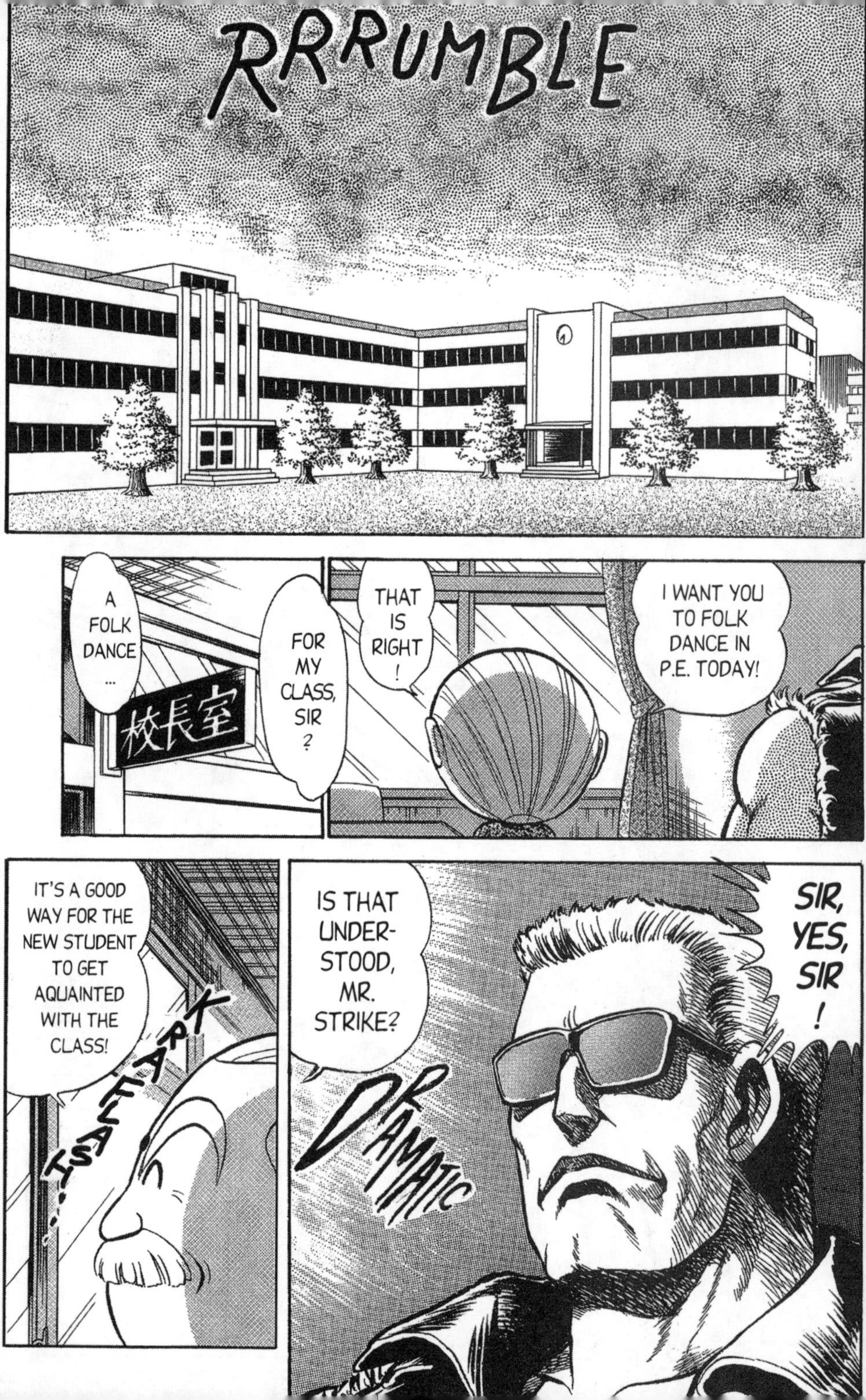
RRRUMBLE
A FOLK DANCE ...
校長室
FOR MY CLASS, SIR?
THAT IS RIGHT!
I WANT YOU TO FOLK DANCE IN P.E. TODAY!
IT'S A GOOD WAY FOR THE NEW STUDENT TO GET AQUAINTED WITH THE CLASS!
KRAFLASH...
IS THAT UNDER-STOOD, MR. STRIKE?
DRAMATIC
SIR, YES, SIR!

Futaba-kun's Wild & Crazy Dance!!

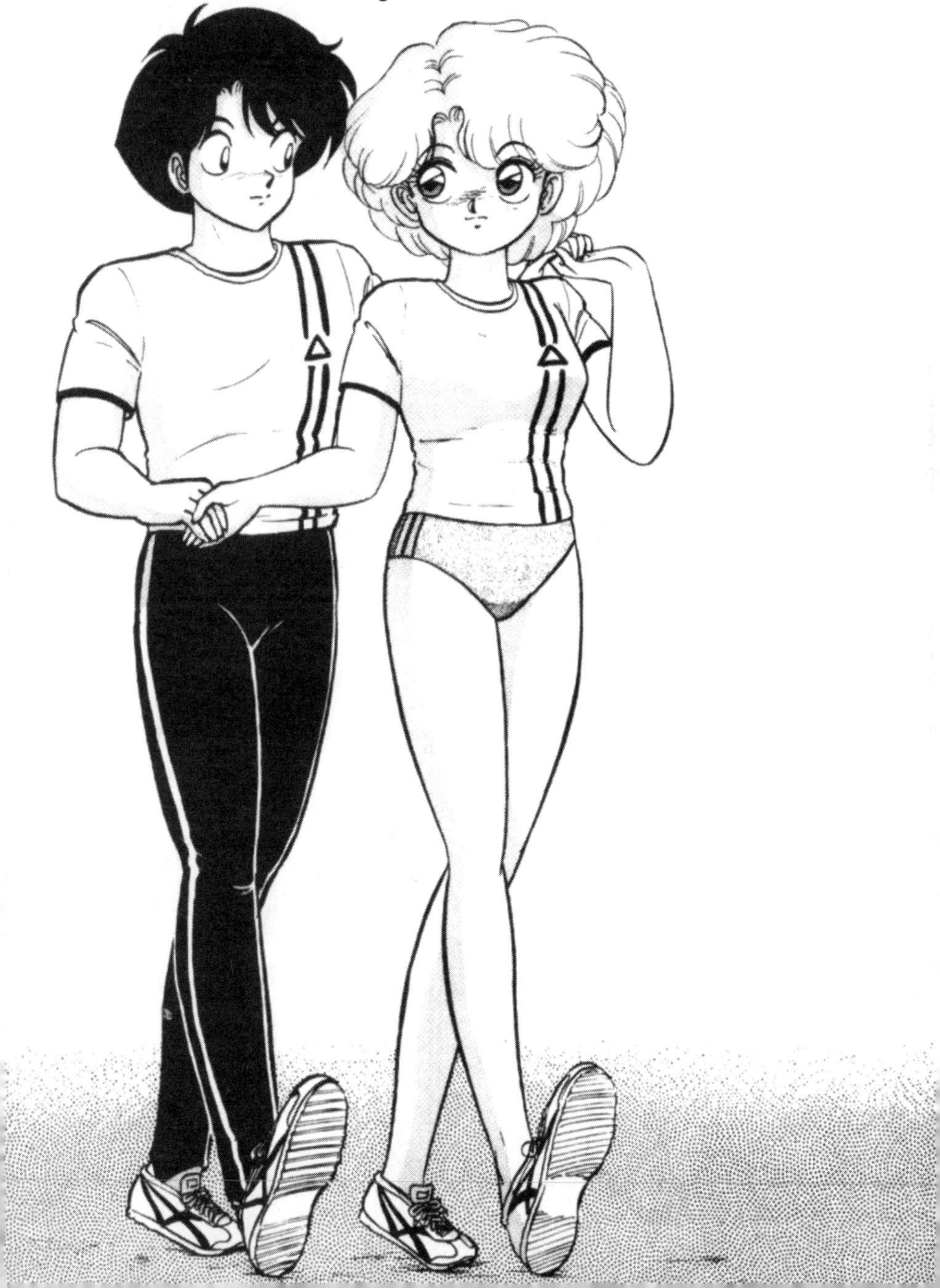

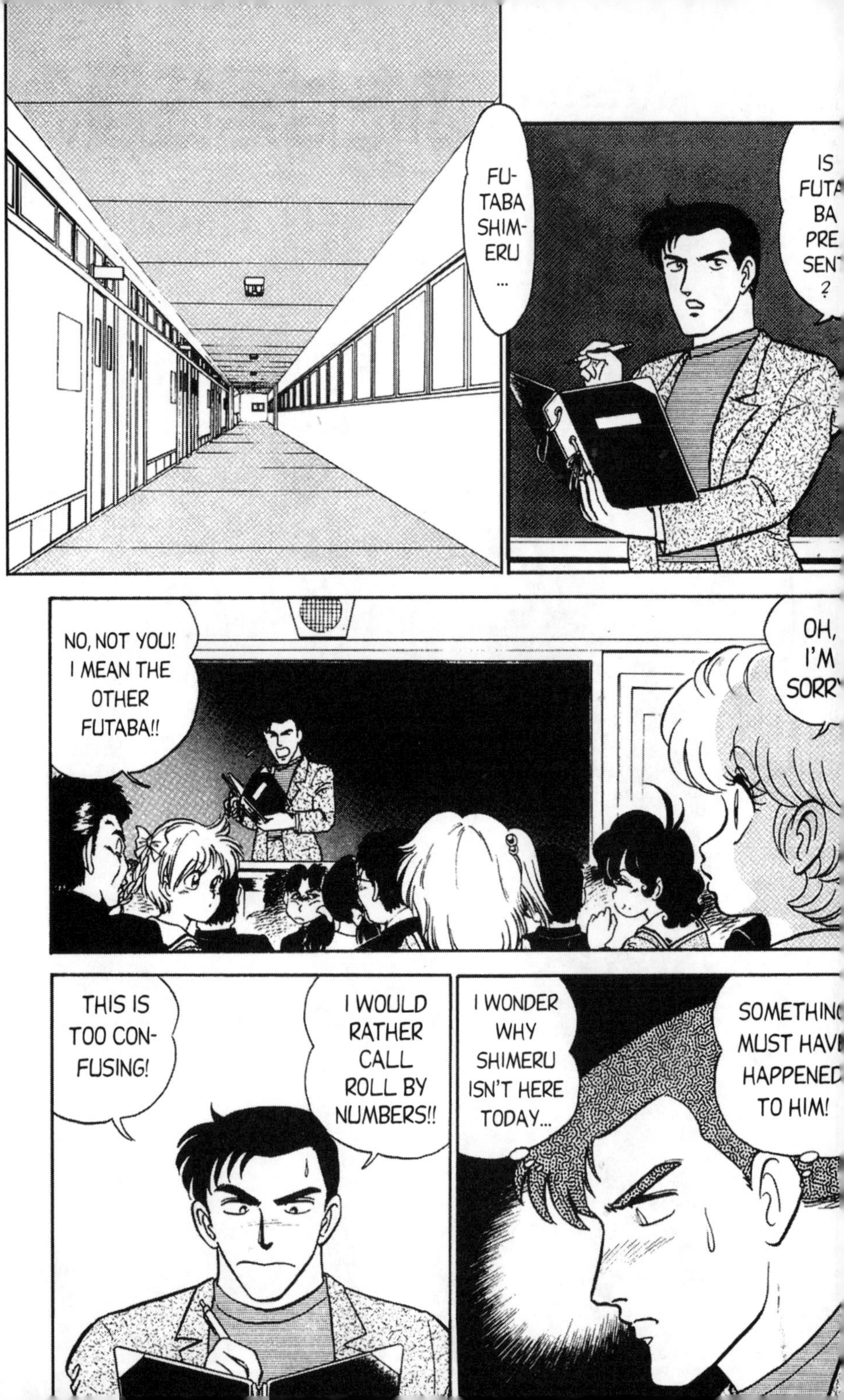
FU-TABA SHIMERU ...
IS FUTABA PRESENT?
NO, NOT YOU! I MEAN THE OTHER FUTABA!!
OH, I'M SORRY
THIS IS TOO CON-FUSING!
I WOULD RATHER CALL ROLL BY NUMBERS!!
I WONDER WHY SHIMERU ISN'T HERE TODAY...
SOMETHING MUST HAVE HAPPENED TO HIM!

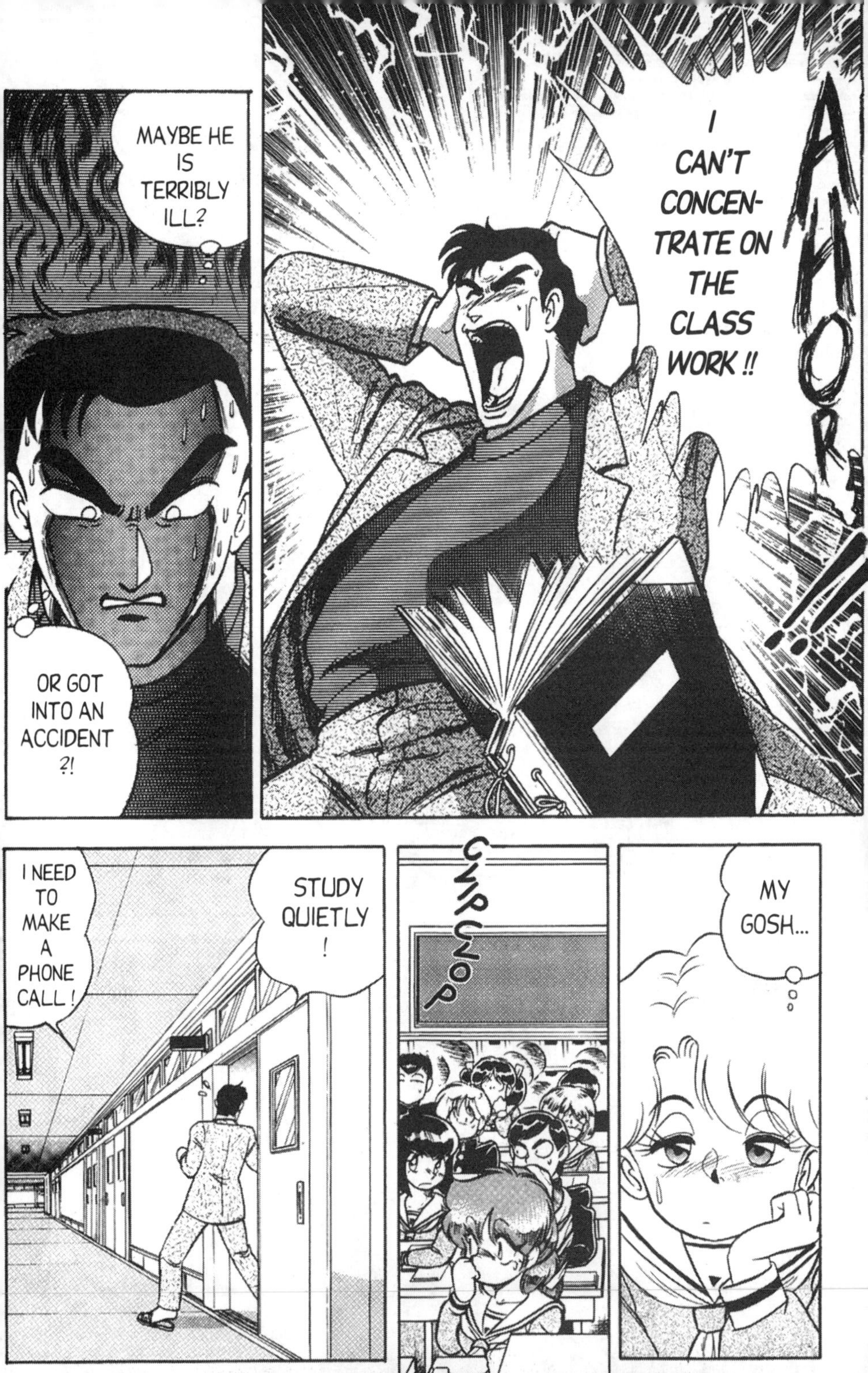
I CAN'T CONCENTRATE ON THE CLASS WORK !!
AHOR!!
MAYBE HE IS TERRIBLY ILL?
OR GOT INTO AN ACCIDENT ?!
MY GOSH...
STUDY QUIETLY !
I NEED TO MAKE A PHONE CALL !

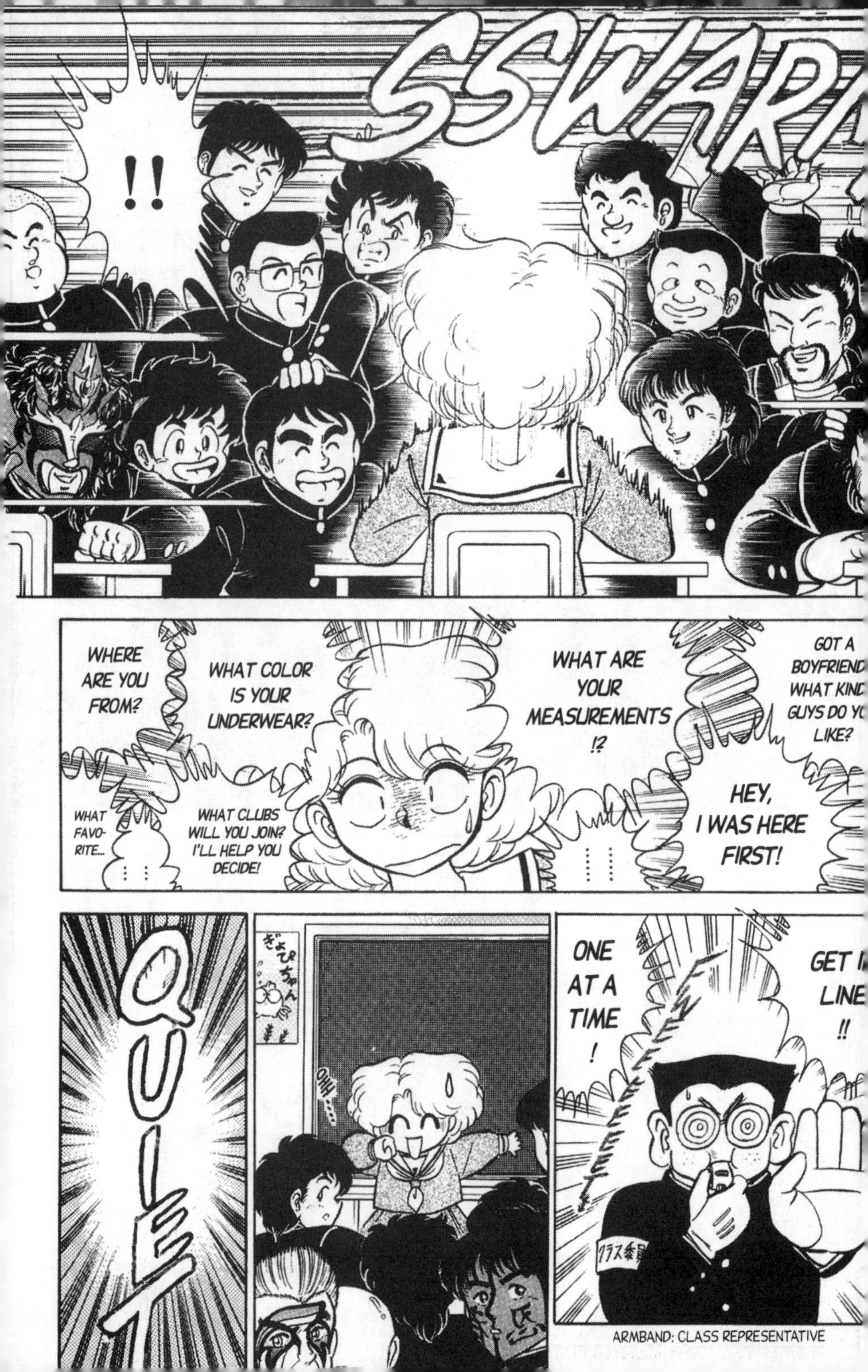
SSWARM
!!
WHERE ARE YOU FROM?
WHAT COLOR IS YOUR UNDERWEAR?
WHAT ARE YOUR MEASUREMENTS !?
GOT A BOYFRIEND WHAT KIND GUYS DO YO LIKE?
WHAT FAVO-RITE...
WHAT CLUBS WILL YOU JOIN? I'LL HELP YOU DECIDE!
HEY, I WAS HERE FIRST!
QUIET
OHH...
ONE AT A TIME !
GET I LINE !!
ARMBAND: CLASS REPRESENTATIVE

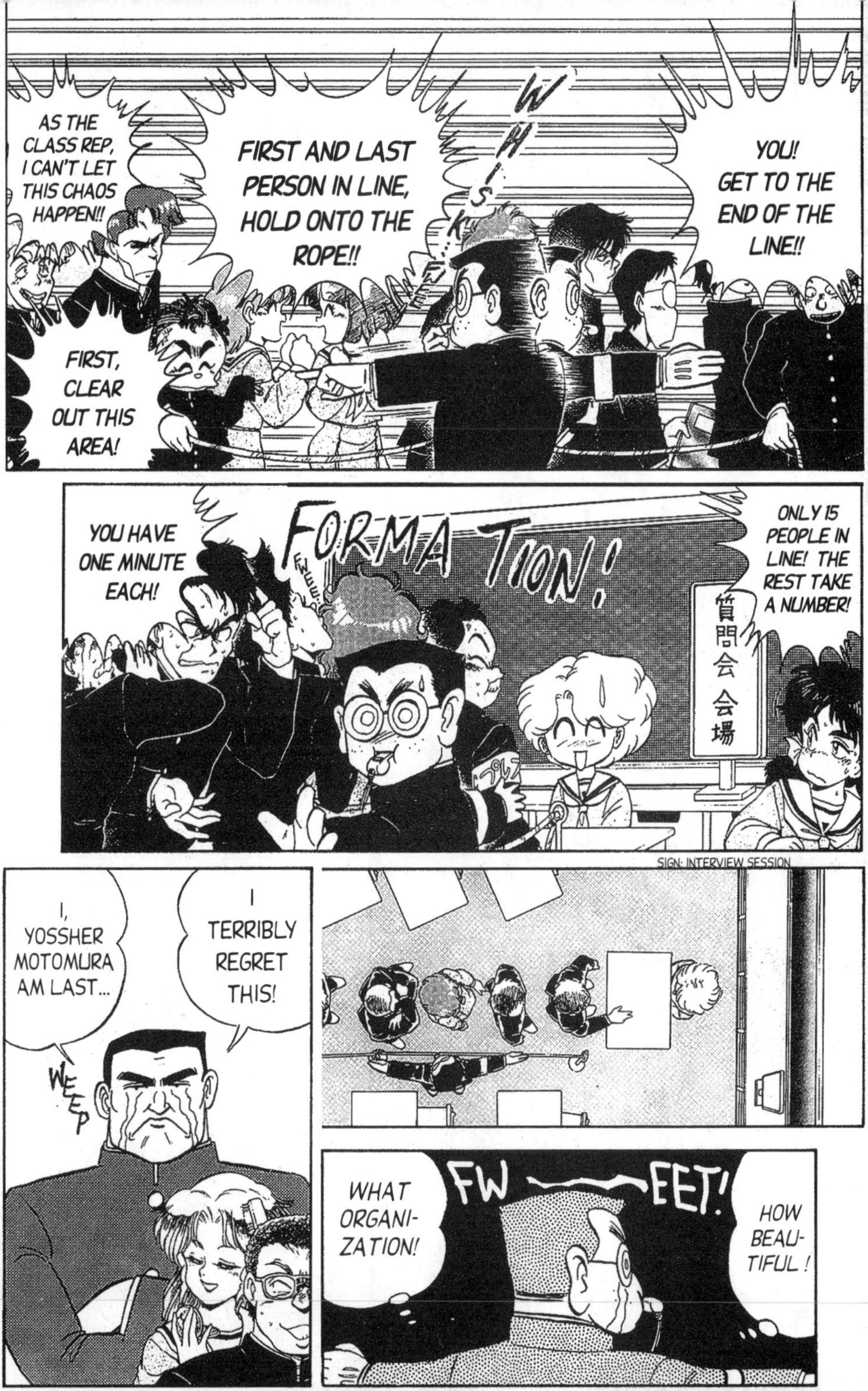

YOU! GET TO THE END OF THE LINE!!
W H I S K... FWEE
FIRST AND LAST PERSON IN LINE, HOLD ONTO THE ROPE!!
AS THE CLASS REP, I CAN'T LET THIS CHAOS HAPPEN!!
FIRST, CLEAR OUT THIS AREA!
ONLY 15 PEOPLE IN LINE! THE REST TAKE A NUMBER!
FORMA TION!
FWEE
YOU HAVE ONE MINUTE EACH!
質問会 会場
SIGN: INTERVIEW SESSION
I TERRIBLY REGRET THIS!
I, YOSSHER MOTOMURA AM LAST...
WEEP
HOW BEAU-TIFUL !
FW——EET!
WHAT ORGANI-ZATION!

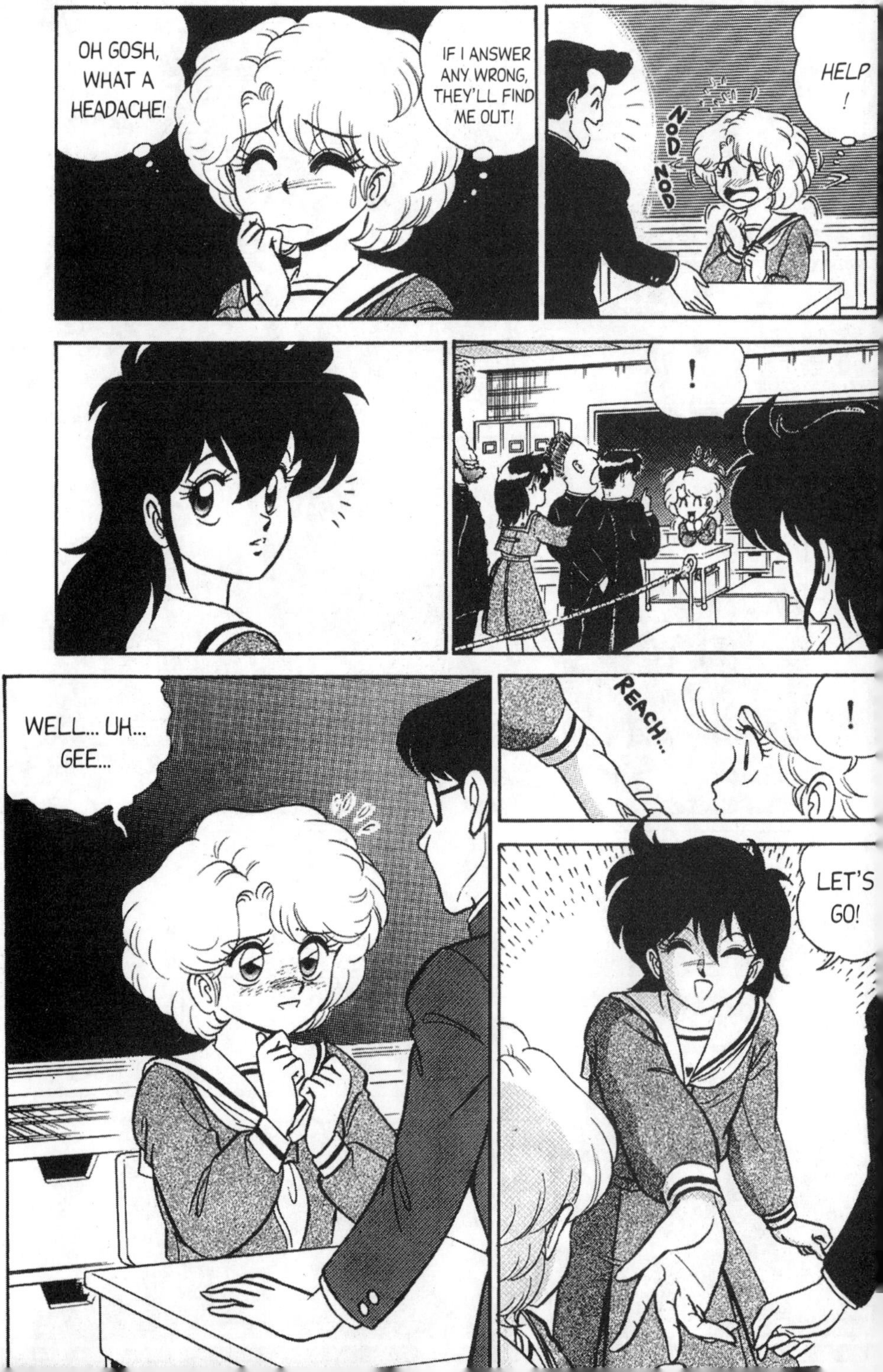
OH GOSH, WHAT A HEADACHE!
IF I ANSWER ANY WRONG, THEY'LL FIND ME OUT!
HELP !
NOD NOD
!
WELL... UH... GEE...
REACH...
!
LET'S GO!

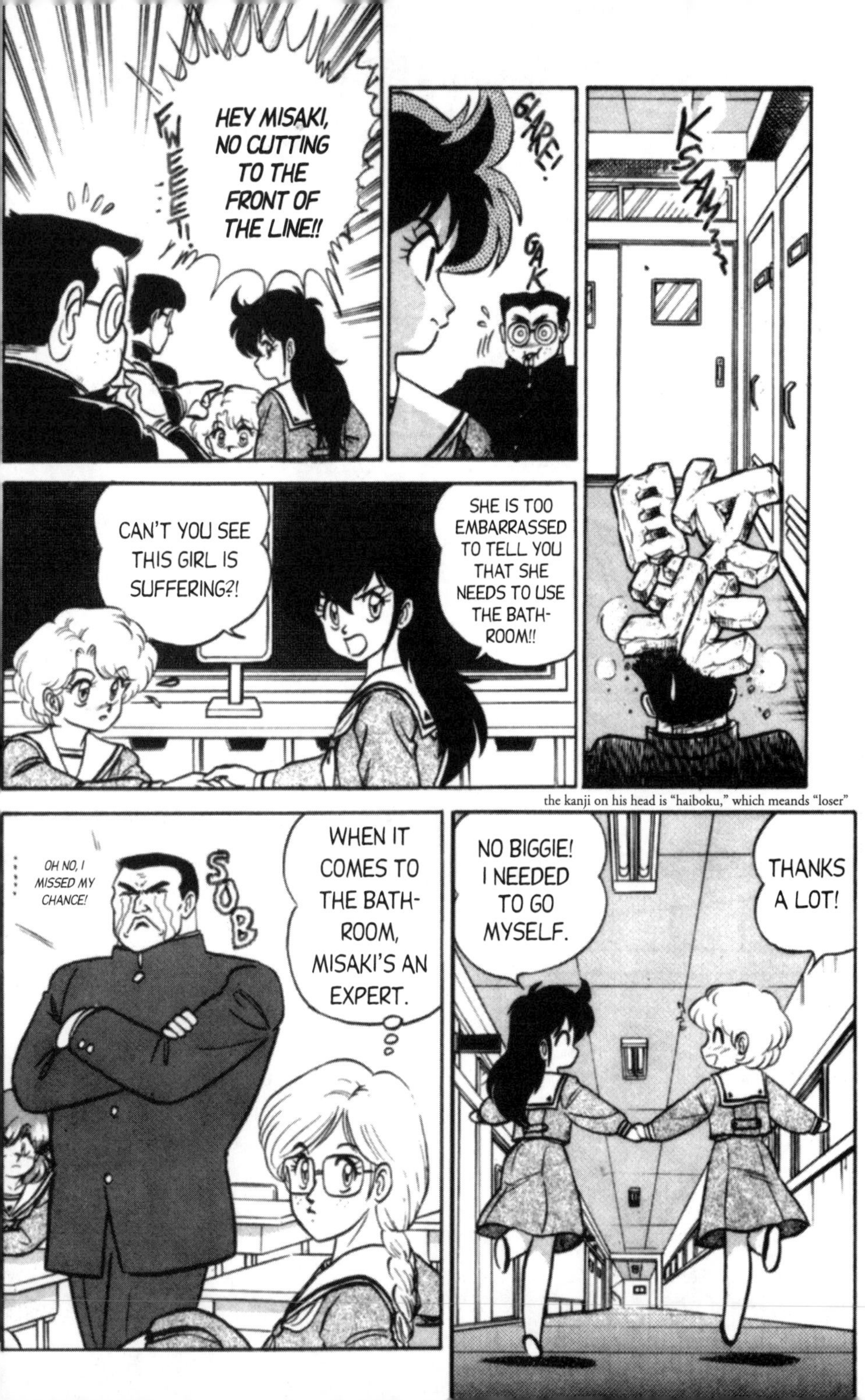
FWEEEET!!
HEY MISAKI, NO CUTTING TO THE FRONT OF THE LINE!!
GLARE!
GAK
KSLAM
CAN'T YOU SEE THIS GIRL IS SUFFERING?!
SHE IS TOO EMBARRASSED TO TELL YOU THAT SHE NEEDS TO USE THE BATHROOM!!
OH NO, I MISSED MY CHANCE!
SOB
WHEN IT COMES TO THE BATHROOM, MISAKI'S AN EXPERT.
NO BIGGIE! I NEEDED TO GO MYSELF.
THANKS A LOT!
the kanji on his head is "haiboku," which meands "loser"

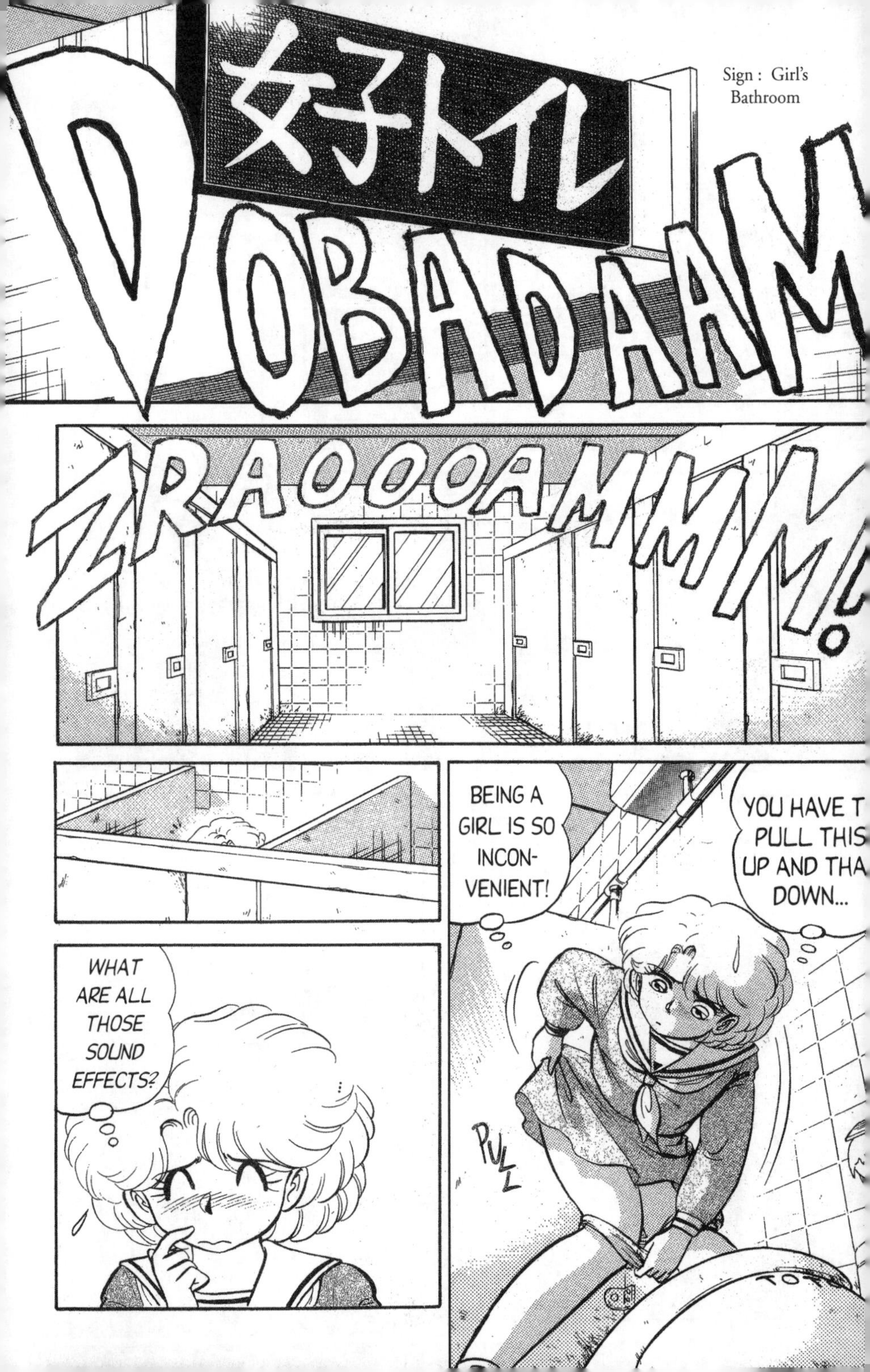
女子トイレ
Sign : Girl's Bathroom
DOBADAAM
ZRAOOOAMMM!
YOU HAVE T PULL THIS UP AND THA DOWN...
BEING A GIRL IS SO INCON-VENIENT!
PULL
WHAT ARE ALL THOSE SOUND EFFECTS?

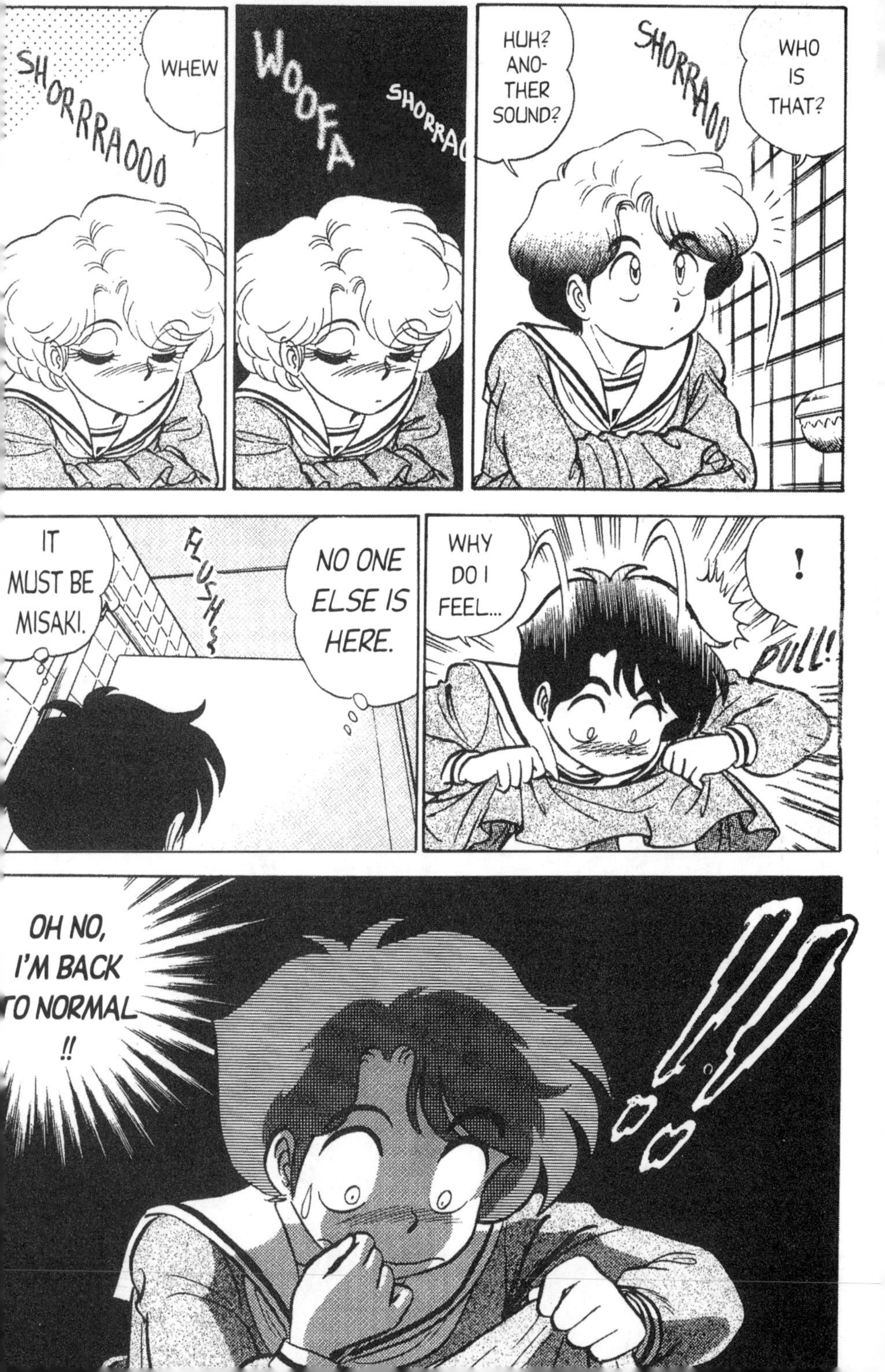

SHORRRAOOO
WHEW
WOOFA
SHORRAO
HUH? ANOTHER SOUND?
SHORRAOO
WHO IS THAT?
IT MUST BE MISAKI.
FLUSH
NO ONE ELSE IS HERE.
WHY DO I FEEL...
!
PULL!
OH NO, I'M BACK TO NORMAL!!

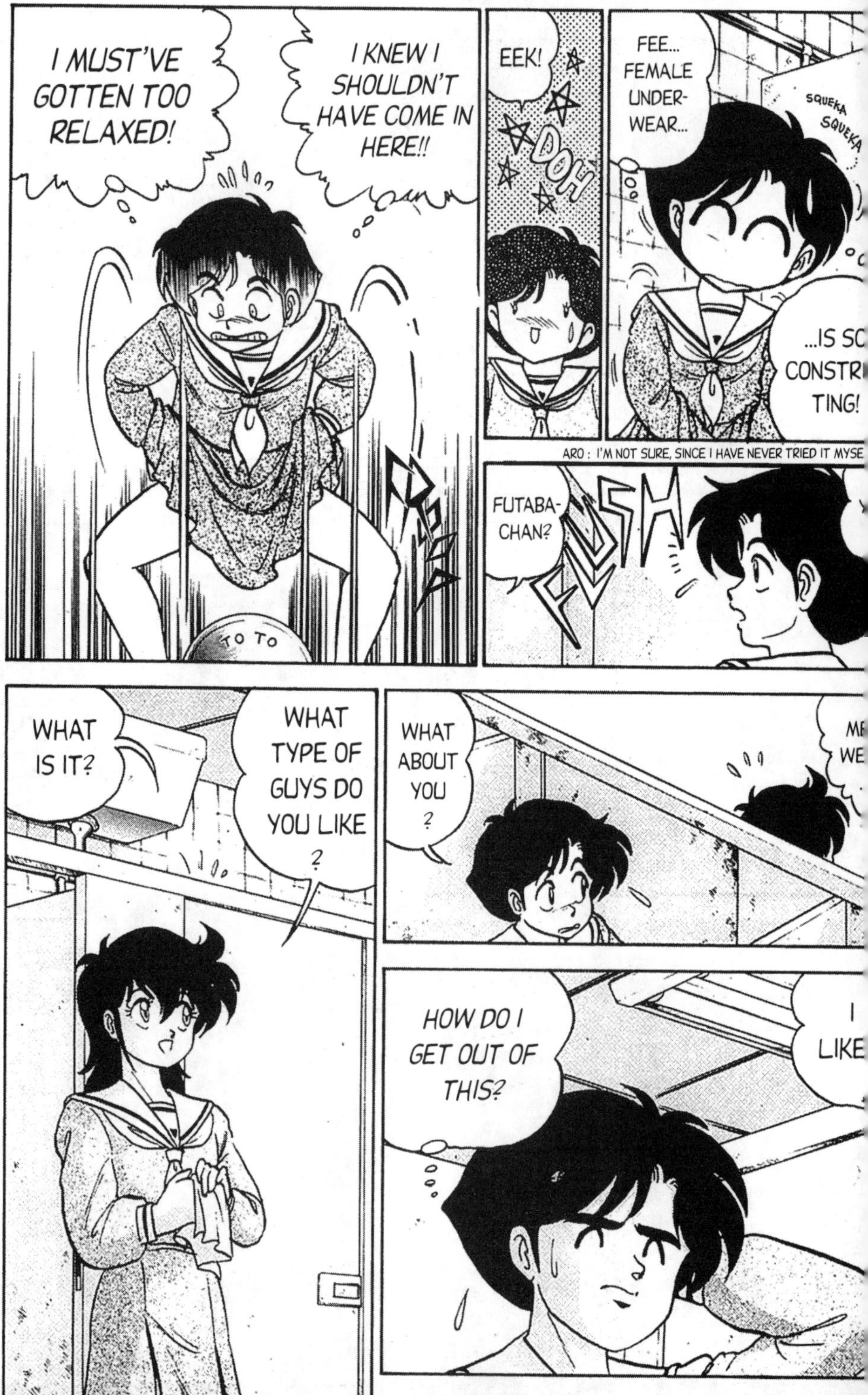
SQUEKA SQUEKA
FEE... FEMALE UNDER-WEAR...
...IS SO CONSTRICTING!
EEK!
DOH
I KNEW I SHOULDN'T HAVE COME IN HERE!!
I MUST'VE GOTTEN TOO RELAXED!
TO TO
ARO : I'M NOT SURE, SINCE I HAVE NEVER TRIED IT MYSE
FLUSH
FUTABA-CHAN?
WHAT IS IT?
WHAT TYPE OF GUYS DO YOU LIKE?
WHAT ABOUT YOU?
I LIKE
HOW DO I GET OUT OF THIS?

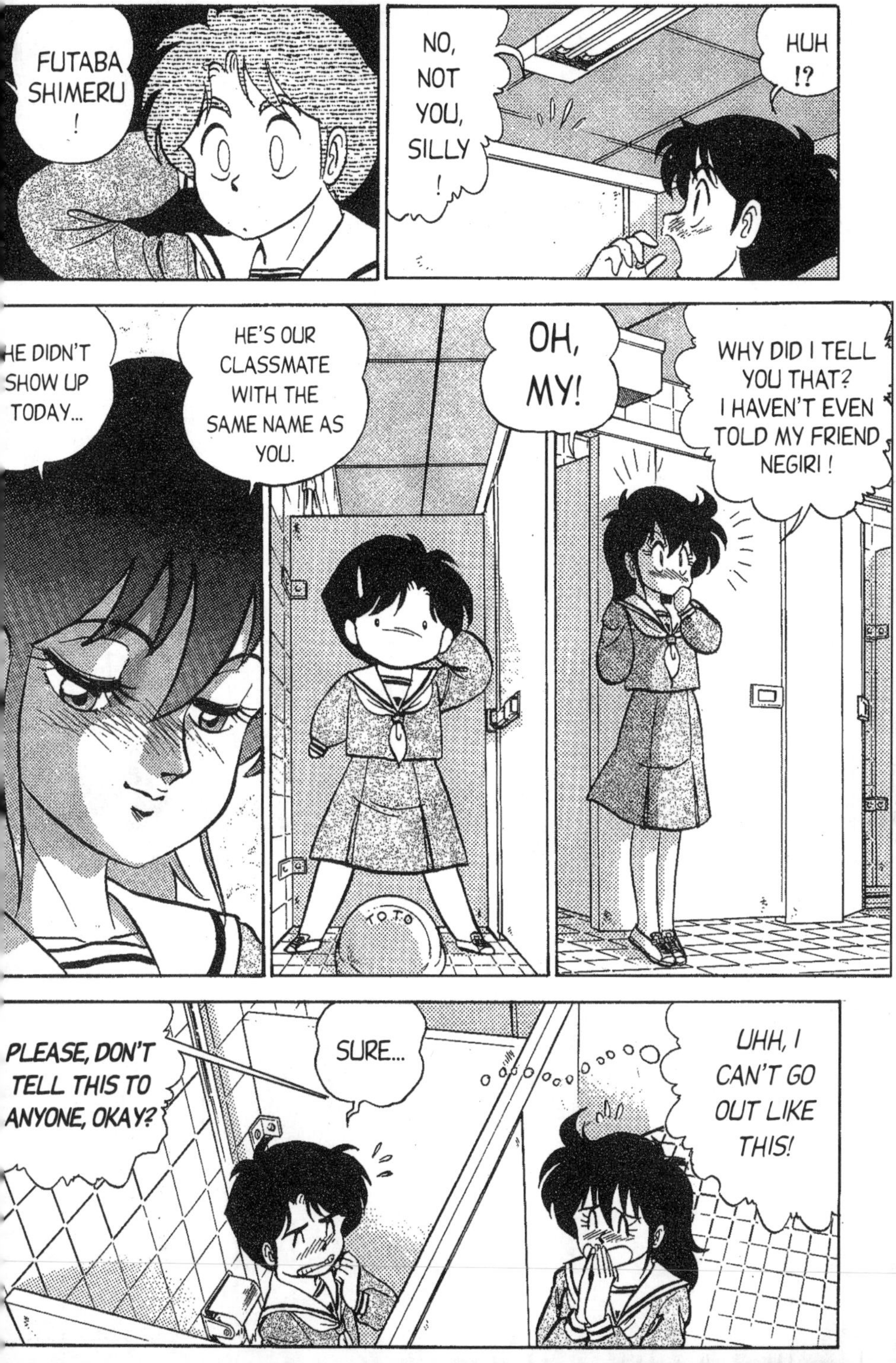
FUTABA SHIMERU !
NO, NOT YOU, SILLY !
HUH !?
HE DIDN'T SHOW UP TODAY...
HE'S OUR CLASSMATE WITH THE SAME NAME AS YOU.
OH, MY!
WHY DID I TELL YOU THAT? I HAVEN'T EVEN TOLD MY FRIEND NEGIRI !
TOTO
PLEASE, DON'T TELL THIS TO ANYONE, OKAY?
SURE...
UHH, I CAN'T GO OUT LIKE THIS!

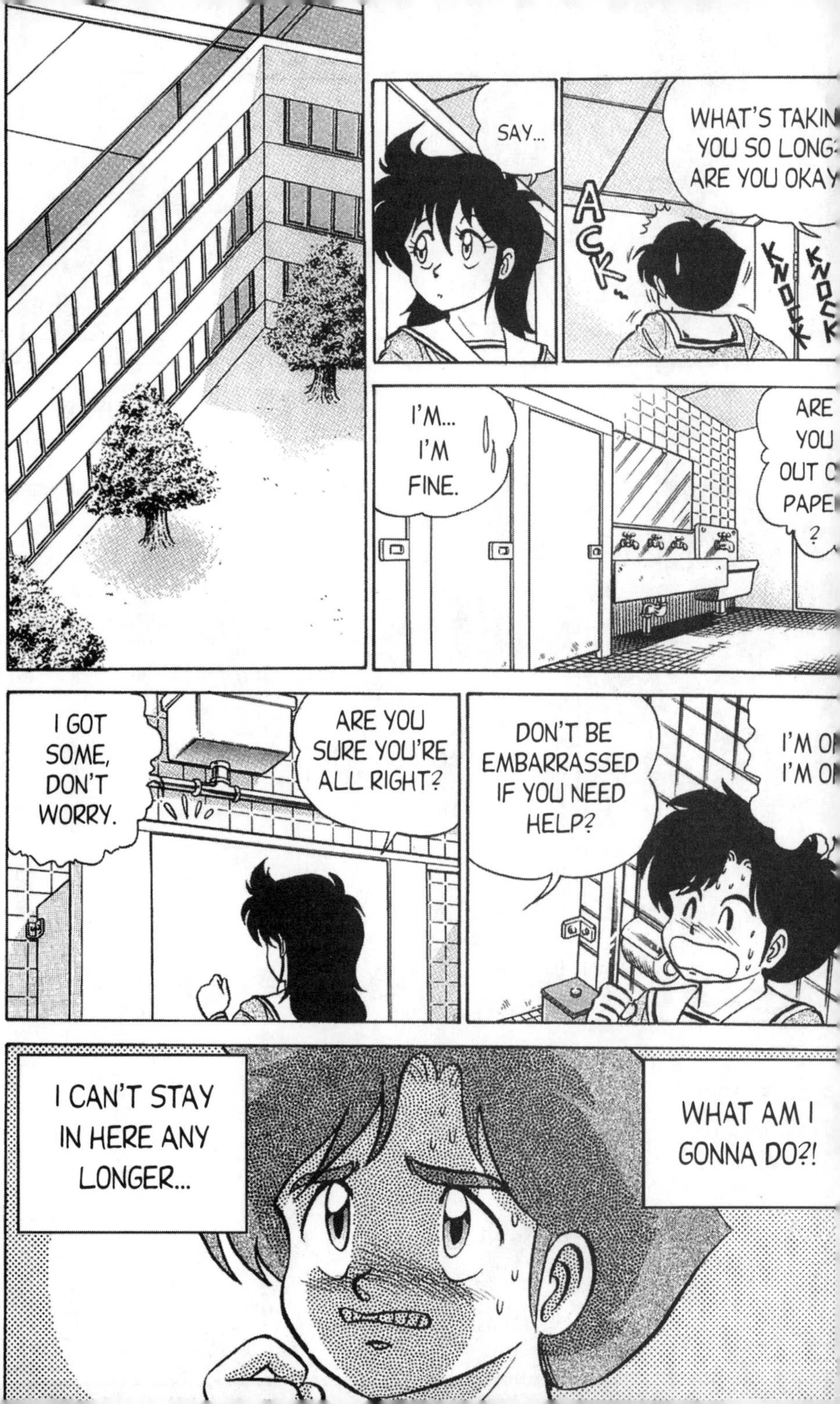
SAY...
WHAT'S TAKIN
YOU SO LONG
ARE YOU OKAY
ACK
KNOCK
KNOCK
I'M... I'M FINE.
ARE YOU OUT O PAPE ?
I GOT SOME, DON'T WORRY.
ARE YOU SURE YOU'RE ALL RIGHT?
DON'T BE EMBARRASSED IF YOU NEED HELP?
I'M O
I'M O
I CAN'T STAY IN HERE ANY LONGER...
WHAT AM I GONNA DO?!

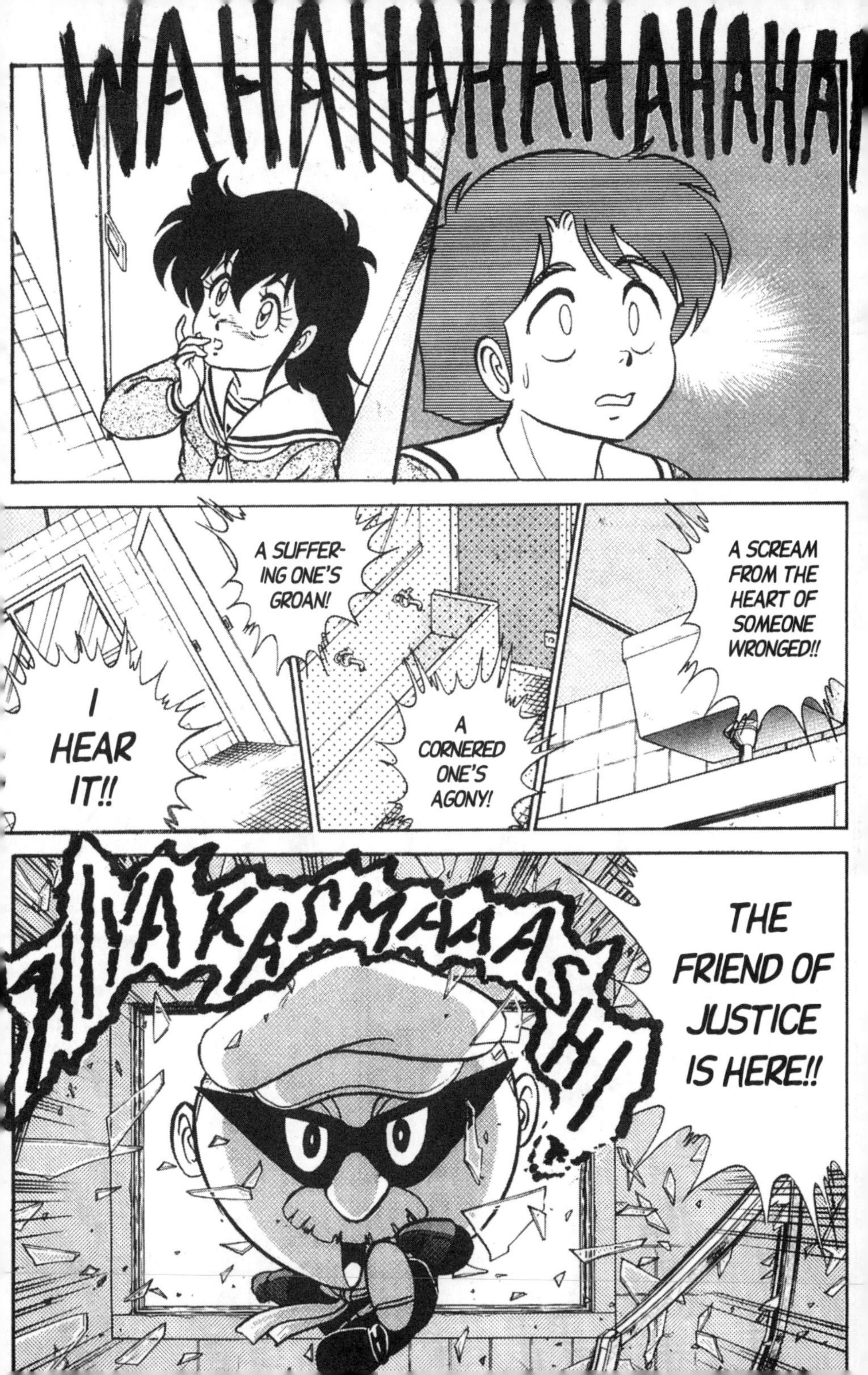
WAHAHAHAHAHAHAHA
A SUFFER-ING ONE'S GROAN!
A SCREAM FROM THE HEART OF SOMEONE WRONGED!!
A CORNERED ONE'S AGONY!
I HEAR IT!!
WAKASMAAAASHI
THE FRIEND OF JUSTICE IS HERE!!

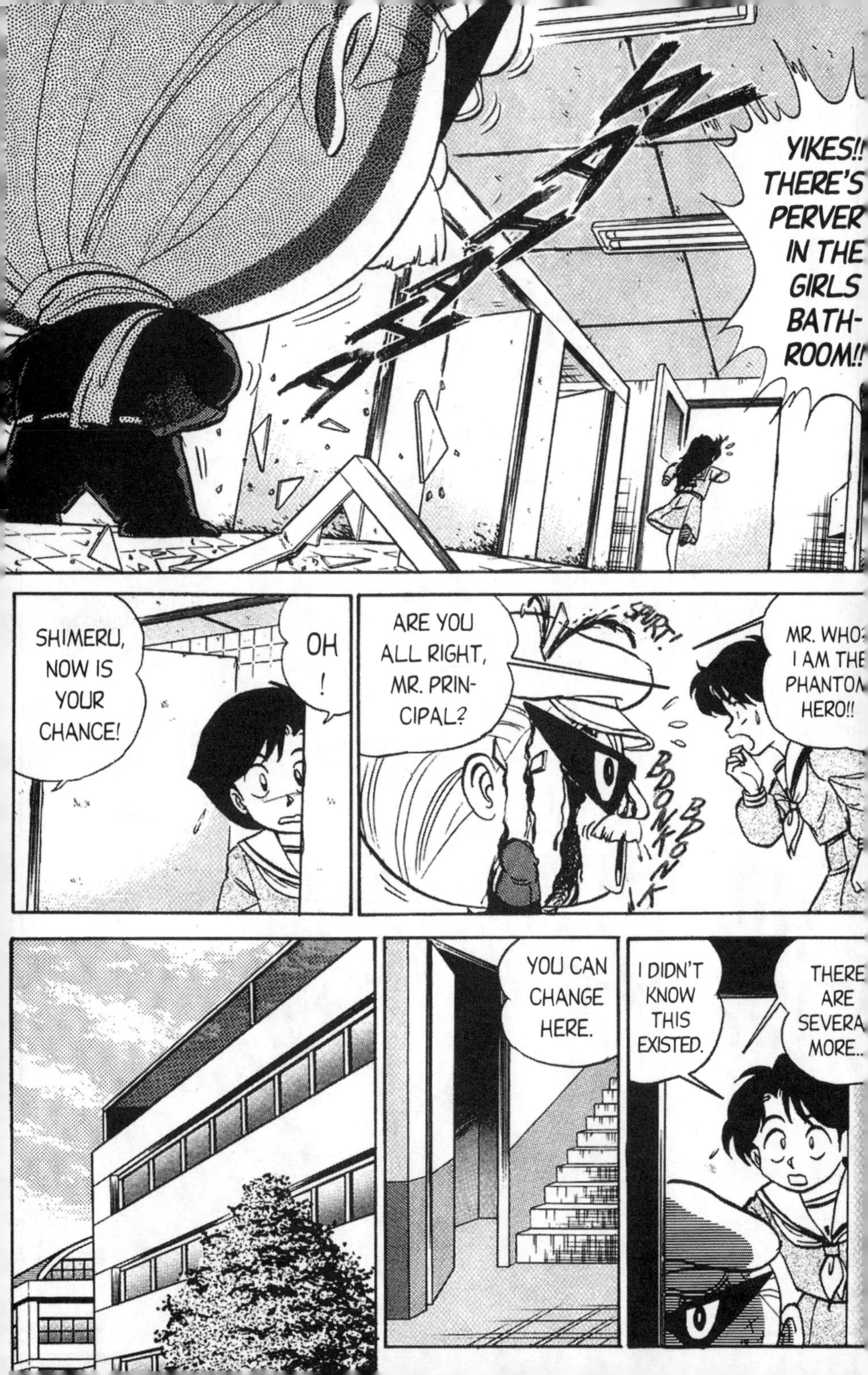

YIKES!! THERE'S PERVER IN THE GIRLS BATH-ROOM!!
AAAAW
SHIMERU, NOW IS YOUR CHANCE!
OH !
MR. WHO? I AM THE PHANTOM HERO!!
SPURT!
ARE YOU ALL RIGHT, MR. PRIN-CIPAL?
BOONK BOONK
YOU CAN CHANGE HERE.
THERE ARE SEVERA MORE..
I DIDN'T KNOW THIS EXISTED.

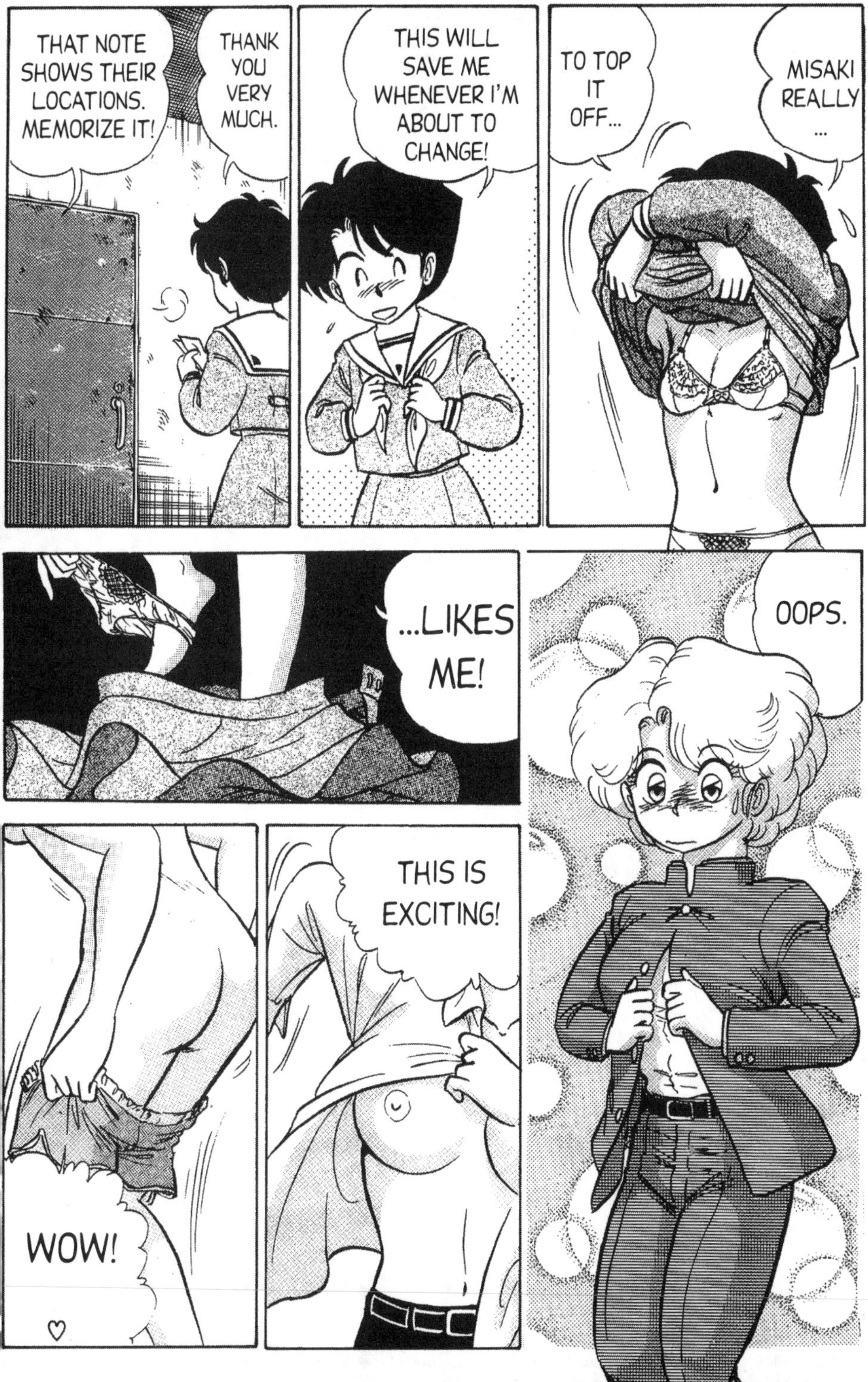

THAT NOTE SHOWS THEIR LOCATIONS. MEMORIZE IT!
THANK YOU VERY MUCH.
THIS WILL SAVE ME WHENEVER I'M ABOUT TO CHANGE!
TO TOP IT OFF...
MISAKI REALLY ...
...LIKES ME!
WOW!
♡
THIS IS EXCITING!
OOPS.

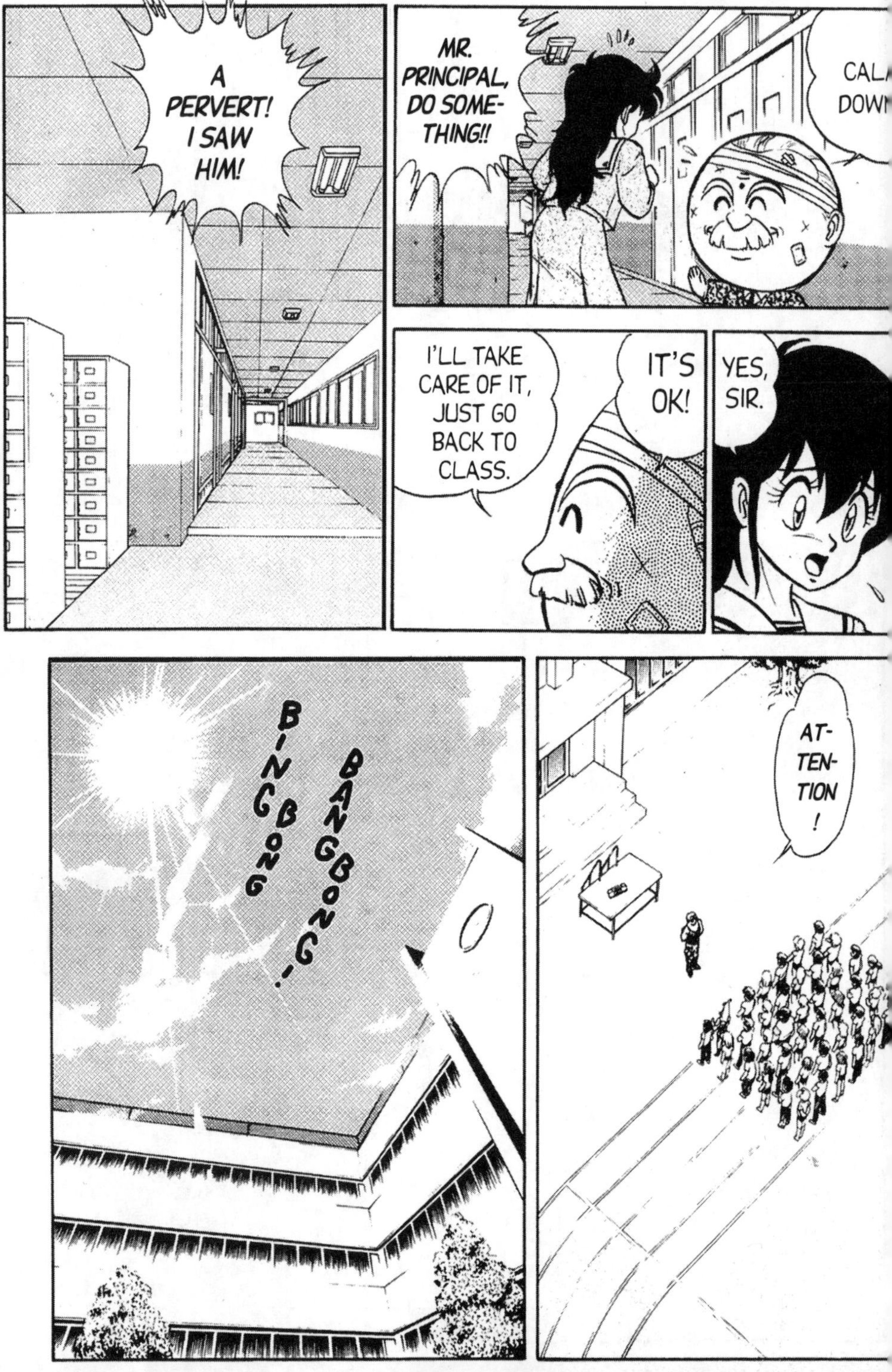
A PERVERT! I SAW HIM!
MR. PRINCIPAL, DO SOME-THING!!
CAL DOW
I'LL TAKE CARE OF IT, JUST GO BACK TO CLASS.
IT'S OK!
YES, SIR.
BINGBONG BANGBONG...
AT-TEN-TION!

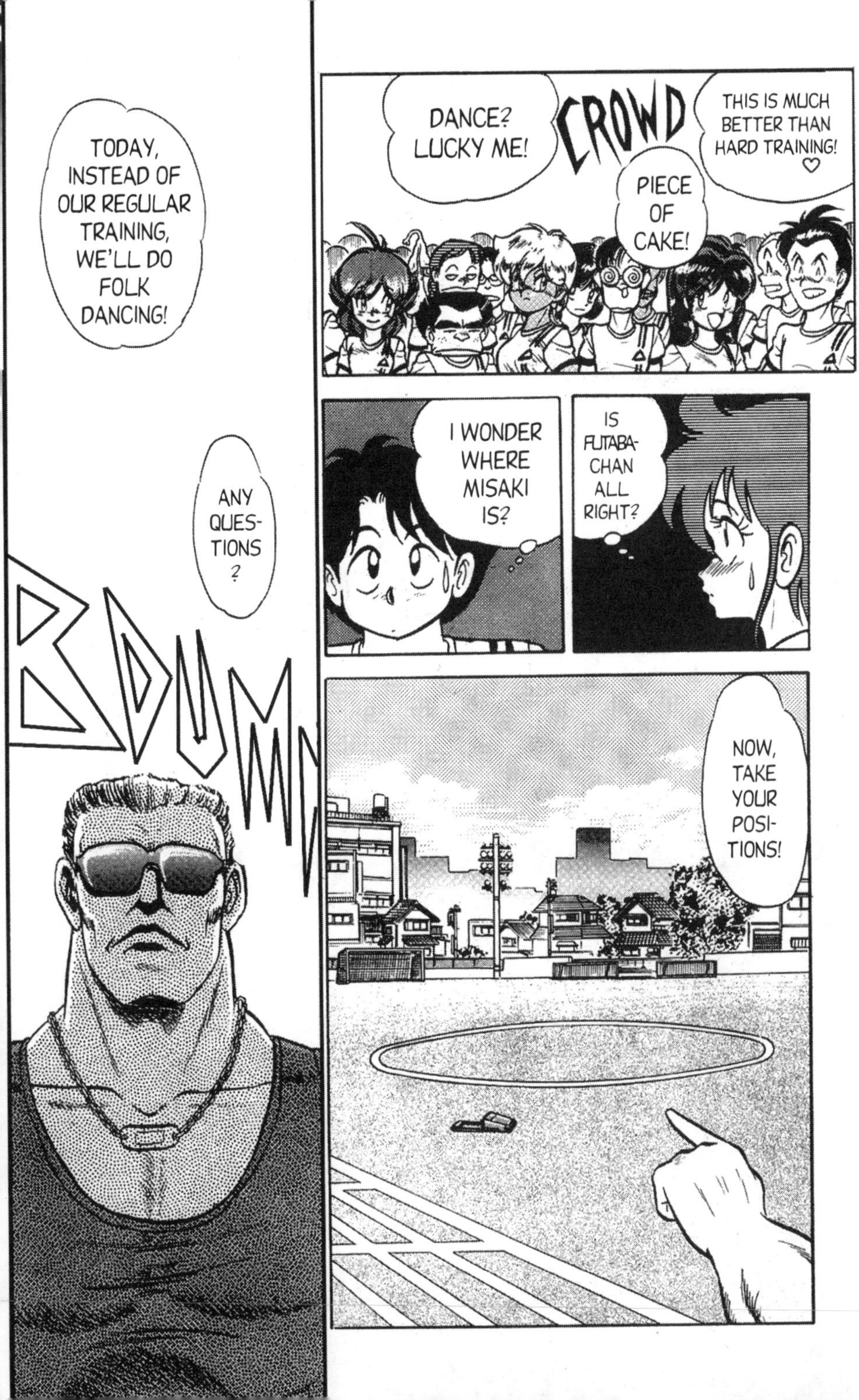

TODAY, INSTEAD OF OUR REGULAR TRAINING, WE'LL DO FOLK DANCING!
ANY QUESTIONS?
RDUM
DANCE? LUCKY ME!
CROWD
PIECE OF CAKE!
THIS IS MUCH BETTER THAN HARD TRAINING! ♡
I WONDER WHERE MISAKI IS?
IS FUTABA-CHAN ALL RIGHT?
NOW, TAKE YOUR POSITIONS!

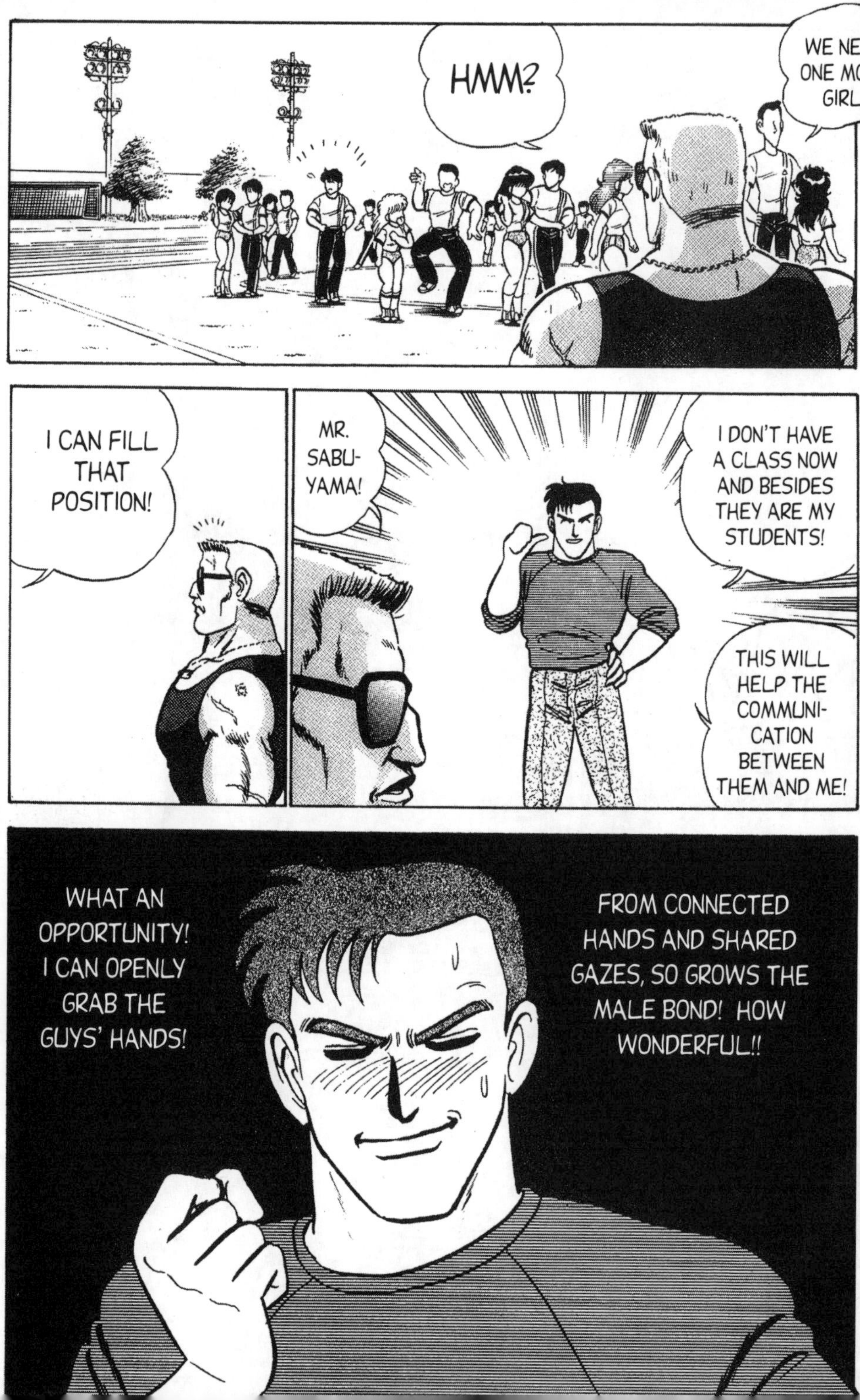
HMM?
WE NEE
ONE MOR
GIRL!
I CAN FILL THAT POSITION!
MR. SABU-YAMA!
I DON'T HAVE A CLASS NOW AND BESIDES THEY ARE MY STUDENTS!
THIS WILL HELP THE COMMUNI-CATION BETWEEN THEM AND ME!
WHAT AN OPPORTUNITY! I CAN OPENLY GRAB THE GUYS' HANDS!
FROM CONNECTED HANDS AND SHARED GAZES, SO GROWS THE MALE BOND! HOW WONDERFUL!!

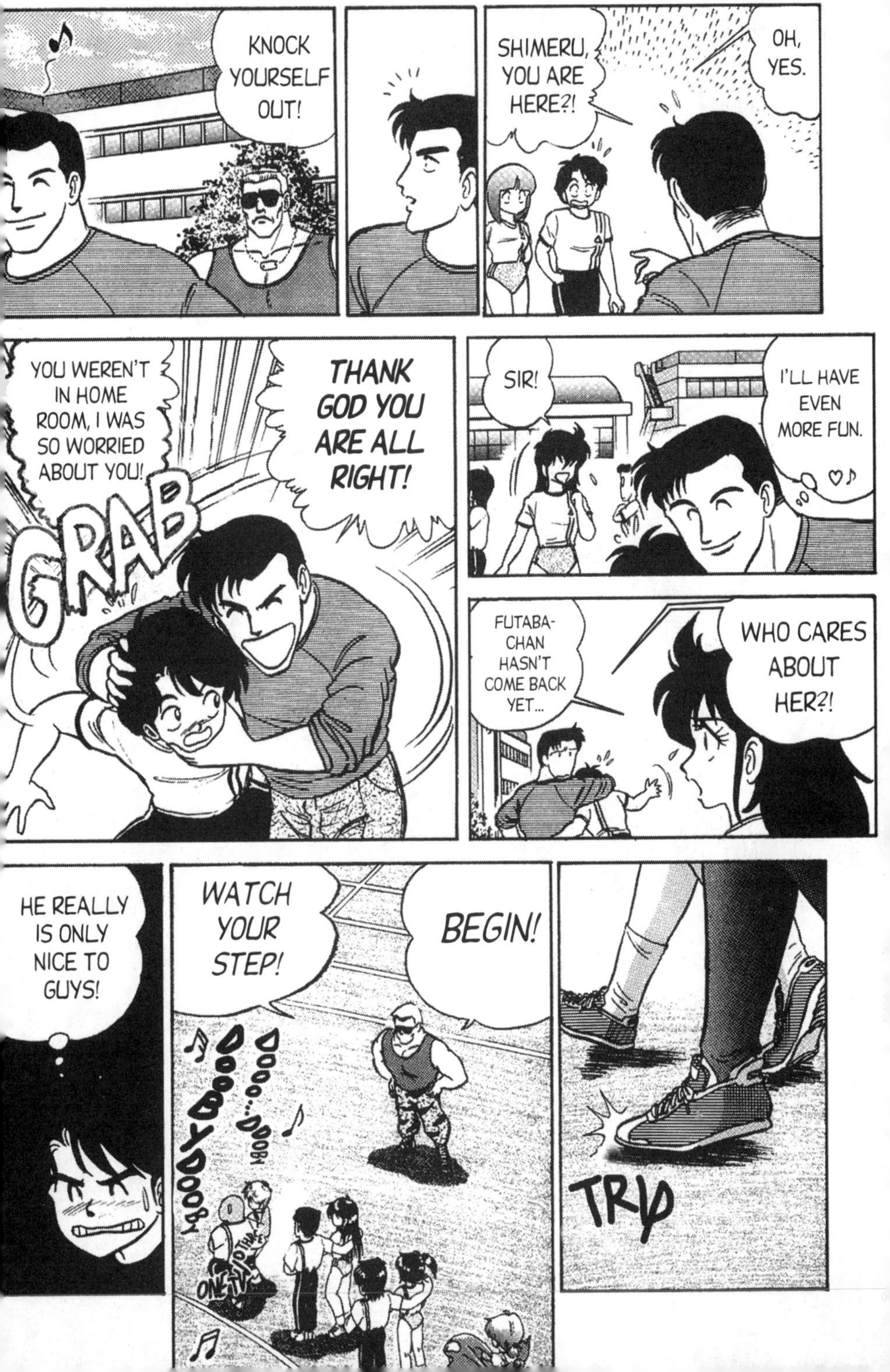
KNOCK YOURSELF OUT!
SHIMERU, YOU ARE HERE?!
OH, YES.
YOU WEREN'T IN HOME ROOM, I WAS SO WORRIED ABOUT YOU!
THANK GOD YOU ARE ALL RIGHT!
GRAB
SIR!
I'LL HAVE EVEN MORE FUN.
FUTABA-CHAN HASN'T COME BACK YET...
WHO CARES ABOUT HER?!
HE REALLY IS ONLY NICE TO GUYS!
WATCH YOUR STEP!
BEGIN!
TRIP

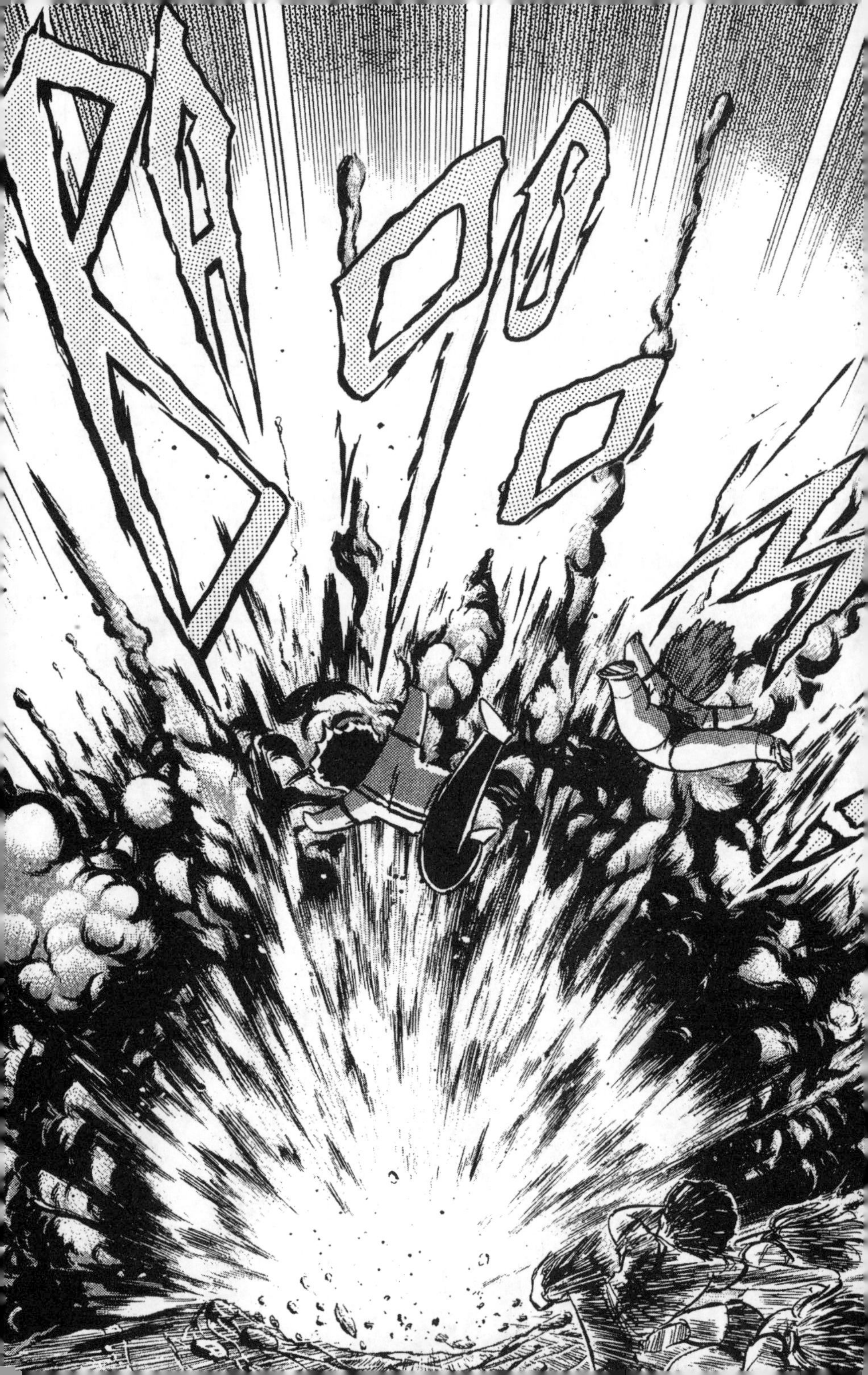

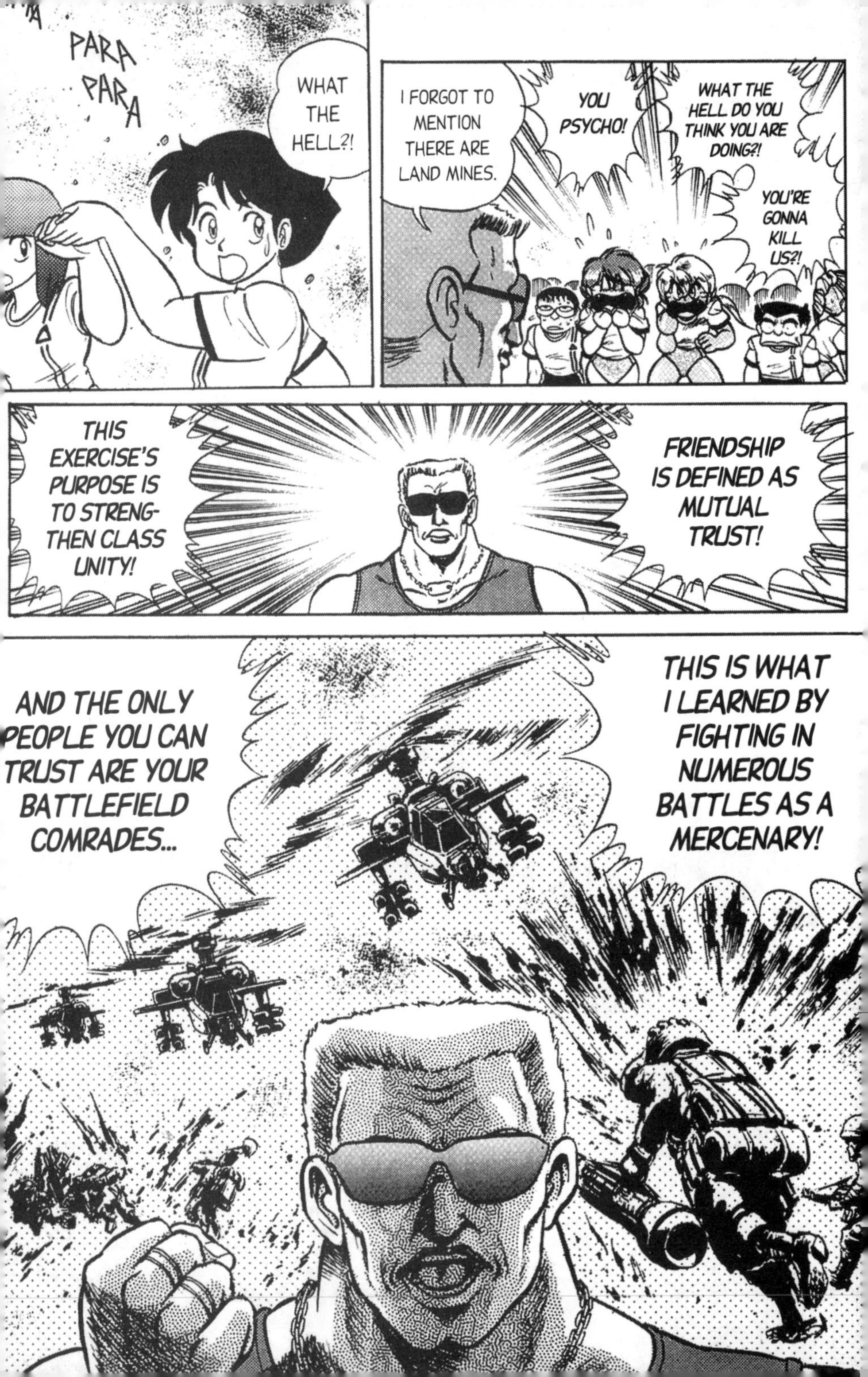
PARA PARA PARA
WHAT THE HELL?!
I FORGOT TO MENTION THERE ARE LAND MINES.
YOU PSYCHO!
WHAT THE HELL DO YOU THINK YOU ARE DOING?!
YOU'RE GONNA KILL US?!
THIS EXERCISE'S PURPOSE IS TO STRENGTHEN CLASS UNITY!
FRIENDSHIP IS DEFINED AS MUTUAL TRUST!
AND THE ONLY PEOPLE YOU CAN TRUST ARE YOUR BATTLEFIELD COMRADES...
THIS IS WHAT I LEARNED BY FIGHTING IN NUMEROUS BATTLES AS A MERCENARY!

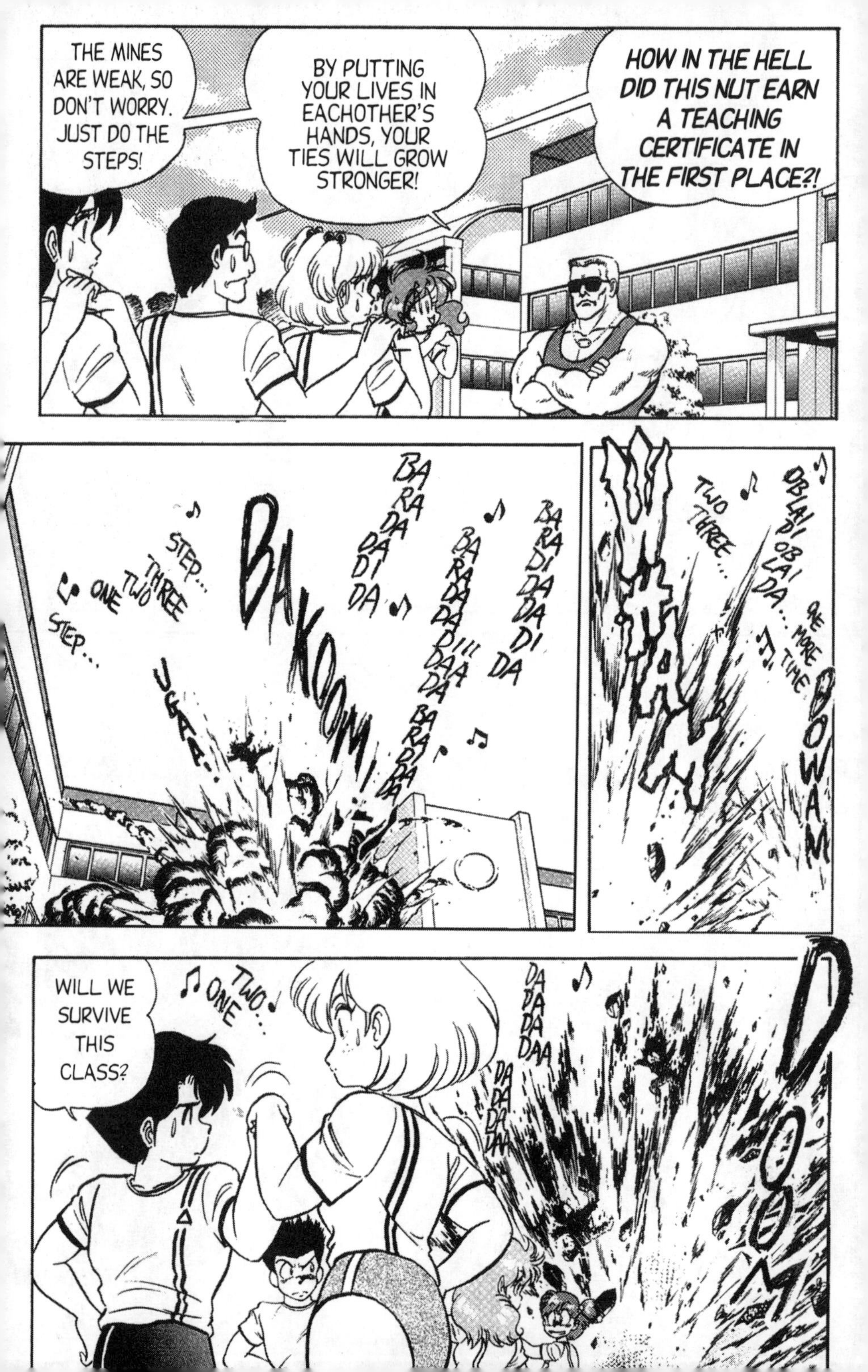
THE MINES ARE WEAK, SO DON'T WORRY. JUST DO THE STEPS!
BY PUTTING YOUR LIVES IN EACHOTHER'S HANDS, YOUR TIES WILL GROW STRONGER!
HOW IN THE HELL DID THIS NUT EARN A TEACHING CERTIFICATE IN THE FIRST PLACE?!
ONE TWO THREE STEP... STEP...
BAKOOOM!!
UGAAA!!
BA RA DA DA DI DA
BA RA DA DA DI!!! DAAA DA
BA RA DI DA DA
BA RA DI DA DA DI DA
TWO THREE...
OB LA DI OB LA DA...
ONE MORE TIME
BOWAM
WILL WE SURVIVE THIS CLASS?
ONE TWO...
DA DA DA DA DAA
DA DA DA DA DAA

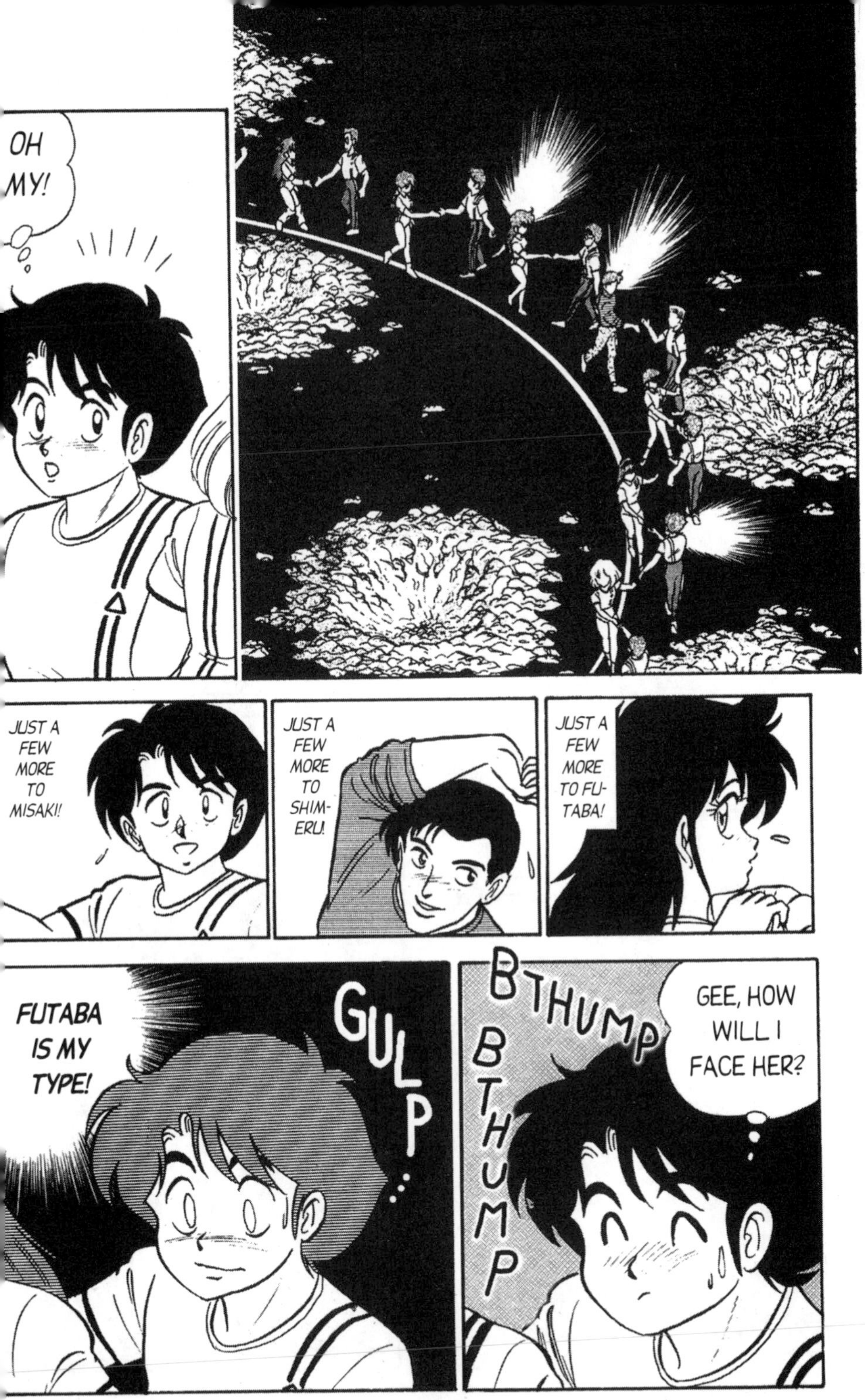
OH MY!
JUST A FEW MORE TO MISAKI!
JUST A FEW MORE TO SHIM-ERU!
JUST A FEW MORE TO FU-TABA!
FUTABA IS MY TYPE!
GULP...
BTHUMP
BTHUMP
GEE, HOW WILL I FACE HER?

KPING

NO!

I FEEL A TRANS-FORMATION COMING!

I'M GETTING TOO CLOSE!!

KATHUMP KATHUMP KATHUMP

KATHUMP KATHUMP KATHUMP

I'M GETTING TOO EX-CITED!

A SECRET ROOM IS CLOSE BY...

SIR

MRF!

I'VE GOT TO USE THE RESTROOM!

OH NO ?!

WHA WHER IS H GOIN NOW ?

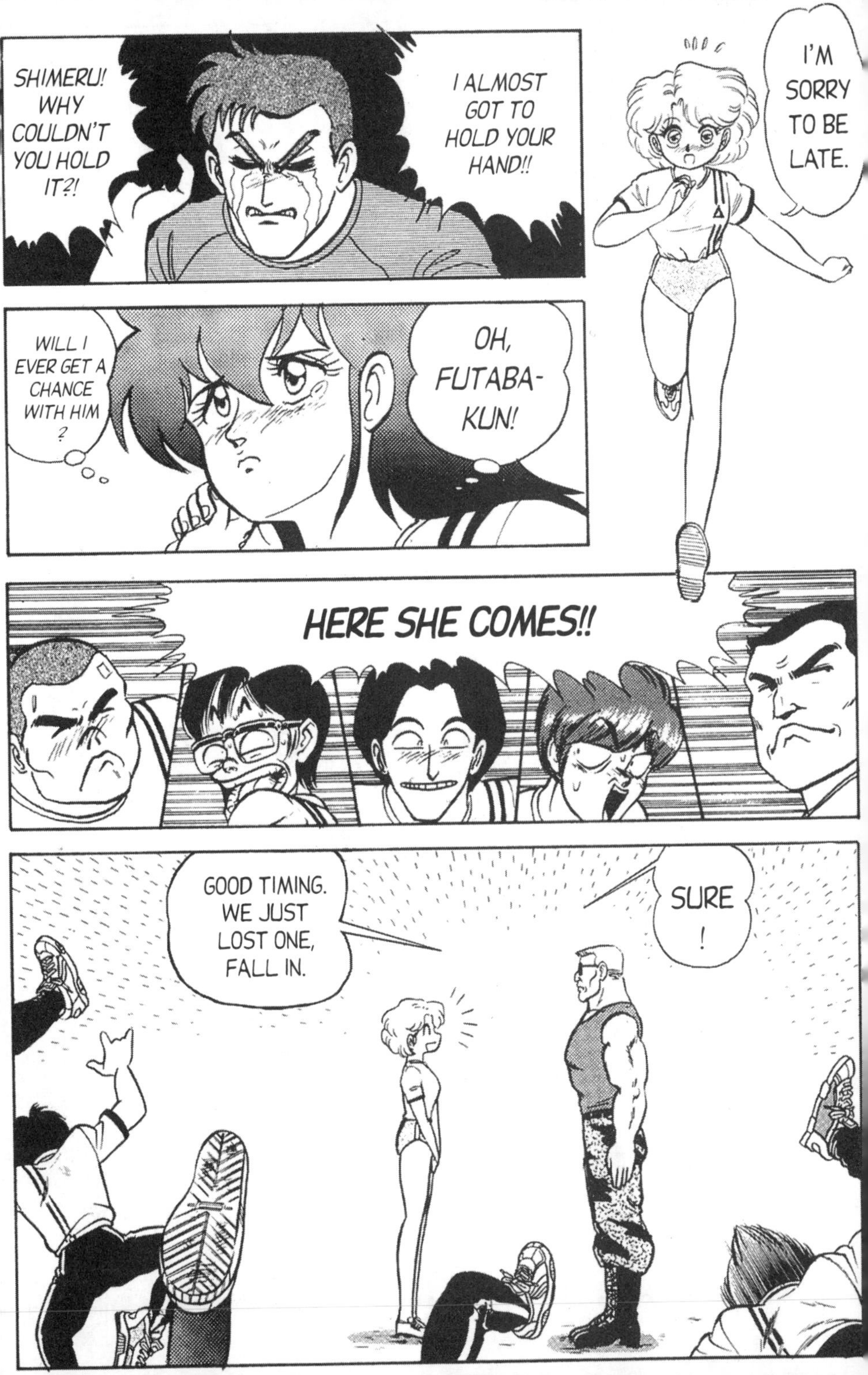
SHIMERU! WHY COULDN'T YOU HOLD IT?!
I ALMOST GOT TO HOLD YOUR HAND!!
WILL I EVER GET A CHANCE WITH HIM?
OH, FUTABA-KUN!
I'M SORRY TO BE LATE.
HERE SHE COMES!!
GOOD TIMING. WE JUST LOST ONE, FALL IN.
SURE!

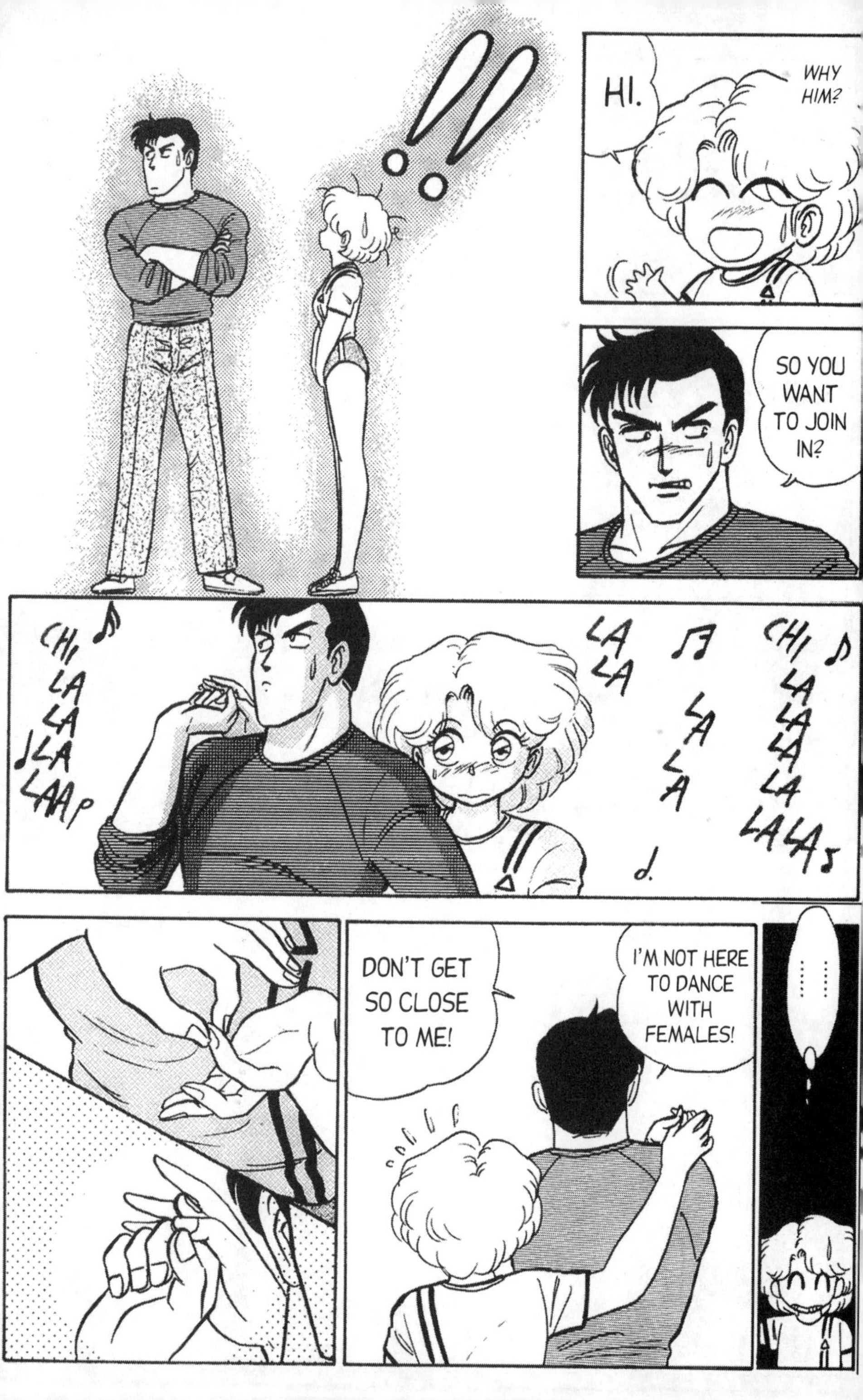

!!
HI.
WHY HIM?
SO YOU WANT TO JOIN IN?
CHI LA LA LA LAAA
LA LA
LA LA LA
CHI LA LA LA LA LA LA LA
DON'T GET SO CLOSE TO ME!
I'M NOT HERE TO DANCE WITH FEMALES!
......

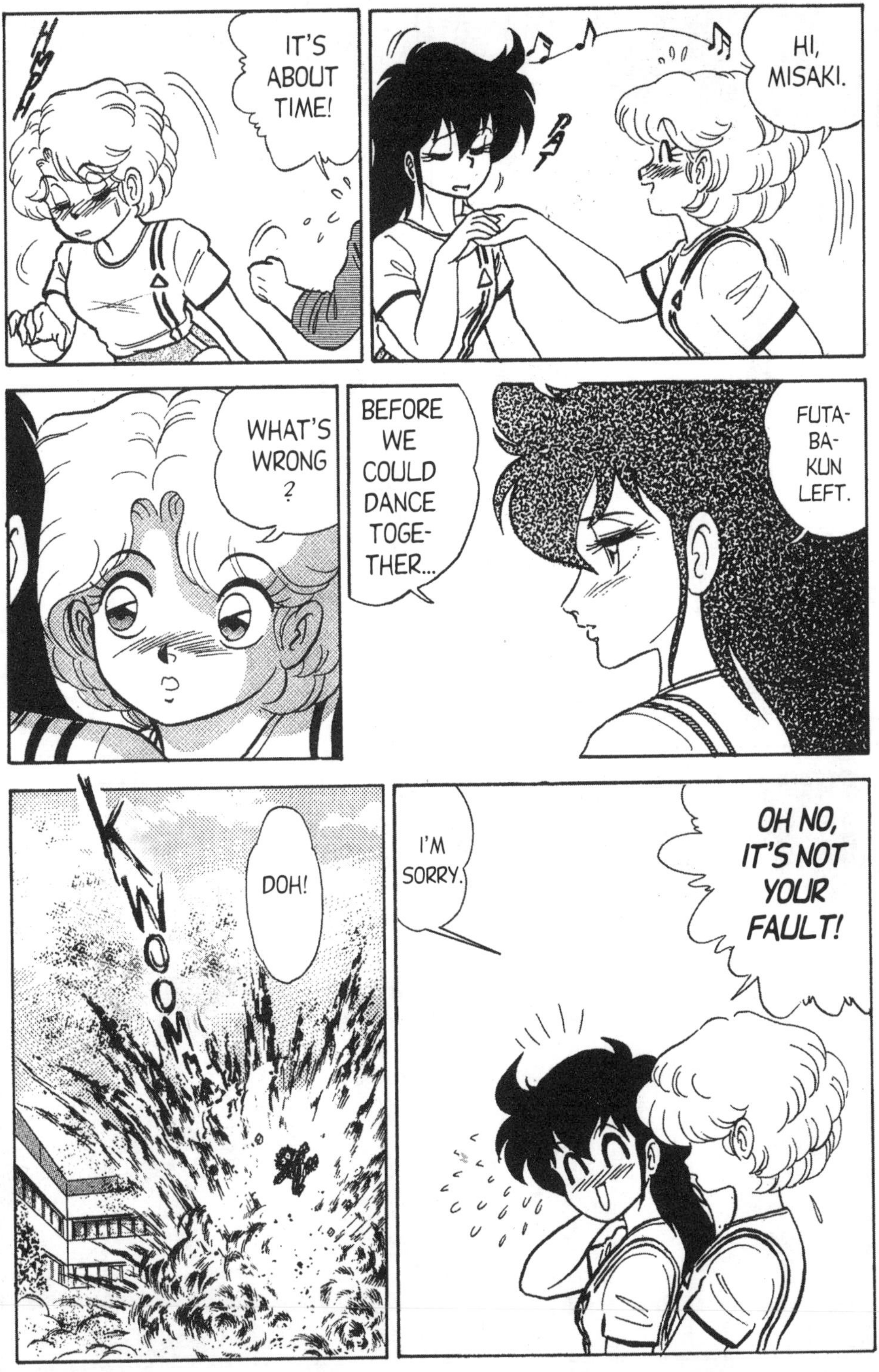
HMPH
IT'S ABOUT TIME!
HI, MISAKI.
PAT
WHAT'S WRONG?
FUTA-BA-KUN LEFT.
BEFORE WE COULD DANCE TOGE-THER...
I'M SORRY.
OH NO, IT'S NOT YOUR FAULT!
KWOOOM
DOH!

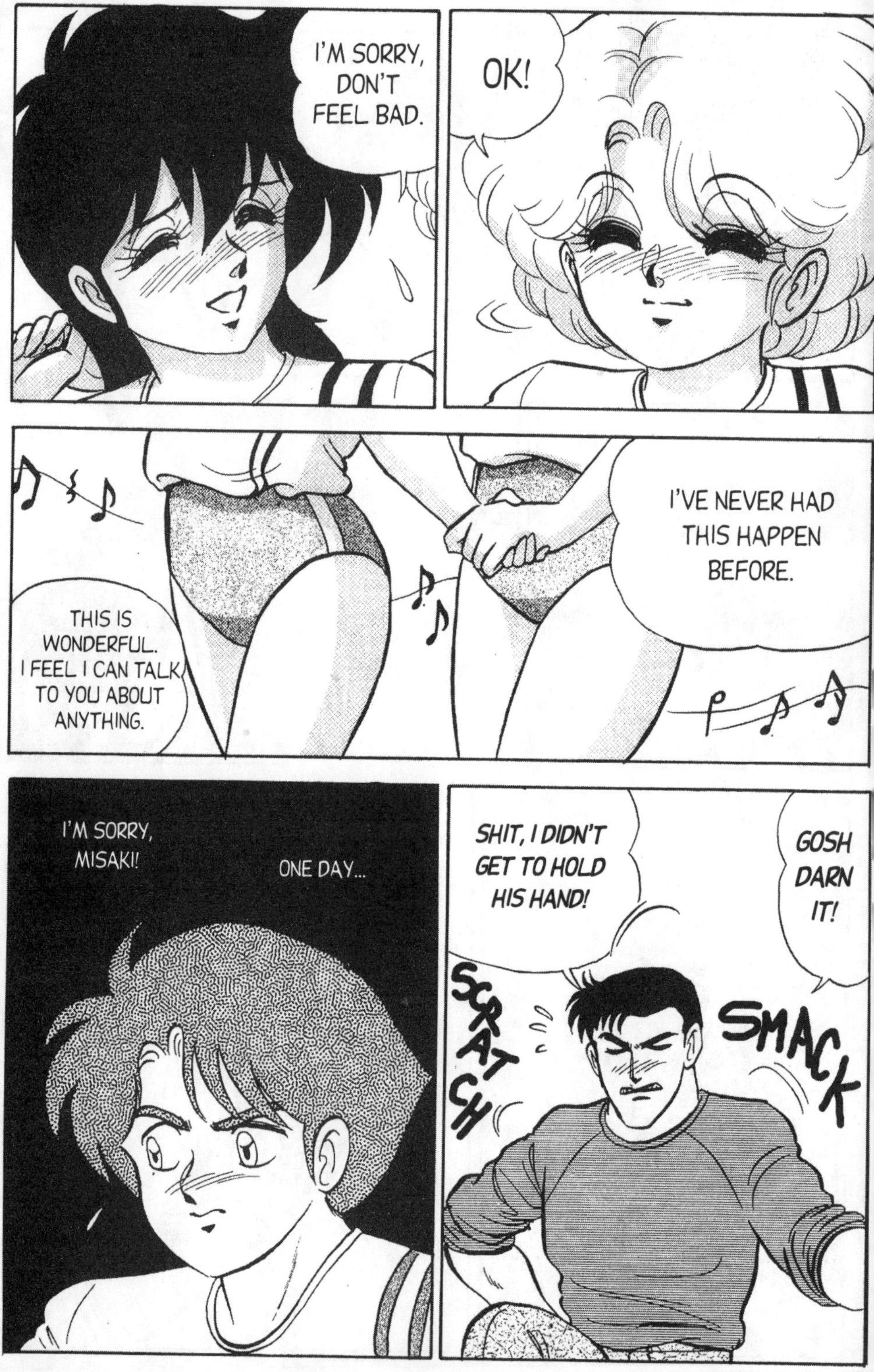

I'M SORRY, DON'T FEEL BAD.
OK!
I'VE NEVER HAD THIS HAPPEN BEFORE.
THIS IS WONDERFUL. I FEEL I CAN TALK TO YOU ABOUT ANYTHING.
I'M SORRY, MISAKI!
ONE DAY...
SHIT, I DIDN'T GET TO HOLD HIS HAND!
GOSH DARN IT!
SCRATCH
SMACK

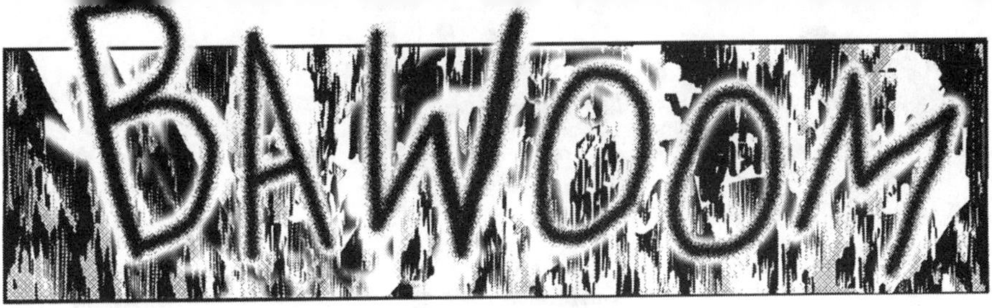
BAWOOM

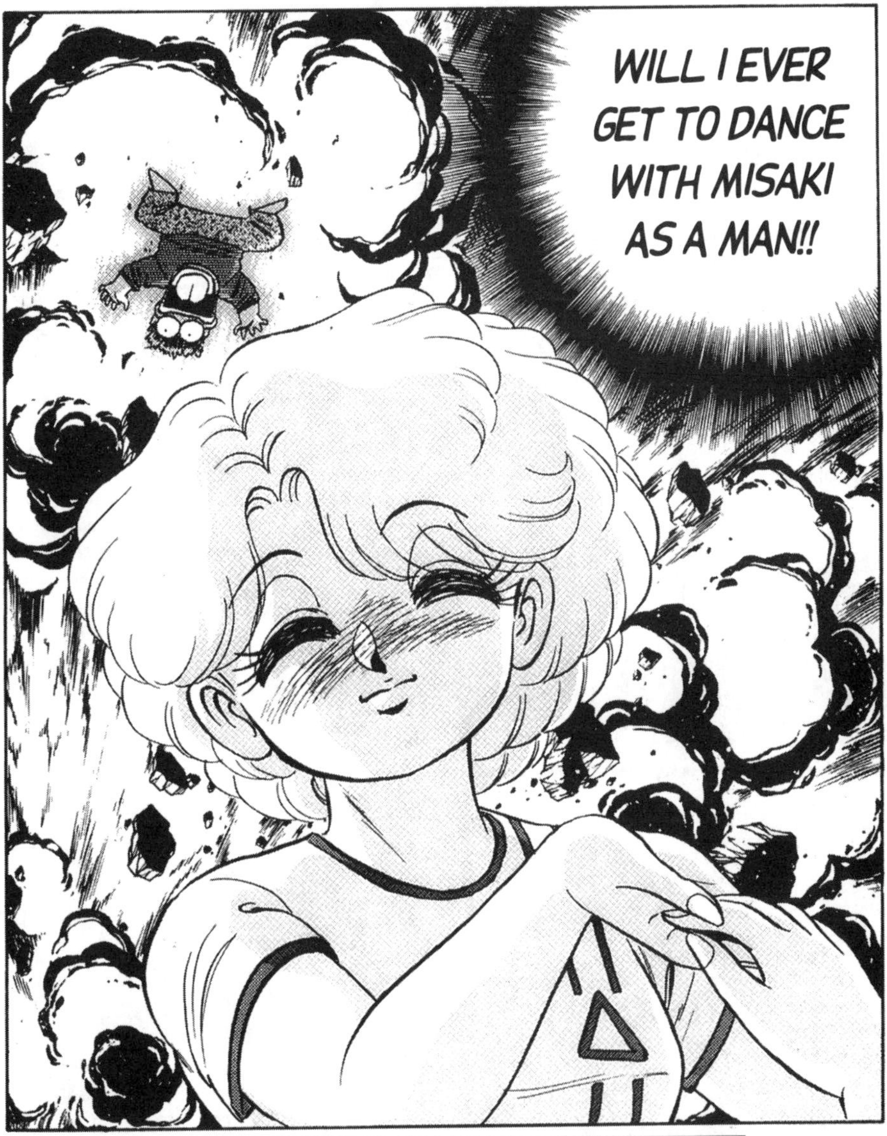
WILL I EVER GET TO DANCE WITH MISAKI AS A MAN!!

End of Volume One!

ワニが翔ぶ

米国のメシはでかかった！の巻

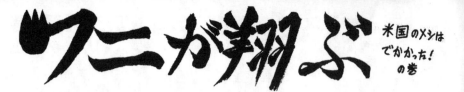

The Flying Alligator (Episode one: Huge American Food)

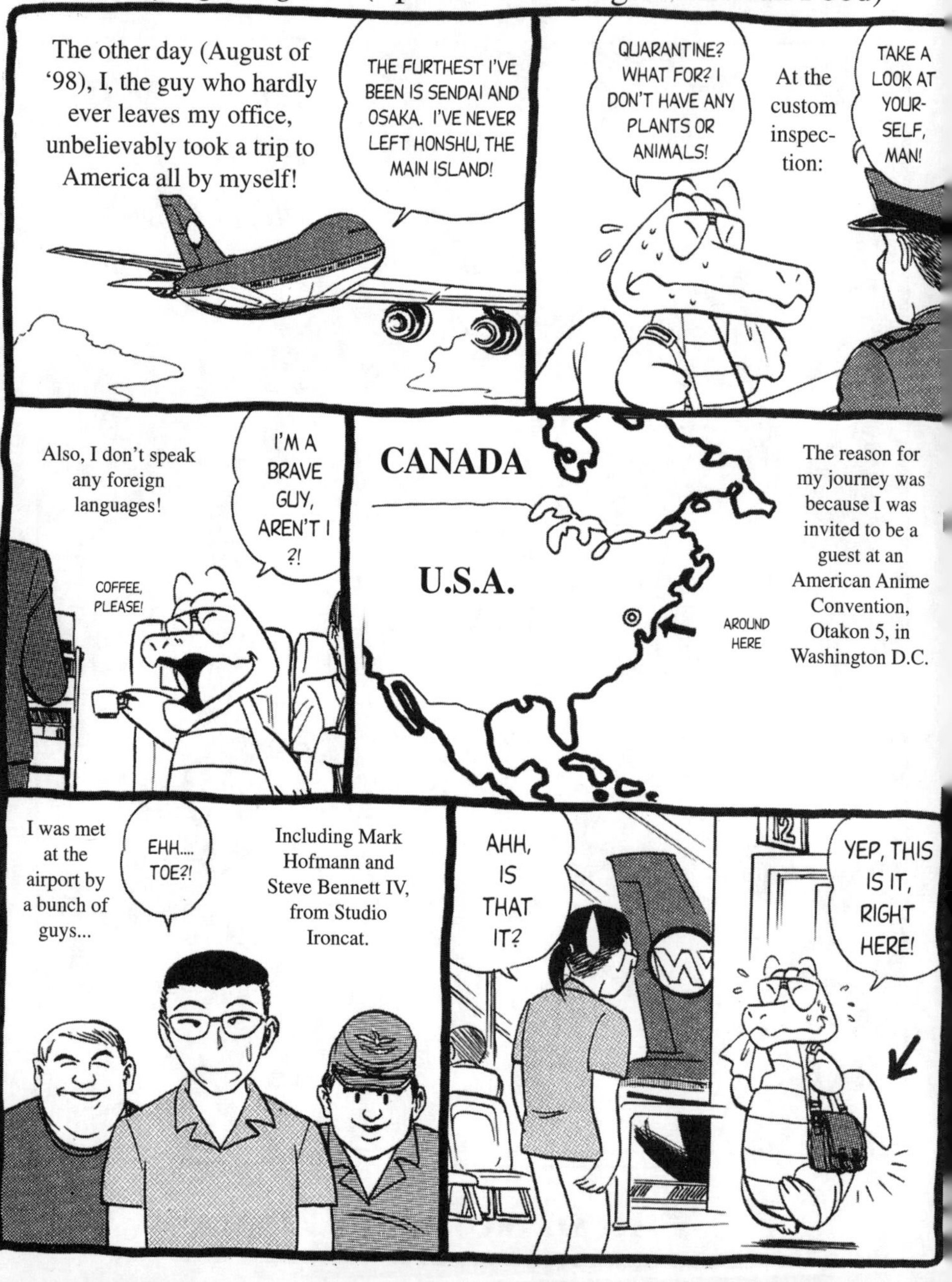

The other day (August of '98), I, the guy who hardly ever leaves my office, unbelievably took a trip to America all by myself!
THE FURTHEST I'VE BEEN IS SENDAI AND OSAKA. I'VE NEVER LEFT HONSHU, THE MAIN ISLAND!
QUARANTINE? WHAT FOR? I DON'T HAVE ANY PLANTS OR ANIMALS!
At the custom inspection:
TAKE A LOOK AT YOURSELF, MAN!
Also, I don't speak any foreign languages!
I'M A BRAVE GUY, AREN'T I ?!
COFFEE, PLEASE!
CANADA
U.S.A.
AROUND HERE
The reason for my journey was because I was invited to be a guest at an American Anime Convention, Otakon 5, in Washington D.C.
I was met at the airport by a bunch of guys...
EHH.... TOE?!
Including Mark Hofmann and Steve Bennett IV, from Studio Ironcat.
AHH, IS THAT IT?
YEP, THIS IS IT, RIGHT HERE!

*coffee comes in tiny cups with no refills and it's really expensive!

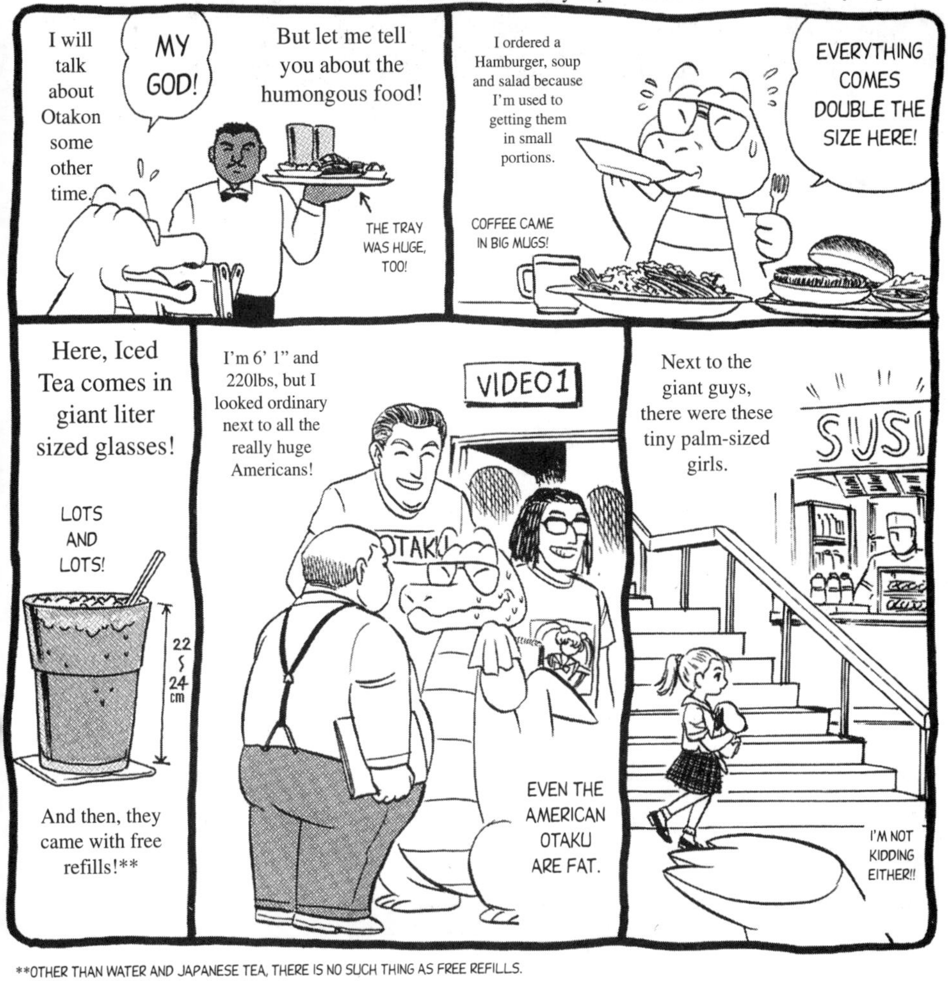
I will talk about Otakon some other time.
MY GOD!
But let me tell you about the humongous food!
THE TRAY WAS HUGE, TOO!
I ordered a Hamburger, soup and salad because I'm used to getting them in small portions.
EVERYTHING COMES DOUBLE THE SIZE HERE!
COFFEE CAME IN BIG MUGS!
Here, Iced Tea comes in giant liter sized glasses!
LOTS AND LOTS!
22 ~ 24 cm
And then, they came with free refills!**
I'm 6' 1" and 220lbs, but I looked ordinary next to all the really huge Americans!
VIDEO1
OTAKU
EVEN THE AMERICAN OTAKU ARE FAT.
Next to the giant guys, there were these tiny palm-sized girls.
SUSI
I'M NOT KIDDING EITHER!!

**OTHER THAN WATER AND JAPANESE TEA, THERE IS NO SUCH THING AS FREE REFILLS.

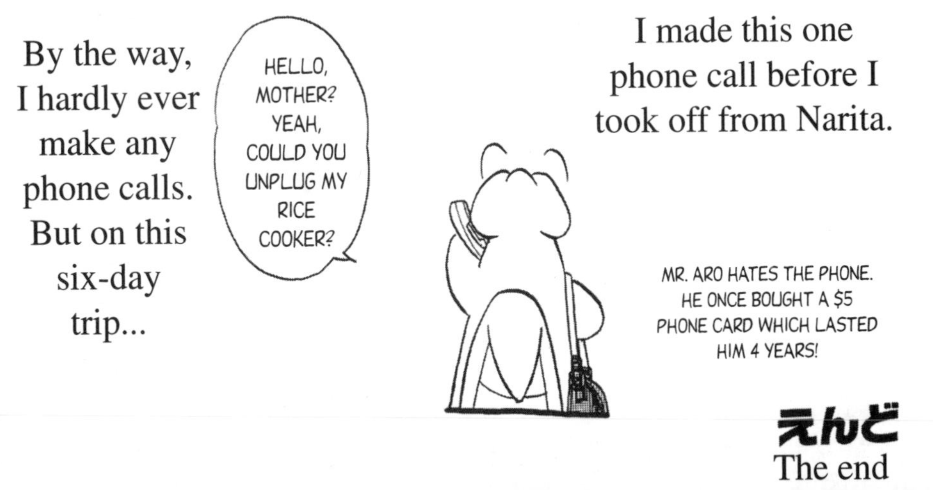
By the way, I hardly ever make any phone calls. But on this six-day trip...
HELLO, MOTHER? YEAH, COULD YOU UNPLUG MY RICE COOKER?
I made this one phone call before I took off from Narita.
MR. ARO HATES THE PHONE. HE ONCE BOUGHT A $5 PHONE CARD WHICH LASTED HIM 4 YEARS!
えんど
The end

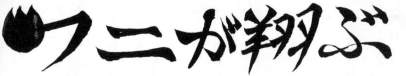

ワニが翔ぶ

米国オタクは熱いぜ！の巻

The Flying Alligator (Episode two: The American Otaku are sizzling!)

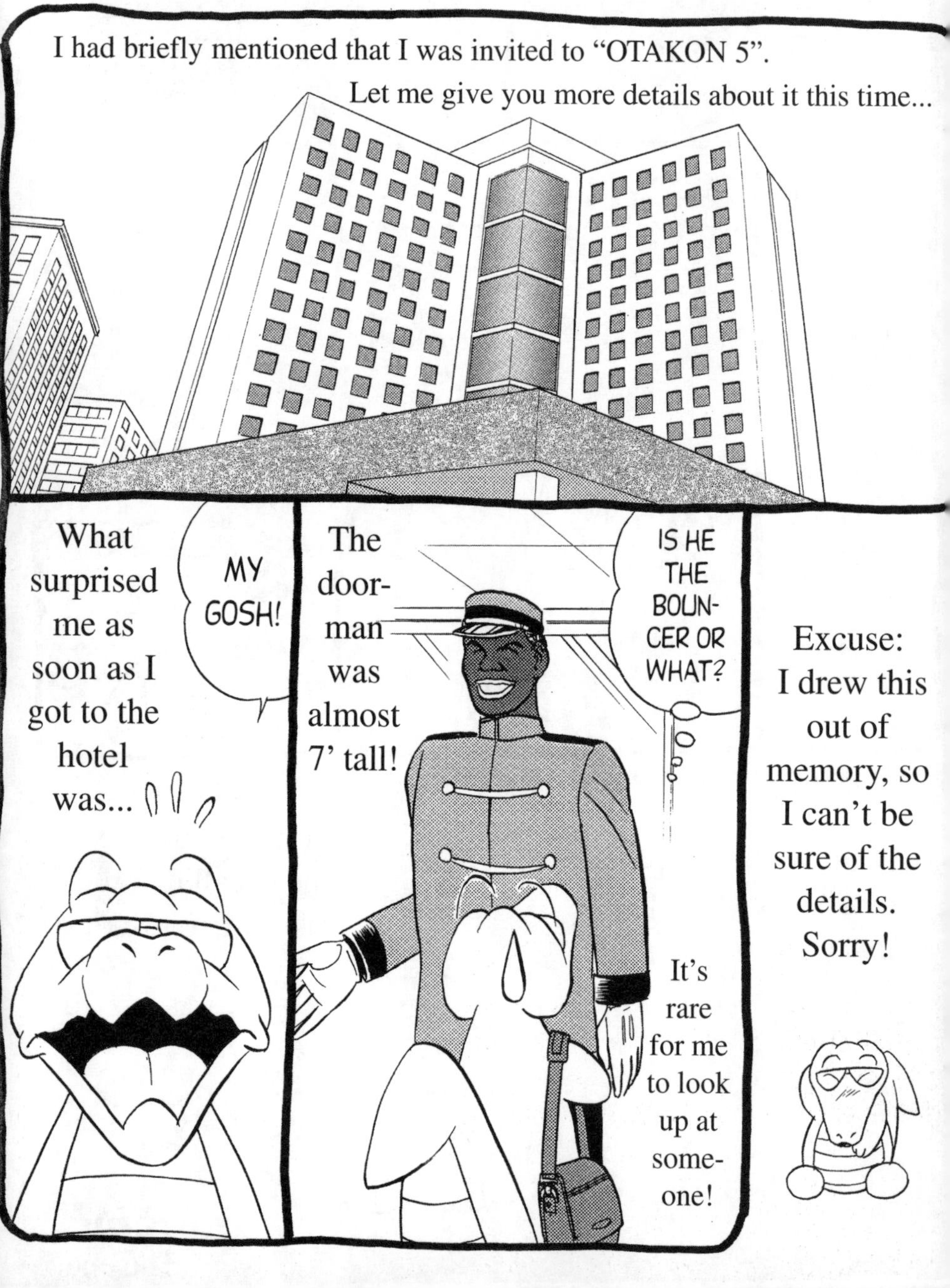

I had briefly mentioned that I was invited to “OTAKON 5”.
Let me give you more details about it this time...
What surprised me as soon as I got to the hotel was...
MY GOSH!
The doorman was almost 7’ tall!
IS HE THE BOUNCER OR WHAT?
It’s rare for me to look up at someone!
Excuse: I drew this out of memory, so I can’t be sure of the details. Sorry!

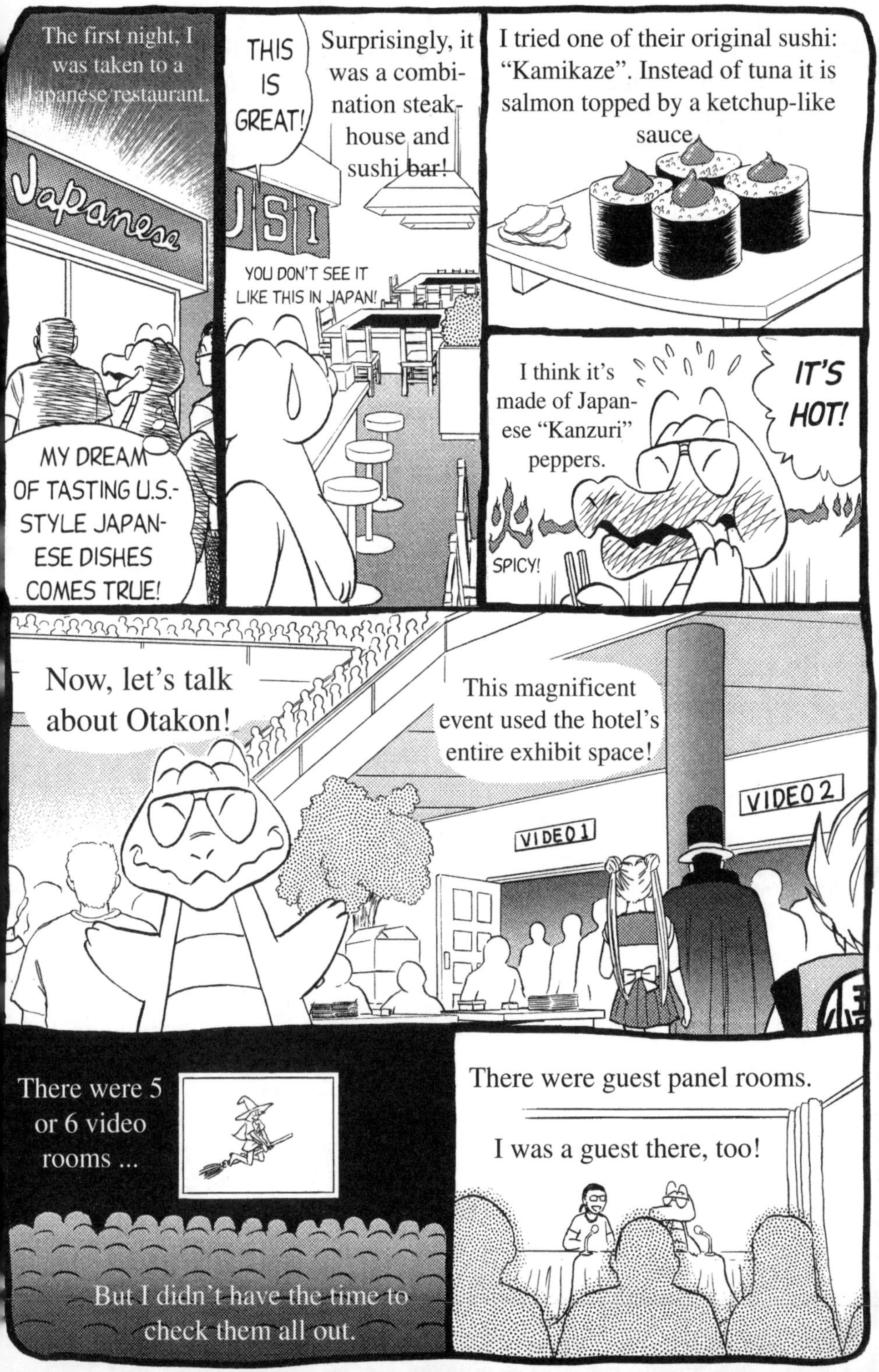

The first night, I was taken to a Japanese restaurant.
Japanese
MY DREAM OF TASTING U.S.-STYLE JAPANESE DISHES COMES TRUE!
THIS IS GREAT!
Surprisingly, it was a combination steak-house and sushi bar!
YOU DON'T SEE IT LIKE THIS IN JAPAN!
I tried one of their original sushi: "Kamikaze". Instead of tuna it is salmon topped by a ketchup-like sauce.
I think it's made of Japanese "Kanzuri" peppers.
IT'S HOT!
SPICY!
Now, let's talk about Otakon!
This magnificent event used the hotel's entire exhibit space!
VIDEO 1
VIDEO 2
There were 5 or 6 video rooms ...
But I didn't have the time to check them all out.
There were guest panel rooms.
I was a guest there, too!

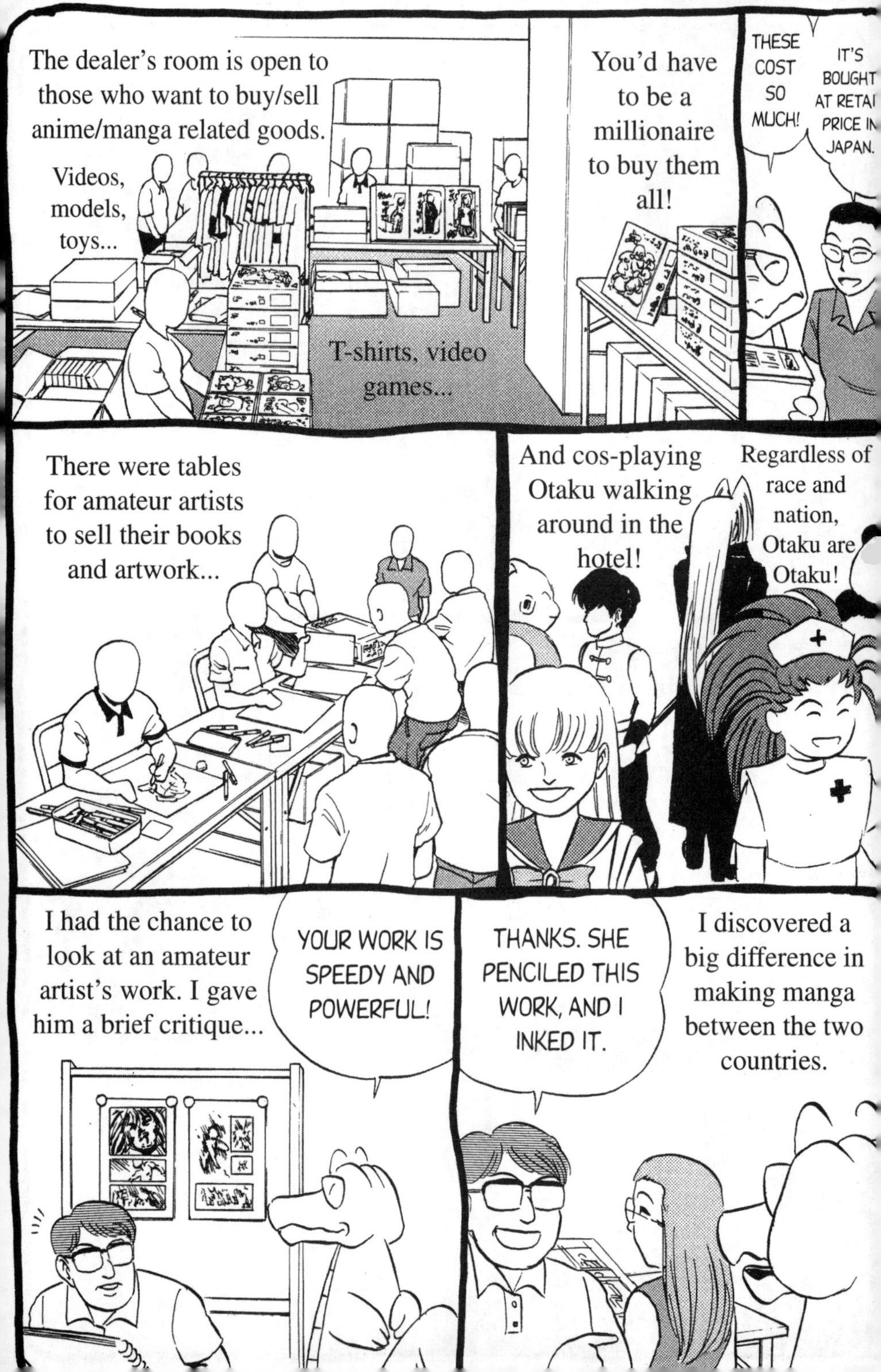
The dealer's room is open to those who want to buy/sell anime/manga related goods.
Videos, models, toys...
T-shirts, video games...
You'd have to be a millionaire to buy them all!
THESE COST SO MUCH!
IT'S BOUGHT AT RETAI PRICE IN JAPAN.
There were tables for amateur artists to sell their books and artwork...
And cos-playing Otaku walking around in the hotel!
Regardless of race and nation, Otaku are Otaku!
I had the chance to look at an amateur artist's work. I gave him a brief critique...
YOUR WORK IS SPEEDY AND POWERFUL!
THANKS. SHE PENCILED THIS WORK, AND I INKED IT.
I discovered a big difference in making manga between the two countries.

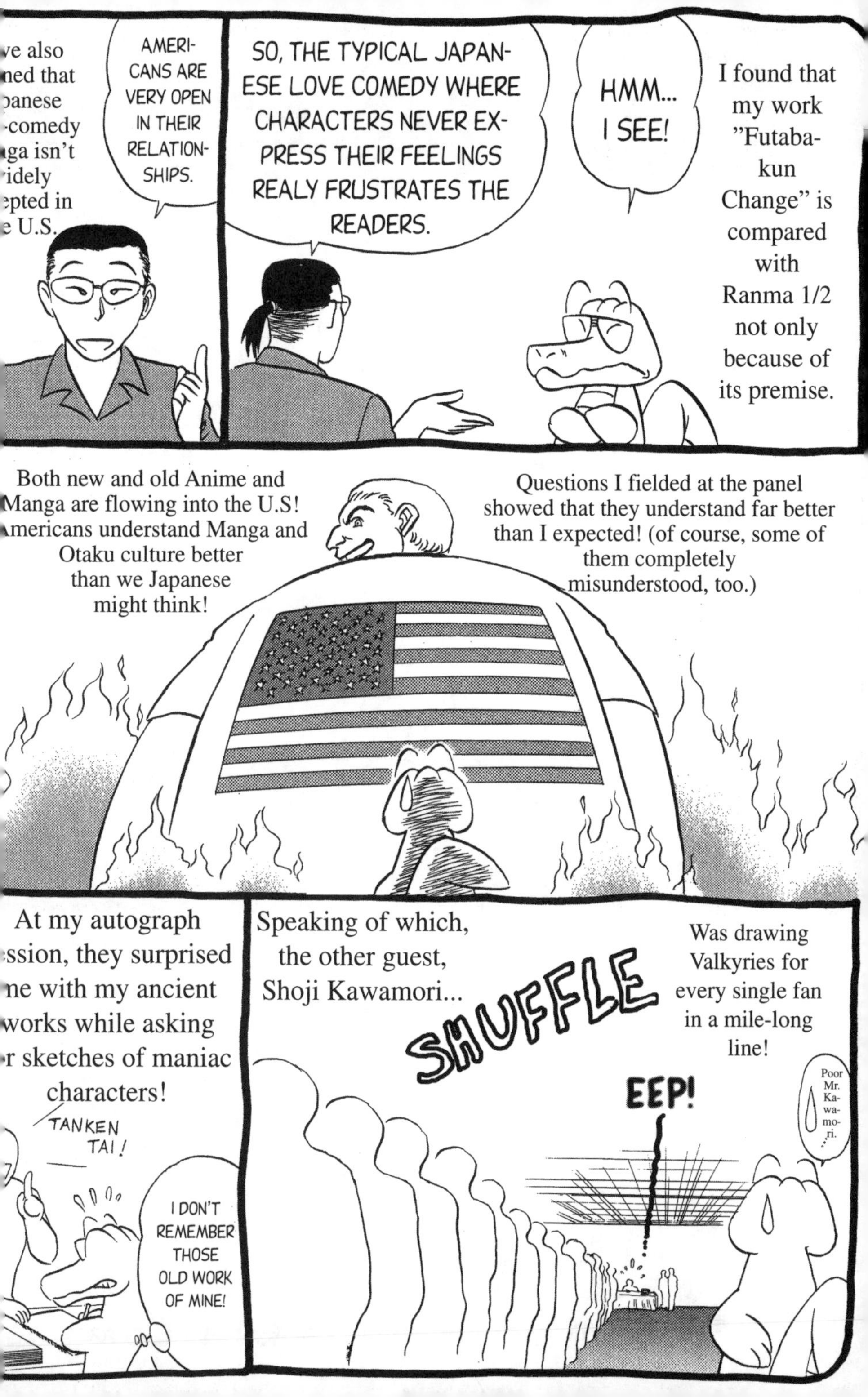

ve also
ned that
panese
-comedy
ga isn't
idely
epted in
e U.S.
AMERICANS ARE VERY OPEN IN THEIR RELATIONSHIPS.
SO, THE TYPICAL JAPANESE LOVE COMEDY WHERE CHARACTERS NEVER EXPRESS THEIR FEELINGS REALY FRUSTRATES THE READERS.
HMM... I SEE!
I found that my work "Futaba-kun Change" is compared with Ranma 1/2 not only because of its premise.
Both new and old Anime and Manga are flowing into the U.S! Americans understand Manga and Otaku culture better than we Japanese might think!
Questions I fielded at the panel showed that they understand far better than I expected! (of course, some of them completely misunderstood, too.)
At my autograph
ssion, they surprised
me with my ancient
works while asking
r sketches of maniac
characters!
TANKEN TAI!
I DON'T REMEMBER THOSE OLD WORK OF MINE!
Speaking of which, the other guest, Shoji Kawamori...
SHUFFLE
Was drawing Valkyries for every single fan in a mile-long line!
EEP!
Poor Mr. Kawamori.

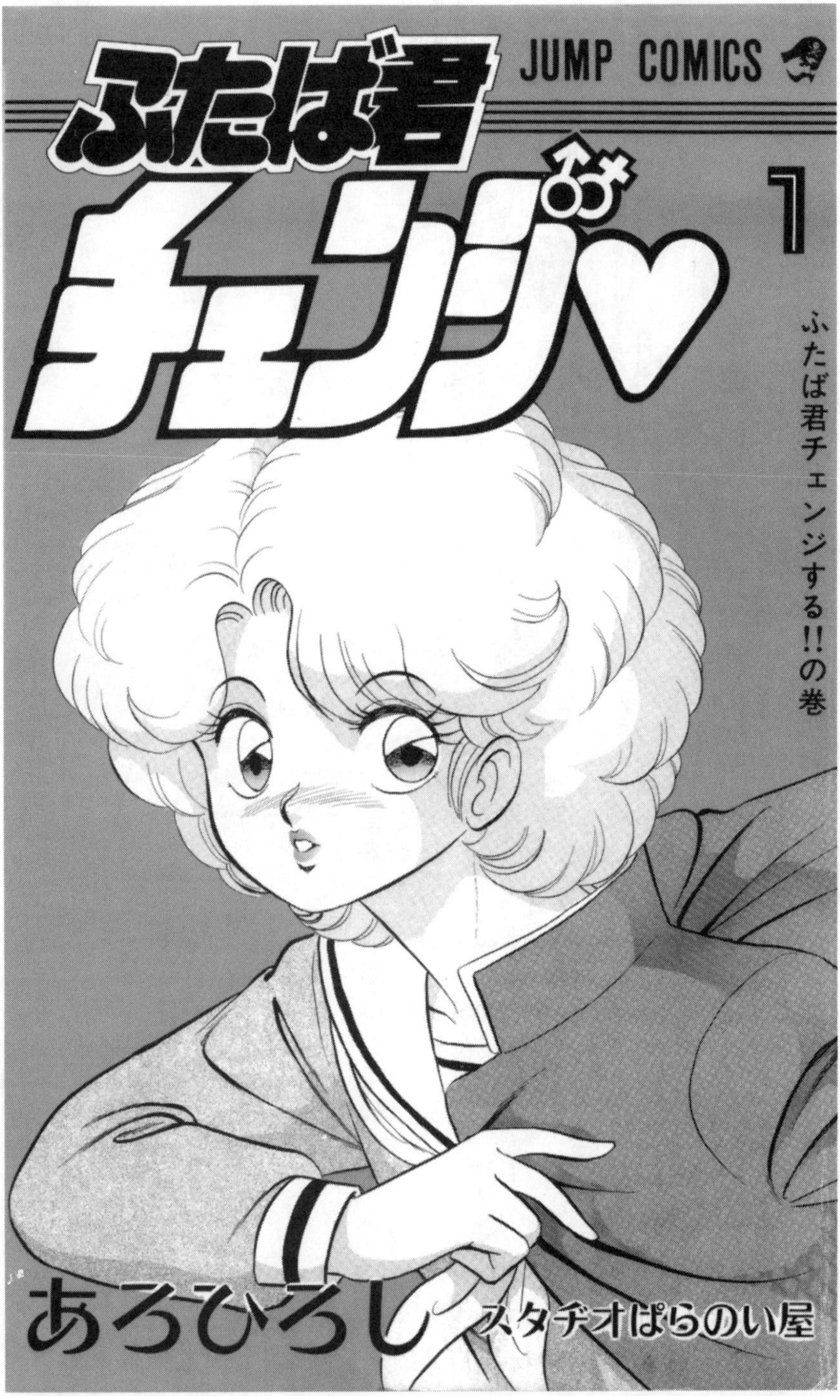
ふたば君チェンジ♥
JUMP COMICS
1
ふたば君チェンジする!!の巻
あろひろし
スタヂオぱらのい屋

The Original Japanese Tankoban Cover